One Good Mama Bone

STORY RIVER BOOKS

Pat Conroy, Founding Editor at Large

ONE GOOD MAMA BONE

a novel

BREN McCLAIN

FOREWORD BY MARY ALICE MONROE

The University of South Carolina Press

Cloth edition published by the University of South Carolina Press, 2018
Paperback edition published in Columbia, South Carolina,
by the University of South Carolina Press, 2018

www.sc.edu/uscpress

Manufactured in the United States of America

27 26 25 24 23 22 21 20 19 18
10 9 8 7 6 5 4 3 2

Library of Congress Cataloging-in-Publication Data for the
cloth edition can be found at http://catalog.loc.gov/

ISBN: 978-1-61117-982-8 (paperback)
ISBN: 978-1-61117-747-3 (ebook)

To my mama, Barbara Ann Kilgore McClain,
who showed me blessed motherhood.

And to my daddy, James Edwin McClain,
who showed me blessed cows.

CONTENTS

FOREWORD

With her bright wit and positive energy, Bren McClain is as much a force of nature as she is a fellow advocate for our natural world. I first met Bren ten years ago at the South Carolina Writers Workshop. I signed a book for her, a fellow writer, and later struck up a conversation. We bonded immediately, sharing a kindred spirit in our love of animals and nature. Our paths have crossed many times over the ensuing years, and each time I became more aware of the novel she was writing. I heard tidbits . . . Mama Red, 1950s era, hardscrabble farm life . . . and I waited anxiously to read it. So it was with great relish and, too, a friend's trepidation that I agreed to write the foreword for *One Good Mama Bone*—this highly anticipated story that had been Bren's personal passion for more than a decade.

I am honored, thrilled, delighted to declare that *One Good Mama Bone* was well worth the wait! This book is everything that Bren is—smart, confident, unflinchingly honest, witty, wise, and possessing a reassuring wisdom and kindness that carries the reader from the story's heartbreaking beginnings to a morally and emotionally satisfying conclusion. Bren McClain's debut novel is a tour de force!

Bren's novel begins and ends with heartrending revelations about the bonds between families, specifically between mothers and children, but ultimately between Mother Nature and all her myriad offspring. In Bren's themes of the power of family to heal and the power of nature to teach, she speaks to the connective threads that I strive to weave through my own novels. What a joy it is then to see a new voice from South Carolina, and one championed by Pat Conroy himself, take up those inspiriting messages in this novel of the Carolina upstate in the 1950s.

This novel itself is the progeny of other stories—of Bren's upbringing on her family's farm in Anderson, South Carolina, of her father's boyhood cattle-show experiences, and of other tales entrusted to Bren as both a journalist and a storyteller. The novel she has crafted here is one of great and lasting truths, be those the hard truths of loss and sacrifice or loving truths about family and fate. This is a story of one place, one time, and three families. Yet, in the telling of it, the narrative echoes and reverberates across the plains of its rural South Carolina setting and comes to speak for many places, many times, and many families. That ability to extract the universal from the regional, and from the personal, is the magical power of story exemplified by my dear friend Pat Conroy, who selected Bren's novel for his Story River Books fiction imprint, giving a literary home to all of the characters whom you will meet in these pages and to the author herself.

With Sarah Creamer, Bren has crafted a compelling portrait of a woman so damaged by the harshness of her upbringing that she is convinced she cannot be a loving mother, that she lacks even "one good mama bone," as her own mother professed. But when Sarah chooses to become a mother to Emerson Bridge, an orphaned child of an adulterous affair, maternal instincts rise up from her very marrow, instincts to protect and foster the young boy that challenge her mother's prophesy. In Emerson Bridge, Bren has given readers the gift of a masterful new vision of rural southern childhood in a character cut from the same rough-hewn cloth as Jean Louise "Scout" Finch, Ellen Foster, Molly Peetree, Lily Owens, and Huck Finn. The bond of mother and child that forms, with some reluctance, between Sarah and Emerson Bridge shows us the capacity for familial nurturing that lies dormant within all of us until called forth. Through this relationship, Bren gives us an insightful depiction of motherhood, of love itself, grounded in the courage to act completely in the interest of another, to give without question and without expectation of receiving the same.

Sarah must learn to be a mother to Emerson Bridge, and, while this at first seems to be an unnatural act for her, it is to nature that she is drawn for instruction. She finds her model of motherhood in Mama Red, the mother cow who has pushed her way through barbed-wire fences and traversed the fields to be reunited with her child, Lucky, the steer the Creamers have bought from the wealthy and glory-mad Luther Dobbins.

Perhaps my favorite sections are the poignant and brief passages centering on Mama Red's animal perspective and Sarah's monologues with Mama Red as Sarah struggles to comprehend the animal's strong maternal instincts even as her own grow and ripen in her breast. This theme of animal as teacher—of following the instructive parallels between nature and human nature—has defined so much of my own writing, and I applaud Bren for the thoughtful and unique ways in which she approaches that message in her novel.

In the contrasts between the impoverished Creamers and the well-to-do Dobbins, and in the compelling connections between Sarah and her son Emerson Bridge and Mama Red and her offspring Lucky, Bren shows us the heart of parenthood isn't rooted in biology or even in species, but in our capacity to love, to change, to give all that we have, to sacrifice oneself for the sake of another. It is a lesson that we need to hear often because it can be difficult to learn and easy to forget, but I believe, as I think Bren must as well, that this spirit of giving and forgiving is the essence of our being. It is the better part of our human nature, and our purpose on this earth of ours is to tap into it within ourselves so that we may share it with others. Bren has done that in her novel, in her art, and, if we can attune ourselves to truly hear the voices we encounter on these pages, human and animal alike, we can glimpse our own potential as well.

There is a pull of destiny in this novel too, of forces aligning just beyond the horizon and guiding characters toward what has been set in motion for them. That pull has been a part of birthing this novel as well. In July 1995, following a talk by Pat Conroy in Charleston, South Carolina, Bren was one of hundreds of eager fans who stood in one of Pat's storied three-hour signing lines. (Pat once told me that at least five marriages could trace their beginnings to his signing lines where future spouses met and, in the course of waiting together for hours on end, realized they had more in common than just a great love of literature.) Simply signing a book for a fan was never enough for Pat. His gratitude to his readers was so deep and genuine that he wanted to get to know them, to treat them as well as they had treated him. He could not meet a reader without striking up a conversation, and this was true of Bren's encounter. She revealed to Pat that she was a writer working on the beginnings of a novel. Pat inscribed her copy of *Beach Music* with this: "To Bren McClain, I hope to read your novel one day. Pat Conroy."

And he did, nearly twenty years later! Pat read the manuscript of *One Good Mama Bone* and selected it with enthusiasm for addition to his Story River Books imprint. At Pat's seventieth birthday celebration in Beaufort, South Carolina, in October 2015, Bren was able to remind Pat of their first meeting and to show him her treasured copy of *Beach Music*. There, at the Pat Conroy at 70 Literary Festival, Pat signed another book for Bren with this: "To Bren, the marvelous writer who is now part of Story River history. Pat Conroy." That part of Bren's history, of Story River's, and of Pat's is now where destiny has placed it, in your hands as the novel *One Good Mama Bone*.

This is a novel that just might break your heart, and it might well heal it too, but with both acts Bren McClain will remind you of why each of us is entrusted with a heart in the first place—to love, to learn, to make the hard choices, and to feel deeply within ourselves the righteousness and generosity of living in the service of one another.

Mary Alice Monroe

part 1

MOTHERS

JUNE 22, 1944

One night, deep into it, when sounds are prone to carry, a baby boy lies crying on Sarah Creamer's kitchen table. He is minutes old, still wet with his mother's blood, and hungry for his mother's milk.

But she does not hear his cries. She is no longer there.

Only Sarah. Only Sarah remains. Her body bent over his, her hands rummaging the wooden planks for a towel still white enough to wrap him in. Blood is everywhere, puddled up as if there had been a hard rain. The smell of it saturates the eighty-one-degree air, pushes aside the dry tang of bleach, and fills the heat with the moistness of a long-shuttered earth, now free.

The baby's cries penetrate Sarah's bosom and bounce around its emptiness.

Her hands are shaking.

A lone light bulb hangs suspended over the table, a pull string running from the base of the bulb. It hangs as still as death. The light casts Sarah larger than she knows herself to be, beginning on the far wall above her husband, Harold, who lies drunk and passed out in front of the open doorway to the porch. Sarah spreads high and wide.

Harold's pocket knife lies atop one of the towels, the blade still open and awash in a red slickness. Sarah yanks the towel towards her, flipping the knife onto the table, still warm from Mattie's body. *"Cut him loose of me!"* Mattie's words to Sarah, who delivered the child. *"Get you a knife and cut him loose of me now."* The towel in Sarah's hands, she twists. The red and white spirals of a peppermint stick. *"What was in my head? I can't keep him. Billy Udean will kill me and this baby, too."* Mattie's voice almost too hoarse for utterance, her legs working to free herself from the table. She drops to the linoleum and heads for the door, crawls over Harold and leaves on him a trail of bright red. *"It ain't the child's fault he was born,"* her last words from the porch, before the darkness drew her.

It ain't mine, either, Sarah thinks now, and wraps the baby in the towel, brings him in close and steps over Harold and into the sweltering night in Anderson, South Carolina, where the moon is on its way to bed, and crickets, a whole chorus of them, sprinkle the farmland in waves.

"Mattie! Sister Mattie!" she calls out, her bare feet scurrying across the dirt yard to the vegetable garden they share, the rows running from Sarah's house to Mattie's. She takes the one between the green beans. They would make in another week or two.

She rushes up the few steps to the front porch and onto the green concrete slab, throws open the screened door, and turns the knob. It's locked. "Sister, open the door!"

Mattie never locks her door. No one does.

Sarah shakes the knob. "I'm bringing him back to you. This is your baby, not mine. Don't you put this on me!"

The door does not open.

Sarah places her ear against the wooden surface and strains to hear Mattie's footsteps inside, hear the creaks her barely one hundred pounds would make. But the baby's cries do not allow for that.

Sarah kicks at the door and beats it with her fist, beats it hard. "I mean it, Mattie. I ain't no mama. You his mama. Bet he's got your dimples. Now come get him. Come get him now!"

Sarah's words come fast like the bullets Billy Udean said he wanted to go fire on the people he called "slant eyes," his arms pretending to hold one of the guns he kept stashed in every room of his house and pointing it like he could see them already. He never broke any of Mattie's bones, but he'd beaten her black and blue. The newspaper the day before splashed a headline that spanned the top of the front page, "War Hero to Return Home," and carried words that said Billy Udean Parnell would be on the train to Anderson the next day around noon. That's in a few hours. "Me and Harold won't let Billy Udean do nothing to you or this baby," she calls through and hopes to the high heavens that is true.

A sheen of sweat coats Sarah's skin, makes it glisten, and keeps fresh the red of Mattie's blood that lines Sarah's hands and wrists and arms. Against the wooden surface in front of her, Sarah lays her forehead, wide like the rest of her, except her eyes, which look almost pinched together, as if huddling. Strands of dark hair, almost black and long loose from her bun, lay stuck to her forehead and neck and sides of her face.

The baby's cries ring in Sarah's ears.

"I mean it, Sister! Come get your baby! I'm going to count to ten, and if you don't open the door, I'm putting him down, *I am.*" Her voice has become shrill.

4

Sarah begins to count. She counts loud.

But Mattie does not come.

"Alright, then," Sarah says and steps back, the screened door slapping shut. She lays the baby in front of it. "He's at your door now, *your* baby is. You the mama, now you come get him. I don't want him. He ain't mine, and I wouldn't make no good mama." The back of her throat feels like knives cutting it. "I ain't playing, Mattie. I ain't!" She stomps her foot. The jowls in her face shake.

The door stays closed.

She takes another step back and holds up her hands in surrender. "Bye, Sister, I mean it. I'm leaving. Now come get him!"

She starts down the steps.

From inside the house, a gunshot blasts.

The sound finds Sarah and lifts her arms like wings.

"Mattie!" she screams and runs back to the door and rams it with her full self. "You playing, right, Sister? Ain't you playing? Tell me you playing!" She grabs the knob and shakes it, then beats it with her fists. "Tell me!"

She listens.

There is nothing.

Blood rushes to her head. The hotness of it, then the coolness like a thousand peppermints jammed inside.

"Mattieeeeee!" Sarah calls out, holding onto her best friend's name as long as she can.

She is a child's toy top spinning. She spreads her feet to steady herself and slaps her flat hands against the screen. "Oh God, no, no, no, tell me no, Mattie. Tell me noooooo!"

The louder Sarah is, the louder the baby at her feet becomes.

But their sounds are just for each other. No neighbors live close enough to hear. Field after field of young cotton surrounds them. The farmhouse across the way has long been abandoned.

Sarah slides down the door, her body folding on top of itself as if she was a knife being put away. Her hands clasp the back of her knees, and she begins to rock. She falls over and draws herself up into a tight curl.

The baby lies just out from her, his cries now wails.

They shake her down to her twenty-six-year-old bones.

Drops of sweat roll down her face. They want to get away from her. She doesn't blame them. "I ain't enough, baby boy, I ain't. I don't know how to be no mama. I wouldn't make no good one. No good one. No good one. No good one."

The towel reveals only his face, the rest wrapped around him like the picture of Baby Jesus she saw in her mother's Bible when Sarah was a girl.

She can see his little mouth working. He is hungry. He needs to be fed.

"Why? Mattie, why? Sister, why?" Sarah's voice is now a whisper. "No good one, no good one, no good one. No, sir. No good one."

He is squirming like he wants to free himself. But he has nothing to free himself for.

Except her. Except Clementine Florence Augusta Sarah Bolt Creamer.

She looks at the screened door behind him. It is closed. She lets her eyes climb the large metal design in its center, a bird, painted white. Billy Udean would always laugh and say it was a pelican that lived along the coast, where he pronounced he would live one day, buy a house on the beach and wait for such a bird to fly by so he could shoot it.

It's a stork, Sarah thinks now, and it's brought a baby. A baby boy.

She can feel light at her back. The sun now is waking. On the baby's face, she sees the light's timid beginnings. The world behind them is becoming midnight blue, the color of God's handoff from night to day, that switchover that appears to occur in a single act, in a single second and setting what was, never to be again.

"No sir," she tells him. "It ain't your fault."

Then she makes herself go still. Just like that, go still.

She rises from the floor and gathers him in her arms. His hair has dried some. It carries a tint of red like Harold's. Around his tiny and heaving back, she folds her hands. They are strong hands. They can cook, and they can clean. Harold called her "handy" once. He was right.

The baby, theirs now.

Sarah bows her head. She can't say who she is praying to. Her mother's Jesus does not know her. But she has to believe that someone, something hears.

NOVEMBER 8, 1950

The mother cow left the herd under a ceiling of darkness, as dots of white, even twinkling white, sprinkled above her and around her in patterns of order and beauty. She headed across the pasture. The light from the full moon lit her way, but she did not need it to see. She knew where she was going. She had made the trip a dozen times before over this familiar land. The other cows did not follow, although it was customary for them to do so when one decided to move. But this early morning, for this mother, none of the others moved.

She crossed the earthen dam that held back the pond's muddy waters and made her way to the creek, where the flow over the years had carved deep and jagged into the red clay soil. She arrived at a spot on its bank near an old cedar tree and dropped to her knees, folding herself onto the earth. At first, she kept her head high, but as daylight dawned, she lowered it, surrendering herself in full.

The mother had come to deliver one of her own.

Neither the farmer nor his workingman had noticed her udder, how it had begun to sack up. Nor had they noticed the top of her tail rising and her lower back softening, her ligaments and tissues becoming supple, so that her babies, twins, lying on their backs and surrounded in fluid warm, could follow their natural course and move from their high place near her tail head past her pin bones to their new place, deep in her womb, where they rotated to their bellies for the rest of their journey.

Like the times before, there would be no mother or sister or friend to instruct her as to what to do. She would know, and it would come from a place deep inside where maternal love lives and maternal love grows, a place that is regardless there, never wavering there, nonnegotiably there.

It lay in her bones.

In the growing light, her uterine muscles began to contract. At first, her squeezes stayed small, but as they became harder, her legs stiffened and lifted. They trembled.

All of this could be seen from above. Life, seen as ripples, moving along the mother's skin.

A single buzzard circled above her. A dark, ragged patch against the beginning blue. The mother cow drew in a breath and released it from her nose and mouth, her breath warmer than what it greeted. It formed a mist that hovered near her face.

From her vulva, a right hoof, the tip of it, appeared. It was midnight black and sheathed in a cloudy membrane. The hoof slipped back in as if timid. She squeezed again. This time, the baby's left hoof joined the right, and together, as if holding hands, they slid under the roof of the mother's lifted tail, along with the tip of its nose. Soon, the rest of the baby's front legs and head came forward in a sack of milky white, transparent and sticky and laced with tiny veins of blood. Already, the baby's nostrils made little sucking noises, popping the white, while its eye lids tried to blink, letting in the first light. From that warmth, steam rose.

The mother cow pulled in her front legs, curled them to her chest and rocked her upper body until she was able to get on her knees. On other days, such would not take much effort, but her advanced age of sixteen years, and having just delivered a calf, made rising taxing. When she could, she lifted into the air her back side and then pushed up on her front legs. She turned towards her calf, wet and bloody and sealed, and leaned down and smelled, beginning at its back legs, then up its body to its face, where her tongue stretched. She began licking in long, slow strokes, lifting its head northward, where a second buzzard, and then a third, now joined the first.

Down its body, she moved her tongue, her young's blood flowing with her. The calf was a male, a bull, and the same color as she, the red brown of their breed, Hereford. But it would be their faces that would summon all attention. They were mottled, carrying a pattern of red brown and white, his, a small version of hers.

The smell of smoke curling from nearby chimneys and woodstoves floated through the air, now filled with light and a fourth buzzard.

The young bull calf curled his front legs, digging into the land. He wanted to stand. He managed to do so, but he could not stay. His legs wobbled. He toppled over.

A fifth buzzard now circled.

The mother stood over him, her mouth nudging him, until he could rise again and stay. This time, he moved his mouth to her underbelly, nubbing along until he came upon a teat, swollen and patient. He wrapped his lips around it.

She bent to the earth and took inside her blades of grass, soon to go dormant.

A second set of hooves emerged from her, dangled like rocks tied to ropes. In a rush of liquid, the rest of the calf's body fell to the ground, landing on its back. The mother jerked her head that way. She had never delivered a second. She turned her body towards it and leaned down and smelled the newborn's face. She began to lick. Her firstborn followed along and continued to drink from her.

A dozen buzzards now rode the thermals above the mother and her babies.

Her tail lifted and exposed a bluish pink bubble, full of fluid and blood and all that had nurtured her young, the bubble's buttons having now disengaged from the mother's womb, the bubble now expanding and extending downward and falling to the ground. She turned again, lowered her head to it and opened her mouth and took it back inside.

The first buzzard landed beside the newborn. The first peck was made at its eyes. The baby jerked its head. The mother cow released a long bellow and charged towards the bird, pulling herself from her firstborn's mouth. The bird hopped back.

By now, the rest of the buzzards had landed. They stood in jagged layers behind the first. The mother ran at them. They hissed and lifted into the air, scattering back a few feet. She ran at them again, her right front leg giving way. She leaned hard to her left and steadied herself and then returned to her new baby, lowering her head and smelling, beginning at its nose. From her mouth, she brought her tongue and drew it up its face. Its head quivered.

Three of the birds hopped towards the mother and her young, the firstborn now on the ground. The remaining birds stood with their wings spread.

The mother ran towards them. They hurled low hisses, flapping their wings and lifting. All except one. It now was near her firstborn, at his rear, pecking.

She ran at the bird. It hopped away.

A patch of tall grasses and young cedars grew near the fence line some fifty feet away. She hard-nudged him with her nose, prodding him until he was able to stand, and then she moved in a slow run towards the patch, her calf following. When they were deep inside the cover, she bore down with her mouth on top of his back, until he laid his body on the ground, even his head, which she pressed to the earth.

She ran back to her second born. The buzzards now surrounded it. The mother charged them.

They scattered.

Most of her newborn's eyes were gone. Splashes of blood and tiny specks of white lined the two hollow holes, both the size of a case quarter. Its eye lashes were still intact.

The mother moved her tongue down her young's body, moved it in long stretches. The calf was a female, a heifer.

A bevy of buzzards fought over what remained of her bubble, their pecks rapid and loud. Two, though, hopped in towards her newborn. On their beaks, traces of red and white were sprinkled about.

The mother began to circle her baby, her sounds gutteral. Her udder, full with milk, swung beneath her. On the rounded ends of her teats, milk seeped. She rammed one bird with her nose. It grunted and hopped back. She moved faster now. Almost running. Charging the second one to her left. Then to her right. Only for a third buzzard and then a fourth to join in. The mother's breathing was hurried. Her mouth dry, bone dry.

Her back left knee hit the dirt. She fell to the ground and rolled. She rocked her body hard but could not get up on her knees. She pawed at the ground, digging grooves, deep ones.

She extended her neck and released a cry, her voice hoarse now. Streaks of sweat in jagged white lines crisscrossed her body. Her second-born lay five feet away. But the mother cow could not see her for the curtain of buzzards.

In time, and it would be just before the sun hit its highest point that day, the mother cow managed to return to her feet and to her firstborn, still in the patch on the ground, his head still against the earth, and his whole being, his whole being still alive and set to carry the prayers of all who would cross his path.

part 2

———

MEET

MARCH 12, 1951

On her knees against the linoleum floor, Sarah Creamer ran her flat hand over the two shelves in her kitchen cupboard, patting every inch of the whitewashed wood as if she was searching for something lost.

She was searching for food to feed their boy.

This was in the early morning, just before the sun showed itself. She would like to have pulled on the light over the table to help her see, but electricity cost good money, and she and Harold were already two months behind on their light bill. She thought about burning the kerosene lamp, but kerosene cost a whole nickel a quart, and only one finger high remained in the jar. So Sarah patted in the dark.

But all she felt that morning was everlasting crumbs.

She had no food for their boy's breakfast. He'd eaten the last three spoonfuls of grits the morning before.

The paper sack to hold his school dinner lay on the table behind her. It held nothing but wrinkles. She would have to give him the same dinner she'd given him the last two weeks and a handful of scattered days before that.

She went to her bedroom, just across the hall from the kitchen. Beneath the chifforobe, three pears lay huddled together. They'd survived the long winter wrapped in newspaper to keep them from ripening too fast. She tucked one in her apron pocket and returned to the kitchen table, where she used her hands like a hot iron, pressing the sack against the hard wood that still carried Mattie's stains. She had tried to wash them out, but the blood had soaked in and made itself a home.

Sarah found that if she pressed her hands long enough, she could make the paper look somewhat presentable.

She wished she had a new one to give him, but that would have to wait until she could afford more food, and that was in question now that Harold had come home with that letter the day before.

She unwrapped the newspaper from the pear and set the pear inside the sack. The paper itself, half of a full page, then half again, she left in the shape it had become, a cantaloupe bloom gathered in to protect. She placed it in the peck basket on the floor by the woodstove. It was the lone piece. She'd used the last one to start the fire that morning.

The school bus would arrive in an hour. With nothing to feed their boy, she would let him sleep an extra few minutes.

She went to the kitchen sink, leaned forward towards the window, and strained to look to her far right at Harold's barn. Light, thin lines of it, traced the door on the front, and in the wood itself, she saw a sprinkling of dots like stars out at night. He'd left his kerosene lamp on again. Some nights he had the state of mind to blow it out before he became too intoxicated. But those nights had become increasingly scarce.

No lights were on across the old garden at Mattie's. Sarah looked for them every day. There had been none since her death. Billy Udean arrived in a police automobile escort a little after half past noon that day, the siren announcing him breaking though the open window over her sink, where she had been standing, keeping watch with the baby in her arms. The sound came in from afar, high pitched and moving in circles. Sarah had thought about running across and telling him, "There was a gunshot, and I think our Mattie might be dead. I couldn't get her to the door, Billy Udean, I couldn't." But the baby was asleep, finally asleep, his belly full of the milk she had driven to town, to Richbourg's, to buy with the change she had found in Harold's overall pockets. No parade was held that day. Since then, the house had sat empty, the garden growing only tall weeds and brush. She and Harold had thought about trying to make a go of one again, but he called the land stained and couldn't bring himself to go get the mule for plowing.

Frost covered the world outside the window that morning, the dirt and grass and weeds, anything bold enough to stay in temperatures that fell into the low thirties overnight. At least the kitchen would be warm for their boy. She hoped it would surround him like a good coat.

She walked down the short hall to his room. His sheets still smelled of the air where she'd hung them out to dry the day before. She took a deep breath and brought the scent into her body. His sheets were clean. She could do that for him.

He lay on his right side, facing the window, where the sun's light, however dim, found its way in. His face showed a feature he shared with his mother, her nose, as delicate as a china doll's. But that was not the most prominent feature he and Mattie shared. He had her dimples.

But they lay asleep.

Sarah folded herself onto the floor, placed her knees on the planks beside his single bed, and called his name, she called, "Emerson Bridge."

His eyes opened, showing her the light green of butterbeans, the ones she and Mattie used to pick. Harold's eyes were that color.

But what she lived for came along next, his dimples. They sank into his cheeks like a finger in biscuit dough, something Sarah loved to make for him, the flour and lard and buttermilk in a big bowl, her fingers bringing it all together. She imagined her finger now dipping into his dimple's curve the way a spoon would, scooping grits. But she remembered she had no grits to feed him, nor any biscuits, and did not know when she would.

"I'm sorry," she told him. She knew her voice quivered. She wanted it strong for him and tried to think of something hard and straight. She pictured the boards beneath her. "But I ain't got nothing to feed you this morning, hon." She managed to keep her voice flat until she said "nothing," and then her voice went wavy again.

"That's all right, Mama," he said.

Mama.

Her eyes flooded. Harold had taught him to call her that. As a baby in his crib, Emerson Bridge would raise his arms, Harold picking him up, their bodies swinging left then right, the two of them, blood kin, moving as one, while Sarah stood alone at the door and watched. She wished he would raise his arms like that for her, let her feel his dimpled face against her bosom. But he never had. He liked to stay private, buddying with himself, except for his papa. They were best friends.

When he passed through the kitchen that morning, she handed him the sack. "You have a good day now, hon." She tried to put a lift in her voice.

From the window at the sink, she watched him run down the dirt driveway towards the school bus. In his little hand, the sack swayed left and right.

He was a boy of only six. His birthday would come in three months, would come in June. He needed food to flesh out that tiny body of his, especially his cheeks where his dimples lived.

The lone pear she'd sent was not enough.

She took in her hand the bottom of the curtains. They framed the window like a child's bangs with a short run of hair along the sides. She squeezed the fabric. She squeezed hard.

She leaned towards the glass and spotted his footprints in the frost just out from the porch's bottom step, his right, then his left and right again. He'd taken his first steps on Father's Day, a week shy of turning a year old, Harold behind him, his hands on Emerson Bridge's sides, Sarah in front, her hands holding the tips of his little fingers. "That's right, come on, let's walk," she had said and wanted to add, "Mama's got you," but she had stopped herself, saying instead, "Papa, Papa's got you, hon." Sparkles, their boy had stepped into sparkles that morning. And they had cushioned him, like his papa's arms.

Maybe, one day, hers.

The mouths of the mother cow and her calf, inches apart, hovered over the newly reawakened Kentucky 31 fescue and ladino clover. Flecks of green glistened on their lips, a testimony to the plentifulness that spread across the seventy-one acres of pastureland like a rug. This was particularly welcome after the long winter when the fields had gone dormant, and they were left to the mercy of the farmer, whose worker on most days had brought them buckets of ground corn and tossed bales of hay off the side of the farmer's truck.

The two were part of a herd of five dozen, all of them grazing and making their way down the sloping land to the pond that sat into the earth like a bowl. The mother and her calf would eat, then walk, then eat some more, all the while keeping their sights on each other. Every few minutes, the calf would suckle her, wrapping his mouth around a teat and pulling hard. Milk, long warmed from her body, poured full inside him. He was four months old and born a bull in the off-month of November, his heifer sister killed when a bevy of buzzards attacked her. But the farmer, a few days after the bull's birth, had his workingman slit the bottom of the calf's sack and reach inside and yank down a cord, which he cut, making the cord fall to the ground and the bull, a steer now, his only use as meat.

He was his mother's first male calf. Always before, she had delivered females and in the early spring, the customary time for births. All remained in the herd with her except two. Each had missed delivering a calf for the farmer's use and was sent to the sale barn for slaughter. The mother cow was old, sixteen, an age unheard of to still be alive. But she had continued to deliver calves, and, for that, the farmer had let her live.

The wailing cry of another steer, this one a year and a half old and the offspring of one of the mother cow's heifers, sounded up the slope near the lot. The mother cow located her own calf, who was at the pond now, taking a drink and splashing water with his head. She looked back the way of the cry. Many of the other cows looked that way, too, but then lowered their heads to resume eating or drinking.

But not the year-and-a-half-old steer's mother. She lingered up the hill, her head high and looking, as the farmer's truck sounded, and from her mouth came her own sound, bellows, which, for a while, her calf returned, until he was carried too far away.

Sarah took herself to the barn. Harold's lamp sat on dirt in the midst of Old Crow whiskey bottles, some standing upright, others on their side, but all empty. Two bales of straw, placed end to end, sat behind the lamp. Her husband lay across them. She had expected to find him sprawled and dangling the way he presented himself most of the time now, but this day he lay as a baby would inside his mother, curled chin to knees, his arms folded and tucked in at his chest.

She picked up the lamp to blow it out but noticed his eyes. They were closed like most mornings, but the crevice in his skin between them looked to be not as deep. Tingles rose to her scalp. He had lost some of his worry. She feared he was dead. She widened her legs, steadying herself in his dirt.

Above his shoulders, clothed in his overalls' denim straps, she held the lamp. Her hand shook, making the light play on him as if it was a bare foot and him a freshly plowed plot of land. "Harold," she said and watched for his rise and fall.

When it came, it was tiny, like a fluttering of a fledgling bird. Sarah dropped to her knees. He smelled of whiskey, saturated like the air in her kitchen used to be, full of grease from fish fried crispy on Sunday nights with Mattie. But that air was beloved.

She shifted the light back to his eyes, buried amidst the hair that began claiming his face the night Emerson Bridge was born. "Harold, it's Sarah, wake up." She shook his shoulder and felt the bones of him, there at the surface like a fish coming up for air.

His eyes peeked open.

Sarah felt every nerve in her body at the edge of her skin. He was alive. He was not leaving her alone. He could find work again. He might not be able to climb poles or work with the telephone wires, but he could drive the truck for someone or how about sitting in the office like a woman and answering the telephone, even become a Hello Girl like the job he had gotten Mattie.

He moved his right arm from near his chest like he wanted to reach for her, maybe even pull her to him and kiss her. Not since the night after they buried Mattie had they lost themselves in their grief with a kiss that told each other they were not alone. Sarah leaned in towards him, but he opened his hand, and there was that letter, his hand shaking so, the paper gave a slight breeze. "I'm sorry," he said.

"They got it wrong," she told him. "You *can* work. Just need to get you through this bad pneumonia and a little cleaned up is all." She began brushing aside his hair. It had grayed more than she'd realized. He was only thirty-nine.

He ground his forehead into the straw. Pieces of it broke loose and flew to the floor.

"All right, maybe not at Southern Bell no more. But what about odd jobs? Like helping that Mr. Dobbins on his farm." Sarah knew she was talking fast, too fast, but could not stop herself. "They got them a little cross, the kind they say Jesus died on, right there on the living room table by a big Bible. They go to church. He's one of them good Christian kind of men."

"Sarah," Harold said, his voice cutting through like a knife. "I said *I'm sorry.*" His eyes no longer carried the white hue of life but now showed the color of egg yolks, the yellow that eggs become when she used to beat them when she had eggs too for them to eat.

He tucked the letter back in against his chest, closed his eyes, and curled back up with himself.

She knew the words by heart. *Dear Mr. Harold Creamer, We regret to inform you that your employment with Southern Bell Telephone Company has been terminated. We appreciate your 19 years of service, however, we no longer can hold your position for you.* They signed off with *Kindest Regards.* But Sarah didn't know what was kind about letting a man go and putting him and his family at risk of losing everything they had.

Sarah got up off her knees. "Reckon they stayed with you as long as they could. You was hit and miss, for sure." At first, after Mattie died, for their boy's sake, he worked steady and used his money for the household. But, over the last two years, his work had begun slowing down like a clock needing to be wound again. Most of the little money he made, he drank.

She thought of Emerson Bridge. "Don't trouble yourself none," she told Harold. "I'll carry it, I will." She blew out the lamp.

. . . . .

Inside the chifforobe, on the bottom shelf and wrapped in a baby-blue blanket, lay something Sarah had never wanted to disturb. Three months shy of seven years had passed since she had folded it and placed it inside for safekeeping. But this morning, Sarah picked up the bundle, held it like a child, and laid it on the bed, where her fingers unwrapped it, revealing the rayon crepe, six yards of it in midnight blue. This was Mattie's material. Sarah had used it to make Mattie's burial dress. She had bought extra, tucking it away like some people keep their husband's first love note or their child's first tooth.

She let herself touch it. It was soft. She pressed on it, felt it collapse to a thin nothing. But when she released it, it sprang back to the shape it once had known. "Mattie," Sarah whispered.

Mr. Dobbins's wife used to give Sarah four dollars over the cost of the material for each dress Sarah made her. But a year ago, she stopped buying from Sarah, saying her husband made her start buying store-bought dresses only.

This was Sarah's only fabric, and there was no money to buy more.

She brought the cloth to her face and imagined it as food on their boy's plate, grits and scrambled eggs, hot biscuits, slices of loaf bread and Treet, spoonfuls of pork 'n' beans, even a box of Hydrox cookies. She would take three dollars now for a dress and add in a dollar and a quarter for the material, so $4.25 tops, and she would be glad for it.

This cloth was fancy. Mrs. Dobbins liked fancy. She liked a collar at her neck, a simple one, an inch and a half in width that laid flat, leaving a respectable "V," yet giving her neck plenty of room to display her pearls. Mrs. Dobbins liked her pearls. She would look at the neck first.

This would be a dress, not of promise, as the others had been, but of hope. Mrs. Dobbins would want this dress. She had to.

. . . . .

Harold stood at Sarah's back. She could smell him. It was late afternoon, and she sat at her sewing machine in their bedroom, pedaling Mattie's cloth through. She had Emerson Bridge's supper, the second pear, waiting for him on a plate on the kitchen table.

"You done said you was sorry," she told Harold and thought he would leave, but she heard no sound towards that. She heard his breathing, labored and full of phlegm.

He began to cry. They were big sobs, not the quiet kind that could be mistaken for a runny nose. These were from way down where lies were no longer welcome.

She turned towards him, his head lowered and his body shaking all the way down his arms. They used to be a strong man's arms. Now they looked small. A quiver of sadness began in the pit of her belly and shot up to her face, which became hot and full.

She rose from her machine, closed the door to their room and got into their bed. She slid towards his side. It felt cool, even cold, through her housedress. "Come to bed," she said and raised the covers with her hand held high.

He did not move.

19

"That other," he said and tried to clear his throat. "I'm sorry about that *other*."

"I am, too," she told him and wished the sun wasn't leaving. He stood just out from the window, where a curtain, yellow with red flowers, had begun to dull in the fading light. At the sun's peak, it would shine through the flowers and set them to spinning. The flowers that afternoon were dead still.

"Come to bed," she said.

"It wasn't but one time. I want you to know that."

She did know that. "Come to bed."

"I'm filthy."

"I am, too." She reached for his hand. It felt crusty. She pulled him towards her until he lay beside her, clothes and boots and all. She moved her mouth towards his and found his lips as soft as a woman's. No longer were they buried in hair.

He cried harder.

Sarah ran her fingers over his skin and felt it covered in tiny bumps. In various places, she saw cuts. He had shaved. Was it for her, because he was staying? Or for God, because he was leaving?

She brought his head to her bosom. Her body shook with his.

It took a while for him to get his words out, but in time, he said, "Reckon you could ever find it in your good heart to forgive me?"

Sarah knew the big word to him was "forgive," but to her it was "good," regardless of what he had put with it. She wrapped her arms around his head and pressed him into her. She thought she could feel her heart coming up through him. "Yeah, I can," she told him. "I sure can. But I know you can't never forgive me back. And that's all right."

"You don't have nothing to be forgiven for," he said.

I don't want him, I don't want him, I don't want him, cycled through Sarah's mind. Emerson Bridge was just a baby the night she'd screamed those words, but, still, he surely could have heard. "But I do. If I just hadn't said I didn't—"

"I love you, Sarah," Harold told her, his head now lifted, his eyes straight on her. "I said I love you, Sarah, Sarah Creamer."

His words ran a stitch to her. "I love you, too, Harold, Harold Creamer."

The sun took itself from their room. It was as if it had visited, eked out a presence and said, *Hey, don't forget me.*

But the words they had just said to each other stayed, and it came to her that, until that very moment, she didn't know her husband any better than the day they had said their "I do's" to a stranger and were pronounced man and wife. What had defined them as a couple were the words they had never said. But now that they had said them, for the first time, she felt alive with him.

· · · · ·

Harold's head began moving above Sarah in short jerks to the left and holding and then to the right and doing the same.

"Harold, what is it? What you seeing?"

But he did not answer her.

Darkness had come full on now. Sarah rolled out from under him and lit the kerosene lamp beside the bed. She cast the light about the room but saw nothing.

She brought the light to his face. His eyes were wide and bouncing. She had not seen them that open since he had looked at Mattie. "Is it Mattie?" she asked, her heart picking up its rate. "She coming for you?" Sarah had heard that the dead do that.

His eyes bounced to the right, towards the chifforobe.

Sarah directed the light there. "Mattie? Sister Mattie, is that you? It is, ain't it?" Sarah thought she could smell potatoes being peeled. "What she look like? She still little and pretty like a china doll? You said that one time, that she was little and pretty like a china doll."

Harold's eyes were bouncing again.

Sarah pictured her own fingers. They were fat like cornbread pones.

His eyes came back around, and this time stopped on her. On *her*, Sarah. She waited for them to move on, but they did not. He began to nod his head like he was agreeing to something. She watched his eyes fill.

Sarah felt light-headed. She had been hoping that death would continue to be a spectator in his life, sit around like it was watching him connect a telephone line. But she knew now there was no more watching.

She blew out the light and made them both naked. She brought his head to her chest and felt his eyelashes stroke her. They were soft like a baby's.

"Tell her I love her, too. And miss her, too, would you?" She thought she smelled catfish frying and heard grease sizzling, it popping up and hitting her hand and Mattie rushing over and wiping it off. But Sarah never minded being marked like that. She wished she could be marked again.

Around his back, Sarah wrapped her arms and pressed so hard, her muscles shimmied. "Don't leave me, Harold. I don't want to be the only one of us left here."

She felt him clutch her, too, their bodies hugging the way they did before Mattie had come into their lives. She imagined him inside her like that first time in that automobile in the woods when she believed he loved her.

"You ain't," he said. "The boy. You got the boy. Our son, Emerson Bridge."

"But he's—" Sarah said.

"He's yours."

But I don't know how to be no good mama, she wanted to say. She knew those words, though, would give him no peace of mind. Or Mattie, either. And didn't they both need peace of mind? "Mine," she told him, "yes mine," and felt every drop of blood rush to her head.

. . . . .

When Harold stopped breathing, Sarah lay beneath him in his silence. She took big breaths, lifting him high and feeling his weight come back to her, until she became dizzy and thought birds fluttered in her head.

She pictured Mattie hovering over them. A thin light ringed her face. It was true. She was still little and pretty like a china doll. And her dimples, they cradled the sides of her mouth. Sarah had always said they could hold a whole lot of happiness. She had used only three and a half yards of Mattie's cloth for Mrs. Dobbins's dress, which left her with two and a half, not enough for a dress for herself. But, still, she had some of Mattie's cloth.

Sarah started to call her husband's name, call him Harold, but, instead, she said, "Harry. Go to her, Harry," said it out loud and let his name carry.

Then she withdrew her arms from him, brought them down along her side and cuddled them up under herself.

She felt him become as light as a piece of thread.

. . . . .

Just before first light, Sarah covered Harold's body with the sheet that had covered them. She would like to have pulled the covers over her, too, but she had a boy to feed.

On her body, still naked and warm, she placed her housedress, wrinkled and cold, and returned to the sewing machine and Mrs. Dobbins's dress. She only had the collar to finish. She would wake Emerson Bridge in time for school.

They no longer had a telephone. It had been disconnected for lack of payment. She would use Mrs. Dobbins's telephone to call about Harold and would put as much of Mrs. Dobbins's money towards the burial as she could.

She began to pedal, her feet working in a rhythm that soon brought the dress home. One day she would buy Emerson Bridge a bicycle, and he would pedal it with a full belly.

She hung Mrs. Dobbins's dress on a hanger on the nail on the back of the door and retrieved her lamp, which she held just out from her creation, there at the left shoulder where the sleeve crested. With her fingers on the seam, she moved in concert with the light, down the curve of the armpit, then down the side of the dress, checking to make sure there were no skips in the stitching, either from gathering in too tight and bunching up or in going long and making holes. Sarah needed them to follow like school children, lucky enough to line up on the Monday after Easter Sunday to march around the classroom and show off their new outfits, the girls in dresses made by mothers who let them go to church and sit on pews and answer the altar call to get saved.

The stitches followed.

She started down the right side. At the waist, she found a hole the size of her finger and removed the stitches on both sides of the opening, catching up under the loops with a needle and pulling them free. If it had not been this dress, she would have done as her mother had taught her and removed only one inch on each side. But it was this dress, Mrs. Dobbins's dress, and it had to be perfect. She removed four inches back and four inches forward and fed the material through again.

She returned the garment to the hanger and ran the light over it again, and not just over the place she had repaired but over the entire dress. One more time.

And then out loud, she said, "Please. Let it be good enough. Please."

MARCH 13, 1951

Sarah stood by Emerson Bridge's bed and watched for his rise and fall. When it came, his tiny breath, she drew it in. His papa was alive when he had closed his eyes the night before. But as soon as she woke him, he would be in a world where his papa was no more. And left only with her. How could she bring him and his dimples into that?

She lowered her head, crossed her arms longways down the front of her body and squeezed in her shoulders. She thought of the smallest place she could tuck herself. The flour bin that no longer held flour. No, the food warmer, the bare food warmer, on the woodstove for biscuits.

"Mama?" she heard. "You cold?"

He was awake. She felt a rush in her nose, a stinging.

"No, hon, I'm just right. You? You cold?" The heat from the fire in the woodstove did not reach his room. She would put an extra blanket on his bed that night.

He pulled the sheet up over his face. Maybe he would go back to sleep, and she could steal away to Mrs. Dobbins and sell the dress. But what if he woke and found his papa in the bed down the hall behind a closed, hard door?

She had to wake him fully.

She wanted to hear him say his name. Harold had wanted her to name him, but she had thought it was his place to. He returned home from work one day, saying he had found a name on a road sign in the southern part of the county, while he was out on telephone company business. The road was Old Emerson Bridge Road. "Because I hope he gets to grow old," Harold had said. She had never wished that more than now.

"What's your name, hon?"

He pulled the covers higher.

He wanted to sleep. Maybe if she closed his door, he would stay in his bed. She looked that way now, but Harold's body lay only ten feet away. She couldn't risk it. "Hon?" she said.

But he said nothing.

She'd heard Harold say the words "I said" when Emerson Bridge didn't do what Harold had asked him to, like go to the road to get the mail or go out to the clothesline and get him a work shirt.

Sarah took a deep breath. "I said *What's your name?*"

His fingers came from beneath and wrapped around the covers. Slowly, he revealed his face, the growing light rushing onto it. On his upper cheek, she saw a small cut and a longer one on his chin. And all about his skin, bumps, tiny and red, lay scattered like polka dots on swiss fabric.

He had shaved. Just like Harold had. They'd done it together. They'd done it while she had sewed the afternoon before.

She tried not to shake all over.

"It's Emerson Bridge, Mama," he said, his voice light, his dimples still asleep.

She couldn't tell him now. She would give him half of the third pear for breakfast and the other half for his school dinner. With Mrs. Dobbins's money, she would buy flour and shortening and buttermilk for biscuits and a can of meat, and she would fill his plate for supper.

Then she would tell him.

· · · · ·

Sarah left in Harold's automobile, a black 1935 Ford coupe, and headed east, towards the Mrs. Luther Dobbins's house in the Centerville community. It was a good four miles away. Sarah hoped she had enough gasoline to get her there.

She parked under a grove of pecan trees that looked as magnificent as the Dobbins house with its thick, white columns on the front. The dress of midnight blue lay beside her, wrapped in a blanket of a lighter blue. She had left it unhemmed but brought needle and thread to finish the job. She had wanted to leave the dress on the hanger to keep it free and flowing, but runs of Harold's whiskey had left dark sticky spots on the long leather seat, coated in dust and the yellow of pollen.

Sarah lifted her gloves from her lap. They were black and carried a silkiness she liked. She slipped them on her hands and opened her fingers like she was readying them to carry a big cantaloupe from the garden, but then brought them together as if praying, her fingers finding the open spaces before them and falling through, tucking in the cloth. A hat, also black, sat upon her head. It was round and short and flat with netting all around, thin black netting, which she had raised to the heavens before she left the house. The last time she wore the hat, she left the netting down. That was to Mattie's funeral.

"A lady always wears a hat and gloves," she said out loud.

On her body, she wore a brown housedress. She would have liked to have worn better, but this was the best she had. She held the blanket against her bosom and, with her free hand, opened the door and stepped out into the Dobbins yard, already a deep green, each blade the same height. Azaleas, a whole crop of them, surrounded the house. They stood tall and guarding and ready to burst with color.

The front door was big and wooden and appeared to be covered in a shine. If this was not the Dobbins house, she would have thought it was grease. It set off the door just right and said *Look at me, I'm worth seeing.*

Sarah knocked. Her hands were perspiring. She hoped Mrs. Dobbins remembered her. "Mrs. Dobbins?" she called through. "It's Sarah, Sarah Creamer."

But she heard no footsteps come her way across the living room floor. She had never spent much time in that room. Mrs. Dobbins always ushered her up the stairs to her bedroom, to the large oval floor mirror made of real cherry wood, Mrs. Dobbins always liked to say.

Sarah felt her heart pick up its pace. Perhaps the woman was not at home.

She knocked again and, this time, heard footsteps. She smoothed down her dress and swallowed, clearing her throat for the words she'd come to say.

The door opened but only about a foot. Mrs. Dobbins stood in the gap and wiped her mouth with the back of her hand.

"Mrs. Dobbins," Sarah said and thought she smelled peppermint.

"Why, Mrs. Creamer." The woman's head peeked out, looking to the left and right. "Big LC didn't see you, did he?" She was whispering.

That was what Mrs. Dobbins called her husband. "I don't believe so, no ma'am."

"Good. He's got his full mind on the catastrophe yesterday with that steer show, so I think we're safe."

The smell of sausage and biscuits filled the air. "Oh, I'm sorry. I didn't mean to interrupt y'all's breakfast," Sarah said.

But the woman shook her head. "Wasn't much eating. Not this morning." She reached into her apron and pulled out a red and white striped piece of candy the size of a marble, a peppermint. "Excuse me," she said and put it in her mouth. "My nerves are bad today."

Sarah could hear it rolling around Mrs. Dobbins's teeth.

She cleared her throat and pushed out, "I made a dress," and extended her arms through the opening. "For you. The dress is inside." Sarah tried to keep her arms from shaking.

But Mrs. Dobbins did not take the blanket. She leaned forward and whispered, "Afraid we have a situation here, Mrs. Creamer. Little LC didn't bring home the Grand Champion yesterday, and Big LC is fit to be tied. I wish I could invite you in, but it'd not be a good thing. Not today."

Sarah thought of Emerson Bridge's empty plate and his ribs she'd begun seeing. She took a deep breath, clenched her fists, and barged through the door and past Mrs. Dobbins. "I'm sorry," she said, "but I came to tell you I'm in bad need of," when a door slammed hard, and Mrs. Dobbins called out, "Oh my heavens," and grabbed Sarah by her arm and tried to pull her back outside.

"Where is he? In his room?" It was Mr. Dobbins coming up the hall beside the stairs.

Mrs. Dobbins let go of Sarah like she'd been holding something hot.

"Uncle said he didn't get on the school bus this morning," he hollered and swung around the banister and headed up the steps, taking two at a time.

"He was too torn up to go to school today, Big LC," Mrs. Dobbins called out. "He's just a little boy."

"You shut your mouth, you heifer you." He was at the top of the stairs now, his finger pointed at her like a gun.

Mrs. Dobbins patted at the pocket on her apron, which looked to be holding something heavy.

"Get out here, boy. Right now!" Mr. Dobbins yelled into a room.

A little boy came to stand in the doorway. He was about the size of Emerson Bridge. He stood at attention like a soldier. Sarah knew this was a private moment and that she should leave, but she couldn't. She needed to sell the dress.

"This is the front page of today's paper, people," the man hollered as if he had a crowd and held up the newspaper. "Do you see your *little boy,* your *Little LC's* picture? No! Because he didn't win. Made me the laughing stock of all of Anderson County. And I won't have it." He ripped the page off and beat it into a tight wad. "Charles would have won."

"But I almost won, Daddy."

"I'd rather have nothing than almost," Mr. Dobbins said and threw the paper over the heads of the two women.

Sarah watched it roll through the open door.

"He wouldn't do right for me, Daddy," the boy said, his head held back and chin stretched high. "Couldn't teach him nothing."

"You listen to me, you can teach a steer to deal cards, if you want to. It's a matter of getting right with them, showing who's the boss."

"But Daddy, that'd be mean."

A cracking sound came from Mrs. Dobbins's mouth like she'd bit down hard on the candy.

"Hey, it's got four feet, two more than you. It could walk away, if it wanted to."

Sarah didn't know what a steer was, but it had four feet. She was thinking it must be a farm animal, maybe a cow or a pig. She grew up in a mill village, and she and Harold had land, ten acres, but no animals.

"You're the last one of us Dobbins men," the man hollered, "and you better bring the almighty blue ribbon home next year, is all I say." He walked down the stairs a couple of steps and beat his fist against an empty space on the wall that carried large glass cases, each displaying the front page of a newspaper and a big blue ribbon."Right here, boy," he said and beat the wall again. "Right here, my next glory, you hear me?"

Sarah brought the blanket in close. She wondered if he ever beat Mrs. Dobbins.

The back door soon slammed.

"I didn't mean to not win for him, Mama," the boy called from the top.

"I know you didn't, dear." Mrs. Dobbins headed up the steps.

"Shortcake tried, too, Mama, he did." Sarah heard tears in his voice. "I'll try to win for Daddy next year."

"I know you will, dear." Mrs. Dobbins had the boy in her arms now. "We all will."

This seemed even more private. But Sarah had to stay. She turned her back to them.

"Daddy doesn't love me, Mama."

"You know he does, dear."

"I don't either, Mama. I don't."

A vehicle rushed past the house. Mrs. Dobbins ran down the steps and to the side window, where she peeked through lace curtains. "It's him," she said. "He's gone now."

The boy took off down the steps and ran out the back door.

"Try to have some fun, dear!" Mrs. Dobbins called after him, then took a skinny dark glass bottle from her apron, unscrewed the top and brought it to her mouth. She took a long swig. "Got that bad nervous indigestion," she said and pointed with the bottle towards the glass cases. "That's what Big LC likes to call the mighty Dobbins Dynasty along that wall there. Some McClain boy won in '41, but that was before the mighty Dobbins arrived on the scene."

Sarah stepped in closer and saw that that each displayed a large photograph of a boy standing beside a big cow. So a steer is a cow, she was thinking.

The bottle was back up at Mrs. Dobbins's mouth now, her head held back. Sarah told herself that when the woman lowered the bottle, she'd outright say what she came to say.

But Mrs. Dobbins kept the bottle at her mouth.

"I don't mean to take up no space here, ma'am, and I know I'm stepping out, because you didn't ask me to do this, but I made a dress for you." Sarah held the blanket towards the woman.

Mrs. Dobbins lowered the bottle but did not take the blanket. Instead, she extended the bottle towards Sarah. "Want some? It's just Retonga."

Sarah had never heard of Retonga and didn't want any. But she needed to sell the dress. She took the bottle and brought it to her lips but kept them closed. She threw her head back like Mrs. Dobbins had.

"I can assure you," the woman told her, "it's a purely herbal stomachic medicine, not that bad alcohol, even though Big LC wouldn't think there was any difference. You know, he's a deacon at the church. Probably the head one, I don't know." She started to laugh.

Sarah handed the bottle back to the woman. She tasted a sweetness and then a bitterness.

On the wall behind Mrs. Dobbins, five stuffed deer heads hung. They had pretty brown eyes and looked scared.

Sarah took a deep breath and held out the dress again. "I made you this."

This time she took it. "Why, aren't you nice?" She peeked inside and giggled and pulled it out.

"Hope you like it," Sarah said. "And *want* it."

The blanket and dress fell to the floor. They made almost no sound. "Why, mercy me," Mrs. Dobbins said and bent to the heart of pine planks, shined to a high gloss.

Sarah had to catch her breath.

Dark blue and baby blue lay tangled up. Mrs. Dobbins grabbed the dark blue, yanking it as if it was a rag from a rag bag, and held the dress by its shoulders.

Sarah kept her eyes on the woman's face, on her eyes, especially, for the verdict. "I thought for something fancy. Like church."

Mrs. Dobbins brought the dress to her face and pressed it in, then her shoulders began to shake like she was crying. She must smell Harold's whiskey.

"I'm sorry, I'll get it cleaned for you," Sarah told her and wished she could take back her words. She didn't know how much it would cost, but even a nickel would be too much.

The woman slid her face around the cloth. Her eyes were puffy. "I want to thank you for not fussing at me just then."

Sarah felt herself relax. "It's all right. It's not something that would break or nothing, ma'am."

Mrs. Dobbins laughed. "Why, Mrs. Creamer, I never knew you to have a funny bone."

Sarah didn't see what was funny about what she'd just said, but she wanted the woman to want the dress, so Sarah began to laugh, too. At first, it was forced and unfamiliar and like she was coughing. But the longer she went, the memory of laughter in her belly returned, and she began to laugh a true laugh. It echoed in the midst of the ceilings that seemed as high as the sky and seemed to fill the space all around her.

Mrs. Dobbins now was skipping about the floor.

Sarah joined her, the bottoms of her black serviceable shoes tap tapping along the wood, until she kicked them off, sent them flying over the coffee table that held the Bible, while her stocking-covered feet popped against the boards from moisture that had collected along her soles. Her hat sloped off the side of her head. She'd used bobby pins to hold it in place, but she saw now that she'd not used enough to accommodate laughter.

But then Sarah stopped herself cold. She came upon the dress and the blanket. They lay in the floor again. Without the laughter, Sarah felt small in the room. She picked them up. "How about us going ahead and getting this pinned for you?" She started up the stairs but heard no footsteps behind her.

"Why, no one's ever done something so nice for me before," Mrs. Dobbins said. "Giving me a dress like this, making me a nice present of it."

Sarah stopped and held onto the railing. It was smooth beneath her gloves. She turned to face the woman, still rooted on the bottom floor. "Really, I didn't—" but Mrs. Dobbins said, "Really, dear, I'm in no shape to get it pinned today." Her words were slurred. "What about coming back tomorrow? The big cattlemen's steak supper is Saturday night, and Big LC will want to go, even if it's just to save face. I think he likes me in blue."

Tomorrow, Sarah heard, *tomorrow.* She pictured Emerson Bridge's empty plate. She couldn't wait until then. "It's not a present, Mrs. Dobbins. I—"

"You're a good friend, Mrs. Creamer, and I thank you. Big LC says y'all aren't churchgoers, but you'd never know." Mrs. Dobbins was spinning like a dancer now.

Harold in the bed. Emerson Bridge returning from school. Sarah's belly knotted up. "Excuse me," she called out, "but can I borrow y'all's telephone for just a minute?"

Mrs. Dobbins spun a few more times, then stopped and pointed towards the wall beyond the stairs, where a telephone sat on a small table.

After Mattie died, Sarah had thought about calling someone to report it, but she decided to leave that to Billy Udean. "Excuse me again," she said, "but who do you call when somebody dies?"

The woman came towards her but not in a straight line. "Why, the preacher's always been with my dead," she said and fingered the string of pearls that circled her neck.

"We don't have one of them," Sarah told her.

"What about the doctor, then, dear?"

"We don't have one of them, either. My husband don't. I left him back at the house cold in the bed dead to come here."

Mrs. Dobbins took her fingers from her pearls and, like a bird, flittered over to Sarah's shoulder. Her hand was little like Mattie's. Sarah wanted to lay her head on it. "Oh dear. Was it sudden?"

Sarah shook her head. "I'd say it's been coming on for as long as he's known me, and that was on the 27th day of April, 19 and 36."

Mrs. Dobbins brought her arms around Sarah. At first, Sarah kept hers to herself, but the kindness brought Sarah's forth, too.

Mrs. Dobbins picked up the receiver. "I'll call my . . . my . . . now who was I calling?"

"I believe you said your preacher or your doctor."

"Oh yes." She dialed a number.

Sarah backed up against the wall.

"Dear, where do y'all live?" Mrs. Dobbins asked.

"Thrasher Road. Second mailbox on the left down from New Prospect Church."

Sarah bowed her head.

Mrs. Dobbins hung up the telephone, spun around once and then sat in the little chair beside the table. "That was Doc Clinkscales." She leaned her head against the wall. "Expect him sometime late this afternoon."

Sarah didn't know how much a funeral would cost, but it had to be plenty. Mrs. Dobbins's eyes looked heavy. Sarah stepped in towards her and held out the blanket. Maybe she could get the woman to see it and change her mind about going up the steps.

But Mrs. Dobbins closed her eyes.

"I can't thank you enough, ma'am, I can't," Sarah said, her voice loud, almost shouting.

But Mrs. Dobbins's mouth soon dropped open, and she began to snore.

Sarah lowered the blanket. *Tomorrow.* Until then, she had nothing to feed Emerson Bridge.

She passed the kitchen on the way to retrieve her shoes. The smell of sausage and biscuits lingered in the air. She peered inside. The room had a tall ceiling, was painted a bright yellow, and was as large as half of Sarah's little white clapboard house. A table sat in the middle, as if on display. On it, plates of food remained, heaped, pretty as a picture.

She stepped inside. There were bowls of scrambled eggs and grits, a platter of fried patty sausage and a basket of biscuits, along with jars of pear preserves and strawberry jam and a full stick of butter on cut glass. Sarah knew she shouldn't be in there, but she couldn't leave.

She lifted a biscuit from the basket and used her fingers like a knife to open it. Inside, she placed a piece of sausage. She had never stolen before, but she had never been without food for Emerson Bridge. She would cut the biscuit in half for his supper and tomorrow morning give him the rest for breakfast. Then she would return to the Dobbins house and sell the dress, and with the money, buy food for his dinner and deliver it to him at school. And she would tell Mrs. Dobbins she had taken the food and ask for forgiveness and subtract a dollar from the cost of the dress.

She placed the food inside the blanket but was careful not to touch the dress.

She found her shoes and put them on.

On the porch, the balled up newspaper lay. She picked it up and placed it inside the blanket. Tomorrow morning she would have paper to burn. Tomorrow morning the kitchen would be warm for Emerson Bridge.

· · · · ·

Sarah ran out of gasoline on Whitehall Road, not too far beyond Emerson Bridge's school. She took off walking towards home, about three miles away.

The day had warmed into the fifties. She was thankful. She had left her house without a sweater.

· · · · ·

At home, Sarah put the sausage biscuit in the food warmer on the wood-stove and the newspaper in the basket. She removed her shoes. She had worn blisters on her feet. They burned.

She stood by the kitchen table and faced across the hall to the closed door of her bedroom.

A chill moved through her. What if she'd gotten it wrong? What if he had just passed out again or was sleeping hard, worn out from the last seven years?

She went to stand outside the door and placed her hand on the door-knob. It rattled like cold teeth on a day that's too cold to bear. She turned it.

The sheet she had pulled over him remained. She leaned forward, and, in the light freely cast through the window beside the bed, she strained to see the rise and fall of his chest. But the only thing moving that early afternoon was the red flowers on the curtains. They were spinning. The sun was out full. Life had carried on. But Sarah wanted everything to stop, just for one minute stop.

She rushed to the window and grabbed the curtains with both hands and yanked them until they were free. And then she threw them in the floor and kicked them out of the way.

She looked back at the window. There was no spinning now. All was still. A kind of reverence for Harold and his passing and his son, who was hers now.

Hers alone.

· · · · ·

Just before four o'clock, Sarah cut half of the sausage biscuit and put it on Emerson Bridge's plate. He would be getting off the school bus in another ten minutes or so. The other half she returned to the food warmer.

She stood at the window and watched. He would see the automobile gone from the yard and think his papa was at work. He would come into the house, tell her hello and then go outside and wait for his papa to come home about 5:30.

The bus stopped at the driveway's edge, and Sarah gripped the sides of the sink and waited for the porch door to open.

But it did not.

She looked outside, and there he was in the yard, running, not from the road, but from his papa's barn.

The porch door opened.

"I got you something to eat, hon," she called out.

"Where's Papa?" he asked, his eyes casting about the room.

Did he not notice the automobile missing? She made herself keep her eyes on him and not look at the closed door. "You hungry, hon?" She pushed the plate towards him. "I got you some meat. Look."

But he did not. He touched his chin where the longer cut was. "Where's Papa?" he said, louder this time. "And why is his automobile way out there on the road? We passed it in the bus just then. Is he here? Did he run out of gasoline again? Where is he, Mama?" He was screaming now.

Sarah felt her face go hot.

He looked at the closed door.

Sarah opened her mouth to tell him, but no words came aloud, only words inside her, *I'm all he's got, I'm all he's got, I'm all he's got.* She stretched her arms his way and moved towards him.

But he said, "I want my papa!" and turned and ran out the door, the screened porch door slapping big, then little, then nothing.

33

. . . . .

Doc Clinkscales came as promised, arrived in an ambulance with the undertaker, a Mr. McDougald.

Sarah stood in the yard near the long automobile, while the two men went inside to pronounce Harold Creamer dead.

Emerson Bridge had not returned.

The two men came from the house carrying Harold's body on a stretcher. A white sheet covered him. They slid Harold into the back of the ambulance.

Sarah walked over to Mr. McDougald. "Can he be buried up there at New Prospect in that part they got on the back?" she asked.

"Come see me tomorrow, and we'll talk about the details, Mrs. Creamer."

He had not mentioned money yet. She asked him, "I wonder if you can tell me how much it's going to cost me to bury him, so I can know how much I need to set by?"

"We don't have to talk about this now. Come see me tomorrow."

"Yes sir, but if I could just set my sights now."

The man cleared his throat and looked to the ground. "I believe we could do something real nice for two hundred dollars, ma'am."

Sarah swallowed.

They closed the door.

The men got inside the automobile and drove Harold away.

In the dust they left behind, she imagined each speck of dirt a one-dollar bill and wondered how high they would be, if stacked on top of each other. She looked above her and saw a sky of gray blue and clouds, she saw clouds, thin and stretching, as if being pulled.

. . . . .

Nightfall returned, but Emerson Bridge did not. Sarah kept watch for him from the bottom porch step. To soothe her blisters, she poured water in the dirt, made a batter of mud and soaked her feet.

The moon did not show itself that night. Pitch black fell, an extra blanket of darkness.

Every few minutes, she called his name, she called, "Emerson Bridge," each time, more piercing.

She heard crickets and dogs howling, but she did not hear what she waited for, "Mama."

MARCH 14, 1951

When the sun came up, Sarah rose from the steps and went inside the house, wet a rag, and washed her face, under her arms, and feet. From the kitchen counter, she took her empty lard can and ran her fingers around its insides, hoping to coat them with any remnant of the white grease. She brought her fingers to her blisters and dabbed. Then, from a drawer, she took two dish towels and went to her bedroom, wrapped one towel around each foot and stepped into Harold's boots, still by the bed. On her body, she put a fresh housedress, green and yellow checks. The stray hair that had fallen from her bun she tucked back in with bobby pins.

In the kitchen, she took one of the sausage biscuit halves from the food warmer and placed it on Emerson Bridge's plate. She had rather wait for him to return home, show him that she remained for him, but she needed to sell the dress.

She picked up the shoes she had worn the day before and the blanket that still held the blue dress, and Sarah walked out the door and into the yard and headed towards Mrs. Dobbins's house. She would remove the towels from her feet and put on her shoes when she started down the Dobbins's driveway. She would hide the towels and Harold's boots among the greeting shrubbery and then retrieve them on her way back home.

She had walked a little more than a mile when an automobile coming towards her passed by and stopped. Sarah had never seen such a pretty vehicle, nor one in that color combination, baby blue and white.

"Why, Mrs. Creamer, is that you?" the driver said. It was Mrs. Dobbins.

Sarah tucked one foot behind the other. "I know I look a sight," her voice hoarse from calling for Emerson Bridge all night. She held the blanket towards the woman. "I was on my way out to see you."

"Why, I was on my way out to see you, too, dear," Mrs. Dobbins said and motioned Sarah inside the automobile.

She had come to take the biscuit back. "I was going to tell you, ma'am, I was," Sarah told her and got inside the vehicle. She would give her the food and ask for forgiveness and hope she still wanted the dress. Sarah did not smell peppermints.

The seats were a dark blue leather. Sarah tried not to touch the clean floorboard with her boots. They were caked in dirt. Mrs. Dobbins's shoes were shiny and a pretty shade of jade green.

Emerson Bridge might be home now. She had kept watch for him as she'd walked.

But Mrs. Dobbins didn't take Sarah home. She pulled in behind New Prospect Baptist Church and inched all the way up to the church wall. "Can't have Big LC catching me, you know," she said.

Sarah put her hand on the door handle and squeezed. "Afraid Jesus don't know me, ma'am." She had never been inside a church.

"I'm supposed to be going to town to the beauty parlor," Mrs. Dobbins whispered, but Sarah thought she looked like she'd just stepped out of one with hair dark, medium in length and curled under the way Scarlett O'Hara wore hers in that one movie Sarah had seen, *Gone with the Wind.*

"He was hungry," Sarah said and looked across to the cemetery where Mattie was buried and where she hoped Mr. McDougald would allow Harold.

"I'm afraid I owe you an apology, dear." The woman was speaking in her full voice now.

Sarah looked back towards her.

"You made me a dress special and came all the way to deliver it to me yesterday, and I failed to give it the proper attention it deserves. Where were my manners?"

Sarah felt her hand relax.

"Can we start over? I've come to ask you that. And pay you handsomely for the dress." Mrs. Dobbins held out an envelope, a white one, the cleanest white Sarah had ever seen. She imagined it as a table cloth and on it plates, heaped, of scrambled eggs and sausage and bowls brimming with grits and hot biscuits.

Sarah reached for the envelope and handed the woman the blanket. Mrs. Dobbins brought it to her chest and held it like it was worth something. Sarah did the same with the envelope and tried not to press on it, but it felt thick. Not as thick as a biscuit but more like a sausage patty. She set the envelope in her lap and took a deep breath. "I'm afraid I owe you an apology, too, Mrs. Dobbins. Afraid I took from you yesterday. A biscuit and a piece of sausage. For my boy. I mean our boy. I mean . . . *mine.*" A heat moved through Sarah and settled in her feet, where she felt the empty space in Harold's boots. "He was hungry." She looked out her window again. She wondered if he would ever return home.

Mrs. Dobbins placed her hand on Sarah's shoulder.

"I'll pay you for it, ma'am—a whole dollar and come cook and clean for you, do your ironing, empty out your slop jars and dust y'all's awards. Please forgive me." Sarah waited for the woman to take her hand back and all of her money and throw her out of the vehicle.

But Mrs. Dobbins's hand remained. "Why, Mrs. Creamer, there's no need for any of that. That food was just thrown into the pig trough. They'll eat anything."

Sarah wanted to thank her, but she didn't think she could talk. She was afraid if she opened her mouth, water would flood her eyes and not stop.

. . . . .

Mrs. Dobbins drove Sarah to her automobile. Sarah did not tell her she had run out of gasoline, only that she had to leave the vehicle by the side of the road the day before. When they passed Drake's store, Sarah noted she would walk back there, buy gasoline and flour, lard and buttermilk for biscuits and a hunk of fatback for some good meat, and then return to her automobile and drive home. She let herself dream that she would find Emerson Bridge in bed, and she would go to the kitchen, cook for him, and fill every empty space inside his belly.

"I can't thank you enough, Mrs. Dobbins, I can't," Sarah said and got out of the pretty blue-and-white and watched it go out of sight. It crossed her mind that they could be friends if circumstances were different, if Sarah had the same kind of life this woman did, one of church and money.

She told herself to start walking to Drake's, and there she would see how much money the envelope contained. But she couldn't wait for that. She opened the door to her automobile, slid in behind the steering wheel, and peeked inside the brilliant white. There, a stack of green greeted her, each bill fanning out like it could breathe.

She lifted them towards her and counted. They were all ones, twenty-eight of them. Twenty-eight whole dollars. In her head, she divided all that money by the price of the dress, $4.25. Mrs. Dobbins had paid her six times over with $2.50 to spare.

Sarah shook. She had never felt such kindness, such outright, unbridled kindness.

"Mama," she heard behind her. It was Emerson Bridge's voice.

She was hallucinating. Lack of sleep and food.

"Mama?" This time louder.

She turned back towards the sound. There was Emerson Bridge, lying in the back seat, his body curled in like a baby's.

She threw open her door and pulled his free.

He was crying now in little sobs, but they grew to big ones, his little body heaving more than a little body should. The sun caught the top of his hair, lit it like a match, the red of him and his papa catching fire and glowing.

She leaned in towards him. "I'm so sorry, hon. I know you and him was tight."

Her hands hovered over him like a bird wanting to land. She didn't know if he would let her touch him, and, if he did, where she should put her hands. She pictured Harold's face the night he died and saw again the cuts on Emerson Bridge. She wished she could have seen that lesson being taught, not been around where they could see her, but be in the shadows the way she liked to be and watched.

And learned.

. . . . .

Emerson Bridge saw his mother's hands above him. They were small and not as rough as his papa's. If they were his papa's, they would bring him in close, hold him against his chest that smelled like straw and not let him go.

He imagined his mother would smell like biscuits.

He imagined her holding him.

And not letting go.

The earth lay ready to receive Harold Creamer's body.

A mound of dirt, as red as it was brown, lay heaped up on one side of a hole and on the other, a pine box, the cheapest Sarah could buy. She and Emerson Bridge stood at the foot of the hole, while the preacher from New Prospect Baptist stood at the head. They were in the church cemetery, after having moved through and past plots filled with a century's worth of dead to an area in the back, where the hill crested and began a gentle slope downwards. There, people whose church membership was elsewhere or no-where, those called "the unchurched," could be laid to eternal rest.

A few men from the telephone company stood off to the side. Harold had no family. He was an only child born to elderly parents.

Emerson Bridge stood in front of Sarah. He smelled of Harold's hair tonic, which, on his own, he had combed through that morning. The scent was musky and filled the space between the two of them. Sarah breathed it in.

He had spoken very little since she found him in the automobile. She had thought he might run away again, but he'd stayed at home, eating very little, only one biscuit, even though she had made a dozen.

Harold's plot lay to the immediate right of Mattie Louise Pender Parnell, a metal marker carrying her name. Sarah had asked that he be buried beside her. She had visited Mattie's grave enough to know that the spot beside her was free. Sarah felt the urge to lean forward towards Emerson Bridge and tell him, *There they are, your mama and papa.* But what if he shoved her in that hole and wished she was the one who was dead?

"Lord Jesus Almighty," the preacher said, "I did not know this man's heart."

Mattie did. And she knew it at its weakest and put a cushion around it, something Sarah failed to do. The Sunday night Sarah had fussed at him for catching less and less fish for their catfish suppers and telling him, "You trying to starve us?" Harold staying quiet but Mattie jumping in and say-ing, "He don't like to kill."

"I did," Emerson Bridge called out, his hand made into a fist and shooting into the air. "I knew my papa's heart."

The preacher cleared his throat.

Winds whipped about around them like they didn't know where they wanted to go. Or how.

"It is my fervent prayer," the preacher prayed, "and I am sure his fami-ly's before me, that Harold Blevins Creamer did, in fact, know the Lord God Almighty as his personal savior, so he can gain entrance into eternity in your sweet presence and not burn in the unholy fires of hell. We lay this urgent plea for the assurance of salvation at your dusty feet because surely, Lord Jesus, you have traveled many miles in your unfathomable love for us this day. Amen."

Sarah's mother told her if you don't go to church, you can't be saved, and if you aren't saved, you're going to burn in the eternal fires of hell. Sarah knew that what Harold had done was wrong, but, for the boy's sake, she prayed, *Please Lord Jesus Almighty, don't let Harold Creamer burn in hell. Let him be in heaven. With Mattie. Amen.*

She watched Emerson Bridge's little shoulders quiver. *I am all he's got now, and that ain't his fault.* She called up in her mind Mattie's and Har-old's faces and held them in her sight. And then she imagined her hands as Harold's and moved them towards his shoulders.

But her hands were not Harold's. They were hers.

. . . . .

Ike Thrasher stood in his room at the McDuffie Street Boarding House and dressed himself in dark slacks, his finest, and a white shirt in the smallest men's size Gallant-Belks sold, a fourteen-inch neck with thirty-two-inch sleeves. An upper-end boy's size would better fit him, but Ike was too em-barrassed to purchase such. He had ironed the shirt the night before with extra starch, repeatedly shaking the liquid onto the garment from a sprin-kler atop a Pepsi-Cola bottle that held the solution and then ironing it smooth. That way, he hoped, the material would look thicker, and, there-fore, Ike Thrasher thicker, even sporting muscles beneath it.

He looked in the mirror on his chifforobe and flexed his arms now, pulling the cloth tight against his skin. He thought he saw the beginning of a muscle just up from his right elbow.

He took a tie from his tie rack, one that carried the dark of his pants and just enough red to give him a spark. On his feet, he slid his just-shined wingtips, his laces new and crisp. It was just after breakfast, and out of the ordinary for him to wear these shoes in the daytime, preferring the night, when it was dark enough for the neon signs to light the world. His favorite was the one above the Greasy Spoon café two blocks over on North Main Street. Some nights Ike would wear these shoes and walk there and watch the spoon, all lit in white and appearing to dance, as specks of red grease flickered around it. There was no music, but Ike always heard music and always the Bennie Goodman Orchestra. From time to time, he would find his feet moving to the rhythm.

Today he needed to move his feet out the door and head west of town to a stretch of land he had not frequented in sixteen years. He applied extra deodorant and hoped it wouldn't leave a ring.

He cranked his Buick and headed out Whitner Street, which took him all the way west, until he cut over on a side road, which led him to Thrasher Road, covered in gravel, his automobile rattling like loose bones in a nervous boy's body. He lifted his just-shined wingtip off the gasoline pedal and pressed on the brake. He was about to approach what used to be his father's place, 107 acres that spanned both sides of the road, with most of the acreage on the house side, on the right, but that never stopped Ike from thinking of this land as a bird, with the road as its body and the two sides of land as its wings. He wished that bird could fly him someplace else that day.

Ike had visited the South Carolina National Bank and discovered that his balance had dropped to $189.02. He knew that to most people, that was a lot of money, but not to Ike. He had no income, having lost his call to preach sixteen years ago and no employment in sight. He had been living off the sale of his father's land, while he passed the time in a boarding house where five other men lived dead-end lives. Ike had kept the house and five acres but sold the rest, splitting the smaller twenty-acre side into two plots and selling them to two fellows, a Billy Udean Parnell and a Harold Creamer. Both men were blushed with love and both wanted to build a house for their intended. Mrs. Parnell's family paid up in full in 1944, after the death of Mrs. Parnell. That same year, the Creamer family began missing payments and had missed the last five months entirely.

Ike was on his way to collect. But it meant coming within fifty feet of something he had not yet earned the right to do, and that was to return home as the man his father wanted him to be. Ike had kept the house and five acres, hoping that one day he could be that man. Maybe if he didn't look at the old home place, but kept his eyes to the left, he could slide by. He gripped the steering wheel and bore down on the pedal, his Buick lunging forward and his tires squealing. He craned his neck hard to the left, seeing only the Parnell place and then the Creamer's, where he turned into their driveway of dirt, his tires sending up dust, lots of it, like some scaredy-cat sissy boy jumping out of his way.

. . . . .

Sarah and Emerson Bridge returned from the burial and found an unfamiliar automobile in the yard. She could see someone inside, someone small, perhaps an older boy. When she approached the window, he jumped as if she had scared him but then collected himself and opened the door and stepped out. He was wearing a nice dress hat, which he tipped at her, and a white shirt that looked brand new. And he had this neat, little trim mustache like the movie star Clark Gable. He wasn't smoking but looked like he should be.

"Mrs. Creamer?" the man said.

"Yes, sir. I'm Mrs. Creamer."

"Ike Thrasher here." He bowed towards her but looked more like he should curtsy.

Sarah had never seen him before, but she knew who he was. He held the note on their ten acres, and she knew why he was there. She sent Emerson Bridge into the house.

"Is Mr. Creamer here?" The man was looking about the yard.

"No sir, he ain't. But I am." She was dizzy now.

"This is men's talk, ma'am," he said and ran his fingers lightly over his mustache. "A matter between me and your husband."

Sarah steadied herself. Her blisters pressed against her shoe leather and burned. "It's a matter between me and you now, sir."

His shirt flapped in the wind. It sounded like bed sheets on the clothesline popping. He might not have been much bigger than a boy, but his face showed a lot of old man living. The lines in his forehead crissed and crossed in various ways, but mostly they lay vertical between bunched up skin like his stitching ran too tight. The tonic on his hair made it shine like a penny.

"I've looked the other way as long as I can. Y'all are behind close to fifty dollars. Going to have to start proceedings, if you can't pay up. In full."

"But we own this house. It's paid for."

"But the land it's on is mine."

Sarah widened her stance, the soles of her shoes pushing aside dirt. Harold had bought the land in 1935 for $36 an acre financed and agreed to pay a dollar and a half a month. She had $15.97 left of Mrs. Dobbins's money, after giving Mr. McDougald $10 and pledging that much every month.

"I can catch up the last five months right now, seven dollars and a half." This would leave her with $8.47. She started towards the house to get the money.

"I'm afraid y'all have gone too far now," he called out at her back.

She put her foot on the bottom step and reached for the screened door. "And I can have more for you in a few days." She was going to make more dresses to sell.

"I'll just wait to talk with your husband."

Sarah wrapped her hand around the handle, slender and running high to low, heaven to hell. "He ain't here. We've just come from laying him in the ground."

She heard the man clear his throat. "I'm sorry to hear that."

Sarah squeezed the metal, worn smooth from hands coated in sweat and dirt, catfish scales, potato peels and flour. And blood. "I'll pay our debt, don't you worry none. I ain't the kind of woman to cut out on you." She opened the door, let its rusty cry fill her ears. She was glad for it. She wished it was louder.

She stepped onto the porch.

Mr. Thrasher stayed in the yard, his hat held over his heart. His hair had more curls in it than a woman's. The wind picked them up and tossed them about. The day had warmed into the upper fifties, but the March wind made it feel much colder. She would stoke the fire she had made that morning in the woodstove. She pushed the door open. "Won't you come in?"

He kicked at the dirt with his right foot. He was a boy at heart. Sarah had stood at the kitchen sink window many early evenings and watched Emerson Bridge do the same thing when Harold would bring to a close what Emerson Bridge loved to do the most, throw a rock back and forth.

Sarah stretched the door wider.

Mr. Thrasher bent to wipe the dust from his shoes.

He followed her into the kitchen, saying, "But, I want you to know, Mrs. Creamer, that I will need the full amount."

Something loud and sharp hit the window. Sarah looked out and saw Emerson Bridge in the yard about ten feet away. The window had a crack in it. He had thrown a rock.

"Excuse me, sir," she said and went outside. Emerson Bridge was running towards the barn.

She wondered if she was fooling herself to think she could ever be enough. She looked across the old garden and thought about what life would be if Mattie had stayed. No burial that day, Emerson Bridge in school, free to learn his lessons, and not loaded with a papa gone way too soon and a mama, a makeshift mama, who'd never once thrown a rock. She'd watched Harold and Emerson Bridge enough to know that you swing your stiff arm back and then bring it forward, letting the rock go. She moved her arm that way now.

The door to the barn slammed shut.

She would let him be.

Mr. Thrasher remained in the kitchen, his arms folded across his chest. He looked cold. The kitchen was cold. The house was cold. Everything cold.

She looked inside the woodstove and found the embers cooling. She would start anew. She reached in the basket for the only paper there, the Dobbins newspaper. No longer was it balled up tight but open. "$680" in big, bold letters caught her eye. She smoothed out the paper against the table, the headline spanning the top of the page, "Grand Champion Brings $680—Dobbins Dynasty Ended."

"Six hundred and eighty dollars?" she said out loud. "They must mean six dollars or sixty."

"For what?" Mr. Thrasher unfolded his arms.

"For the grand champion at some kind of cow thing yesterday. But that can't be right. That's more money than Harold made all last year."

"Grand Champeen," he said and made a big sound with his nose. "You don't say."

"From what I heard, they have a big cow show, and one of them gets a blue ribbon and a big write-up in the newspaper with a photograph. But I didn't know they got big money, too."

He moved his flat hand over the top of the page, trying to smooth it out more.

"I can't believe it." Sarah said.

"Believe it," he told her and grabbed the top of his pants, pulled them up with a force. "Yep."

The photograph showed a little boy standing beside the animal. The words "Ain't It Wonderful!" ran beneath and said the winner was a Herron boy, seven years old.

"My boy's almost that age, seven," Sarah said.

"That's right, you got a boy."

"I do." And Sarah had to feed him, put gasoline in the automobile, pay for his papa's burial, catch up the light bill and now pay for Mr. Thrasher's land.

The man took off in a flash, headed for the porch door.

"Wait! Your money," Sarah said.

"I'll come back around tomorrow." The door slammed shut.

Tomorrow. She knew that word.

She looked at the photograph again. Mrs. Dobbins had called the animal a steer. The boy and the steer stood close to each other. They looked like they were friends. She imagined the steer following the boy around the

44

yard like a dog and sleeping outside his window at night, even walking him down the driveway to the school bus and waiting there for his return.

Goosebumps ran up her arms and climbed her neck and face. What if she got Emerson Bridge a steer? It would bring in money to feed him. For a long time. Every morning, she would have hot biscuits, a whole basket of them, and a bowl of grits heaped so high, some would spill over the sides. There would be scrambled eggs cooked in butter and on the soft side the way he liked them and sausage patties she'd mashed and formed with her hands and fried to a crisp. And for his school dinner, she'd have a piece of fried meat between a cold biscuit and, for a surprise, would include a Hydrox cookie. On Sundays, she would make him two cobblers, strawberry and peach. And they would go fishing together and come home and fry what they'd caught crispy, and she'd make coleslaw from a good head of cabbage and have fried potatoes cut longways like fingers.

Fingers. On her hand. Both hands holding him, his belly full.

. . . . .

The shaving kit that Emerson Bridge and his papa had used remained on the bale of straw. There were no windows in the barn, but enough light slivered in through the old wooden boards for Emerson Bridge to see. The kit looked like his papa's boots, dark brown leather and covered in scratches long and deep.

He wondered if this was the last thing his papa had touched. He had seen his papa set it on the bale before Emerson Bridge left the barn that afternoon. He never saw his papa alive again. He'd gotten off the school bus and run to the barn to tell him "hey," but that afternoon he didn't find his papa laying across the bale or on the dirt, but standing in the back, propped up against a pole, and, in his hands, the shaving kit.

"For when the time comes," his papa had said and instructed Emerson Bridge to stand on the bale.

"What time, Papa?" he'd asked.

But no words came, only his papa taking a thick, white cup from the kit and pouring in water from a mason jar. He spilled more than made it in. Then round and round with a little brush his papa stirred, until white lather rose up like a puffy cloud, and his papa put his eyes on Emerson Bridge and said, "For when you're a man, son."

A jolt shot from Emerson Bridge's feet skyward, lifting him on his tiptoes. Even with the foot and a few inches tall bale, he still wasn't as tall as his papa. He couldn't wait to be.

His papa gathered lather on his fingers and smeared it on his beard, dipped his razor in the water and began moving the blade southward, his hand shaking. His papa was teaching him to shave. He bet none of the other boys at school had papas who had done that.

A John Deere tractor mirror hung about eye level on a nail on the post in front of him. It used to hang higher for his papa. "Why you teaching me now?" Emerson Bridge asked.

His papa cut his eyes at him. The sound of the blade against his papa's skin, a scraping sound, cuts breaking out along the way.

Emerson Bridge felt a knot in his belly.

"Now is all we've got," his papa said.

Emerson Bridge swallowed saliva to keep from throwing up.

His papa made two more swipes with the razor and then held it out for Emerson Bridge. "You're the man of the house now, son."

A ray of light fell in beside them, and in it specks of dust tossed back and forth. They were rocks, tiny ones. He wanted to run and get a rock and play. But in his papa's hands was something straight and sharp, a razor. Not a rock.

Emerson Bridge took it, gathered lather, and imagined his hands as his papa's. He brought the blade to his face.

"And I hope you'll be a better man than I was. The Bible says to be kind. 'Be ye kind, one to another,' it says. I wasn't always, but I hope you will be, son." His papa's breathing had sharp edges like it could break something. The way a rock could.

The sound of an engine cranking drew Emerson Bridge back to the world where his papa was no more. It was that man's automobile. He hoped he wasn't going to be his new papa.

He placed his hands on both ends of the shaving kit, imagined his papa's hands there, and thought about kindness. Throwing a rock against his mother's window was not kind. He brought the kit in close, placed it against him like his papa's chest. "I will be kind, papa. Yes, sir. I promise you."

· · · · ·

From River Street, Ike spotted the steer out front of Richbourg's, just as the newspaper article had said. The animal stood to the left of the double glass doors and appeared as big as Ike's Buick. "There he is," Ike whispered. "The Grand Champeen."

He surveyed the lot for the closest empty parking space and found one on the front row beside a tractor, one space down from the steer, no more than six feet away from Ike's front bumper. The animal jerked his head high and pulled on a rope that ran from his halter to the tractor beside Ike, the steer's nostrils flaring wide, as did his eyes, showing mostly white.

A large glass wall ran behind the steer and carried large sheets of white butcher paper, showing the store's specials in splashes of bright red and deep yellow. Duke's mayonnaise thirty-nine cents a pint. Beef roast fifty-three cents a pound. And then directly in front of Ike, the front page of the Anderson Independent, along with the store's advertisement, topped in big block letters "Grand Champion steer shown at Fat Cattle Show & Sale now appearing outside our store. Come see him now and then visit him in the meat department in the coming days. Quality beef for your family."

Quality, indeed.

Ike studied the steer's thickness, his muscles, especially. "All man," he said and ran his hand down his thigh. He felt nothing that counted. He was all bone.

He squeezed the steering wheel, the big round black circle that it was, and felt his fingers afloat in the grooves. They fit the way a girl's would. A boy's would fill the space. Ike pressed down, hoping to fill with his flattened flesh. He pressed until his fingers went numb. He wanted to call out, *"Daddy, look, I can fill it up,"* but the door near the steer swung open, a young boy shooting from it towards the animal, which shifted Ike's way and pulled on the rope so hard, the tractor beside him shook. Manhandling, Ike was thinking. *The Grand Champeen is manhandling a whole tractor.* Ike wanted to say something to the animal, maybe call his name. But he couldn't remember reading what his name was.

"I want to pet you," the boy called out and stretched his arms towards the animal's face, now thrust high into the air, the animal's eyes wide and cut towards Ike. Ike had seen eyes like this before when he was a preacher, from people who'd walked the aisle at his church and proclaimed they were sinners in need of saving. When the numbers were sufficient, Ike would take them to his father's pond, which he would enter first, the water nipple high as the sinners came, one by one, his right hand placed behind their head, his left in the small of their back, and he would say, "I baptize you, my sister or my brother, in the name of the Lord Jesus Christ Almighty, who died for our sins that we may spend eternity with him in glorious heaven." And Ike would lower them backwards into the water and then restore them upright.

"I'll save you, boy," Ike called out to the animal and moved his hand to the door handle and pushed down, his left leg shoving it open. In no time, his left shoe hit the pavement.

But the child now was jumping up and down and squealing. Ike wanted to tell him to stop, that that's how girls act, that squealing.

But Ike did not tell him that. Ike simply brought his leg back in and closed the door. And to the steer, whose eyes remained on Ike, he said, "It's me, old boy, it's me. You got to save *me.*"

Sarah needed a plan to pay for the steer, and she wanted to write it down. She'd been carrying around figures in her head like groceries in a sack. She would take them out one by one and set them on pretty blue lines as straight as the stitches she tried to make. She took a sheet from Emerson Bridge's blue horse school tablet he kept atop his dresser. She hoped he wouldn't mind, that and borrowing his pencil for a few minutes.

The window beside the dresser was open. He'd gone outside that way. The wind blew the curtains in towards her. Maybe it would blow him in, too.

She sat on his bed. He would see her and trust that she waited on his return.

At the top of the page, she wrote Mrs. Dobbins's $28.00. Under it, she listed $2.53 for Drake's Store, $10 for Mr. McDougald, and $7.50 for Mr. Thrasher. She had $8.47 left. She would make one dress a day and charge a flat $3, which would mean clearing up to $2 a dress or upwards of $14 a week or as much as $56 a month. Subtract out the monthly $17.50 for the land and burial, $5 for food and gasoline, and another $3 for the light bill, which she was behind already $9. They could continue to live without a telephone.

She did the arithmetic. She should have $32.50 in clear money each month.

She didn't know how much a little steer would cost, but it had to be a lot less than the $680 a big one cost. There would be feeding the animal, but she thought they ate grass, and they had grass. She wondered how little they could be, if maybe like a big dog, something to buddy with. Every child needed an animal to buddy with. And what if she could surprise him on his birthday, have the little steer outside his window on the morning of June 22nd. She would stand at his door and let the animal's sounds wake him and watch his dimples spring forth. But, mostly, he would know that Sarah wanted him. She could get him to trust her this way.

"Mama?" she heard. It was Emerson Bridge, climbing back through the window.

She stood, her body perched forward, her mouth rushing out the words "What if I got you a little cow to buddy with? It's what they call a steer. You could love it and it love you."

"That wasn't kind what I did with the rock. I'm sorry." His words came just as fast.

Then silence. It hung in the air like a third person.

She saw his eyes swollen and his cheeks flat. "That rock don't matter, hon. Just you."

He wiped his eyes with his coat sleeve. Four inches at least of his wrist showed. He'd had the coat for close to two years. She could buy him a new one with the money they'd make with the steer. She'd look for a nice green to set off his eyes.

"What about that little steer, hon? Would you like you one? There's this big cow show, and the best one gets a nice blue ribbon and y'all would have your picture on the front page of the newspaper together. Y'all would be famous." She started to say "And we'd get a lot of money," but that was her worry. He was just a boy.

He kept his arm over his eyes and began to nod, the red of his hair vibrant in the midday sun that lit up the room. "I'd be kind to it," he said.

Harold had done well with him. "I know you would. You're a kind little boy."

He slid his arm down his face and peered over it. "Why did Papa die, Mama?"

This was the first question he'd asked since she'd found him in the automobile. "Hard times, hon. He died of hard times."

He slid his arm back over his eyes. She wondered if he would ask what that meant. She didn't want to tell him his papa couldn't live with what he'd done and drank himself to death. She'd just say had he that bad phlegm.

His eyes peered over again.

She swallowed and readied herself.

But his eyes looked heavier than that question. They looked to be carrying something more, like he wanted her to hold him.

The curtain behind him whipped his way, but Sarah felt the urging at her back. She stepped towards him. *But what if he didn't want her to, but was just wondering why she didn't.*

She moved in no further.

She could not delay getting the steer. He needed a buddy and now.

Maybe Mr. Dobbins would sell her one and let her pay on it like she was doing for the land and burial. She recalled the $32.50 she would clear each month. She would go to see him the next day and pledge $30 a month. They could live off her dressmaking until the steer won the cow show. That was one year away.

She sat back down. She'd made wrinkles in his bedspread. She ran her flat hand over it, smoothing it out. She would make it clean, wash it and hang it out to dry.

MARCH 17, 1951

LC lay under his bed that early morning in darkness, save for the light from his horse lamp on his night table. He lay with his arms tucked tight beneath him, his legs pressed together. He thought if he could fold up into himself, he might disappear.

"Get your hard clothes on, boy, not that baby git-up your mama lets you wear." It was his father, shouting up the stairs.

On LC's pajamas, little brown horses ran sprinkled about and free. He pictured the one on his pocket over his heart. He looked like he might run the fastest. LC named him Shortcake.

"He's too little, Big LC, *don't,*" his mother said.

Yeah, *too little,* LC thought, but Shortcake would protect him. The horse would take him some place far away. LC jumped on. They went galloping off across pastures and creeks.

"But LC's not Charles, Big LC. And Charles was older and wanted to and asked for it the first time."

His father's boots slapped the wooden steps. Indians with their hard hands slapping against their open mouths, a steady yell calling through. Shortcake was running now. LC, his knees bent, and holding on.

"Hey, boy!" his father called from the door, his big boots showing through the fringe on the bottom of LC's bedspread, Shortcake's mane. Shortcake outrunning the Indians, the wind blowing back the dark hair of his mane. LC blew on the fringe, making it move in the wind.

"Get out from under there." His father stuck his long arm through. Tomahawks now raised, Shortcake running harder.

His father yanked him to his feet. "Today's the first day of your education. Today you start being a true Dobbins man."

The Indians' faces marked with red stripes. LC thought it could be blood.

"You a man?" his father asked.

LC wasn't, but told him, "Yes sir."

"What kind?"

He recalled his father's exact words. "A Dobbins man. A true one, Daddy."

His father thumped LC's shoulder. "The truck'll be leaving in ten minutes."

LC bent his knees like he was in a saddle.

He and Shortcake would go again.

· · · · ·

LC's father put the shotgun in LC's arms. It was heavy. LC had never held one. It felt cold and hard like the devil he'd learned about in Sunday school.

They were at Parson's Mountain, an hour south of Anderson. Daybreak was on the cusp with the first hint of light showing itself. They stood in cover at the edge of the woods, a field of green before them. LC had on corduroy pants, a flannel shirt, and a denim jacket.

"That's a 16 gauge there, a Browning, the best there is," his father told him and slapped him on his back, the front of the gun flipping up and hitting LC in the forehead.

His father got in behind him and helped him get the gun back on balance. "Nature's got its own rules, boy. Number one is not to have no racket out here. No deer's gonna come up with racket. You understand me?"

LC nodded. His arms shook.

His father pushed LC's left hand out along the barrel, until it reached a wooden holding place, his arm stretching so far, it hurt. Then he placed LC's index finger on his right hand against the trigger. It was curved like Shortcake's tail when he ran real fast. Like now. They were running fast together. "It's all about lining up. Look down the barrel there, and put it dead on one of them hardwoods across over there." His father now guiding his arm to the left. LC lining up with a big tree, the kind they had in the yard, the kind he liked to climb and hide in.

"Now we just wait. They like young grass," his father said. "Then he's ours."

LC imagined his knees bent, a bad man chasing him and Shortcake. Run faster, Shortcake. Faster. The horse's hooves digging into the ground, throwing up clumps of grass, the bad guy tripping and falling, LC and Shortcake running free.

"There he is," his father whispered. "Shoot it."

A small deer bent to the grass about twenty yards away, snapped off several blades with its mouth and then returned its head high, making quick movements left and right, while it chewed. A few blades hung from its mouth.

"I said, 'Shoot it.'"

His father's arms around him tighter now the way LC's legs wrapped around Shortcake, him and Shortcake good pals. The bad man was back on his feet, his arms extended towards the horse's rear end and LC.

LC closed his eyes.

He pulled the trigger. The blast scaring Shortcake.

The deer went down.

LC's knees giving way, his father catching him and going down with him.

The sound of the gun echoing.

· · · · ·

Ike Thrasher walked out of the dressing room at Sears & Roebuck in a new denim shirt and rider jeans so stiff they could stand by themselves and in pointed-toe black cowboy boots so shiny he could see himself curling his mustache in them. On his head, he set a cowboy hat, also black. It was too big for him, but he hoped no one would notice.

Just outside the store, on the square in downtown Anderson, under a sky of unfettered blue, sat his new pickup truck, a '47 Ford, fresh washed and green with black fenders. He'd bought it that very morning at Scarboro Motors on South Main, traded in his Buick for an even swap. He had thought that they would call him back into the store and tell him that it was all a tease, that there was no way that Isaiah Ferdinand Thrasher belonged in a truck like that. But he had gotten away with it. They let him drive it off the lot.

He laid the sack with his old clothes and wingtips in the floorboard and then scooted his slick-bottomed boots up front to the hood, where he tried to lean as if he'd been leaning there his entire life. His clothes, though, being skin tight and of the western fit, kept him from accommodating much of a slant. He crossed his fingers that someone would notice, like one of the men at the McDuffie Street Boarding House two blocks east.

But no one did. What thrilled him, though, was that no one pointed at him and laughed. Or called him names that he himself used to laugh at, but not when he was alone.

The big clock on the courthouse showed almost ten o'clock. It was Saturday, and typically he'd be at the cowboy picture show at the State Theatre, his favorite cowboy being Roy Rogers. But this day he had something more important to do, strike a deal with Mrs. Creamer.

He'd begun his preparations the afternoon before. After seeing the steer at Richbourgs, he visited the Agriculture Department on Towers Street and found out that the biggest cattleman in all of Anderson County was a fellow named Mr. L. C. Dobbins, Sr. His older son, Charles, had won a string of Grand Championships. Ike then made one other stop, the South Carolina National Bank, where he'd withdrawn a crisp one hundred dollar bill. His balance showed only $89.02, but the steer was worth it.

That morning, he allowed himself one more thing. He scooted to the back of his truck, which he imagined as Roy Rogers's horse, Trigger, and saw himself do what the cowboy king liked to do in the movies, go airborne over the animal's rear end, only to deliver himself into the saddle. He was ready now to head out to the Creamers. He would liked to have rolled his window down, not because it was on the verge of being warm, but because he'd seen other men ride with their windows that way. But the wind the open window would bring might blow his hat off, and that was reason enough to keep his windows where they were, closed and tight and safe.

When he approached his father's land this time, he looked to the right side of the road, at the eighty-two acres Ike had sold to another cotton farmer. The land was fresh-plowed and ready for planting. But the old home place up ahead he could not see for the trees and overgrown shrubs and weeds that stood tall and unsupervised. He inched his truck forward, letting it take him within a few feet of the dirt driveway, where he could see part of the house, the once white boards showing the worst kind of gray and the roof on the front porch sagging deep.

He parked his truck along the road and stepped towards the driveway, stopping just short of its edge. He aimed the tips of his boots towards an address that once carried love. Didn't it? Didn't the address of Mr. Isaiah Ferdinand Thrasher, Sr., Route 2, Anderson, S.C., once carry love?

And like no time had passed at all, Ike became a boy of four and five and six, each version of himself rising higher among his father's stalks of cotton. "Take a look, Junior," his father would say, "one day you'll be the King of Cotton in all of Anderson County, just like me." The laughter would come next, first from his father and then Ike following and mimicking. It was ever growing, their laughter, so much that people all around could hear. Couldn't they hear?

But in Ike's seventh year, the laughter stopped one Saturday morning when he was riding in the back of his father's wagon, Ike and a boy named James, a tenant on his father's farm. They were on their way to pick cotton in early September, one of those mornings that offered a glimpse of the relief from heat that was to come. The light showcased James's jaw, the line of hard bone that girded the muscles flexing from the apple he was eating. Ike felt his own jawbone and found it unsubstantial like a match stick in the tin container by his mother's woodstove. But it was James's eyes of blue the light favored the most, carrying the powdery quality of Ike's mother's talcum and falling somewhere between a soft baby and a deep royal. To Ike, it was the blue of bluebirds, the most beautiful color God had created. Ike kissed the boy on his cheek.

His father stopped the wagon hard, and both Ike and James fell to the ground. His father grabbed James by his shirt. "You say a word about this, and you and your people will be out of here so fast, you'll feel like a chicken with your neck ringed." Then his father threw Ike into the back of the wagon and whipped the horses with his reins until they got to the church up the road, where his father dragged Ike inside to the altar and threw him to the floor. "I know you're pushing all the boy you got, but the Lord's going to have to help you push some more."

Ike didn't know what was wrong with kissing a bluebird, but his father did. Ike decided to become a preacher that day. On his father's deathbed some twenty-five years later, his father told him, "You never fooled me once. You been wearing a preacher's git-up all this time, but until you become a real man and can look in the good Lord's eyes and not have him spit on you, you better not step one blame foot on this place, not even the tip of your fancy wancy wingtips. If there was another soul on earth I could leave all this to, I would. But I'm stuck with you." The next Sunday, Ike quit preaching, and, within six months, he had sold all the land except the house and five acres.

The smell of dirt found its way to Ike's nostrils. It surprised him, how familiar the smell was. He'd been thinking he'd taken nothing from his past.

He called up in his mind that steer and ran his hands down his thighs, his hands at first held flat, but they became fists, which he squeezed, until he felt a toughness rise up in him. "Not yet, Daddy," he said out loud. "But almost. I'm about to be a real man. A *cattleman*." He turned back towards his truck and began to run, holding onto his hat and listening as his soles slapped the hardness beneath him. He wondered if this was how Roy Rogers's boots sounded and let himself believe it so.

· · · · ·

Luther Dobbins went to the center of his big lot out from his barn, turned on the spigot at his watering trough for his cattle, and placed his hands under the running water. They were covered in deer blood, dried hard and cracking on his skin. "Rule number two," he had said to his boy when they both were able to gather back on their feet, "got to give each party its due." Then Luther picked up the gun and walked with LC to the deer, lying on its side. Inside the animal's wound, at its neck, Luther sunk his fingers and brought them, warm with blood, to his boy's face, running them first along his forehead and then down each cheek. Luther dipped his fingers in again, and this time brought them to the gun, to its barrel, and said, "Y'all are marked now."

A breeze brought the scent of pine his way, pungent against the smell of blood, musky and dank. A whole strip of pines grew at his back, beginning a few yards behind him on the other side of the hammer-mill shed and stretching past his house to the road. They were planted as seedlings, upwards of fifty of them, close to seven years ago, soon after LC was born. His wife, Mildred, had begged him to plant them, said she wanted something special to mark LC's birth. But Luther didn't like pines. Pines were weak. They let the wind blow them however the wind wanted. He only agreed to plant them to shield his big house from Uncle's tenant house across the field.

LC was no longer with Luther. He was inside the house. He had run there as soon as they returned home. Mildred was probably in there scrubbing his face and hands raw. Luther had wanted to start on LC's second lesson of the day, learning how to help Uncle operate Luther's prized hammer mill, the only one in Anderson County. It ground his corn into fine, edible specks for his cattle. And then he'd planned to take LC down into the pasture, walk among his herd of five dozen Herefords, and show LC the steer that was certain to be the next 1952 Fat Cattle Show & Sale Grand Champion. Luther had picked it out himself. The animal was one of five steers, each a year old, the prime age for feeding out. It was wide between the eyes, which would mean broad in width and frame. All of Charles's winners had looked that way, and he'd won Grand Champion every year since 1942. Charles was Luther's older boy, a student at Clemson College and too old to compete. Charles always had selected his own steer, but he didn't pick out LC's for the last show. Luther had.

And Luther had let LC run on.

Why had he done that?

He pulled his hands from the water. Ribbons of red, some wide, others in strings, swirled in his wake. The red-and-white-striped top LC used to play with when he could barely walk, Luther with him on the floor, the top beside them, Luther priming the long knob in the middle, making it spin faster. The two of them laughing. The top slowing and stopping and LC pointing to the toy and looking at Luther as if Luther could do all things. Luther priming. The top spinning. His boy laughing. Luther was beating the top and winning.

He looked back at the pines, tossing in the breeze, free to go here and there without fear of losing. They could be playing. Couldn't they be playing? A boy should be playing.

He imagined his boy running to him. To him, Luther Dobbins. Running without being called, prodded, urged, shouted at, demanded. Running because he thought his father could do all things.

Luther took off running to the pine that was the tallest, the strongest, the one with the most to show. It grew the third from the road. But he stopped at the first one from the shed, the weakness, the littlest, the one that had to try the hardest. There, on the bark, he saw ladybugs, a whole procession of them marching up the trunk like they were going to a burial. He wanted them to play and put his finger beside one, pushing it out of line in a playful shove. But the bug lay tilted on its right side, its left legs in the air and spinning. Luther was too rough with it. LC would not be so rough, not nearly. "LC!" he called out. "LC!" he called again, this time louder and kept his eyes on the back porch screened door, some fifty long, bloody feet away.

But LC did not come.

Only Mildred rushing out that same door and a late model automobile driving into the backyard and Mildred hollering, "I tried to tell her not to come back here, Big LC!"

The automobile stopped a few feet short of Luther, and out stepped a woman and a young boy about the size of LC.

Luther glanced over at the porch door.

"Mr. Dobbins, sir," the woman said, "I'm sorry, I don't mean to barge in on you, but I need to buy my boy here one of your little cows, a steer, for that cow show next year."

"Where's LC?" Luther called towards Mildred, who stood behind the woman and boy. She was wringing her hands, but she had no blood to be rid of.

"I told her it's too early, Big LC," Mildred said, "that y'all don't start fooling with the show until the fall."

"I can't wait that long, sir." The boy came to stand in front of the woman, no more than a foot away. She and the boy were close.

Luther aimed his eyes towards the porch and saw nothing but screen.

"My boy here needs him an animal right now, sir. To buddy with."

Buddy with. Before LC started feeding out his steer last fall, he and Luther were buddies.

"I got money," the woman said.

Luther looked her way. She was holding out a five dollar bill. All the fertilizer he'd just put on his pastures had set him back.

"Can start on paying you. I'm good for it over time."

"Emerson Bridge," he heard called out from the house. It was LC at the screened door, and there was a lift in his voice.

56

"LC," Luther said and raised his arm his boy's way. He tried to see his face, but the screen was in the way.

"Hey, LC," the woman's boy said and waved towards the door.

So the boys knew each other. Luther didn't know if from school or church.

Luther stepped towards the woman and boy but kept his eyes on LC. "I've done picked out the winner for next year. Picked a good one, too, for my boy there. Y'all are wasting y'all's time here."

LC ran back inside the house. Luther heard his little boots against the floor, taking him further away.

"Oh dear," Mildred said and cleared her throat.

Heat shot up Luther's body, his face on fire.

Out of the corner of his eye, he could see the woman and boy, still standing close. Luther stood alone, the space around him wide and empty, any sound he'd make echoing.

They looked poor, their shoes, especially, hers scuffed and run over, his beat up and too small. Luther believed his boy could outrun him. He summoned saliva to his mouth, as much as he could hold, and sent it forward. A spot of white bubbles, the size of dimes stacked, landed beside the woman's shoes. "Don't sell to no woman," he said, glad that she wasn't a man. What excuse for his feelings of unadulterated envy would he have then?

Luther was too far away to smell body odor, but he bet they hadn't bathed in a while. He should offer up his watering trough to them. It was round and cut from a terracotta pipe as big as the trunk of one of his mighty oaks in the front yard. He'd had it built after Charles won two Grand Championships in a row and made his farm a real show place. They would see he was rich and would tuck tail and run.

Another vehicle came into the yard, this time a truck. It came up fast like somebody wanted to run him over. Luther clenched his fists and was ready to put the driver in his place, but a little man in a big cowboy hat leaped out and said, "You Mr. LC Dobbins, Sr., the most important cattleman in all of Anderson County?"

Luther felt himself relax. "I am."

The man was wearing a new denim shirt and jeans, and his boots looked to be fresh-polished, if not brand new. Luther was dressed in denim, too, overalls. But his denim was covered in blood.

"Ike Thrasher," the man said and extended his hand.

"Thrasher," Luther said. "Isaiah Thrasher, big cotton man Thrasher?" He had never had any interest in competing in cotton.

The man cleared his throat and looked away. "My father," he said in a voice so light it could have been LC's.

The blood on Luther's hand had washed away. Luther obliged him.

The man's truck looked shiny. Luther's was a dull black, but it had no blood on it. Luther had left the deer and the gun on Parson's Mountain.

"I aim to be a cattleman like you," Thrasher told him.

That'll be the day. But this man did come from winning stock, albeit cotton.

"But mainly I aim to have the Grand Champeen next year." The man yanked at his jeans and about pulled himself off the ground.

He must have been adopted.

"Mr. Thrasher?" It was that woman.

"Why, Mrs. Creamer," the man said and removed his hat.

Creamer. This was the woman who was not a churchgoer and who had dared make dresses for his wife. He recognized her now. Luther crossed his arms. Selling to a woman aside, this was a heathen woman. He shot Mildred a look, but she missed it. She was slouching towards the house.

"Why, I've just come from y'all's place," the man told the woman. His head looked like a peanut. The two of them huddled together and began talking low like they were in cahoots.

Luther always thought that God made his right eye the way it should be, to look at things straight on. But, his left eye, God had made special. It sat cocked off a tad to the left and up a little high and helped him be watchful for whatever was coming up behind him or from the side or from above. This one helped him see what people really were up to. "Hey," he said, "y'all have y'all's little hen gathering someplace else. I got important doings. My boy Charles is due here anytime now."

He started for the house. The Cattleman's Supper was that night, and this would be the first time he'd not be there as a winner. He imagined the smirks and whispers that would break out when he walked into the room, growing into all-out laughter and fingers pointed, the word "loser" hurled his way. His stomach knotted, his breakfast sausage trying to come high. He bent forward and crossed his arms down low. Maybe he wouldn't go. Maybe he'd say he was sick.

But then he thought of Charles, the all-time winning Charles, who would be there with him. Everyone would want to see his elder son, the closest to a star anyone in Anderson had ever known. They would flock to him the way they flock to football heroes or movie stars. Luther would stay by Charles's side all night. Maybe then Luther could bear his embarrassment.

"Me and Mrs. Creamer and the boy here," Thrasher called out, "we want to buy the nicest looking steer you got, Mr. Cattleman, sir."

Mr. Cattleman.

Luther uncrossed his arms and straightened his body. He was a tall man, the only good trait he'd gotten from his father.

"And he's a man," he heard the woman say. "You can sell it to him."

Luther kept his back to them. "This ain't no beauty contest. It's a steer show, people."

"That's right, I am a man." Thrasher's voice had gone deeper.

"Please sell us one, sir." It was the boy now. There was something about him, the way he spoke up, a strength to his voice. Luther wanted that for LC.

He turned to look at the boy, and there was Thrasher, holding a one hundred dollar bill as new as Luther had ever seen. Luther pictured his bank account. It was so low, the teller surely had called the bank president to gawk at it. He felt his stomach tighten again.

Now that he thought about it, he did have a steer he could sell. It belonged to an ancient mother cow, sixteen years old, ugly with a splotchy face like none he'd ever seen. Always before, she had dropped heifers and did so in the spring of the year when she was supposed to. Girl calves grow up to be mothers and produce more calves, which was why he'd kept her around twice as long as most farmers would have, besides cows pay for themselves at age six. But she messed up last November, way out of cycle, and dropped twin calves, one the buzzards got and the other a bull calf, something Luther didn't need. He had Uncle cut his balls, making it a steer whose fate would be the butcher block as soon as he was weaned from his mother and fed out some. She was headed for the block, too, and the only thing she was good for now, hamburger meat. He was doing the old cow a favor. With her age, he feared if she became pregnant again, she could have trouble delivering, and that could leave her paralyzed and unable to stand. The steer wasn't but four months old, which was at least two months too early to wean, but that hundred dollars could put Luther back in the comfortable category. And if he sold the mother for another two hundred at next week's cattle sale, he'd be sitting high again. The calf might die without his mother's milk, but that wasn't his problem.

He removed his can of Prince Albert's tobacco from a pocket high on his overalls and a pack of rolling papers. He selected one piece, and with his forefinger, tapped the side of the can, forcing the crushed brown leaves onto the paper, which he brought to his mouth, and licked the outside edge and rolled it all together.

The three people before him reminded him of the Three Stooges, an oddball comedy act of three idiots he'd seen from time to time at the State Theatre. He put the cigarette in his mouth and lifted the bottom of his boot and struck a match. The man stooge was waving the money like a flag. Little did they know they had surrendered.

The searing sound of the match was brief as it lit its intended. He dropped it to the ground, part of his seventy-one spectacular acres of Kentucky 31 fescue and ladino clover that helped tack down the earth and keep it from blowing away. He was doing important work. He stepped on the match with his boot, a real cattleman's boot, dirty and carrying a smattering of blood. He twisted the stick into the earth and tried not to, but he looked back at his house to see if his boy was watching.

The mother cow heard the automobile's engine before it came into view up near the barn. The sound was not one she recognized. She began moving in a half circle, bringing her offspring along with her, until he stood behind her, tucked in. She lowered her head back to the tender grass, while her calf clamped his mouth around her teat and pulled.

When the second vehicle sounded, another she did not recognize, she did not lower her head to eat. She kept it high in the air.

The third sound was one that she knew. It was the farmer's truck. She turned towards it and watched for it to come around the barn. She walked that way, her calf following. The sound could bring them food.

The truck stopped beside a tree that gave the mother and her offspring shade. The workingman stood in the back and began swinging something that caught the neck of her calf, who tried to run. The man jumped from the truck and tied her calf to the tree.

The mother cow ran towards her calf, the two of them bawling in a rhythm that went back and forth. She circled the tree and her calf. She circled again and again.

Other cows raised their heads and watched. Some moved in closer.

The farmer sat on the tailgate. "Just let it wear itself out. The mama, too. She'll wear down after a while."

The while came, the animal's voices no longer strong, the sun having peaked and begun its slow crawl towards the horizon. The workingman grabbed at the calf's flank where its back leg joined its body and then rammed his knee up into it hard, pushing the three-hundred-pound animal onto the ground. He tied its back legs and moved to the steer's face, where he placed a halter.

The mother cow continued to circle. Her gait had slowed but not her frenzy.

The farmer no longer sat on the tailgate. He made a ramp of two long boards off the back of the truck.

The workingman untied the steer's legs and rope from the tree, then started with the animal towards the ramp, grabbing its tail and twisting it hard, then yanking it high and holding. The steer moved forward into the bed, five foot high wooden railings surrounding him. He moved from side to side, looking through the holes between the slats. The mother cow rammed the side of the truck. The railings shook.

The two men drove her offspring away.

She chased after them, running free for a stretch but found the barbed-wire gate closed and sitting snug in wire loops. She rammed it with her 1,008 pounds, her chest pressing into the barbs. They pierced her and brought forth blood.

The fence was made to hold. She pressed harder.

Her cries were loud, and, as light faded and darkness turned bold, they grew deafening.

That evening, the winds became high. She was accustomed to wind. She'd come from it, was born into it. Every now and then, there would be a short break, and in that space, the wind delivered to her, his voice.

She bellowed back, still pressing. Like his, her sound stretched long.

Sarah, along with Emerson Bridge and Mr. Thrasher, had been waiting in the yard for more than two hours when Mr. Dobbins's truck pulled into the driveway. "Where's the lot to keep it in?" he called from his open window as he passed Sarah. She pointed towards Harold's barn.

They all chased after him, even Mr. Thrasher, who had been quiet during the wait, his head lowered, his hat on the verge of falling off. Mr. Dobbins had refused to let him bring the steer home in Mr. Thrasher's truck, saying he did not have what Mr. Dobbins called "bodies." They were railings that would protect the steer's safety during transport.

When Mr. Dobbins came to a stop, Mr. Thrasher shouted towards him, "Hey, I want you to know I'm going to get my own bodies."

But all Mr. Dobbins said was, "Where's the fence for this baby beef?" He sounded mad.

"We don't have one of them," Sarah told him. "What about him just staying out in the yard like a dog?" The steer was larger than any dog she'd ever seen, by three or four times. It stood pressed to the railings on the right side of the upper end like it was scared and made sounds, deep ones. Emerson Bridge stood just out from the animal, his head tilted back, chin in the air. Sarah wondered when he'd want to touch it. The railings allowed room for such between the boards, as much as four inches.

"I said *where?*" Mr. Dobbins shouted.

"Well, let's see." Mr. Thrasher had his hands on his hips, his body pivoting on the heels of his boots. "Cows eat grass, so we need a place where there's grass."

Mr. Dobbins slapped the outside of the door with his flat hand. "Tie it to that water oak over there, Uncle, and let's get out of here." He was talking to another man inside his truck, a negro and on the skinny side.

He got busy doing what Mr. Dobbins asked.

Emerson Bridge walked up to the truck window and asked, "What's his name, sir?"

But Mr. Dobbins waved him off and revved his engine. And when his helper got back inside, he backed up into the yard and left.

The animal pulled hard on the rope. Sarah hoped he would like his new home.

He had to.

Emerson Bridge stood near the barn, about twenty feet away. "You like your new buddy?" Sarah called out to him.

He plopped down in the dirt and leaned back against the wooden boards. "My papa's my buddy."

The steer's bellows were becoming more shrill. Sarah wondered if she'd made a mistake bringing the animal there. She felt needles in her face and head.

Mr. Thrasher was walking beside the barn, appearing to study some cedar trees growing in a line and then back a ways. He put his hands on the trunk of one down low.

Sarah took a deep breath and thought about all the goodness she had seen that day. She'd taken needle and thread to hem Mrs. Dobbins's dress, but she already had it hemmed in town. And Mr. Thrasher had offered to buy the steer outright and suspend her payments on the land, until after they won, if she let him participate. With the extra $7.50 she now no longer owed him, she had $15.97 to pay the light bill down and buy notions and fabric and gasoline and food for Emerson Bridge. "You're a good man, Mr. Thrasher," she called out.

She saw her words move through his body, cause him to jump into the air the way she had seen schoolgirls jump rope. She was glad he could play. She wondered when Emerson Bridge would.

"Reckon we should build a fence," Mr. Thrasher said. His hands were back on the cedar trunk. "Reckon how you do it?"

Reckon how you pay for it, Sarah wanted to say, but that was no one's problem but hers.

· · · · ·

62

"They don't have a shot in hell, do they?" Luther asked Uncle as they drove back home. "I mean, could you find three bigger clowns or what? A jelly, a woman, and a snot-nose." Luther began chuckling and waited on Uncle to join in, but Uncle stayed quiet. Luther gave him a quick push on his upper arm. "What? Cat got your tongue? I've asked you two questions."

Uncle cleared his throat. "I feel for them, Mr. LC."

"Feel for them? Well, I *feel* for that steer. God help it. With no mama's milk and no pasture, it'll be dead before summer."

Uncle shifted in his seat.

"You ain't going soft on me, are you? You know those people have no business messing with my Fat Cattle Show. They're an embarrassment. And where's that woman's husband? You know jelly's not him."

Uncle had his head turned towards the side window. Luther let out a huff and gritted his teeth. *How dare Uncle take their side.*

Luther slammed on the brakes. "Get out! Get the by God out right now."

Uncle stepped out.

Luther peeled off. *How could Uncle be so ungrateful when Luther had built him a tenant house and let him live free from day one on Luther's land?*

He watched Uncle get smaller in his rearview mirror and told himself that the steer didn't matter, and neither did those people. They had as much of a chance of winning as Uncle did, which was zero, since he wouldn't be allowed to enter, only the Negro Fat Cattle Show & Sale, which was a pitiful knock-off.

Luther needed some air. His window was down, but Uncle's was rolled up. *What was it with negroes and not wanting to be cold?*

He pulled off the road and stretched across the long seat and rolled Uncle's window down. He could smell the man, the smell of oil and the scent of fire burning and sweat. And Luther could feel him, the indention his rear end had made over the years. Luther put his hand there. It was still warm.

· · · · ·

At the Calhoun Hotel that night, Luther Dobbins and his family sat at the large round table on the last row. The table up front was reserved for the winner and his father. He'd thought about sitting on the second row, but that was where the pitiful sat, those who'd never had any kind of shot at glory and never would. He told himself he'd better get a table with plenty of room around it so people could talk to Charles. That meant the back row.

He'd placed his younger son on his left and, on his right, leaned the back of Charles's chair against the table to save his place. Charles had not yet arrived. Luther sat so he could easily see the door and his boy walking in. Mildred sat on the other side of LC. Another family filled the rest of the seats, except the one beside Charles. Luther had it reserved for the county agent, Paul Merritt.

Mildred wore a dark blue dress, one of those rich blues that Luther liked. He couldn't say she was a pretty woman, but he wasn't embarrassed to have her sit with him. He didn't know how much she weighed, but it wasn't much and not even close to what she weighed when they married. Back then, he had something to hang on to. He missed that, but at least she wasn't fat like Merritt's wife.

The room had an elegance to it, especially the chandelier in the middle, as fine as he imagined any home in Anderson possessed, even the rich people who lived in homes along the Boulevard or Murray Avenue, but also the walls with their sage green wallpaper that appeared as satin with its high shine.

"So, how does it feel sitting out all the way in the back pasture with the rest of us?" It was the man across from Luther. He'd seen the man before but had never thought him important enough to remember his name.

Luther slapped the back of Charles's chair. "My boy Charles won nine years in a row. He's probably getting him a parking place at this very minute."

The county agent walked in. Luther rose to his feet and waved him over. The man did as he was told but shook his head the whole way there. "You know I got to sit at the head table, Luther."

Luther liked that Merritt had to raise his chin in order to look at him. Luther wanted to tell him, *You mean the grand champion's table,* but was afraid his voice would catch. So he said, "Thought you might want to talk to Charles. He's coming, you know. You might learn something." Then Luther sat and tucked the white cloth napkin at his throat, letting the rest of it hang down over his high-dollar tie that went with his high-dollar suit. "Wonder when that steak's coming?"

A waitress set a small wooden bowl of tossed salad with French dressing at each place. Then came plates filled with steaks and small Irish potatoes, boiled and already buttered. "Looks like sirloins," Luther said and took his knife and cut into his. The meat looked to lack sufficient marbling. He put a piece, a small one as if sampling, in his mouth and chewed but soon reached for his iced tea glass and took a big swallow. He was right. "This ain't a Dobbins steak. Tough as shoe leather. Somebody pass me the Heinz 57."

Merritt stood at the podium and began talking. Luther knew he was only a few minutes away from asking the grand champion and his father to stand. "Yeah, my boy Charles," Luther told the table, "is a big college man up at Clemson studying what they call animal husbandry. That's a fact."

"Big LC," Mildred whispered and nodded with her head towards the front.

"Yeah, he'll probably come back when he's finished and take that man's job up there." Luther had the attention of several people at tables nearby. "He already knows how to put an X on a cow's forehead and kill it with a ten-pounder." Luther put his arm around the back of Charles's empty chair. "And can you believe I ain't having to pay for all that? He's on scholarship he's so smart." He took a big gulp of his iced tea.

"I did something today," his younger son said.

Luther spewed tea from his mouth across his plate of food.

Applause broke out around the room. This year's grand champion and his father were standing now. The crowd joined them, even Mildred. But LC stayed seated, as did Luther, his boy's eyes fixed on him. Luther could feel rings of sweat beneath his armpits.

The crowd sat, the room becoming quiet, except for the flashes from the newspaper woman's camera. Luther cut an extra big piece of steak and put it in his mouth.

"I killed a deer today, my very first one," LC said, his voice as loud as Luther's had been. "I'm marked now." His boy looked at him straight on. He had washed up clean. All that was left could appear as a slight sunburn.

"I didn't know it was deer season, Big LC," Mildred said. "Charles always killed his in the fall of the year."

Luther raised his hand. He noticed it was shaking. He put it back down and cut his eyes to the people around him. Most shifted in their seats.

Mildred put a peppermint in her mouth.

Luther looked towards the door. *Where was Charles?*

The steak was still in Luther's mouth. He tried to swallow, but the meat wouldn't go down. He took a drink of iced tea and tried to swallow again, but the steak seemed stuck. He took another big drink.

Nothing.

He brought his fist near his upper stomach and tapped it there as if he had just bumped his hand. He wanted to do it harder, but he didn't want anyone to know he was in trouble.

His heart rate picked up to a near frenzy.

He got up from his seat and hurried out the door to the lobby to an area off to the side.

He was choking. He was going to die. And die a loser. And do so in front of his boy, whose love he did not have. And Mildred, he was leaving Mildred with a house and a farm she believed was paid for. But it was not. And then there was Charles, who did not need him and never had.

He dropped to his knees. He did this on a rug more plush than he could afford, and all of this in front of a settee, covered in velvet the color of blood. His body fell forward, his upper stomach hitting the mahogany arm railing hard, the chewed piece of sirloin now dislodging and coming back into his mouth.

He looked around. No one was there.

He coughed the chewed meat forward, the dark, ugly mass hitting the wall a couple of feet in front of him and then began sliding down the green satin shine. Luther wiped his brow with the back of his hand, his brow slick with wetness, his throat on fire and burning.

He was being punished. He had called that woman, Mrs. Creamer, a "heathen." But that's what he was. God had let him taste hell, let the flames of fire in the devil's house lap at his heathen heels and climb his heathen legs.

He heard applause inside the room. That's where everyone else was, his boy and the grand champion and his father, a man who had not pushed a ladybug over that day, nor was he a man who had put a gun in his boy's arms and forced him to kill, knowing his boy was too tender for that.

Wasn't he too tender for that?

. . . . .

Emerson Bridge, darkness having settled in, remained outside with the steer, off to the side, sitting in front of his papa's barn. The steer's sounds had been loud in the daytime but now had become a scream. Emerson Bridge cried louder at night, too.

He thought of his papa's urging to be kind. His mother had delivered a bucket of water to the animal soon after it arrived that afternoon, but he had done nothing to make the steer's way better. He had thought he wanted an animal to be his friend, but seeing it and hearing its cries reminded Emerson Bridge that his papa was gone.

He recalled the animal's face, white with a brownish color scattered about, and his hair had looked fluffy, like it might be soft. His papa's beard, before he shaved, was soft.

He looked towards the tree, where the steer was still tied. He could see its dark shape. It was alone, too.

Emerson Bridge rose from the ground and went to the animal, nudged closer the bucket of water and stood still. The steer backed up to the tree and made a sound with its nose like it was pushing air through. Emerson Bridge thought he could smell it. There was a sweetness.

The moon hung high in the sky behind them. It lit the steer's face, that fluffiness, that softness. Emerson Bridge lifted his hand towards the animal, held it still in the growing cold, and said, "It ain't your fault my papa ain't here no more."

The steer seemed to hold on Emerson Bridge, their eyes about level. "And I'm going to be kind to you. I promise you that."

The steer released its scream again. Emerson Bridge didn't know what the animal was saying, but he knew it was important. No, more than important. Necessary.

Emerson Bridge wondered what was necessary for him to say. He could smell the fatback his mother had fried for his supper. He had not been in to eat, and she had not bugged him about coming in. The word "lucky" came to him. He was lucky to have her.

And lucky to have a new friend, too. He wondered if the steer knew how to play throw-the-rock, and then he let out a giggle, his first since he lost his papa.

"Lucky," he said aloud and knew he'd said the animal's name. "Lucky, you're my Lucky boy."

. . . . .

The steer's bellowing did not let up. It rumbled like thunder in the pitch black.

Sarah lay in bed and wanted to sleep, but she was feeling what the steer was sending forth in her toes. It made the bottoms of her feet sweat and rise up her body in waves.

She got up, lit the kerosene lamp, and went outside to the steer. Emerson Bridge was no longer with the animal. She'd heard him come into the house about midnight.

"Sounds like you're calling for somebody. Who you calling for?" Sarah's voice was like a child's, large and full of wonder.

She held the light at its face and saw mostly white but also a pretty red brown that started at the bottom, near its nose, and ran ragged on a diagonal towards its right eye. Over its left, a dot of that same red brown like somebody had dropped a speck of red-eye gravy.

The animal raised its chin into the air and released his long, slow resonance, and, this time, Sarah's legs began to tremble. The utterance was not one she recognized in her head. But in her bones, where it had lain since her beginning days, she did.

MARCH 18, 1951

Sarah woke in the early morning light to a pin-dropping quiet.
The steer's sounds were no more. *Had it died? Or broken free of the rope and run away?*

She rushed to her window, threw it open, and held herself.

But she heard nothing.

She ran through the house and out the door, running barefoot, the ground cold and hard.

With the sun rising at her back and her eyes straining toward the tree, she saw the shape of something large. She came to see it was a cow but much bigger than the steer, maybe three times. The animal shifted backwards and revealed a smaller one, its rear end aimed Sarah's way and its head tucked beneath the larger one. She heard slurping sounds, hungry ones. The small one was nursing. A rope extended taut from the animal to the tree. *This was Emerson Bridge's steer.*

The larger cow's face looked at Sarah, straight on. It carried the same two colors and markings she'd seen on the steer the day before, only more pronounced. *This was the steer's mama.*

She looked around the yard for Mr. Dobbins's truck but did not see it. She wondered if he dropped her off sometime in the night. But why would he pick such a late hour? And would he expect payment? The cow would likely cost triple what the steer had cost.

All up and down the mother cow's neck and chest and legs, Sarah saw cuts, many appearing deep and in long, jagged runs like someone had taken serrated knives and sliced. Most of the blood was bright red, but some was almost black. She hadn't seen this much blood since the night Emerson Bridge was born.

She recalled the fence of little x's at Mr. Dobbins's farm the day before. She and Emerson Bridge and Mr. Thrasher had stood behind it and watched his truck move into the pasture to get the steer. She had touched one of the little x's. It was sharp. It could pierce.

Chills spread over Sarah's body. *The mama cow had broken free and come for her calf.*

Sarah had taken her child away. She took a step back. How could she have done that?

The mother cow held her eyes on Sarah, circles of soft brown that welcomed, not chided. The cow began to chew, her mouth moving in a rhythm, slow and steady. It was one Sarah recognized. It was the rhythm of her arm, stirring a pot of grits. It was the rhythm of love.

"How'd you know?" Sarah's voice full of hush. "That's a long way for you to come. And in the pitch black, too. How'd you know?"

The mother cow raised her chin and sent forth a sound, a short one, yet deep, even vibrating. The sounds the steer had made were deep like that, but his were long, intended for the long haul, for his mother, who heard and who came. Sarah knew now who he had been calling. His mother. Such acts had never occurred to her. Neither a child's calling nor the mother's coming.

She thought of Emerson Bridge and looked back towards the house, to his window, where six feet away, he lay. "I got a boy, too."

The mother cow's neck now was stretched to her far right, the bottom of her mouth and chin moving along the ridge of her calf's back near his tail. She began to lick, making long runs with her tongue. Her breath, hot against the cold, hung in a mist. And then rose high in the growing light.

Sarah stepped forward and leaned in, in the hopes that the mist would come find her, that it would trudge across however far it needed to come, even knock down a fence or two, to come find Clementine Florence Augusta Sarah Bolt Creamer.

The mother cow heard a squeaking sound behind her and then a slap slap. Her calf's head was beneath her, nursing. She turned to face the sound. He lost his grip on her teat but caught it again.

The day's light had begun to appear. Someone was moving towards them, someone the mother cow did not know. She positioned her body so that her calf was tucked in behind her, protected. He was not free to run like she was.

This someone wasn't as tall as the farmer or his workingman. This one moved slowly the way a gentle wind blows grass. The mother cow was not afraid. She straightened her body, bringing her calf within view of the gentle wind that came to stand just out from them.

There was a stillness now. Blood from her wounds had started to dry, but now that she had moved again, the cuts on her front knees oozed. She had broken free of the farmer's fence just as the moon was losing its orange and becoming white. Her calf's cry drew her across lands that were foreign, open fields of wheat, the green sprouts rubbing her belly, and across stretches of grass, just reemerging to the promise of warmth.

When she'd come within a half mile of her young, she could smell him. She bore down, the wind in her face.

When she found him, she'd sniffed just up from his mouth, where she ran hers, parched. And then she began licking him, as she was licking him now.

The gentle wind was making sounds. They came from her mouth.

The mother cow continued to lick.

Sarah returned to her house, to Emerson Bridge's room. He was asleep, his body curled in tight under a thin sheet. She pulled the bedspread up over him and got on her knees and called up in her mind the mother cow, how she had moved her mouth along the top of her calf's back. She was saying, *I love you, boy.* She didn't have to say, *And I hope you know I want you.* The calf already knew that. His mother had come for him.

Sarah brought her hand up and touched her own mouth. Then she moved her face, pushing aside the inches between her and boy, to his cheek, where her lips hovered above his silent dimple. She lowered herself to him and found his skin as soft and warm as the inside of a biscuit.

She felt him stir and drew her face back. His eyes were open and on her.

She scooped him up, brought him full to her chest.

Around her neck, hard and fast, he wrapped his arms.

She released a sound she had never made. It carried both a low end and a high, like she had lost her breath and spotted it in the distance.

They began to rock.

She had always thought she lived to see his dimples. But it was this. This is what she'd lived for. *This.*

You done started on your teaching of me. With my boy. Can I tell you that, girl? I don't know your name. What's your name? Mine's Sarah.

I come back out here to thank you. I'm six days now into having to be his mama full on. But can I tell you something? I don't know how to be. *I don't mean to be whispering, but them words—be a mama—they scare me. I'm lost. See, if me and you was a long piece of cloth, you'd be one end with me clear across the whole wide world on the other, trying to hang on to a skinny piece of nothing. Because as good a mama as you are, I'm that, that . . .* I don't know how to be a mama.

You can sure tell your boy there is yours. Them two colors on y'all's faces, that pretty red brown and that white. And both of them arranged in that same exact pattern, except his is littler. Like his ears and his forehead is stamped in that red color across the bottom of your face. Like his shadow has fallen on you for all time. So that you won't never leave him. No ma'am, Mama Red, you don't. Mama Red. *Can I call you that?*

See, my boy don't look like me. That's because he's not my flesh and blood.

Oh, to say those words out loud.

Not another soul that's alive on this earth knows that but me. The two that did are dead.

I see you holding your head just as still, listening to me with that good kind of mama way you got. This ain't the first time I've seen it. The first time was when I was a girl, six year old. An old mama dog showed it to me. She come across our backyard one afternoon. I spotted her out the kitchen window when I was making some cornbread for Mama before prayer meeting. "Get it smooth now, girl!" Mama hollered down to me. She was upstairs on her sewing machine. "Don't want to see no pones, no big fat pones, sticking up out of it."

I took off out the screened door after that dog. But I didn't see her nowhere. I wanted to call out "Hey, girl," but I kept quiet. Mama's room was right up over me, and her window was open. It was hot and in August right before I started to the first grade. Then I heard this sound like a steady beat from under the house, so I crawled up under it, and there she was. That was her tail I was hearing. She was wagging it. And I believed it was for me.

But then her legs went to lifting up, holding them out stiff like broom handles, and she let out this squeal and stretched her head back towards her tail that was all hiked up, and there she come back holding something in her mouth by her teeth and started shaking it hard like she was mad at it. But she wasn't mad, she'd had a puppy, Mama Red. She laid it real soft in the dirt and got her tongue and licked it and then took her nose and tucked in that baby up to her teats, so she could get her a good drink. My eyes started filling up in buckets.

She had four more of them. I scooted back that way, so I could watch. I wanted to see it all. And just like you would, Mama Red, she welcomed every one of them like she was saying to them, "Hey there, I'm your mama, and I think you're good."

But then my mama started calling my name. I didn't want to leave, but I knew I had to go. Before I left, I soaked up how still that mama dog was, and that made me get all still, too. I whispered to her, "I love you." She held her eyes on me like I might matter. And then I crawled out, and Mama yanked me to my feet and told me, "You ain't got no time to be playing, girl."

"I wasn't," I told her, "I was watching a mama dog have puppies."

"Don't you talk back to me!" she said and slapped a fly swatter up against my shoulder.

"It was sweet, Mama, what I seen," I told her.

"Sweet? It's just having babies. Anything can have babies. That ain't nothing. And you so fat, you'd smush them." Then she brought that swatter down and hit me on my arm. It stung some but not like the words she said to me next. And with every one of them, she timed out a slap. She said, "You-ain't-got-you-one-good-mama-bone-in-you."

I felt like a knife had sliced me open, cut part of me out and flung it to the winds.

"And nobody wants to see no crybaby," she said. "You better learn to carry it, is all I say."

Papa come home from the mill that night, and she made him get the dog and the puppies and carry them off somewhere. We never did have no more talk about it.

But I'll tell you this now, mama's words to me was the first stitch on a garment that I would wear for the rest of my born days. And once that stitch got to running, it kept going more and more off seam. I let her words take up housekeeping inside of me.

They inside of me now. But I don't want them to be.

MARCH 18, 1951

Luther did not enter the church sanctuary that Sunday morning in his usual fashion, from the hall that led into the front near the pulpit and choir loft. He would have to face people that way, men from the Cattleman's Supper the night before who saw another father and son crowned winner and people in general, good people. He entered on the opposite end, through the outside door and walked the center aisle, stretching twenty five rows of pews, putting the congregation's backs to him.

This was no usual Sunday. Luther wanted to get saved. God had brought him back from almost dying the night before and given him another chance to be a better man. Even though he'd gotten saved when he was a boy, when the preacher gave the altar call at the end of the sermon that morning, Luther would answer, and LC would witness his father humbling himself. Yes, Luther could do this.

He thought about sitting on the first row. That way he would have only three or four steps to make when the altar call was given. But that would signal he was up to something, since Mildred and LC were already seated in their usual spot, fifth row back. Luther decided to join them, but, instead of sitting between Mildred and LC, as he typically did, he motioned for LC to slide over and let him sit at the end the pew on the aisle. Neither questioned him, nor did they question finding him in the lobby after the supper the night before.

LC sat with his hands folded on top of his Bible. The look of sunburn had faded. No one would know he had killed a deer the day before. Except Luther.

The preacher walked in, and the organist began with "Up from the Grave." Luther's stomach knotted up. One hour lay between him and the altar call. He wondered if his family and the whole church would faint when he answered the call, because next to the preacher, the head deacon was considered the next most godly.

When the ushers began passing the offering plate, Luther took his bill-fold out and tried to catch his boy's eyes, turning his head towards LC and leaning in. Luther had never tithed his ten percent before, always putting in a dollar bill and making sure it lay on the bottom beneath the tithing envelopes. But this Sunday, Luther took out ten one-dollar bills, his tithe of the money he'd received for the steer the day before and put them in one at a time in an envelope with his and LC's name already on it. He held it out for LC to see. "Mine's on it, too?" LC said. Luther nodded and dropped in the envelope and thought about showing his boy the ladybugs soon.

The sermon began, but Luther did not listen. There was no need to until the end for the call. He looked down at his shoes. They were black dress shoes, his most expensive. The first time he answered the call, he'd worn boots, white ones with tassels. He was a boy of eight with no shoes to wear, and cold winter had set in. He and his family were white but lived in a tenant house on a rich white man's place, a Mr. Joseph Allgood. They lived beside another family, this one negro. This was Uncle's family, and back then, Luther called him by his name, Emmanuel. Luther's mother cleaned for the Allgoods and saw a pair of girl's boots, white with tassels, in a paper sack by the front door. Mrs. Allgood was going to throw them away but gave them to his mother. "Nobody'll know, son," his mother told him. But a boy in his Sunday School class said, "Hey, ain't them girl's boots?" Luther slid his feet back and told the boy, "Naw." "They are," the boy said louder, "and they've got jelly tassels." The boy laughed. The preacher's sermon that morning talked about getting saved, saying that God protected the saved with a shield. Luther wanted that shield. So when the altar call was given, little boy Luther yanked on the bottom of his pant legs and walked the aisle and told the preacher, "I need one of God's shields around me."

Luther wondered if the preacher that morning would use that kind of language. He wasn't sure if God had given him a shield back then and taken it away. Or if God never had.

"The time has come," the preacher said, and Luther felt a wave of sweat move over him.

"We talk of 'once saved, always saved,' brothers and sisters. *But are you sure?* Are you sure that if you died going home this day, are you sure you would escape the eternal burning fires of hell and spend eternity with our blessed savior and Lord, Jesus Almighty Christ?"

No, I'm not sure, Luther screamed inside.

"Because if you're not," the preacher said, his hands now raised, "why don't you come forward and have all your sins forgiven and be washed in the blood of our almighty Father?"

Yes, I want to be washed in the blood.

The congregation now was standing. Luther burst into the aisle like he'd been shot from a gun. He took two steps and thought he heard smirks and whispers. *Is that Luther, the head deacon, stepping out as a sinner?* He took another. *You're a fake, Luther Dobbins.* The words now in full voice. *You mean you've been living a lie all this time?* Laughter breaking out, coming in waves, big ones. Luther taking long strides now and within reach of the preacher's hand, now extended towards Luther. *You running tuck-tailed to the Lord now that you're no longer Grand Champion?* Screams now.

He turned and headed to the door past the pulpit and choir loft, and then to the bathroom, where he stood at the sink and turned on the hot water faucet.

He ran it until it burned.

Into that fire, he placed his hands.

He wanted to sear them.

. . . . .

Ike Thrasher told himself he would not show his face at the Creamer's until he had properly outfitted his truck with bodies, but he fell short of that pledge that Sunday morning as he traveled west on Portman Highway in his "unequipped" truck, as Mr. Dobbins had called it the day before. But the steer needed a fence.

Harold Creamer had always looked to be a real man, so likely he had materials in his barn Ike could use to build the fence, although Ike had never built one. By the time he was old enough to learn from his father, Ike had kissed that boy and was told to stay in the house and be a girl like his mother. Ike knew he could learn a lot from Mr. Dobbins, and now that he had seen the cattleman had a helper, Ike set his sights on becoming one. Roy Rogers called them hired hands. "Yeah," he said aloud, "this future hired hand is riding out to build a fence for the Grand Champeen."

He drove up close to the tree where the steer was tied and saw the steer nursing a bigger cow.

"Mr. Thrasher!" It was the boy near the barn, holding something with both hands. It looked like a thick stick, and he was swinging it.

"What's that big cow doing here?" Ike called out his window.

"That's his mama," Emerson Bridge shouted. "She loves him."

"Loves him? A cow?"

The boy came towards him. It was an ax he was holding, one almost as tall as he. "Yes sir, Mama said the cow loves him so much, she broke out of the fence at Mr. Dobbins's and walked all the way here in the night. Four miles." He took a big swing through the air with the ax. "But I think Lucky, that's what I named him, I think Lucky just needed his mama."

The steer's head was still beneath the big cow. "Hey, this ain't no sissy boy needing his mama." Ike got out of his truck.

"And she got cut up so bad, Mama put some medicine on her to help heal her up."

Ike slammed his door.

"And Lucky's getting him a fence, too. That nice man Mr. Emmanuel from yesterday's going to build it."

"You mean Mr. Dobbins?"

"No sir, Mr. Emmanuel, the one that did all the work."

"I thought his name was Uncle."

The boy hunched up his shoulders. "Told me his name was Emmanuel. He walked all the way here this morning rolling that little wagon over there with a big ball of barbed wire he kept underneath a coat. Said the wire was a toss off, that Mr. Dobbins didn't think it was shiny enough."

"Where's your mama?" Ike asked.

"In the house, sewing. Mr. Emmanuel had to leave but said he'd be back."

Ike marched towards the house. He started to knock on the porch door, but the matter was too urgent. He went inside, and from the kitchen called "Mrs. Creamer." She didn't answer, but he heard the sewing machine across the way and followed the sound to a bedroom. He stood in the doorway and saw her hunched towards the machine. He was aware he still had his hat on and that gentlemen did not do such inside a house, but it made a statement of serious intent.

"I've come to say that mama cow out there's got to go," he said in a loud voice, which startled him.

She stopped pedaling and jerked her head his way. "No, sir. No, sir." She came towards him.

"Yes ma'am, yes ma'am, she does."

"No sir, she don't." She was standing in front of him. She was barefooted. With his boots on, he was a tad taller. He wanted to make himself even higher. He raised up on his tiptoes.

"I aim to go to Mr. Dobbins today and not leave until he's said I can buy her," she told him.

"Where you getting the money? I'm not giving it to you."

"I'm making a dress right now to sell, and when I finish, I'll get on another."

She held her eyes wide like a fishing net the Bible talked of to catch fish. That's how his congregation looked when he had hit the height of his sermon, and he knew he had them with his words about righteousness and filthy selves and spending eternity in hell. After that, they would soak up anything he would say. He took a deep breath and mustered all the volume he could. "I said we ain't going to have no sissy boy needing his mama."

"And *I said* I'll pay for her."

He watched her neck to see if she would swallow hard. He'd learned to put his eyes there when his parishioners would talk of their troubles and then ask him to get the Lord God Almighty to help fix them. Their necks showed if they believed or not. If they swallowed, they were in deep, both in their troubles and their belief in divine help. But, if they did not, they were skimmers and shut off from any help that could come.

Mrs. Creamer swallowed hard.

"I'll pay for her and my debt to you, too, if it means I don't eat nothing but cold loaf and the pads on chicken's feet, if I can ever afford a chicken again, and give my boy all the good vittles."

Ike felt a tremor move through him. Her boy was right. This woman did love him. Ike's mother had loved him like that. He could smell his mother's talcum now, fragrant as her red roses growing up the trellis by the side of the house, the way she'd sprinkle the powder on her body after a bath. The time his father had gone to the cotton gin, and she let him sprinkle some on him, lavender snow, he had thought of it, the lightness of it like his father's field dust, but the talcum didn't have to be washed off, it could stay. His mother let it stay.

He came down off his tiptoes. He was thinking now that maybe it wouldn't hurt the steer to have his mama around.

He reached up and took off his hat.

· · · · ·

Luther took his seat at the dinner table that Sunday and wrapped his hands around his iced tea glass, letting the condensation on its outside sooth his skin.

"Here's your favorite, the pulley bone, Little LC," Mildred said, her body leaned over the table with a platter of fried chicken.

"I told you not to call—" Luther started.

"Don't call me that no more, Mama. I ain't little." LC's voice was louder.

Luther shifted in his seat. He had laid in bed the night before, thinking about what he was creating in LC, a small version of himself. The cold look in his boy's eyes told him that, but Luther could only see them sideways. He wanted his boy to look at him straight on.

A knock came at the front door. Luther saw an old black automobile out the window behind him. It was that heathen woman, Mrs. Creamer. She was on to him about the steer being too young and wanted to get that man's money back. But that wasn't going to happen. The note on his place was due that coming week, and the $90 he had left would cover it.

Mildred got up from the table.

"Tell her a deal's a deal," Luther called out.

"I bet Splotchy took off over there after her calf," LC said.

"Thought I told you not to name them cows," Luther said.

"I got to talk to him," he heard, footsteps, loud ones, coming his way. He slid his chair back and started to leave the room, but Mrs. Creamer met him in the entrance. She was holding out money.

"I'm sorry to barge in here, but my boy's steer's mama has come for him, and I want to buy her from you."

Luther saw a ten, a one-dollar bill, a quarter, and two dimes.

"This ain't enough, I know," she said. "But it's a start."

"One of my cows got out?" Luther yelled. "There's a hole in my fence?"

"Uncle's down there fixing it," LC said.

Luther whipped his neck back towards the boy. "How do you know?"

"While mama was cooking, I went down to see the cows and saw him."

Luther waited for someone to laugh at him for being the last to know and for having a hole in his fence and for not riding herd over his own cows.

But no one laughed.

LC was looking at Mrs. Creamer.

Luther blew air through his nose and told the woman, "That's my cow. I'm coming to get her."

"No sir, please don't. I want her." She pushed the money closer.

"If you *want her,* then you can go see her at the Greasy Spoon at the end of the week. Order you a hotdog—extra chili. I'm selling her at the sale Tuesday for scrap, the only thing she's good for now, ever-loving hamburger meat. She's worse than broken mouth, she's a gummer, used up, empty, spent, open, and her udders ruined." He knew his words had come fast. Once he'd mentioned the sale, he had to keep going for fear that LC or Mildred would ask him why he never took his cows himself, always making Uncle do it, while Luther found something "pressing" to do, such as need-ing a haircut for a special church meeting. The truth was Luther couldn't bear to see them being herded into the ring and sold to the highest bidder and then carried away for slaughter. Occasionally, though, on days when his own cattle were not being sold, he would make a show of going and milling around with other farmers and talking price on the hoof or price hanging.

"Excuse me," Mrs. Creamer said and ran from the room.

He had scared her off. Maybe he could get LC to look at him now.

Luther returned to his chair. He wanted to lean over and whisper, "I've picked better for you this time," but what came out was "So you went to check on your steer, Mr. Grand Champion Man? Good to see you taking that kind of interest."

LC brought his eyes to him, just like that. *So all it took was a question?* But then they started to fill. "I was wanting to see something still alive."

Mildred gasped, her hands flying to her mouth.

A shot of heat rose through Luther and settled in his hands. They were on fire again. He wanted to run from the room, run down his sloping land to the pond, where a preacher would be standing, his hands outstretched, welcoming Luther for a saving, then a baptism, and saying, "I baptize thee, my brother, Luther Charles Dobbins, Sr."

"Why, Mrs. Creamer," Mildred said.

The woman stood in the entranceway again, her head bowed as if in prayer. *Wasn't that what he had been—in prayer?* He wondered if she was joining in his, or had she heard what LC had said? Luther put his eyes on his boy, whose head was bent low, too. But Luther didn't have to wonder about his boy's prayer. His boy was praying for a father who could be a good man.

The preacher's words "washed in the blood of the Lord" flooded his mind. *The Lord could use blood to cleanse?* Luther looked at his hands, the pink of blood, its stain, lying just below the surface.

Mrs. Creamer dashed towards him and laid something shiny beside his plate. It was a key. "To my automobile," she said. "I want to trade it for Mama Red."

Luther imagined his hands cleansed, put his eyes on LC, and from his mouth came, "Keep that mama cow."

He watched for his boy to bring his eyes to him, wide open eyes. Because it would be safe to now. His father could be a good man.

"Oh, Big LC," he heard Mildred say. She was swooning like she did before they married. Maybe she might love him again, too.

"No sir, it ain't right for me to give you nothing for something worth so much." Mrs. Creamer said.

"No, keep the cow. I don't want your automobile."

There they came, his boy's eyes. And they came wide. Luther wanted to jump inside them, soak up his boy's goodness and the two of them run to that pine tree to look for ladybugs.

"No sir, wouldn't be right," Mrs. Creamer said and laid the money she had been holding on top of the key, then headed back to the entranceway. Mildred offered to drive her home, but the woman said she preferred to walk. "Feel what it's like for a mama to go that distance for her boy."

Luther stood at the window and watched her leave. He had thought the calf would be dead by summer. He changed his mind now. It was the mama that would be, not by summer but by winter. This woman would not know

79

to wean the calf from the mama in a couple of months, so the calf would continue to nurse, and with the cow being old and having no good grass to eat, she would have nothing to replenish herself. Being the good mother that she was, she would not tell her boy no. She would let him nurse her until she was skin and bones and dead.

Luther told himself he should stop Mrs. Creamer and tell her this.

But he did not.

He looked back at his boy, who was looking at him. *Distance for her boy. I'll go the distance for mine.*

He would not leave his boy's eyes.

. . . . .

It took Sarah Creamer an hour and a half to return home.

She spotted Mama Red and the steer first, standing near the tree, where she'd left them. She broke into a run. "You can stay, Mama Red," she called out, her voice high and clipped, her breathing hurried. Still, her legs whirled like a handle she was turning on her flour sifter, preparing to make biscuits for her boy.

He was near the barn, swinging something. Mr. Thrasher was bent towards the ground.

"We're making a fence for Lucky and his mama!" Emerson Bridge yelled and ran towards her.

Sarah knelt to the ground, her arms held wide.

But he stopped in front of her, his eyes past her. "Where's the automobile, Mama?"

"I traded it for her."

The sun caught the red in his hair just right and lit the space around him. "I know I can't never take your papa's place," she told him, her mouth dry, "but I want you to know that I'm going to try to be more than just a hired woman around here. I'm going to try to be a mama to you."

"You are my mama."

Sarah looked over at Mama Red. The mother cow's eyes seemed to be on her. Sarah moved her hands to the top of her boy's arms, curling her fingers around the soft curve of him.

He did not move away.

"I mean a good one."

part 3

TEACH

SEPTEMBER 21–22, 1951

"You only have one job to do with your steer, boys," the county agent, a Mr. Merritt, said to the room of nine 4-H boys, including Emerson Bridge, who sat on the outside row. This was the third Friday in September and the first 4-H meeting of the school year. It was also the official kick-off for the 1952 Fat Cattle Show coming up in March.

The man held up one finger in the schoolroom air, still full of flecks of chalk dust, floating from the lessons of the day. "And that is to finish him."

The way Mr. Merritt said the word "finish" told Emerson Bridge the word was important. Some boys must lose interest along the way. He balled up his fist on his right hand, making his knuckles pronounced. With his left index finger, he began counting the months until March, touching the rise and fall of his bones. He counted seven, and part of that time would be through the winter, which would be cold. He could see why some might not want to finish. But he would. He and Lucky had become best friends. He wanted to say that out loud. He wanted to raise his hand and be called on and say those words.

But this would be unusual for him. He'd never raised his hand without the teacher first asking a question, and he was in a room full of strangers, except for this one boy, LC, who was sitting beside him. They'd been in the first grade together and now in the second. LC used to be nice, but he had gotten mean.

"Looks like we have only one boy new to the steer project this year," Mr. Merritt said.

This was his chance. He put his arm up in the air. "Emerson Bridge Creamer, sir. And I want you to know that I aim to *finish*."

"Pear boy!" LC called out.

The boys all turned his way and laughed.

Emerson Bridge nodded. His mother had just harvested the new pears on their two trees. He was thankful he had them to eat.

"I aim to finish, too!" another boy called out from the front row. Emerson Bridge had seen him at school. He was in a higher grade.

"Crybaby," LC said.

"Now boys," the county agent tried to say.

"Ain't no crybaby," the boy said.

"You are, too," LC said. "You can't lose no sleep over what we're doing. If you ain't cut out for it, you ain't cut out for it."

"I *am* cut out for it, too," the boy said. "I've grown up over the summer."

Mr. Merritt stepped in closer. "Growing up is certainly what the 4-H helps you boys do. The beauty of the steer project is that it teaches responsibility and taking care of another living creature and seeing it all the way through."

Emerson Bridge raised his hand. The man nodded towards him. "I'm doing it for the money. For me and my mama."

"Us Dobbins men do it for the glory," LC said.

Emerson Bridge saw dried blood on LC's arm. He'd been in a fight that day.

"You didn't get no glory this year, did you, big talker, *Little* LC?" that boy up front said. "You won't ever catch your big brother." Many were laughing.

But Emerson Bridge did not. He didn't see what was funny.

"Now, boys," the county agent said, but LC cut him off. "Next year is what I'm talking about. Y'all better watch yourselves *next year*."

"My dad went all the way to the North Carolina mountains and bought mine," one of the boys said. "They got good minerals in the ground up there. Dad says 284 different kinds."

"Mine is from the Dobbins stock," LC said. "And that gives my baby beef a leg up."

"I see we have some friendly competition this year," Mr. Merritt told them. "You all should have your project steer by now. Should have chosen him for his good muscle in his forearm, rib, loin, hip, and stifle quarter and also have a square rear end and an overall good wide base. If you don't see it now, you won't see it down the road when he's finished."

Emerson Bridge pictured Lucky. He had a lot of muscle and seemed pretty wide, too.

"He should be in the five-hundred-pound range at present," Mr. Merritt was saying, "and be anywhere from a low end of six months to a top end of a year old."

Talk about a leg up. Emerson Bridge had already spent six months with his steer.

"As for his feed, you should have him on full dry, boys, with a balanced ration of small grains and some kind of meal."

Mostly, Lucky liked to nurse his mama, but he did eat grass, too, out behind the barn where the fence was. But Mr. Merritt said Lucky also needed a "meal." Emerson Bridge and his mother barely had enough for themselves, but he would start sharing what he had with Lucky.

There was applause in the next classroom over where the 4-H girls were meeting. The windows were open, so the sounds came in easily. The girls talked of sewing, of salvaging their mothers' scraps of fabric and making them into something useful. That's what his mother did with the dresses she made. All day long and way into the night, she sat bent over her sewing machine. Sometimes, he'd make himself quiet and stand in darkness just outside her door and wonder if her back hurt. He couldn't wait for Lucky to win.

Since the school bus had already left, he would need to get home on his own. His brogans were too little to run in. He would remove them when Mr. Merritt dismissed the meeting and take off running.

· · · · ·

Sarah Creamer pulled up out front of Emerson Bridge's school that Friday afternoon in a new automobile, a black 1929 Model A Ford. He was inside, attending a 4-H meeting. She had just come from town, where she'd bought it on credit at Scarboro Motors. Mr. Thrasher had found it in a newspaper advertisement, "2 door. 2 new tires. Runs. $49.50." She'd paid $10 down and promised $5 a month. In seven months, she would have it paid for. She knew she was splurging, but she'd taken advantage of Mr. Thrasher's goodness to haul her and her boy around long enough.

Three other automobiles were parked near her. She hoped they belonged to the teachers. She was there to try to sell them dresses. Six lay beside her, each folded top to bottom. She would have preferred to lay them flat, but that was not possible, since the automobile had no back seat, only a rumble seat, and that was unfit to carry them. Folded down, her dresses would be crushed. Kept open, they would fly out.

She was down to $2.14 to her name. The most she'd been able to sell was a dozen a month, mostly to Mrs. Dobbins's friends. Sarah had tried to sell them out front of Gallant-Belks in town, but she was run off for interfering with the dress business inside. Now, with the automobile payment, she needed to sell at least a dozen and a half a month.

Three women emerged from the schoolhouse. They had to be teachers. They were carrying books and all well-dressed and of average size. Her dresses would fit them.

Sarah waited until they were close and then opened her door and said, "Excuse me, Ladies." She crouched low and kept her voice to just above a whisper. "My name is Mrs. Sarah Creamer, and my boy goes to school here. He's inside at that steer meeting right now. I've made some dresses, some nice ones I hope, and I was wondering if y'all might be interested in buying one." Her hands perspired beneath her gloves.

"My mother makes all my clothes," one of them said. She was wearing a long dark skirt and a heavily-starched white blouse, high at the neck.

"She done a good job," Sarah told her. Sarah's own house dress, a washed-out brown, hung loose on her body from lack of eating. What if they thought she couldn't sew? She should have taken the time to sew a cinch belt for her waist.

The two women who remained wore dresses, a dark green and a medium blue. One didn't look old enough to teach. The other looked too old.

"May we see them?" the older one said.

Sarah scooped them up and presented them as if on a platter. "I don't mean to sneak so, but I don't want my boy in there to see me with all them windows across the front. Don't want to embarrass him to have his mama out here having to sell dresses."

The two women looked at each other. Sarah had made them uncomfortable. Now she had lost any sale she may have had. Her hands shook.

The older one cleared her throat and bent towards the dresses like a person would bend towards a child. The younger one picked up the top dress, a rayon butcher linen in a pretty shade of green and held it by its shoulders. The older teacher did the same with the light-gray linen. The fabrics were so thin, Sarah could almost see through them. "I'm sorry," she told them, "but they're more for summer wear, as y'all can see."

She hoped they wouldn't put them back. The four that weren't picked up yet were made of either gingham or seersucker, summer fabrics as well. "As soon as I sell these, I'll have money to buy some nice fall and winter gabardines and that very ladylike fine corduroy and maybe worsted wool."

The older picked up the light blue and white gingham and the younger, the pink and white seersucker. The women passed the dresses back and forth.

"You are an exceptional seamstress, Mrs. Creamer," the older one said. "How much are you asking?"

Sarah swallowed. She needed more than the flat $3 a dress she had been charging. For her boy's sake, she closed her eyes and pushed out, "Would $4 a dress be too much to ask for?"

"That's all?" the younger one said. "For this fine work?"

They opened their pocketbooks and put in Sarah's hands several bills and coins. They took all six dresses.

"I can't thank y'all enough, I can't," Sarah told them and closed her gloved hand around the money. She now wished her skin was naked so she could feel.

$$\cdot \; \cdot \; \cdot \; \cdot \; \cdot$$

LC bolted from the schoolhouse. He wished he could run somewhere far away, but his father would hunt him down and hurt him.

An old timey automobile was parked out front with a woman standing beside an open door on the passenger's side. This was the Creamer boy's mother. She had come to his house twice, and both times, she was nice. His father had her old automobile parked behind his barn. She must have bought a new one and come to pick Emerson Bridge up. LC's own mother was not there. She had come to pick him up the year before, but his daddy had stopped it this year, saying that LC needed to grow up and get home on his own.

LC got in behind the bushes beside the front stoop and hid. He thought that Emerson Bridge would run to her, and she would hug him. Right out in the middle of the world, hug him.

There came Emerson Bridge out the door. LC jumped up and shoved him off the other side and took off running. When he passed the boy's mother, he yelled, "That automobile's dumb. And ugly, too."

He could have yelled to the boy, *I appreciate you not laughing at me in there,* but he did not.

$$\cdot \; \cdot \; \cdot \; \cdot \; \cdot$$

That Saturday morning, Sarah rose early to make Emerson Bridge a surprise. This was a day of celebrating. The county agent was coming by to look at Lucky for the first time. Sarah was making her boy biscuits. She'd stopped at Drake's Store the afternoon before and spent $1.32 of the $24 her dresses had brought. In her dough bowl, she put two cups of flour and a good fork's worth of lard. Then, she trickled buttermilk from a quart bottle on top of the mixture, while her fingers began working it, bringing it all together, making what was separate, one.

There were two more reasons the day was special. It was Harold's birthday and the day Emerson Bridge was conceived. Sarah had made biscuits that morning, too. Harold going out the door to work, driving his automobile over to Mattie's and picking her up so they could ride to the telephone office together, while Sarah stayed behind, her kitchen rich with the smell of bacon, eggs, grits, and biscuits. Like the smells in her kitchen that Saturday morning. She'd also bought eggs and grits and bacon, two strips, cut extra thick, Mr. Drake's dial showing they weighed close to a sixth of a pound, a whole dime's worth.

Sarah covered her hands in flour and sprinkled a layer on a wooden board, then gathered the ball of dough she'd made and placed it in the middle. She had a rolling pin but preferred her hands, at first using her palms to press the dough to a half inch thick. Then she turned a drinking glass upside down in the flour, coating the rim, and brought the glass to the dough, where she cut out circles, ten of them. And then came what she'd waited for. With her hands hovering above the ten, her fingers spread wide and ready, Sarah, one by one, pressed her fingertips into the dough, making little dimples. She'd made them that September morning in 1943, too, but they'd been Mattie's that day.

When she served Emerson Bridge his breakfast that morning, she watched him bite into one. "You happy, hon?" she asked.

He giggled and nodded his head, biscuit crumbs falling from his mouth down his chin. She watched him take his fingers and scoot them back into his mouth. "I'm going to give half of my food to Lucky, Mama," he said and moved his fork down the middle of his plate, making two sides. She liked that he wanted to share.

Before he went outside, she combed tonic from Harold's bottle on his hair. She combed it like Harold used to, parted on the left side.

"I know about the money we need, Mama," he said.

"Oh, hon, no, no." She tried to keep her voice calm. "We're fine."

She ran the comb through his hair again. "Don't you worry none about that. That ain't for you."

"I ain't worried. Me and Lucky's going to win, and we'll be rich." He ran out the door.

He had a scrape on his elbow from falling when the Dobbins boy the day before must have wanted to play and got a little rough and knocked Emerson Bridge off the stoop. She had wanted to apply a second dose of mercurochrome on the wound. She would do that later.

Mr. Thrasher would be there soon. He came every Saturday and Sunday to see the steer, but Sarah suspected it was also to see Emerson Bridge, who called him Mr. Ike now. They enjoyed each other's company, which she understood. Her boy needed a man around, and Mr. Thrasher might need a boy.

She went outside and stood at the fence and watched Emerson Bridge inside with Lucky. Mama Red stood a few yards away, eating grass. A hard rain had come overnight and left a big mud puddle near the middle of the lot. Lucky was playing in it with his head, splashing water. Any time it rained, Lucky played like that.

"Watch, Mama!" Emerson Bridge called out and held part of the biscuit in front of Lucky's mouth. But the steer continued to play.

Sarah loved seeing him enjoy something so much. She tried to think of a time when her own mother may have felt that way. Sarah had loved to look out her bedroom window at the colored glass in the windows across the street at her mother's church. "I see you looking out your window, girl, every time I walk over there," her mother told her one night after returning from a service. Sarah was in bed and braced herself for a whipping. But all her mother said was "They's a big picture of Jesus hanging behind the preacher's head and he's got him on a pretty white robe and what looks like an angel's halo around his head. You heard of angels, girl?" Sarah nodded. Her papa had told her they're something that she couldn't see, but they were around her and looked out for. She and her mother were in darkness, and Sarah couldn't see her mother's eyes, but she imagined they were sparkling. "And that pretty colored glass all around out where the crowd sits, they's three windows right beside each other, and right in the middle of all three, they got flower petals. Four of them. Two straight up and one on the right and one on the left. It looks like a cross, the kind Jesus died on for our sins. For our real bad ways. He wiped them all out. All the bad we do. Every bit of it," her mother said. "Every blame bit of it."

Emerson Bridge now was laughing so hard, it rang out like a church bell. His steer now was licking his face, doing so in long swipes. "It's rough, Mama, and it tickles." He threw his head back like he was happy, like there was nothing more in the whole wide world he wanted.

"Look at you with your giggle box turned over," Sarah told him, and he laughed harder and louder. She looked Mama Red's way and began to laugh, too. She let herself inside the gate, went to her boy and with her fingers, tickled his belly like she had seen a mother do in the Piece Goods department at Gallant-Belks. Sarah did this without thinking and started to stop when she caught herself with such display, but he bent forward towards her touch, closing in over her like he wanted her to stay.

· · · · ·

Mr. Thrasher had just pulled up near Sarah and her boy when the county agent drove in.

"I can't wait to show you Lucky, Mr. Merritt," he called out and started jumping up and down as the two men approached the fence.

Mr. Merritt had a nice smile on his face that reminded her of Harold, way back. No wonder Emerson Bridge had talked so highly of him.

But the smile left. "What's that mama cow doing in there with your steer? And *nursing* her?"

"He missed her so much, she come for him," her boy said and opened the gate for them all to go in. "Four miles."

"That's right, four of them," Sarah told him and followed them all inside.

Mr. Merritt lifted his cap, then set it back down. He was shaking his head. "No sir, son, we can't have this. That steer's got to be separated, weaned off his mama. That's the first order of business."

Sarah rushed towards him. "No sir, we can't do that. That was tried once, and both of them pitched a fit." The thought of taking Mama Red away from her calf again made her dizzy.

Mr. Thrasher made a show of clearing his throat. "I told them way back we didn't need no sissy boy still with his mama."

They were all standing near Mama Red and Lucky, who continued to nurse as Mama Red chewed grass. "Separating is the natural course, folks," the county agent was saying. He now had an edge to his voice. "A project steer still can't be nursing."

"But will he have enough to eat?" Sarah asked. She couldn't see that there was enough grass out there to fill them up.

"It's the natural course."

"Natural," Mr. Thrasher said and spit on the ground.

Sarah had never seen him do that.

"Y'all can do what's known as 'fence weaning.' It's not as severe. Just run a fence between them."

Sarah thought about the money it would cost to do so.

"Your steer needs to be on small grains, son, three to four gallons a day, and all the dry feed it wants, plus some kind of meal like I said yesterday. You can get all that at the FCX near town. He's got to feed out to around a thousand pounds by the time the show rolls around, and that's just six short months away."

Sarah was only getting about six hours of sleep a night. She'd go to five and make more dresses to sell.

"All right, sir," Emerson Bridge said, "but I wanted to tell you that Lucky don't like biscuits. But I'll see if he'll eat a bite of whatever Mama makes for supper."

"Excuse me?" Mr. Merritt said.

"You said feed him some kind of meal."

"I'm talking about *linseed* meal or *cottonseed* meal." Mr. Merritt took a deep breath. "Where's your pasture, son?"

"You mean where they eat?" the boy said.

"I mean *pasture*. Where Kentucky 31 fescue is planted or some other kind of grass, along with some clover like ladino."

Emerson Bridge was looking at Mr. Thrasher with eyes that Sarah recognized. They were asking for help. He used to look at his papa that way.

Mr. Thrasher hunched up his shoulders.

Emerson Bridge told the man, "All they've got is this grass. Don't know the name of it."

Mr. Merritt squatted down in front of him. Harold used to do that. "Son, listen, I don't know where you got this steer, but I'm afraid this might be too much for you." His voice had softened. "What you have is not a pasture. I've got to tell you most of the boys have a year-around pasture, a permanent pasture. It would take you a good year, if not two, to get you a good stand."

"Why, we got him from the biggest cattleman there is, Mr. Luther Dobbins," Mr. Thrasher said.

The county agent jerked his head Mr. Thrasher's way. Emerson Bridge put his hands on Mr. Merritt's face and turned it back towards him. Sarah thought he was going to throw his arms around the man's neck, but her boy kept his arms down and told the man, "Lucky's special, sir. You just wait and see."

Mr. Merritt touched the top of Emerson Bridge's shoulders, then rose to his feet and tapped the top of his head.

"We'll sure get us one of those pastures for our grand champeen," Mr. Thrasher called out. He'd already left the lot and was standing by his truck, which carried bodies now. He wanted the county agent to see them.

Mr. Merritt told them, "Mama cows don't know how to tell their younguns to stop. They're not like birds that just stop feeding their young, so they'll leave the nest." And then he took a bucket of grain from the bed of his truck and kept holding it in front of Lucky, Mama Red trying to get in between them, until the steer followed him out of the gate and back to the tree, where it had been tied before.

Mama Red stood at the gate. Sarah wondered if she would try to break out. She had noticed the mother cow's ribs showing, but she had been thinking, with the hot summer they'd had, the mother cow didn't feel like eating so much. She lined up in her head all that they were doing wrong and brought her arm around her boy's shoulder and pulled him to her.

. . . . .

Luther Dobbins yawned and covered his mouth, making sure his back was to his boy, who was about to swing open the big wooden gate on the barn to let his project steer into the lot. Luther had had little sleep the night before. Paul Merritt was due out any time now to see LC's steer for the first time, give the animal an assessment, which meant assessing Luther. He'd lain in

91

bed practicing his words. "The big one there," he would say and point to the steer, "your next grand champion, don't you think? An easy feeder, for sure. Look at that back. Water already runs off it. It's as straight as they come."

Luther turned towards his boy and the lot and saw two steers head for the water trough. The bigger one, the better one, was his son's. Luther had the other there to provide competition, to make his boy's steer eat more. He pulled a cigar from his overall's front pocket and tried to keep his hand from shaking so he could light it. He saw his boy coming towards him. He turned his back again.

"I'm going to cream everybody this year, Dad," LC told him, Luther cigar's catching fire. "You just wait. It won't even be a contest." This was the first time LC had called him what Charles had always called him, Dad.

It being a Saturday, Uncle had the hammer mill in full operation, the tractor that powered it sputtering and shooting black smoke through its stack."We're not like the others," Luther told LC. "No other boy has their very own grinder." He pulled a long draw from his cigar and sent it into the air above his son's head. He wanted LC to see him send the smoke at least as high as the tractor's, even beat it.

LC's hair was cut close, because Luther preferred it that way, since Luther was mostly bald, with only a semicircle that ringed his head like someone had thrown a horseshoe. He always wore a hat to keep it hidden. LC's hair was sandy blond, the color of Luther's when he was that age, but over his thirty-seven years, Luther's had turned a shade of brown that carried hints of both light and dark.

For the first time, he could see what Charles had always claimed, that LC looked more like Luther than Charles did. LC had Luther's nose, its narrowness that ran to a sharp point and flanked by a squatty roundedness on each side. Charles had Mildred's, that simple kind, as if God had made theirs in his sleep. Luther thought of his boy's name, Luther Charles Dobbins the third. Mildred had tried to dissuade him from having a second namesake, saying it wasn't proper, what with Charles already being Luther Charles Dobbins, Jr. But Luther wouldn't hear of it.

LC picked up a rock and threw it hard against the side of the hammer mill. It bounced back about halfway. LC looked at Luther. "You like that, Dad?"

Luther did not like it. The rock had likely put in a dent in his machine. But LC began to laugh, and Luther had not heard laughter like that since before the deer. He thought of the ladybugs. He'd not yet shown them to LC. "Come on, let's go see something," he said and started for the pine trees, his arms motioning wildly for LC to follow, Luther feeling like a boy himself.

But LC did not follow. "You really mean it?" LC called out, his voice climbing higher with each word.

Luther stopped. LC did not believe him. If Luther was Luther's boy, he wouldn't believe him, either.

A truck pulled around back of the house. It was Paul Merritt.

Luther dropped his arms and bit his teeth around the cigar, before taking it from his mouth. "About time you showed up," he told the man and nodded towards the lot. He would wait until Merritt got out of his truck before saying the rest.

But Merritt stayed in his truck.

Luther walked over to him and slapped his hand against his door.

Merritt jumped. "Sorry, Luther. Thinking about those people I just left. They're earnest people. And he's a little shaver of a boy."

"What people?"

"The Creamers."

"That Roy Rogers wannabee?"

"Don't say that, Luther."

"Why? That's what he is. And that's just being polite. If I weren't such a good Christian man, I'd call him worse than that."

Luther dropped his cigar, ground it into the dirt with his boot, and motioned LC over. He could feel the bottoms of his feet sweating. "The big one there," he said and pointed towards the lot. "Your next grand champion, don't you think? An easy feeder, for sure. Look at that back. Water already runs off it. It's as straight as they come."

The county agent, though, was not looking. He was shaking his head. Luther shoved the flat palm of his hand against the man's shoulder. "Hey, what's the matter with you? You better remember where your bread is buttered." Luther had helped get Merritt his job.

"Think I'm going to have to do something this year I dread. Think I'm going to give the boys a paper to sign, saying they know this is a terminal event, that they acknowledge the steer will be sold for slaughter once the show's over."

"Everybody knows that," Luther said.

"Yeah, everybody knows that," LC said.

He spoke up like that Creamer boy had back in the spring. Luther balled up his fist and tapped his boy near his shoulder. LC would thank him one day for toughening him up.

"The Prater boy didn't. After the sale last time, he asked me when he could buy his steer back, and when I told him he couldn't, he cried. And then there's the new Creamer boy this year."

"Jellies," Luther said.

"Hey, heard you sold the Creamer boy his steer," Merritt said.

"So what if I did? It was just a throwaway."

"Did you take a good look at him? He's thin now, but—"

"But what?" Luther said.

"But he might be an easy feeder, a real down-the-roader. Wide in the eyes and looks to have the base for finishing out top of the line."

Top of the line. Luther felt lightheaded. He wanted to ask, *What about my boy's?* He lit another cigar and took a long draw.

"They're in over their heads, though," Merritt said.

Luther wondered if he was, too. But he'd done better selecting his boy's steer this time. *Hadn't he?* LC would see that his father could be a winner. *Wouldn't he?* Luther blew a smoke ring and watched it fall apart.

"No pasture to speak of, no mineral lick, no hay, no grain, no kind of meal, only a little bucket to drink water out of, and to top it off, the steer's still nursing his mama. Had to separate them. And what's she doing over there, anyway?"

Luther began to chuckle. *What had he been worrying about?* And the mother was still alive.

"Let's just call it charity," he said and blew another ring.

"Didn't have the heart to tell them all I could, though."

There was more?

"The boy's already named him. *Lucky,* of all things."

Naming him. The death nail. Luther took his cigar out and began to laugh. When his boy joined in, Luther's laughter grew, becoming loud and hard. But it was not the laughter Luther had imagined with the ladybugs. They had wings and could fly. Luther had seen them do it. The sound of the ladybug laugh would be more light. More free. Him and his boy taking off and going up, up and away, soaring over God's earth.

The mother cow stood at the far left side of the fence, pressing against it and bellowing for her young, standing near a tree where she had found him after he was taken away. This was as close to him as she could get. He kept trying to return to her.

Tall shoots of Johnson grass in the midst of a few trailing vines of lespedeza clover surrounded their hooves. Flecks of pink and purple from the clover's flowers peppered her mouth and his. Mostly, she ate the clover, since it was soft, unlike the Johnson grass, which was hard to break off, since she had worn what remained of her bottom teeth down to almost nothing and had lost six of her eight altogether. She'd lost another tooth that day. Mostly, she brought gum to gum when trying to take food into her mouth.

94

The gentle wind stood beside the mother cow, while the gentle wind's little one remained with the mother cow's young. Earlier, the gentle wind and the little one had made sounds, light ones, that floated to the heavens. Now, they made none.

Behind her, unfamiliar men tore holes into the earth and placed in them parts of trees.

Inside the mother cow, a new baby was growing, three months old and the size of a newborn puppy. Just that day, it had crested the mother's pelvic rim and moved into her womb. A neighbor's bull had jumped a low place in the fence and mounted her while the stars sprinkled above.

Me and my boy, we got a fence running between us, too, Mama Red. You just can't see ours.

I didn't come by being a mama like you did. I bet yours was all quiet. I come by it loud, with a gunshot, Mattie's. That was my boy's mama. She took her own life the night he was born. I ain't proud of how I carried myself that night. Can I tell you that? You never would have done what I done, said what I said. It's eating me plumb up. See, I never did get saved by my mama's Jesus, so I'm going to spend eternity in what my mama called "the fires of hell." Reckon I could tell you about it? How I got over here. If I could just stand here with you, girl, and tell you.

A handsome man come knocking on my mama's door one afternoon in Gainesville, Georgia, where I grew up. I'd just come from a memorial service for my papa. A bad tornado blew him off somewhere. We never found him, like a lot of people they didn't find. So they just had a casket with a blue cloth over it for the men and a pink one for the ladies.

The man said he had a telegram for the family of a Mr. Claude Bolt. That was my papa. Condolences from President Roosevelt himself.

I offered him some sweet tea, and he said, "You know how to make sweet tea?"

I told him, "I sure do. Know how to cook, too."

Mama hollered in, "He can tell that by the way you look, girl. Either that, or I know how."

But all he did was smile and say, "That's awfully kind of you."

He said his name was Harold Creamer and was from over in South Carolina, a place called Anderson, and that he worked for the telephone company, and they'd asked for volunteers to come over to Georgia to help out. He told me, "You right handy around the house. I like women who are handy around the house."

I noticed his eyes on me, especially on my bosom.

He come back the next day about suppertime, wanted to know where a fellow could get good eats. Mama pulled me away from the door. "I know you ain't never been around no boys before, but don't go hog wild over the first one that crosses your pig path."

He left but wrote to me he was coming to see me Saturday night week, for me to be ready at six o'clock. I'd heard girls at school talk about wearing tight tops that showed off what boys liked to look at, so I put on a dress that was too little for me up there. We went to a café, and his eyes kept dropping to where he liked to look. He said he'd sure missed me, and I told him I'd sure missed him, too.

After we ate, he drove us somewhere and pulled off the road and reached over and kissed me right on my lips. I'd never been kissed before.

Before I knew it, he was touching where he liked to look. I thought about stopping him, but I didn't. It felt good to be touched, Mama Red. And I didn't stop him when he dropped his hand lower than that and not even when he did something to me boys wasn't supposed to do, not until you're married. It wasn't my first choice to have done what we did, but I told myself that Harold Creamer loved me.

He come back to see me that very next Saturday and next two after that, and we put it all on repeat.

But then I missed my monthly. And one night, when I was in bed, I felt a warmth come over me, and I knew I had a baby inside of me. I put my hand on my belly and felt a little spark growing off to my right side. It was like a tiny bubble, and it was trying to get my attention and say, Hey there, Mama.

When Harold come back that next Saturday night, I told him. He went to beating the steering wheel.

In a couple of weeks, he sent me a letter. Said he wasn't the kind of man to run out on me but he didn't love me. Said he'd be over to get me that next Saturday, would pick me up at four o'clock and for me to find us somebody to marry us. I filled up a pillowcase with my clothes, and just before four o'clock, told Mama, "I'm marrying Harold and moving over to South Carolina."

"Ain't no man would have you," she told me.

"One did, and that's all it takes," I said.

I was almost down the front steps when Mama called my name. She was at the door holding out a black hat and gloves. "A lady always wears a hat and gloves," she said.

I ran back to her and wanted to hug her for being so nice, so I leaned in, but she pulled back from me.

I put them both on. The hat had black netting with little squares that fell all around my face. I put my mama in one of them squares to try to catch her and keep her.

I started down the hill and couldn't be sure, but I was thinking I'd seen tears in Mama's eyes, and I got to tell you, Mama Red, that about made me turn around and go back and tell her You know what? I believe I just might stay.

But I kept on walking.

Harold pulled up. I got in. A stranger married us. We crossed the state line and come right to that house I'm still living in. He went to work, and I set up housekeeping. I found a photograph of him and a girl, a pretty, skinny girl, in the bottom of his chifforobe. Harold had a big smile on his face. On the back was the names Harry and Ellen. When he came home that day, I asked him who that girl was.

"Ellen," he said. "The girl I wanted to marry. Built this house for."

I asked him why the name Harry was on the back. "That's what she called me," he said. "And it was good that she backed out on me, because I'd have had to pay a colored woman to help her out. She's not handy like you."

OCTOBER 18–19, 1951

Sarah went to her room, to her chifforobe, and took from the baby-blue blanket a rock. It was one of several she had seen her boy play with. She'd been practicing with it. So far, she had managed to toss it as high as three inches and still catch it. But she would risk more this time. She tossed it twice as high, and with her hands cupped like a bowl, she caught it and giggled, so much that she fell onto her bed and kicked her feet like a school-girl. At that moment, Sarah was young again and watching other children on the playground tossing a ball at recess. She had no ball herself, but one day she thought of her mother's pin cushion and hurried home and took it from her mother's sewing table and tossed it hard, up high. It slammed into the ceiling at the same time her mother walked into the room. Her mother whipped her hard with her hand and told her, "If I ever catch you playing again and with *my* belongings, I'll get me a hickory and leave marks on you that you won't never forget."

That morning, Sarah stopped kicking and giggling. She got off of her bed and put the rock away.

· · · · ·

Sarah was on her way to the road to get the mail when she heard Mama Red call to her from the lot. "Why, hello there yourself," Sarah said and walked to the separating fence, where, down about ten feet, Mama Red and Lucky stood near each other, the wire running between them, Mama Red bent to the grass, while Lucky splashed water in the big wash tub he now drank from. That was another thing Mr. Merritt had advised they do, give each a bigger drinking container. "Look at you playing, making a mess."

Mr. Merritt had sent two men to run the fence the same day he'd sepa-rated Mama Red and Lucky. Both were Mr. Merritt's friends from church. They wouldn't take a dime from Sarah.

Mr. Thrasher's truck pulled up to Sarah's house. He came every day now to check on Lucky. He had retrieved the mail for her, one piece, from the Farmers Cooperative Exchange, the FCX, a bill for $22.55 and marked Past Due in red. Buying all that Mr. Merritt had advised had cost more than her dress money brought in. Mr. Thrasher had put their entire purchase on credit.

"I got eight dollars and a penny," she said.

· · · · ·

The FCX sat in a low place near town. Sarah was the only woman in this place of business. Two men stood behind a long, wooden counter. The young one glanced at her but went back to sorting papers, laid out on top. The other man, much older, stood behind the cash register, holding onto the sides with hairy hands as if he loved it. He never looked Sarah's way.

She carried the letter in her hand. "Excuse me, sir." The younger man raised his eyes. He wore black glasses like Harold, but the glass in this man's was thick, making his eyes look as big as fifty-cent pieces. "I come to see about paying some on my bill here." She set it on the counter and un-snapped her change purse and took out a silver dollar. A teacher at the school that week had paid her that way.

"Creamer," the man said and looked to be studying the bill. "Route 2. You're not the Creamer that Luther Dobbins sold that old mama cow to, are you?"

"I have a mama cow from Mr. Dobbins, yes sir. Mama Red."

He pressed his middle finger against the bridge of his glasses. His eyes looked even larger now. "She got funny markings on her face?"

Sarah didn't like how interested this man was. She squeezed the silver dollar in her hand. Telling a lie was not something she liked to do, but she felt she had to. She shook her head.

"Must be another Creamer, then. You'd know what I mean by funny markings."

Sarah felt her body flush, especially her head, where she imagined her jowls flashed shiny spots of red.

"That'll be $22.55, ma'am."

Sarah showed him the large coin that lay in the palm of her hand. "It's all I can part with at present." The silver stood out bold against the black cloth of her gloves.

He didn't reach for it. Instead, he appeared to look around the store, she assumed for the older man, who must be his father, who no longer stood at the counter.

Her change purse carried two more silver dollars and a folded five dollar bill for Mr. Scarboro. She needed a dollar for food. She'd begun buying cans of Vienna sausage for her boy for twenty-one cents each, along with saltines for twenty-eight cents for a good-sized box. On Sundays, she served a can of "star quality" Treet, which always set her back forty-seven cents. She could offer one more silver dollar. She set one on the counter.

But he did not pick that one up, either. He looked around the store again.

In his eyes, in their largeness, Sarah saw something small, like he'd been hurt before. She wondered if his father had done that. "What's your name, sir?" she asked.

"Allgood."

"That your given name?"

"No ma'am, it's Jeremiah."

"Jeremiah. Sounds old, like it comes from the Bible."

"It does."

"Mine don't," she told him. "It's Sarah."

"That's in the Bible, ma'am."

"My name? My name come from the Bible? My mama give me a Bible name?" Sarah was talking loud.

The man nodded.

She wrapped her arms around herself. "About that mama cow," she said and wished she could take those words back. His niceness had made them slip out.

He pushed on his glasses again. "She's part of my boyhood." Across his face came a grin. "One hot summer day in '34, I was a boy of eleven then, Pop brought me to town, to the train tracks over there." He pointed out the side of the store. "They were unloading cattle, skinny as a rail, a heap of them from the state of Oklahoma, where they'd had bad dust storms and no rain for months, so all the pastures had dried up. President Roosevelt paid the farmers out there a dollar a head and brought the cattle east in carloads. Five hundred and fifty came here to Anderson. Pop took thirty of them and got paid fifty cents a head per month to pasture them until just before Christmas when the government slaughtered them and then canned them for the poor people to eat."

The word "slaughter" cut through Sarah.

"That mama cow I was asking you about come off that train. She'd just been born before they left out there, but her mama didn't survive the train ride. Left her a bum heifer."

Sarah felt her stomach knot up. She didn't know what "bum heifer" meant, but she knew it wasn't good.

The young man removed his glasses. His eyes were no longer large. "I'll never forget her face. The white of it was the prettiest white I'd ever seen, whiter than Pop's cotton. I begged him to let me bring her home, promised to bottle feed her and raise her up."

Sarah pictured the mother cow's face. The white on it had a gray tint to it now. Her calf's face, though, still carried that pure white the young man had seen.

"But when it came time for them all to go to slaughter, the government spared her, said they'd give twenty-five of the cows to poor people. I begged Pop to tell them to please make one of them that calf. And they did. She wasn't but four months old."

The thought of almost missing Mama Red made Sarah tremble. She'd thought she didn't like his father much, but now she did.

"So y'all was poor, too?" Sarah said.

The young man shifted his body. "No ma'am, *we* weren't, but we had people, tenants, that were. Pop finagled somehow to give that calf to one of the families on our place."

"Then how did Mr. Dobbins get her?" Sarah asked.

The man did not answer. He put his glasses back on and rang up the cash register. A big "2.00" appeared at the top.

Sarah had been on the verge of telling him that the mother cow was at her place now, and she was living out her days in love. But all she said was "Thank you, kind sir."

She would go now and pick up her boy, and they would go home. All Sarah wanted to do was place her hand on the mother cow's face, let it rest in her hair, already thick for the long haul of winter.

The mother cow and her calf stayed close, their heads bent to the earth almost in concert. Occasionally, the calf tried to stick his head between the rows of barbed wire that separated them and grab onto a teat. Their bawling back and forth had continued for two days, but, by the third, their sounds had started to fade, and after one week, they had all but stopped.

Buttons, little buttons of red, an inch and a half apart, lined the inside of the mother cow's membrane sack, snapping it onto to her womb, where the baby now lay, the buttons holding the sack in place and allowing the mother's food to pass to her baby, now about a foot in length and weighing close to two pounds.

"By now, boys, you should be seeing a pretty good poundage gain on your steers—two, even three pounds a day." Mr. Merritt was talking as though LC did not know that. LC started to tell the county agent that they weren't babies, but, first, he'd look around to see if anybody else had a frown on their face like him.

He stopped on the Creamer boy, whose face carried not only a grin but a contentment, even though he sat by himself off to the side. Either he was shy, or he thought he was better than the rest of them. And he sat with his shoes off. The top part near the toes had an opening, like a knife had been taken to it, the shoes directly beneath his feet like he didn't trust that they'd stay safe. His feet hovered over them like a mother cow, the way they protect their young. The boy's socks were a dingy white and looked to be too big with extra cloth bunched up at the end. LC wondered if he wore them like that on his own or if his mother had wanted him to have that extra. He believed his mother wanted him to have extra. He'd seen the way they looked out for each other. *Yeah, that Creamer boy must think he's better than anybody else.*

"Boys, it's time now to step up your mixed grain feeding by another pound or two this month," the county agent said. "Do it gradual now. Too much too soon can make your steer sick."

"We already know all this," LC said, his words whistling through the open space in his teeth. He'd lost a tooth that morning but didn't tell anyone. The tooth fairy was for babies. He'd thrown the tooth in the trash can.

Mr. Merritt cleared his throat. "Not everyone does, LC."

LC looked at the Creamer boy and hollered out, "Hey, when are you going to give us that paper?"

But all the man did was talk fast and loud. "I'm especially pleased with the quality of the cattle this year, boys, and believe they'll all be well-finished for the show. All are shooting towards that down-the-road prime category, instead of a canner."

LC didn't believe for one minute that everyone's steer was looking good. He wondered why the agent didn't talk like a man and tell the truth. LC would ask the question again, but he would wait for the right time. Maybe when the Prater boy opened his crybaby mouth. Since he had messed up so bad the year before, he might try to offer some real competition this year. But probably it would be last year's winner, the Glenn boy, a twelfth-grader now, who would really turn it on and try to make it two years in a row. The others in the room mattered not. There was no fire in their eyes.

Except for the Creamer boy, who held his eyes wide like he wasn't afraid, like he was free to go stand in a field, since there was no one there holding a gun. But it was dangerous to hold your eyes that way. No, the Creamer boy was going nowhere. Besides, he'd named his steer. LC knew better than to do that this year. He'd heard Charles talk of boys that named their steers what they would soon become. "T-Bone is my steer's name," LC called out.

Snickers broke out around the room, all except from Emerson Bridge.

The county agent shot him a look and in a loud voice said, "Part of your job of finishing your steer, boys, is getting him to do everything you' ask him to do over the next few months. I'm talking about building trust."

LC had begun rolling his eyes, but when the man said "trust," LC stopped cold.

"We already have that," the Creamer boy said. "He lets me throw a rock up in the air right beside him."

LC felt a rush of heat rise through him.

Mr. Merritt cleared his throat. "Like I was saying, the first part of building that trust is with your steer's food, by feeding him in the same place and at the same time every morning and every night."

Before now, LC had been thinking that what had made him so sad about losing his steer in March was that he'd named him. But Mr. Merritt had just put his finger on the rest of it. LC had gotten his steer to trust him.

"So, boys, this next part is getting him to trust that you are going to take care of him. I'm talking about brushing him, touching him every day. You want him quiet in the ring, because I got to tell you a quiet disposition goes a long way with the judges. In fact, the ideal words from the judges are 'Quiet and broken to be led.'"

LC ran from the room and out into the hallway. He moved down a ways in case anyone came after him. But no one did. He no longer had any friends. The air smelled of sweaty children, know-it-all kids who liked to ball up their fists and hit something. Like himself. And even from days past, like his father, who had attended Centerville, but that is all he knew of his father's early days.

He thought he smelled his father now and balled up his fist, which he wanted to ram down his father's throat and make him choke like he had done at the Cattleman's Supper the day he'd made LC kill that deer. LC was glad he'd choked. He hit the wall. It was made of wooden boards running the way he was not, towards the front door, where there was light.

The door to the classroom behind him opened. The boys were coming his way. He crossed his arms over his stomach and bent forward like he was sick. A couple of boys laughed as they passed.

He waited until he heard no more footsteps and then freed his arms and started for the front door himself.

"Hey," he heard at his back. "You all right?"

It was that Creamer boy. LC turned towards him. He had his shoes on.

LC nodded and watched him pass. Then he called out at the boy's back, "Hey, my dad's got y'all's automobile at our house."

"I know," Emerson Bridge told him and kept walking.

"*And* my steer's going to beat your's tail." LC brought his fist up to slam the wall.

"No, he's not," the Creamer boy said and stepped out into the light.

LC ran after him and found him walking towards an automobile parked in front of the school. It was the same one from before, and the boy's mother stood beside an open passenger door. She wasn't nervous like his own, but appeared anchored like a rock that couldn't be moved. She saw him, he thought, and even smiled at him.

LC smiled back. He did it easily.

"Hey!" he called out and ran hard towards Emerson Bridge, who looked back at him. LC was glad. He was afraid the boy might not. LC wanted to tell him in a strong voice, *Don't name your steer,* but what came out of his mouth in a whisper was, "I named mine last year. I named him Shortcake."

"I like that name," Emerson Bridge said.

"I like it, too."

"We supposed to keep their names a secret? That why we're whispering?"

LC knew he should tell him to get rid of the name altogether, that calling him a name would make it hurt even more when he had to say good-bye. But LC couldn't do that. Not now. It felt like he was visiting someone he used to be, and that felt good. "Yeah, a secret," LC said.

"Mine's Lucky," Emerson Bridge told him. "I mean that's *his* name, Lucky."

The boys giggled.

Then something spilled forth from LC. He threw his arms around Mrs. Creamer, who hugged him back just as hard. She didn't smell like his mother's peppermints.

Then he took off running home. He ran among the late autumn colors, the oranges and yellows and reds of the leaves, and it occurred to him that, just before their death, they become their most bold.

· · · · ·

"It's dumbfounding, actually," Merritt told Luther as they stood outside Luther's lot where his boy's steer was eating a bale of hay.

Luther had had Uncle place the bale against the far fence, the best spot to show off the steer's growing body. "Yeah, dumbfounding," Luther said and admired the weight gain on the steer, which he figured was close to seventy pounds since Merritt had seen him the month before. Luther had been imagining that the county agent would say, "Now, there's the one to beat," but he would take "dumbfounding." And he had done it without Charles.

"Yeah," Merritt said, "I never thought it'd be possible with their inferior conditions to put meat on that steer's frame. But, God help them, they're doing it."

Luther wanted to hit him. Merritt was talking about that Creamer boy's steer.

"Like I've said, he's got the right frame for feeding out. Just a matter of getting it on him."

"They poor as mud," Luther said. "You know they can't afford to keep it up. And he's not even on full feed yet."

"Full feed is next month." Merritt now was walking towards his truck. "Better get on to the next boy."

"What you mean *get on?* You ain't gotten to mine yet." Luther looked for LC. "Hey, boy!" LC was supposed to stay out there with him after he'd helped Uncle run the hammer mill early that morning, but he was nowhere in sight.

Merritt opened his truck door. "There's nothing I can tell you that you don't know, Luther."

"Hey, boy! Get yourself out here. Mr. Merritt wants to brag on your steer!"

Merritt slammed his door shut and cranked up.

Luther held up his arm to signal for the man to wait, but he pulled away. But not Merritt's words. They stayed behind with Luther. *There's nothing I can tell you that you don't know.* Merritt thought Luther was smart. He wished his boy had been there to hear that.

"LC!" Luther hollered again. His boy had been minding him. This wasn't like him.

Luther picked up a stick and began whipping it in the air above him, moving it in a circle like buzzards when they find something dead.

LC came from behind the barn. He came in a slow walk.

"On the double!" Luther called out, but the boy kept the same pace. Luther went towards him, swirling the stick and slapped it against the boy's arm. "I called for you, and you didn't come. You know how that makes me look? Like I'm a nobody. Is that what you think I am?" Luther hit LC again.

"No, sir," his boy said.

Luther noticed LC's shirt was wet. "What you doing back there?"

"Washing that automobile."

"That Creamer woman's?" Luther shoved the boy's shoulder.

"It was dirty."

Luther brought his hand up to the boy's face. "You touch that thing again or don't come when I call you, and I'll knock you to kingdom come. I'd do it now, but you got a show to win in five short months, and I don't need you to be recovering from nothing."

His boy's lip was quivering. That made him even more mad. He balled his fist up.

But then it came to him that this was good. Luther had broken him. Now he could begin to work with him. "You ain't started trying to put a halter on it yet, have you?"

"Mr. Merritt hasn't—" the boy tried to say.

"Mr. Merritt nothing. I'm the one that knows how to build a champion. He said so himself just then. You missed it by not being here. Now go start getting a halter on him, for God's sake."

LC ran towards the barn. Luther walked to the automobile. The top and back half carried a high shine. He gave the back panel a good kick. If he had a hammer and nails, he'd slam them in and imagine they were slamming into that steer. It needed to die.

. . . . .

"I've come back to ask you to hire me on as your hired hand on the mighty Dobbins cattle ranch." It was Mr. Thrasher. He'd come to see Luther the day before, and Luther had run him off.

But this day Luther wouldn't do that. He didn't need a hired hand, but he sure could use a hired mouth. Luther had just come from cranking the woman's automobile, letting all the gasoline run out. A brilliant move, he was thinking. The sound of the engine would drown out Luther's words and keep his boy, who was standing thirty feet away with his steer, from hearing.

"This is your lucky day," Luther told Thrasher.

The man jumped into the air.

"But you got to keep it quiet," Luther leaned in and whispered. "There's another fellow who's been wanting the job. Not nearly as strong as you. Don't want to disappoint him, if word gets out."

"No, sir. I wouldn't want that, either. When do I start? Today?"

"No." Luther's voice was loud now. Merritt made his visits on Saturdays, so the next work day after that would be Monday. He started to say only the Monday after Merritt's monthly visits, but that would be too obvious. "Just need you on Mondays. Report at 8 A.M."

"Yes, sir. Mondays. Got it, Mr. Boss Man."

"Don't mean to rush off," Luther said and made a couple of steps but made sure his words were not rushed. "I need to go pick up my boy's mixed grain feed at the FCX." Luther was certain Thrasher didn't have enough sense to know that Luther ground his own feed and had no need to buy it. "Got to hurry before they close at noon and get a heap of bags of it. Time for *full feed,* you know. But I'm sure you're already on top of that, being the cattleman that you are." Luther studied him hard for any sign that he'd heard the words Luther had planted on purpose.

Thrasher adjusted his hat. "Yeah, I'm on top of it, all right."

"On top of what?" Luther quizzed him.

"On top of the feed."

"What kind of feed?"

"Full feed."

Luther realized he might be smiling too much. He made himself pull back a bit.

The man leaned in and said, "You really think I'm a cattleman?"

"Think it? I know it."

What little chest the man had swelled out, and he began working his mouth such that a big spot of white bubbles landed beside Luther's boot.

Luther could do better than that. He gathered as much saliva as his mouth could hold and sent it forward in a straight shot like a bullet. It overshot the man's.

If only his boy had been there to see it.

. . . . .

Ike Thrasher stopped by the FCX and looked for his boss man's truck but did not see it.

"Hello there, Mr. Allgood," Ike said to the young man behind the counter. "I need the back of my cattleman's truck out there filled with as many bags as you can of y'all's mixed grain."

"This is for the Creamer account, Route 2, right?" the man asked.

"One and the same," Ike told him and used his deepest voice.

"That account is closed. Pop says it's got to be paid down before I can put any more purchases on it. Y'all still owe $20.50."

Ike had gone by the bank the afternoon before and withdrawn a twenty dollar bill to buy the boy his own Rider shirt and jeans, which he had surprised the boy with earlier that morning. The two of them were going to the State Theatre to see Roy Rogers's new movie, *South of Caliente.* This would be their first cowboy picture together and the first meeting of the Roy Rogers Riders Club. The outfit had cost most of five dollars. Ike would need a dollar for the picture show and refreshments, which left him with $14.02. Mr. Dobbins had not discussed his pay, but Ike was sure it would be quite hefty, given his new boss man's stature in Anderson County, the beef capital of South Carolina. Ike took his billfold from his back jeans pocket and took the ten and four ones and from his front pocket, the two pennies and put the money on the counter. "This is all I have."

The man adjusted his glasses and spoke in a soft voice, "Forgive me here, but in full swing, it's going to cost y'all upwards of $70 a month to feed your steer, what with the mixed grain, linseed meal for sheen, and bales of hay."

"Don't you worry none, I'm Lu—," Ike started, but he told himself a promise is a promise. "I'm lucky. Real lucky and you'll have your money."

Mr. Allgood looked around like he was trying to spot something, then took a fifty-cent piece from his pants pocket and his own billfold from his back pocket and laid the coin, a five and a one alongside Ike's money.

Ike could feel little shakes breaking out all over his body and wondered if this is how his parishioners had felt when they talked of the Holy Spirit visiting them, an experience Ike had never known. He had always told them, "That's our Lord saying 'I'm right there with you.'" Ike told himself those words now. The acts of kindness that day came before him, getting hired on with Mr. Dobbins and Mr. Dobbins giving him the knowledge about full feed and now Mr. Allgood's assistance. "I want to thank you, kind sir," Ike told the man and tipped his hat towards him.

Mr. Allgood told Ike to pull around back for the feed and then added, "How's that mama cow doing?"

Ike wondered how he knew. Maybe the Creamer ranch was becoming the talk. "Doing good," he said. "Real good."

Before Ike turned into the Creamer driveway that morning, he stopped in the road just out from his father's place and stretched across the seat and hollered, "Almost, Daddy. Almost. I'm a hired man now on a real cattle ranch." And then he imagined the steering wheel as reins and turned up the drive and found Emerson Bridge ready in his Roy Rogers outfit by the side porch.

"Howdy, partner!" Ike told him when the boy climbed into the truck.

"Look, Mr. Ike." The boy held up both hands."Got my Roy Rogers Riders Club pin and card in the mail with that dime you gave me." He sported a smile as big as the western sky.

"Swell! You're a real cowboy now."

"And I've already memorized the Roy Rogers Riders Rules. But I got a favorite." He closed his eyes like he was concentrating hard. "Be kind to animals and care for them," he said, giving each word its own space. Ike thought the boy could be a preacher one day, if he wanted to.

Ike's belly flipped just thinking about the surprise that was waiting for Emerson Bridge. When a new boy joined the Roy Rogers Riders Club, the owner, Mr. Sanders, called the boy up on the stage and put the pin on the boy's shirt. Ike was itching to tell him, but he made himself wait.

Instead, he motioned with his head towards the back of the truck. "Hey, look at the grub we got for our herd."

The boy followed his lead. Ike leaned over and whispered, "I've got some secret inside knowledge that we need to go ahead and get our Mr. Lucky started on what's known as *full feed.*"

The boy smiled and brought his hands up to his mouth like he couldn't believe it. Ike wanted to keep going and tell him the rest of his good news. He even felt his lips quivering like they were Trigger, ready to get going. But he pulled back on his reins and stayed quiet and spun the truck around in the yard and shouted, "Come on, Trigger! Take us away!"

Emerson Bridge giggled, and he giggled loud. This pleased Ike more than he ever imagined. What a day this was. He wished he could turn a big mason jar upside down on it and capture it like he used to capture butterflies when he was a boy, pretty ones with brilliant colors of blue, especially.

. . . . .

As soon as Emerson Bridge left with Mr. Thrasher, Sarah drove to see Mrs. Dobbins. For almost twenty-four hours now, all Sarah could think about was her name. She needed to finish the dress she was making, but she also needed to know who Sarah was in the Bible, and the only person she knew to ask was Mrs. Dobbins.

Sarah parked and hurried to the front door and knocked.

When Mrs. Dobbins answered, Sarah told her, "I don't mean to barge in, but I know you to be a good Christian woman, and I was wondering if you know who that woman Sarah was in the Bible? Her heart, I mean, what kind of heart she had." Sarah had left her manners at home. She'd not even said hello. "And I meant to say, Hello, Mrs. Dobbins."

"Why, hello back, Mrs. Creamer. Please come in."

They sat on Mrs. Dobbins's couch, surrounded by the smell of something fried and corn and biscuits. Mrs. Dobbins had skipped a buttonhole at the top of her dress, making some of the material billow like a sheet on the clothesline when the wind gets up.

"Why, dear, I'd say Sarah had a generous heart."

Sarah fixed on the woman's words like an iron to a garment.

"Because she put up with a lot." Mrs. Dobbins took her Retonga from her apron and held it in plain sight. "The first thing Sarah had to put up with was being called her husband's sister. Sarah was so beautiful that her husband, Abraham, feared he'd be killed because all the men would want her." Mrs. Dobbins took a big swallow.

Sarah knew she couldn't claim beauty. In fact, most people would say she was ugly. Her mother didn't give her that name on purpose. She knew this now. She'd wasted Mrs. Dobbins's time. Sarah moved to stand, but Mrs. Dobbins pulled her back. "But the biggest thing was Sarah was barren and Abraham wanted a baby, so she offered up her girl servant to her own husband for the girl to conceive and give her husband a child."

Sarah leaned back on the couch.

"But then Sarah regretted doing that and became angry at the girl and banished her from the house. Then God told Sarah *she* would conceive, but she didn't believe it, because she was ninety years old and her husband was one hundred." Mrs. Dobbins turned her bottle up to her mouth.

"So Sarah had a child?" Sarah brought her body forward.

"A son, Isaac."

Sarah felt a warm flush move all through. She had heard of people wanting something so much, they called it into being. She wondered if she had called Emerson Bridge into being.

Mrs. Dobbins was tapping Sarah's arm now and holding out the bottle.

But Sarah did not take it. All she wanted to do was thank her mother. Sarah had sent her a letter soon after Emerson Bridge was born, but it went unanswered. She had never tried to telephone her and didn't know if her mother even had one. "I know it's long distance and that costs good money, but is there any way I could ask you if I can try to call my mama?"

Mrs. Dobbins rose immediately and went to the hallway, to the telephone. Sarah gave her mother's name and address, and the operator got Sarah's mother on the telephone. This was a miracle. Sarah held onto the receiver with both hands.

"Hello, hello," she could hear her mother in there saying.

"Mama, it's your girl, Sarah."

"Ain't got no girl," her mother said. "She up and left me."

"You do, Mama, *me*. You know I got married."

"I know she up and left me, almost fifteen years ago to the day."

"I sent you a letter, Mama. In June of 19 and 44."

"Then you sent it to a wrong address."

"It never came back to me, Mama."

Mrs. Dobbins stood beside Sarah and held onto the spindles in the staircase.

Sarah backed up to the wall and took a deep breath. "I was calling to thank you for giving me a Bible name."

"Bible name? I didn't pull from no Bible."

110

"Sarah, Mama. Sarah's from the Bible. Abraham's wife. Had a boy named Isaac. You know Sarah." She wished she was in private. She put her back to Mrs. Dobbins.

"What about them other names, then? That Clementine Florence Augusta I give you. You seen them in there?"

Sarah swallowed. "No, ma'am."

"I just pulled them out of the air. Sarah don't mean nothing. None of them do."

Sarah let her arm holding the receiver fall down her body. She let go of it. It hit the floor. Her mother was still talking, her voice faint, even scratchy like a radio station whose signal was fading.

Mrs. Dobbins picked up the receiver and slammed it back into the holder and opened her arms.

Sarah laid her head on the woman's shoulder.

Mrs. Dobbins did not take her arms away.

Mrs. Dobbins told her, "My name's Mildred."

"Mine's Sarah, but you already know that."

"I do, and it's from the Bible."

My mama named me four girls' names. She named me Clementine Florence Augusta Sarah. She said she did it, because she wanted to get rid of all the girls' names that popped in her head. She didn't want no girls, Mama Red. She wanted boys. Only boys. After my mama had me, she didn't have no more babies. Said she was afraid she might have her another slittail. That's what she called girls, slittails. I sure hate to say that word around you, girl. In y'all's world, girls are thought a whole lot of, because they can grow up to be mamas, and that's a good thing. Maybe the closest to my mama's Jesus anybody could ever be.

The first time she called me that was about a month before I was to start to the first grade. It was the Sunday after that mama dog come and got took off. I was upstairs in my room, looking out my window towards my mama's big church across the road. I was trying to spot me some children about my age, some I might be going to school with, maybe even one or two I might could make friends with. I didn't have no friends.

I was waiting on my mama to call me to breakfast, but she never did that morning, so I went on down there myself. Mama and Papa were sitting at the eating table, her on one end and Papa on the other. I always sat in the middle, but that Sunday, there wasn't no place set for me.

"Where's my plate, Mama?" I asked.

"You don't need you nothing to eat. You too fat, girl," she said. "They going to laugh at you at school as it is." She cut her off a big piece of sausage and dipped it in some redeye gravy and put it in her mouth.

"But, Mama, I'm hungry," I told her.

She slapped me across my mouth. "Take that if you want something in them big chops of yours. You ain't nothing but one big pone, look at you. And a slittail, at that."

Papa lifted up off his chair and said, "Now, Teeniebelle."

"Now nothing," she went. "I spared her the pain all these years of folks making fun of her at the church, but I can't spare her the pain at school. She's got to go there. It's the law."

My papa sat back down.

I said, "Mama, I was hoping you'd let me go to church with you this morning. Let me meet some of the boys and girls I'm going to be in school with."

She held up two fingers and told me, "You twice they size. And church people don't want to see nobody waddling down the aisle, it's embarrassing. And you'd take up too much room on them pews, too." She sopped her up some gravy with one side of a biscuit and took her a big bite.

I went on back to my room and stood by my window and waited for the church bell to ring. The church was almost straight across from our house and set up high off some steps that led up to it. Me and Papa'd go over there sometimes when Mama would be at work at the sewing plant, and he'd be off from the mill. We'd go and step them and count them. There was twenty of them, Mama's twenty steps to Jesus is what I called them.

That Sunday morning, the church bell started ringing. Mama soon came into view. Her hair was all done up in a bun that pressed close to the back of her head and was pinned for good keeping. It looked like a sawed off peacock tail, if you looked at Mama straight on. That's what me and Papa always would say. But nobody over at the church could see her hair. She always wore a hat.

I watched the boys and girls gathering over there, and I saw that none of them was fat, they was all skinny. I started trying to hold in my belly. I found if I took a deep breath, it wouldn't stick out so much.

Papa called me to come to the kitchen. He had me a plate of sausage and eggs setting where my place was. I wanted to eat, but I'd seen them skinny children, and I said, "I'm fat."

He told me, "No, you ain't. Them other children's poor. Now eat. Enjoy yourself, hon."

I hugged his neck and kissed his face. His whiskers were rough. I liked that. It meant he wasn't going to work that day, and he'd be home with me.

When Mama came back across the road, me and Papa was sitting in the front room waiting for her to tell us about Jesus in her heart and for her to take her hat off, so we could see her hair and try not to bust wide open.

There she went. She told us, "Got the love of Jesus in my heart, people," and me and Papa held hands and squeezed hard. Then she took off her hat, and there was her sawed off peacock tail. Me and Papa had to squeeze harder.

I was expecting her not to set a place for me to eat, but Mama did. She set me a place for dinner and then again for supper, heaping helpings.

The mother cow's calf no longer sneaked his head between the wires to drink from her. Nor did he place his head near hers to eat from the earth. He made sounds that made her keep her head high and not leave the barbed wires between them.

As soon as school was dismissed that Friday, LC ran to the back of the schoolhouse. Overgrown shrubs, much taller than he, lined the back wall and gave teachers switches to use on disobedient children like himself. He reached inside the second shrub and retrieved a paper sack he'd hidden when he'd first arrived at school that morning. It held a gift for Emerson Bridge.

"Hey, what you got in there? A snake?" the Glenn boy asked when LC started down the row in the classroom. The monthly 4-H meeting was about to begin.

But LC gave the boy no response and walked past him, LC's eyes cast for Emerson Bridge. LC had a seat near him and slid the sack under his desk.

"Boys, this is a big day," the county agent said. "With two months of controlled feeding under your belt, it's time now to get your steer on full feed and give him all the mixed grain and dry hay he can eat. It's called 'Full Choice' from here on out."

The Prater boy raised his fist in the air and hollered, "Yeah!"

"Had a teacher up at Clemson tell us 'The eye of the master feeds his flock.' He was talking about finding the right amount of food to give your steer without being wasteful, because it can run into big money when you're having to buy it."

Emerson Bridge sat with his feet out of his shoes and his hands folded on his desk. Where his shirt buttoned up the front, small holes puckered like tiny mouths held open to eat.

"It's going to be a big change, because I'm talking about easing him into a full fifteen to eighteen pounds of grain a day, boys, instead of the mere three or four you've been giving him."

LC didn't know how Emerson Bridge would be able to afford all that feed. But it wasn't only the money that worried LC. He worried about the boy's heart. LC knew him to have a tender one. He wondered if there was a minimum weight requirement for the show and, if there was, maybe Emerson Bridge's would turn out to be too little. Maybe the animal's name would turn out to be true. But that would never be the case for LC's own steer, thanks to his father's hammer mill grinding a never-ending supply of corn. Tears started to well up, but that could not be. He took a deep breath and hollered, "It takes a real knack for knowing how much. A real knack."

"Yeah, and don't you wish you had it, *Little* LC, like your big brother Charles did?" It was the Prater boy.

"Now, boys," the county agent said.

But laughter filled the room, every little space around LC. The only one not laughing was Emerson Bridge.

"At least I didn't think I could buy him back," LC said and watched the Prater boy's mouth close. LC opened his to send out his own laughter, but he saw the boy's eyes, how small they had become. They could have been his own that early morning in March when he stood behind his father in the barn and watched him twist Shortcake's tail, forcing the animal up the cattle chute and into the back of the waiting truck. LC had wanted to shout *Stop!* But he did not.

Emerson Bridge's eyes were still wide and still unafraid. LC wondered how much longer they could stay that way.

"Besides getting your steer on full feed," Mr. Merritt was saying, "it's time to build on that trust I hope you've all established by getting him used to your touch. Everybody doing that?"

"Made mine so gentle, I can ride him!" the Glenn boy called out.

"Mine's my friend," Emerson Bridge said.

The boys all looked Emerson Bridge's way. A few nodded their heads but a couple smirked and moved their arms as if dismissing him. But not the Prater boy. He stayed looking at Emerson Bridge and said, "Yeah, until he ends up in somebody's deep freeze."

"Yeah, there's a deep *freeze* called for tonight, sure is," LC said as loud as he could. He was standing now and keeping his eyes on Emerson Bridge, who had a smile on his face as if he thought the exchange was funny.

"Let's get serious, boys." The county agent put his two fists beside each other like he was holding onto something. "It's time now to begin the next part, and that's breaking him." When he said the word "breaking," he moved his fists like he was popping something open.

LC felt his head jerk.

"So, boys, before I dismiss you, let me advise you to go ahead and get a halter on him and get him used to wearing it."

Emerson Bridge was bent over, putting his feet back in his shoes, the tongue, wide and extended, as if hoping to catch some food.

LC leaned over and undid his own laces and began tying them back. "I appreciate you not laughing at me," LC told him.

"It wasn't funny," Emerson Bridge said and reached beneath his desk for his clutch of books. He started for the door.

LC slid out his sack and caught up with Emerson Bridge in the doorway. "I've been wanting to make friends with you," LC told him and extended the sack the boy's way. The sack was shaking.

Emerson Bridge took it.

LC had never noticed his dimples. "Look inside."

The Creamer boy pulled out a halter.

"It's for your steer."

"For Lucky," Emerson Bridge said.

LC nodded but did not repeat the animal's name.

"That's real kind of you. Thank you. Now Mama won't have to buy me one."

They took off outside together. Emerson Bridge's mother was waiting with his door open.

"Mama, look what my friend gave Lucky!" Emerson Bridge held the halter up for her viewing. It was made of rope, what LC's father called an everyday one. LC had sneaked it from the barn the afternoon before as soon as his father made his usual trip to the garage to his bottles of RC Cola, which he kept out in the open and his bottle of whiskey, which he did not. A half dozen rope halters hung from nails in the tack room. He wouldn't miss one of them, but he might miss one of his six show halters, made of brown leather with a fancy chain that hung beneath the steer's chin.

Mrs. Creamer held her hands flat to her mouth like she couldn't believe it.

"It goes on him like this," LC said and took the halter and held it by the two long sides. He made sure Emerson Bridge was looking, but mostly, he wanted Mrs. Creamer's eyes, not to watch how he was going to demonstrate, but to watch *him*.

He believed it so.

· · · · ·

116

A heavy frost covered the ground that early morning at the Creamer place. Emerson Bridge liked the way the little white sparkles covered the grass and dirt and even rocks as if they were having a party to celebrate something good. He sat on the porch steps, waiting for Mr. Merritt's monthly visit, his third. He wanted to show the county agent how big Lucky had grown and how much Lucky trusted him. He had practiced putting the halter on him as soon as he got home from school the afternoon before.

Mr. Ike stood by the front fence with Emerson Bridge's mother. They giggled a lot. Emerson Bridge liked hearing them do that.

When Mr. Merritt turned into the driveway, Emerson Bridge ran towards the barn and stood ready by his steer. As soon as the county agent came through the gate, he lifted the halter from the fence post, where he'd hung it the night before, and whispered to the animal, "Hold still, boy." Emerson Bridge made sure Mr. Merritt was looking and then slipped the halter on the steer's head. Lucky didn't move. He only let out a low moan. "See how much he trusts me?" Out of the corner of his eye, he saw his mother and Mr. Ike waving from the fence, and then they both started to clap.

But Mr. Merritt was shaking his head.

"Oh yes, sir, he does, too." Emerson Bridge started removing the halter, so he could show the county agent again.

But Mr. Merritt wasn't watching Emerson Bridge. He had his hands feeling along the top of the animal's back. Lucky raised his chin and made that low sound again. "He's lost weight, son."

"Oh no, sir. We've been feeding him more than ever. As much as he could eat, too, didn't we, Mr. Ike?" Emerson Bridge called out.

"Full feed! Tell him full feed!" Mr. Ike came running their way.

"Full feed?" Mr. Merritt said. "You've had him on full feed before I told you to yesterday?"

"Why, yes sir," Emerson Bridge said.

There was a frown on the man's face, and his hands were now feeling down lower on the steer's side.

"Exactly what's the situation here?" Mr. Ike said.

The county agent now was touching Lucky's ears and his legs and even looking at his hooves.

Emerson Bridge felt dizzy. "He's not sick, is he?"

"Son, I'm afraid he's got the bloat. You don't see how poked out his sides are?"

Emerson Bridge didn't know what the bloat was, but he knew it wasn't good. "Thought he was getting fat like y'all wanted him to."

Mr. Merritt moved behind the animal and looked at Lucky's rear end. "And he's got the scours, for goodness sake." He sounded mad now.

Emerson Bridge felt his stomach knot up. His mother was standing beside him now. He didn't dare look at her or his lips might start to quiver.

"Son, you have got to follow my instructions, especially when it comes to food."

Emerson Bridge nodded and let his eyes drift over to Mr. Ike, who stayed at the fence. Emerson Bridge wanted him to ask him why he'd said to put Lucky on full feed the month before, but Mr. Ike was fiddling with his yellow scarf he had tied around his neck.

"We've got to get rid of all that mixed feed in his trough," the county agent said, his words coming fast. "Dry feed only right now. I'm talking hay. That's *all.*"

Mr. Ike took off towards the feed trough.

"Y'all got any Pepsi-Cola, ma'am?" Mr. Merritt asked Emerson Bridge's mother. She had her eyes cast down and was shaking her head. Emerson Bridge didn't know what a Pepsi-Cola was.

"Then, can you go to the store and get me two right now?"

His mother started running.

"You got any money, Mama?" Emerson Bridge called out.

She raised her hand, which he took to mean she did. But this was his steer. He ran inside the barn to his papa's straw bales, where the shaving kit remained. He unzipped it, moved his fingers past the brush that had dried hard and past the mixing cup that contained cracked remnants of their last shave, to the round coin he'd been saving, the fifty-cent piece from the tooth fairy the month before. He took off outside with it and saw his mother getting in the automobile. "Mama! I've got some money!"

But she told him, "That's yours, hon." She took off out the driveway.

He ran back to the lot. Mr. Merritt and Mr. Ike were scooping grain from the trough with their hands and putting it in his papa's wheel barrow.

Lucky was tied to the fence post with a rope. Emerson Bridge told him, "I'm sorry, boy, I didn't know." His papa's words about being a better man, Emerson Bridge had not understood, but now that he'd not taken good care of Lucky, he wondered if that's what his papa had thought about himself. "Papa was wrong, though. He didn't make me sick. I've made you sick."

His mother pulled up to the fence in a cloud of dust. "Got Mr. Drake to go ahead and open them," she called out and hurried their way, each hand holding a glass bottle filled with dark liquid.

Mr. Merritt worked to get the steer's mouth open. "His tongue's hot."

Emerson Bridge had felt that but had not thought much of it. He took a step back.

"Son, I need you to pour one bottle at a time on his tongue, and be easy with it." Lucky was trying to jerk his head. His mother held one of the bottles Emerson Bridge's way, but he did not take it. "Son, we don't have time to be standing around."

"He don't trust me no more."

"He trusts you, son, now come on. Now's the time to stay strong."

Emerson Bridge reached for the bottle and poured it on and watched the liquid bubble up. He poured in the next one.

"Let's hope this makes him belch and get rid of his gas." The county agent wiped his hands, coated in slobber, on the legs of his khaki pants.

Emerson Bridge felt his eyes start to fill. "Is he going to die, Mr. Merritt?" he whispered.

The county agent leaned towards him. "This is big boy's work, son, fooling with a steer. So I'm going to talk to you like a big boy, even a man. Feeding him too much too soon, yes, could kill him."

Emerson Bridge felt his knees go weak.

"You make sure you keep him on his feet, all right? That's why that rope's got so little play in it."

Mr. Merritt was leaving. Emerson Bridge didn't want him to. It had never occurred to him that he might not be enough for this animal, but it occurred to him now.

He looked along the ground. The sparkles had all gone.

· · · · ·

Luther put his hand on the back of his boy's steer, the animal's head bent low to the trough, heaped with Luther's ground corn and oats and milo. Luther had started the steer on full feed the day before. He ran his hand along the ridge, then down the steer's sides, feeling for meat. He wasn't sure what to feel for. *Was it hard like muscle or soft like fat?* He tried to remember how Charles's steers had looked with only four months left to feed out, but Luther had never bothered to pay much attention, since Charles had never needed him to. LC was with Uncle running the hammer mill behind Luther, holding the sacks under the funnel to catch the grain. Luther was glad his boy was not with him to witness his father's unknowing hand. He bent towards the animal's ear and whispered, "Eat up, boy, please," and reveled in the loud grinding of his hammer mill, let it fill his ears with something he could claim as having done right. The decision to buy it had been his and his alone.

Luther shoved his hand into the trough, pushed the tiny bits of grain around, making them go wherever he sent them. He looked back towards his house. Merritt was late with the news that Luther had been waiting on, whether the Creamer steer had the bloat or whether his plan had back-fired and the steer had packed on more even more weight, putting it even stronger on the path to becoming champion and Luther Charles Dobbins, Sr., a total nobody and failure in his boy's eyes.

Luther's own belly had bloated. It began as soon as he tasted Mildred's sausage that morning and then chased it with orange juice. His belly protruded like a woman's, the fleshiness of their middle, but his was swollen hard. He hoped no one would notice.

Merritt drove up. LC came running towards the lot. Luther pressed on his belly.

Merritt apologized for being late. Luther told himself not to act too interested in the reason, but when the county agent said, "Afraid the Creamer steer has the bloat," Luther chuckled.

"That steer could die, Luther."

"It's got the bloat?" LC said.

"What? You think I'm an idiot, Paul? That I don't know that? I've had my share of cows with the bloat and I've seen them die from it." Luther's voice was weaker than normal. It hurt to talk too loud.

"It's not going to die, is it?" LC said.

Merritt touched LC's shoulder like he was the boy's father. "Hey, that's my boy," Luther told him and slapped Merritt's hand away, then put his hand where Merritt's had been. The boy was thin. Charles had a lot more meat on his bones when he was LC's age.

"Sure hate to, but reckon I'll pass out that paper for the boys to sign at our December meeting," Merritt said and started towards his truck.

"Don't think you need to do that, Mr. Merritt," LC yelled and ran that man's way.

Luther followed. "Hey, you're not going to say anything about how my boy's steer is finishing out?"

"He's looking good, Luther."

"Some details, Paul, details."

Merritt was inside his truck now.

Luther thought if could get the county agent to say exactly what looked good, he would know what to concentrate on. He motioned for him to roll down his window.

Merritt obeyed but said, "I made it clear to them that they must keep him on his feet. God help them."

Then he backed up and left.

LC, though, remained by Luther's side.

His bloat was lessening. "Listen and learn, boy. Grand champions are made between the holidays, Thanksgiving to Christmas. Your competition's going to slack off, but the mighty Dobbins are going to step it up even more."

Merritt hadn't realized he'd given Luther an early Christmas present. *Keep him on his feet,* indeed.

· · · · ·

"I know you told me not to come around here on no day but Monday," Ike called from his truck to his boss man, who was in the pecan grove with his boy and Emmanuel. "But our steer's got something bad called the bloat. We give him two Pepsi-Colas to drink, but I was wondering if you know anything else to do, because he might die."

Mr. Dobbins made no response with words, only blew smoke from this cigar in little short bursts like he was kissing the air.

Ike knew he was talking fast and that his breath was foul from the vomiting he'd done over the mistake he'd made. "I said, the steer has—"

"Heard you the first time, for God's sake." His boss man's words carried an edge that he had become familiar with. "I don't know of nothing."

Ike looked at Emmanuel, who had his head down. "I put him on that full feed like you said, but—"

"Full feed?" Mr. Dobbins hollered.

"Yes sir, full feed."

"I never told you that."

"Yes, sir. That day you hired me on as your hired hand."

His boss man had his eyes on his boy, who stood within a couple of feet of him. "Everybody knows—*everybody,* right, LC?—that you don't put him on full feed until November." He slammed his hand towards the ground, sent some pecans bouncing and hitting his boy's leg. "You must have misunderstood me."

His boy moved away from him.

"Yes sir, I reckon I did. I'm sorry about that." Ike wanted that whale in the Bible to open his mouth and swallow him like he did that man, Jonah, but he wanted the whale to go ahead and chew him up, too.

"I'll just see you on Monday, Mr. LC," Emmanuel said and held up his hand. He tipped his cap towards them all and started towards the road.

"LC, why don't you run on, too," Mr. Dobbins said and pushed him aside and started for Ike's truck. Ike wished now that he'd taken time to stop by Drake's for some chewing gum.

"If you're going to be my hired hand," his boss man was saying, "you're going to have to start listening with two ears. I've got a reputation in this county. Even this whole state."

"Yes sir. For where *two* or three are gathered together in my name, there am I in the midst of them. Matthew 18:20. Yes sirree."

"What's the matter with you? You talking like a preacher. That's blasphemy."

Ike shook his head. "Oh, no sir. I'm a hired man through and through." He felt perspiration in his arm pits and kept his arms down by his side.

Mr. Dobbins glanced around like he was looking for something and then leaned in towards Ike. "I reckon the biggest thing I can advise you is to try to get it to lay down. So it can get some rest."

His voice was so light, Ike could have missed his words. "Lay down. That what you said?"

"That's right. Get it to *lay down.*"

"*Lay down,*" Ike repeated. "Get the steer to."

Mr. Dobbins removed his cigar and raised his chin. He released a slow and steady stream of smoke. Then he returned the cigar to his mouth, bringing his chin down.

Ike took that as a nod. He had gotten it right this time.

He told his boss good-bye and left the driveway even faster than he'd arrived. Up in the distance he spotted Emmanuel, whom he assumed was walking to town. Emmanuel motioned for him to stop, which Ike did, but he leaned across the seat and told him, "Wish I could take you, but I got to get back to the Creamer place in a jiffy."

"Reckon that boy's mama's got an ice pick?" Emmanuel's voice was low.

"Reckon so."

"Think I can help you." Emmanuel hopped into the bed of the truck, but Ike threw open the passenger door and hollered, "Get up here with me, or I won't take you."

Emmanuel got in the cab. He smelled like the wind.

Ike felt like they were on a secret mission together. Here he was with this man who knew something more than his boss man and didn't want to show him up. Ike tried to think how an ice pick would help. Maybe to chip up a block of ice to hold on the steer somehow? Or eat it as a way to get water in the steer? "But I don't know if Mrs. Creamer has a block of ice," Ike said.

"Won't be needing ice."

The steer was on his feet when they arrived, the boy and Mrs. Creamer standing beside him. Ike would let Emmanuel do what he needed with the pick, and then he would share his special advice with the boy. "Emmanuel's going to help us," Ike hollered, "and he needs an ice pick right quick."

Mrs. Creamer started towards her house in a run.

Emmanuel called after her, "And can you boil it good, please, ma'am?"

She raised her hand in the air.

Emmanuel ran his flat hand over the steer's side. The animal moaned.

"Please don't let him die," Emerson Bridge told him.

Ike loved that the boy was free to be honest. He wished he could be a boy again.

Mrs. Creamer returned with the pick, wrapped in a dish towel. Emmanuel held it by its handle, long ago red but now a dull gray. The sharp metal part, those four inches, appeared clean and glistening in the sunlight. "Y'all might want to step back," he said.

But no one did.

He put his flat hand up high on the steer's side in the triangular area between the hip bone and last rib and moved his hand in a circle, then made a fist and hard tapped the spot as if his hand was a child's pogo stick. When he made the stab, it was fast and deep. The steer adjusted his feet and tried to pull away from the post. Ike heard the boy draw in a breath. Mrs. Creamer held her hands over her mouth. Ike swallowed.

Emmanuel leaned down and held his ear just out where the pick had been. "Here it comes, some air. I hear it."

"Mama Red!" Sarah called out and started the mother cow's way. She stood on other side of the fence. "Your boy's going to make it!"

"Ma'am, he—" the man tried to say, but the boy hustled over and put his ear at that place. Emmanuel held the pick out to his side, the metal part covered in blood.

"Sounds like a little wind, a baby one," Emerson Bridge said, and then a smile came across his face, the sun seeming to throw a spotlight on his dimple like the lights on the stage at the State Theatre. It wasn't looking like they would make the Roy Rogers Riders Club meeting this day.

The boy wrapped his arms around the man's waist. "Thank you, sir." Emmanuel held his arms out from the boy but did not touch him. They were not of the same skin color. Ike had held his arms out from the boy like that, too, but he didn't have that excuse. The truth was, if Ike ever hugged the boy back, he might not let him go.

"But he ain't out of trouble yet," Emmanuel said.

Emerson Bridge bent his head back and looked up the man's long body.

Ike wanted to be tall like that. He pressed down on the front of his feet and reared up on his toes.

When Emerson Bridge released Emmanuel, Ike motioned for the boy to come his way and then bent towards him and whispered, "Got us some more secret knowledge, but this time I got it right." He concentrated hard on his words. "We need to get him to lay down. Give him some rest."

The boy made no comment, though, and ran back to his steer and Emmanuel.

Ike waited for the boy to make the steer lay down.

But the boy did not do that. The boy laid his head against the animal's side and stretched out his arms to hold him.

Ike waited for more than an hour.

But the boy never did.

Ike returned to his truck and left the driveway. When he came to the road, he pressed his eyes shut, squeezing out water that ran down his cheeks, shaved as smooth as a baby's earlier that day but now carrying stubble that he was always thankful for. But this day he dug his fingernails into his skin, trying to scrape off what surely God had meant as a joke. "You were right, Daddy. I ain't no man. Ain't no cattleman, either."

He drove to the boarding house and shed himself of his hat and boots and rider jeans and rider shirt and neck kerchief.

He got in the bed.

Then Ike Thrasher began to shake, not of being cold, but of being nothing.

· · · · ·

As soon as Mr. Thrasher left the driveway, LC saw his father walk towards the barn and heard him call for him. LC was hiding behind a tree and had overheard his father telling the man to do something that LC knew to be wrong. He needed to warn Emerson Bridge to not do what his father had said. He had seen two of his father's cows lay down from bloat, not because his father had made them, but because they could no longer stand. Neither ever got back up.

He stayed quiet until his father reached the barn, and then he made a run for the house and tried to telephone Emerson Bridge. But the operator said the number had been disconnected. LC would have to sneak over there. He knew where they lived. Uncle had told him one Saturday when they were running the hammer mill. LC figured the sooner he could satisfy his father, the sooner he could break away. He ran out the back door and let the screened door pop loud.

"Where you been, boy?" his father asked. He was standing beside LC's steer.

"Working on my lessons."

"The only lesson you need is with your beef here. Going to teach you how to do like Charles." His father slapped the steer's rump and made the animal lunge forward. But LC put his hand on the animal's face to calm him.

"Hey! You going soft on me?" His father shoved LC towards the fence.

LC felt the barbs in his back. His mother had tried to get him to wear his coat, but he'd thought the afternoon temperature would rise. "No, sir."

His father lit a cigar and put it in his mouth. LC wanted to shove it down his throat.

"I'm talking about breaking him, boy. Breaking him to lead with his rope, breaking him to start following you. The trick is to put an apple in your back pocket. They'll walk over nails to get to that apple."

LC already knew this. He'd practiced with an apple last time but left the apple at home on the day of the show, because doing such was against the rules. He looked towards the house, hoping his mother would be standing outside. *Come get your coat, dear,* he wanted her to say. But she was cleaning the house. She would not be coming for him.

LC went through the motions with his steer, marking time until his father opened the side door of the garage for his afternoon secret drinking. And when his father did, LC made a run for the road.

He was barely out of the yard, when he heard at his back, "Boy! Where you going?" It was his father, and he was standing beside the house.

"To check the mail!" LC turned and ran hard to the mailbox, which he'd just passed. The box was empty, as he knew it would be. His mother always got the mail. "Mama must have gotten it!" he called out.

His father now was coming his way. LC began skipping towards him like he was playing. This would signal that he was not scared.

But his father grabbed his arm. "I asked you where you were going."

"I told you, Dad. To get the mail." LC knew he'd hesitated. Lying did not feel good to him.

"I believe you're telling me a story, boy."

"No sir, Dad, I'm not." LC told him faster this time.

His father slapped his mouth. "That's to remind you that you better not be telling me no story, because if I catch you, you're going to wish you'd kept on running wherever you were headed."

LC tasted blood. It tasted like deer's blood.

· · · · ·

Luther watched his boy go inside the house, and then he returned to his garage. He'd already had his one drink for the day, had wrapped his glass in one of Mildred's dish towels and set it inside an empty lard can behind LC's old tricycle. But he took the glass back out and poured in the rest of the RC Cola he'd already capped and had waiting for Monday. He tried not to drink on Sundays.

He kept his pint of whiskey hidden behind an old hub cap that leaned against the back wall. Uncle bought the whiskey at a store in town. It was easier for negroes to buy it. People expected negroes to drink.

He pictured his boy's lip, the blood on it. He wished he'd not done it. Why couldn't he have invited his boy to go see the ladybugs? They could have run there together and watched the insects play.

Luther poured in a shot of his whiskey.

Luther suspected the boy had somehow overheard what he'd told Thrasher about the steer and his boy was headed to the Creamers. But what if LC really had been getting the mail? That's where Luther was headed. Mildred had not had time that day. She was getting the house extra clean. He liked it extra clean.

Luther held his bottle over his glass and tipped it all the way up.

. . . . .

LC lay in his bed with the covers pulled high to his chin. On his body, he wore his clothes from the day, his jeans and flannel shirt and even socks and brogans. The time was close to his father's bedtime, nine o'clock. His mother had already kissed him goodnight and closed the door.

He had butterflies in his belly. He'd never sneaked out before. Boys at school had talked of it and said a boy may as well be a girl if he'd never done it. But, when the bragging words came this school year from boys like the Prater boy, LC had laughed and called them jellies, telling himself that he'd skipped that stage and gone straight to manhood. But now that he had the opportunity before him, LC saw the escape not only as a way to help his friend, but also as a means to be a boy again.

Taking the stairs and leaving the house by way of the front or back door was too risky. The stairs liked to creak, like they were doing now. His father was coming to bed. He'd be passing LC's room. LC closed his eyes and lay as still as a corpse.

The handle on his door turned. LC sucked in his breath as the darkness in his eyelids went light and then dark again. His father's shadow had fallen on him.

"You asleep?" his father said.

LC tried not to breathe.

His father stepped closer. "Huh? You asleep?"

His father's voice didn't carry much of an edge, but, still, LC was thinking, *Here it comes.* He listened for the sound of his father's belt sliding through his loops on his khaki pants. LC felt his body sweating.

But he didn't hear any such sound, only that of his father clearing his throat. "Boy, you know—" He heard his father swallow. "You know I love you, don't you?"

LC's eyes flew open, but he squeezed them shut again and hoped his father had not seen. *No,* he wanted to say, *no sir, I do not know that. I think you hate me.*

"I know I'm hard on you, and I'm sorry for that. But I want you to have it better than I did."

LC wanted to say, *Then stay off my back.*

His father took a deep breath, the smell of whiskey in the air between them, and then LC heard his footsteps take him away. LC allowed his eyes the slightest crack and saw his father's shoulders slumped, his head hanging low.

The door closed.

The light went out in the hallway.

The door to his father and mother's room beside his closed.

LC exhaled.

His father knew that LC had heard him. His father's bent body told him that. Now LC wished he'd answered him, because what if his father laid in bed and cried?

His father wasn't a bad man, LC tried to tell himself. He just liked to win, like Roy Rogers liked to win when he fought with the bad guys for stealing another man's horse or cows or tried to cheat somebody out of something. As far as he knew, his father had never done those things. He'd only told the man to get that steer to lay down. But those words were meant to kill his friend's steer.

His father was a bad man. He was the bad guy.

LC threw the covers off.

He raised the window a little at a time, all the while listening for his father's sounds. When he freed about a foot of space, he stepped through, placing his feet on the tin roof. It made a dull cracking noise. With his foot, he tapped along the tin until he found a run of wood beneath, and then he placed his weight there, following the beam towards the front of the house. He walked as if he was a 4-H girl, his arms held by his side like he was balancing a book on his head the way he'd seen the girls do to learn correct posture. At the end of the roof, a big oak tree rose tall into the air. Its limbs, barren of most of its leaves, provided him a helping hand.

He jumped on.

· · · · ·

Luther heard a noise outside his window and reached under his bed for his pistol, a loaded .32 with a pearl handle. He sneaked over to the window to look outside and saw nothing to his right towards the garage and barn, nor in front out in his field. But to his left, he saw, walking along the roof like a ballerina, his boy. He'd been right that afternoon. His boy had heard him and was headed to the Creamer place. Luther knew this as well as he knew his name.

What a fool he'd been to go soft. It crossed Luther's mind to fling open the window and aim right at him. Shoot him dead the way Luther made Uncle shoot hogs with that pistol. Go ahead and put him out of his do-good misery.

But Luther decided to let the boy go on. He would be back soon. He was too much of a baby to last out there by himself in the cold dark.

No, Luther would be waiting for him when he returned. He'd even give him enough time to get back inside his window and return to his bed. Then Luther would start the night over. He'd climb the stairs again, and, again, open the door to LC's room. But this time Luther would not tell his boy he loved him and give LC the opportunity to pretend sleep and shun him.

· · · · ·

LC ran, cocooned in twinkle stars that night.

He arrived at the Creamer driveway out of breath but paused only a few seconds to aim his eyes towards the answer he'd come seeking. He took off towards the barn and found the steer standing, along with Emerson Bridge, who stood beside the animal and Mrs. Creamer close by, sitting. His eyes had grown accustomed to the darkness.

"Why, hon," Mrs. Creamer said. "What you doing way out here?" She was standing now.

Her kindness made tears puddle up in his eyes. He was glad these people could not see him clearly. When he could, he told them, "Just come to check on y'all. Heard your steer had the bloat."

"Why, hon, we thank you, we do. But in the night? You come in the pitch black cold night? And on foot? And that far?"

"I was worried, ma'am," LC said. "Didn't know if y'all knew to keep him on his feet or not, but I see you do. You got to keep him on his feet."

He felt her arms come around him, and he knew that whatever happened to him when he returned home that night would be worth this.

"That's what Mr. Merritt told us," Emerson Bridge said.

But what about that cowboy, LC wondered. Surely, he came here and said. "But if anybody tells y'all to get him to lay down, don't do it, OK?" He searched the faces of these two people, who stood beside each other now, both nodding. In the spare light, he could see a mother and her son.

A cow mooed behind them. It was Splotchy pressed to the fence a few feet away. LC would know her face anywhere.

"Reckon I'd better get on back home," he said and started for the road.

"Wait!" Emerson Bridge called out, "want to hear him whistle?" He motioned LC over and pointed to a place up high on the animal's lower back. "Right there's where that ice pick went in him."

"Ice pick?" LC said.

"Yeah, that Mr. Emmanuel come and helped us with that."

LC didn't know anyone with that name.

"Put your ear there and listen," Emerson Bridge told him.

The air tickled LC's face.

Emerson Bridge leaned in, too, and whispered, "I'm scared."

"Just keep him on his feet," LC whispered back.

"Not that, I know that," Emerson Bridge said. "I'm scared that everything I do for him comes up short."

LC wanted to tell him *then don't do it, stop it now, run while you still can.*

Emerson Bridge wiped his coat sleeve across his eyes and showed a wrist so skinny, it looked like a bone. And the boy's mother, LC had felt how thin she was, the bones of her back still in his arms' memory. Emerson Bridge was right when he'd said they needed the money the steer would bring. Maybe that would be enough to carry them through all that it would cost them.

At that moment, LC vowed to help Emerson Bridge win. "Did that cowboy man come back here and tell you to make him lay down?"

Emerson Bridge nodded.

"Then you know enough," LC told him. "You knew enough not to listen to him."

LC ran his hand along the top of the animal's back. What he felt would make his father angry, but it made LC glad. "You got a winner here," he said and picked up his friend's hand and set it where his had been. "Feel how straight it is? He's got what the judges look for. You'll hear them say, 'This one won't hold water.' They like that. Can you feel it?"

Emerson Bridge nodded.

"And I see you got that halter on him. Pretty soon, start walking him, get him to follow you. Put an apple or a pear like you like to eat in your back pocket. He'll walk over nails to get to it."

"Thanks," Emerson Bridge told him and stretched his arms around the animal's neck. "He's got to live. I love him."

LC's stomach churned. He understood that kind of attachment, but he also understood that if his friend was going to make it through the next four months, he would need to think another kind of way. LC told him, "You're doing a swell job raising your *project.*"

He wanted Emerson Bridge to say the word back, but all he said was, "I just hope Lucky thinks so."

Telling him about his steer's name was the biggest thing, but it seemed too much right now to lay all that on him. But wasn't all of it too much? LC took a deep breath. "It'd be better if you could stop calling his name."

"Why?"

LC cleared his throat. "It just is. It'll make you stronger."

"What would I call him, then?"

"Nothing."

"Nothing?"

LC would try one more time to get him to say the word. "It's good that we have a *project* that could bring so much money."

"Yeah, project," Emerson Bridge said.

There it was. LC had begun his friend's education. In the pit of his belly, he felt a deep sadness. But he remembered these people's bones and let it be.

A vehicle's engine sounded near the house. LC saw headlights moving towards the lot. A rush shot up his body. His father had come for him. The vehicle stopped just out from the fence but did not sound like his father's truck. A door creaked open. It was Mrs. Creamer. "Let me run you home, hon. I know you must be cold."

He was cold but mostly he wanted to spend time with her. "That would be real nice." He climbed in.

They started for home.

"I didn't want to say this in front of Emerson Bridge, Mrs. Creamer, but his steer's mama's done lost one. It was that steer's twin. I mean it, y'all got to keep this one on his feet."

"They was twins she had?" Mrs. Creamer said.

"Buzzards got to it when it was born. All that was left of it was a little rug."

He heard her make little whimpering sounds.

His father called them heathens for being unchurched, but LC knew better. He'd felt their hearts. And in his few short years of life, he already knew that's where all truth lies.

· · · · ·

Luther waited, deep in the shadows on his front porch. He waited with a belt, his thickest, wrapped around his fist and coiled like a snake.

He couldn't spot the moon from where he was sitting, but he could see a scattering of stars, peppered above his trees, and appearing to wink at him as though they shared his secret. Luther and all those stars in cahoots. It had crossed his mind to go roust Uncle and tell him to come chop down his boy's escape tree. But Luther knew that Uncle liked to have his whiskey

130

on Saturday nights, and, at this late hour, he'd probably be drunk as a coot and trying to have relations with his common law.

He thought he heard noises coming from that way now. Uncle's tenant house was set off to Luther's right and far enough back so it wouldn't be in the line of sight with his house, but close enough to the road for people to see that Luther had a tenant family. Luther had built the house new when Uncle came to work for him, which was soon after Luther bought the place.

No, it was laughter that he heard coming from Uncle's way that night.

Luther stood. He had not always called him Uncle but by his name, Emmanuel. They grew up together, lived side by side in tar-paper shacks on Mr. Joseph Allgood's place. The name Uncle came when Emmanuel went to work for him. That's what white men of means did, call grown male negroes "Uncle." Luther had sneaked out when he was a boy, too. Growing up, his and Uncle's shacks were so close, a grown man would barely fit between them. Laughter always lived at Emmanuel's house but wasn't welcomed at Luther's, his father greeting such with a strap as if Luther was an animal. The only time Luther was free to laugh was with Emmanuel, when they were in the fields working. But the laughter they shared was nothing like what Luther heard that night when he was a boy, so strong, it drew him from his floor pallet, his bare feet sneaking across the rough boards and outside to Emmanuel's window. There was his friend and Emmanuel's mother beside him in a rocking chair, both with their heads thrown back in raucous fun, her hair as white as cotton and not a tooth in her head. In her arms lay a baby, a white baby. Luther took off running to the Allgood house that sat in the midst of a grove of pecan trees. The sheriff came and took away the baby and also Emmanuel's mother. Within a day, Mr. Allgood moved another family in and sent Emmanuel, barely a teenager, on his way. Luther watched him leave and wanted to tell him good-bye but was too ashamed of what he had done. Emmanuel's mother died not too long after that.

Luther now saw two headlight beams cutting through the night and coming his way from Whitehall. They stopped up the road near the far end of his pasture, and he heard a vehicle door open and could have sworn he heard "Thank you, ma'am." He could have sworn it was his boy's voice. Sounds carry in the night. And then another voice came his way, the Creamer woman's. She must have gotten a new vehicle somehow. Maybe his do-gooder boy helped her buy it.

The word "good" hung in the frosty air around Luther, then jumped onto him, marched up him like a ladybug, then descended him and sank like a rock, a heavy one, the kind, if tied, would drown a person. He felt a gathering around his eyes like parishioners around a baptism pond. He'd been thinking all this time his boy was becoming a small version of Luther.

But he'd been wrong. His boy was a larger version, much larger. He'd sneaked out like Luther had, but his boy had sneaked out to do good.

Luther unwrapped enough of his belt to free a foot or more of the tongue. And then he shoved his fist high in the air and brought it back down, slapping his own thigh and leaving a heat that soon became cold.

He dropped his belt on the floor.

. . . . .

In the early morning darkness, Luther walked among his cows. They lay not out in the open pasture but nestled under trees that lined the trickle of a branch that ran from his pond. In the moon's light, he saw most lift their heads, the pure white of their faces more prominent now. They had no need for what Luther came seeking. All cows had to be was cows, no pressure at all to be a head deacon. Or boss man. Or husband. Or good father.

If he was Uncle or either of his boys, the cows might think he came carrying some kind of grain, and they would push themselves up and stand. But he was Luther, and they would expect nothing. They all stayed on the ground.

The sun was just beginning to rise over his pastureland that morning. Over the pond, a mist rose like a fog. One of his cows drank at the water's edge. His boy would know her name.

He went there, let the tips of his boots touch the water and then stepped onto the muddy bottom. Already he could feel the shape of their hooves beneath his soles. If the weather was hot, they would stand out in it as if they were preachers, waiting for a sinner to baptize. He could have thought of them the other way, as sinners, but, in his two decades with cattle, he had never seen any darkness in them, only light.

Luther had come to their water, intending his own salvation. He ached to be somebody in his boy's eyes, looked at the way his boy looked at Uncle, his eyes fixing on him and not letting him go. Even the boy's mouth, the way it'd be slightly ajar, as if he was amazed. But mostly it was that smile that would come across his boy's face when he talked to Uncle that dug a home in Luther's skin. His boy always looked as though he could break into laughter.

Luther took himself into the water, until he was waist high and then raised his right hand as if he was the preacher, while he placed his left on the shoulder of the man he imagined turned sideways in front of him. He was that man. Luther closed his eyes and recalled the precise words that would make it official. "I baptize you my brother, Luther Charles Dobbins, in the name of the Father and the Son and the Holy Ghost."

Then Luther dropped his hand and took a step forward, assuming the position of the man being saved, folding his fingers over his nose and squeezing, waiting for the preacher to place his hand in the small of Luther's back and his other over Luther's nose, so the preacher could take him backwards into the water.

But the preacher's hands never came.

Luther would have to do it himself. And the only way he could, would be to fall, to completely fall. He would have to get on his knees and tip over backwards. He got down on his knees and tipped over backwards, forcing himself into the waters, where he sank to the bottom of the pond and lay in mud and cow dung. He worked to free himself, and when he did, he ran back to his land. Water, now full of himself, fell from him in streams.

He was cold. The sky now was beginning to brighten, but the sun brought no real warming. And Luther Charles Dobbins was still not saved.

In the air, he saw buzzards flying. He wondered if they were coming for him.

They would not be for his boy. He was in bed asleep. Luther had stayed in the shadows and watched him climb the tree and listened to the creaks the tin roof made as LC's little body, light with goodness, danced across it.

· · · · ·

The church bells had just sounded that Sunday morning and found Sarah Creamer's ears, when she heard her boy scream, "Mama, I don't hear it no more!"

Sarah had nodded off against the barn. But when her boy's words came, she shot up from the overturned bucket and ran to him, his finger pointing to that place on his steer. She put her ear there.

"You hear it, Mama?"

She wanted to tell him yes, yes, she heard the whistle, but she did not hear it, nor did she feel what had become the familiar tickle of the little wind against her skin. Still, she told him, "I'm listening" as she tried to think what she would say. This was what she had feared, that it would stop on his watch. Each time her boy had taken his turn, she had tried to lengthen her stay by telling him, "I don't believe my time's up yet." But each time her boy would say, "It is, Mama. It's mine now."

"I bet this is just part of it," she told him. "Lucky's just needing to rest. Like we do. Maybe we should go in the house and take a nap. What d'you say?"

Her boy leaned in towards her. "I ain't supposed to call his name no more," he whispered.

133

"What you mean? What you supposed to call him then?"

He hunched up his shoulders.

"That don't sound right to me. Everything God made deserves a name."

He spread his arms like angel's wings around the animal's neck.

She wondered if he knew what an angel was. "You know what an angel is, hon?"

He shook his head.

"It's something that you can't see that looks out for your good, gives you extra help."

"Like Papa??"

She nodded. She wanted to tell him about a second one. She wanted to say, *You got you two, hon.* But that might break something loose inside of her. And him, too.

If she took him to church, he would know about angels, and he could get saved when the time came. But that would mean she'd have to step inside one.

She thought about getting a rock and tossing to him, see if she could get a back and forth going, but this wasn't a mood for play. She could sing. She sang, "Jesus loves me, this I know." It was a song she had heard the other children sing when she was a schoolgirl. They had learned it at church, but she learned it at school, hearing them sing it every morning.

Her boy joined in. He not only knew the words, he claimed them. He must have learned it in school, too.

What Harold had started in him, maybe she was helping move along too.

So you lost you a baby, too, Mama Red? Lucky over there had him a twin? And buzzards got to it? Oh, girl, I'm so sorry. You come by being a mama loud, too, didn't you?

Can I tell you I lost me one, too? But whatever got to mine didn't come from the skies, it come from me, way down inside.

I told you I was carrying, and that's why Harold Creamer married me. One day not too long after I moved over here, I was making up our bed and felt something move down in my belly, a little jab. And I got this picture in my head of a finger, a little one, held up at me like it was trying to catch my attention. It was my little baby. Her touch was real light, and I knew that was in case I didn't catch it. That way she could tell herself she didn't do it on purpose, she must have just bumped into me. But I did catch it, Mama Red. I did. I ran my hand up under my dress and put it flat where I'd felt her and waited for her to touch me again so she could see that I was there. I kept on doing that.

Harold took me to town to a doctor, said I had four more months to go. I'd never been so happy. But on the way back home, I let my mama's words about me not being a good mama come to me, and I grabbed onto the door handle with one hand and with the other grabbed Harold.

"What's the matter?" he said.

I didn't want to tell him all that was in my head, so I just said part of it. I said, "I'm scared," and I let go of him in case he wanted to beat on the steering wheel. But he didn't do that. He picked up my hand and said, "I am, too."

We went home, and me and him got in the bed. If I was a swearing woman, I'd swear that Harold Creamer that afternoon loved me. I liked when we had relations, because it give me somebody close, even if it was just for a few minutes.

"What we going to name her?" I asked him that afternoon.

"Her?" he said.

"Yes, her. What about Little Claudia after my papa, Claude?"

"What if I want a little boy to follow me around so I can teach him things like how to shave and play?"

"Reckon we'll have to have us another one, then," I told him.

We laughed, and the sound of it filled that room like nobody's business.

In the days out from that, Harold would ask, "Heard from Little Claudia today?" and we'd both get real still and put our hands on my belly and wait. It didn't happen every day, but when we did, we had us a connection that I believed was strong enough to take us through.

But there come a time when we didn't feel her move no more, and I started to bleed. Harold took me to the doctor, and he listened to my belly and didn't hear nothing either, so he told me to go home and get in the bed, that I was so deep into it, I'd have to wait on my time to come. I felt like somebody had put me in hot grease and then thrown it in the deep freeze.

It took two weeks for my time to come. The doctor come out to our house. And I was right, Mama Red. She was a girl. And she was blue in color. I had to plead with him to let me hold her. I did it loud and hard the way you would, but he wouldn't let me. He said, "You might get attached," and kept her in his stiff arms. All I wanted to do was put my mouth up to hers and blow in it. I wanted to see if I could wake her up.

He asked us what church we went to. I told him we didn't. He said he knew of a place south of town that would take her and then said, "Best you forget about all of this, Mrs. Creamer," and walked out the door with her.

When my milk come in, my bosom swelled up hard as rocks, and I felt a pain that I don't have no words for. Harold would hold me until it all went quiet. Then a bad infection set in and took away any chance of me ever carrying again.

My mama was right, I told myself. I wouldn't make no good mama, and my little girl knew that.

NOVEMBER 18–19, 1951

The envelope was pink and lay on top of the light bill in Sarah's mailbox. She'd not taken the time the day before to check her mail, since she and her boy had stayed with Lucky, who was still on his feet and alive, but his whistle had not returned. Sarah's eyes were tired, so she couldn't be sure, but it looked to be a personal letter with a large "S" that started off the first name. Could it be Sarah? Or Sister? Mattie's favorite color was pink. Sarah felt a surge rise to her head.

She reached for it. There was her name, the "C" of Creamer standing tall like the "S" and both taking up space. The return address showed Mrs. Luther C. Dobbins. Sarah put her finger on the letters and traced them, letting herself follow the woman's rises and falls.

She felt a tightness in her belly. What if Mildred was writing to say she no longer wanted to help her find buyers for her dresses? Sarah thought about putting the letter back in the box. But what if it was something good?

She opened it. The letter inside was of that same pink and carried a border of red roses. The paper was more delicate than any she'd ever seen. She held it lightly. "Dear Sarah," she read, "I have a special surprise for you Monday morning. I know it's late notice, but it would delight me to pick you up at your house at fifteen minutes past 9. However, if you do not choose to answer your door, I will understand that you do not desire to go. Sincerely, Mildred."

Of course, she desired to go.

She wanted to scream and tell someone. Emerson Bridge was in the lot with Lucky. She opened her mouth and drew in a breath, made a gasping sound, the kind her boy had first made when he was days old. Harold was holding him in the kitchen, and Emerson Bridge was laughing and Sarah noticed his dimples, for the first time, noticed his dimples. She blew on his face like a gentle wind, but he gasped and Sarah feared she'd hurt him. His laughter, though, resumed, his dimples sinking deeper into his soft flesh.

Sarah knew then that he was filled with more capacity for joy than she'd thought was possible for one living soul, much less one so new to this world.

Sarah now began to laugh. She laughed hard and loud and spun around like a schoolgirl. But she lost her balance and fell to the dirt. When she got on her feet again, she was facing the garden and, on the other side, the house that used to hold Mattie.

She felt Mattie's eyes on her. They were sad. "You're still my friend, too," Sarah called out and took off running to Mattie's, to the front steps, once painted a pretty green but now faded and cracked. The screened door with the bird on it had rusted. Sarah had not stood on this porch since the day Mattie died, and the ambulance carried away what was left of her.

She put her hand on the handle. "I don't mean to take away nothing from what was ours, Sister. But I got me a new friend now, and I need you to bless it."

Sarah waited, her ears tuned to the little pitter patter of Mattie's feet and her voice, high and hushed.

The wind picked up at Sarah's back, making the skirt of her dress billow and her apron flap against the door. Mildred's letter lay in her front pocket. It could blow away. She pressed her hand against it, the words "do not" from the last line coming to her. She removed the letter, her eyes moving to the words. "But if you do not choose to answer your door, I will understand that you do not desire to go."

"Do not, that's right," Sarah said out loud. "If you *do not* want to do it, Sister, do not want to give me your blessing, I will understand." She spread her arms across the screened door, leaned her forehead against the top of the bird's beak. The metal felt cold and rough against her the way Harold's hands had felt, crusty from the years he'd spent working outside on telephone poles and consuming enough whiskey to fill a sky and dry his body like slivers of apples in the sun. She could feel his hands clutching the sides of her naked hips, Harold at her back and her leaning against their bed. The first time he'd wanted it that way, she'd thought he was too tired to turn her around and lay her flat. But after the second and third times, she knew this was the way he preferred it now, maybe even needed it. She knew she was not a pretty woman. Sarah could not remember the day Harold began this, but it was after Billy Udean left for war and he and Mattie began working together.

The bird had warmed beneath her. It would cut her, if she moved.

She moved. She moved her forehead to the left and then dragged it across to the right.

She took herself from the door. Where she'd scraped her skin felt cool and began to burn. But it felt alive.

She balled up her fist and hit the door. "Why can't you, Mattie? Why can't you just do this one thing for me? I ain't never asked you for nothing."

Sarah held herself still and listened.

But the wind was all that answered her.

She descended the steps and returned to the mailbox and took out the light bill. It was stamped Past Due, Second Notice. Maybe she shouldn't go with Mildred now. Maybe she should finish the dress she was making before Mr. Merritt told them the bad news about Lucky. She had already lost a day's work.

No, she would not be answering the door when Mrs. Dobbins knocked the next morning. By the time Mrs. Dobbins set her delicate hand to rap, Sarah would be onto her third dress.

· · · · ·

The steer's front knees dropped to the ground. The rope, with its short run and scant play, thrust his chin high into the air and held it there. He released a long moan.

Emerson Bridge jumped up from the bucket. "You got to stand up. Come on, stand up!" He was careful not to call Lucky's name. His hands and arms worked hard to try to pull the animal to his feet. But he could not make him budge.

"Mama!" Emerson Bridge screamed. She was in the house sewing.

He thought about untying the rope, but then he would lie down for sure and die. The animal made a gurgling sound. He was choking. "Come on, get up!" He gave Lucky one big yank, but he stayed on his knees. He thought of his papa's words. *Be kind.* Choking is not kind. He should untie the rope, but it was too tight.

He ran to the barn, got his papa's handsaw and began moving it back and forth over the rope, his hand becoming his papa's. He sawed harder and faster.

The saw cut through.

The animal went down on his back knees, then his whole body to the ground. Emerson Bridge dropped down beside him and placed his knees against his steer's side to try to keep him from rolling over. "Please don't die. Please give me another chance for you to trust me."

Nighttime was almost full upon them. The air was chilled. He could see his breath.

Another deep freeze was on its way.

· · · · ·

"Mama, what's a deep freeze?" Sarah heard at her back. She stopped pedaling.

Her boy stood in the doorway. She had to adjust her eyes to see him. Her lamp was turned low.

"You talking about a place to keep food, hon?"

"If that's what it is. A deep freeze."

"It's like an ice box that rich people keep their food in."

He brought his arms up and folded them across his chest. They'd been hanging free by his side. She wished she could buy him a new coat, but that would have to wait until she caught up on the light bill. "You cold, hon?"

"What kind of food, Mama?"

"Beans, corn. Even meat, for people who can afford meat. You hungry, hon?" She knew he had to be sleepy. Hungry, too. He'd not wanted any supper.

"So it ain't a big frost like we had last night?" he said.

"Why, yes, that could be a deep freeze, too."

"It could?" There was a lift in his voice now.

She'd always known he was smart. Mattie was smart. She could add figures in her head without writing them down.

"How's Lucky, hon? I mean—" She wanted to honor his not wanting to call the animal's name. She feared he was trying to distance himself, thinking the steer would die. "Everything all right out there, hon?"

"What kind of meat, Mama?"

She took that as a good sign. He would have said if something had changed. "All kinds, I reckon."

"What about that fatback and Treet we have sometimes. Are they meat?"

"You hungry, hon? We got a strip of fatback in the woodstove. Let me get it for you." She slid her chair back.

"I ain't hungry. Just wanted to know if that's meat." He was talking fast.

"Why, yes, hon. And that's as good as I can do right now. I wish I could—"

"Where does it come from?" He'd never run over her words before.

"George Drake's, mostly."

"I mean, from what *animal*, Mama?"

"Why, fatback's from a hog. I think that's right, I didn't grow up in the country. And I don't know about that Treet, but I think that's meat too. I sure intend it as such."

Emerson Bridge stepped away from the door and into the hall's darkness.

Sarah stood. "Why, hon? You got a lesson on that at school?" She wanted to go to him, but she heard him take another step back.

139

"I don't want no deep freeze. Ever!" He turned and ran.

Nobody in the whole world could ask for a better boy. He never asked for anything, always accepting however little she could give.

She began pedaling again, the hum of it like a train going down the tracks, taking passengers to someplace they used to know. Like Gainesville, Georgia. But Sarah didn't want to go there. Trains also take passengers to someplace new. Like Mildred's house. But she wouldn't need a train to take her there. She wouldn't even need her automobile. She would just need to be in her kitchen, ready.

She wondered what time it was. Harold's watch by their bed showed it was shortly before eight o'clock. In thirteen hours, Mrs. Dobbins would be at her door. Sarah could smell peppermints. She could hear laughter.

She stopped pedaling. She could spare a few hours from her sewing, couldn't she?

She went to her chifforobe. Her rack of dresses, the checks of red and green and brown and yellow, the brown solid and the green. She was on the lookout for special. But she saw none.

Her eyes fell to the baby-blue blanket. She let herself pick it up and, from it, take Mattie's cloth. She held it up high by one of the long ends and let the rest fall to the floor, where it puddled up.

Sarah closed the door and looked past the brown specks of tarnished glass in the mirror at the house dress on her body. She took hold of the dress at her waist and began pulling it away. Close to two feet of space lay between her fingers and her body.

She allowed herself to have a thought. *Reckon Mattie's cloth would be enough to span Clementine Florence Augusta Sarah Bolt Creamer?* She brought the cloth to her body and held it across her. It more than spanned her. Her hands began to shake.

· · · · ·

Emerson Bridge stood in the yard between his house and the lot where his steer lay on the ground. He had not wanted to leave him, but what he had started to think could not be true. They wouldn't do that to the grand champion. *Make meat out of him?*

He told himself he was just tired from lack of sleep and scared that the animal he had come to love would not recover. It was making him think funny. And not say his name? What if someone had told him not to say "Papa" on that last day when they had shaved? That would be wrong.

He turned towards the lot. He would not only call Lucky's name, he would scream it so loud, his papa would hear him.

"Luckeeeeeeeey!" he yelled and ran to his buddy.

. . . . .

Sarah held her breath and fed her arms through the bottom of Mattie's cloth, lifting them as if giving praise. Down her body, the material fell. It made the whole journey.

She looked at herself in the mirror. Morning had come, and its light filled in the space around her. She placed her flat hands on her hipbones and then brought them, stiff with measurement, to her reflection. Nineteen inches, she looked to be. She used to measure twice that.

It was almost nine o'clock. She set her hat upon her head. It had to be positioned just right, since her forehead had scabbed up. She lowered the netting to just above her eyes. She'd never seen a woman wear it like this, this halfway style. On her hands, she placed her gloves, and on her feet, her shoes. They had holes in their soles now.

This was a good day. Her boy had wanted to go to school. He had told her, "Lucky's going to be all right, Mama." He had called his steer's name.

. . . . .

The knock came at 9:15 exactly. Sarah smoothed down the sides of her dress and opened the door to the porch and on it stepped. Mrs. Dobbins stood on the other side of the screened door, which Sarah swung open, her eyes falling to the pretty blue and white. "Why, I ain't never seen a prettier automobile," Sarah told her. "Reminds me of a movie star's, what that woman that played Scarlett in that picture I saw one time must drive out there in Hollywood. Can see her now with her scarf and big sunglasses riding around." Sarah knew she was talking too much and told herself to be quiet, that she was in the presence of a rich lady. All she really wanted to say was *thank you*.

Mrs. Dobbins headed towards town. Sarah didn't wonder where they were going. She didn't care. But soon the woman turned onto Dixon Road and then into her driveway. Mrs. Dobbins was taking her to her house.

They went inside the back door and stopped in the hallway beside the telephone. Mrs. Dobbins looked at her watch. "We're a tad early," she said and turned on a radio that sat on the table. Sarah didn't remember the radio being there before.

"I want to thank you, Mrs. Dobbins, for whatever the surprise is," Sarah told her.

"Mildred, call me Mildred."

"Mildred, yes, Mildred, I remember. Thank you."

"And I want to thank you, too, Sarah. You gave me the courage to say my piece around Big LC. I told him I was going to bring you over here, and he said nothing against it."

Sarah was glad about that, but she had her mind on her and Mildred's outing. She wondered what they were early for. It appeared to be a telephone call. Was Mildred going to call Sarah's mother again? She felt her stomach knot up.

But Mildred was giggling and fingering her pearls. "Oooh, it's that music," she called out and turned up the radio.

A man began talking. "Ladies, I hope you are by your telephone." His voice was deep as a good well. "It's time for Shoe of the Week, sponsored by our good friends at Welborn's Shoes on the square in Anderson, where you get exclusive but not expensive footwear." Mildred's eyes sparkled. "For all of you ladies who put your name and telephone number in the registration box at the store last week, get ready. I'm about to draw a name."

Mildred was holding a folded piece of paper.

"I'm now placing a call to the lucky lady, and if she can describe the shoe of the week, she wins that shoe in her lovely size."

Sarah knew what the surprise was now. Mildred thought she might win and wanted Sarah there to share in the joy.

The telephone began ringing. Mildred screamed and reached for the receiver. Sarah screamed, too.

"Hello," Mildred said. Her teeth were as white as her pearls.

The man on the radio said, "Is this Mrs. Sarah Creamer?"

Sarah's heart jumped.

"Why, she's right here." Mildred passed the receiver to Sarah.

"But I ain't never been there before," Sarah whispered to Mildred, who held the telephone at Sarah's ear.

Mildred pointed towards Sarah's mouth. "Say hello," she whispered.

Sarah swallowed. "Hello?"

"Mrs. Creamer?" the man said.

"This is Sarah."

"Mrs. Sarah Creamer, can you name the shoe of the week?"

Mildred was pointing to the paper she was holding and mouthing out "Read!"

Sarah shoved the netting on her forehead up. "It's the, the—Du—," she read.

"Spell it," Mildred whispered.

"It's the D-u-e-t."

"Ladies, we have a winner! The featured shoe is, indeed, the Duet, one of the genuine Logrollers, by Sandler of Boston, made with a hand-sewn vamp and back. Mrs. Sarah Creamer, congratulations!"

Mildred was jumping up and down.

"Thank you, sir, I want to thank you for that, I sure do." Sarah held the telephone up against her mouth with both hands.

"You are mighty welcome. Be sure to go by Welborn's Shoes on the square and tell them that Marshall Gaillard at WAIM radio declared you this week's Shoe of the Week winner."

"Yes sir, I will, I sure will as soon as I get me some gasoline money."

An advertisement for the store came on. Sarah thought she might faint and backed up to the wall. Mildred took the receiver from her and said, "Let's go!"

Sarah saw the woman's eyes on her forehead.

"Why, dear, did you fall?" Mildred asked.

"Kind of, but I'm on my feet again." Sarah lifted the netting all the way around.

Mildred drove them to town and parked in front of Woolworth's. They crossed Main Street and walked inside Welborn's Shoes, where Mildred introduced Sarah to the clerk as this week's winner. He motioned for Sarah to have a seat in one of the chairs, and then he scooted a stool for himself her way. It had a ramp up the front and on it a large measuring plate, which his manicured hands held in place. Sarah removed her shoe and placed her foot there. The metal felt cool. She hoped her foot didn't smell. She'd not taken the time to wash her feet that morning, only under her arms and her neck and face. But her stockings were clean.

The clerk moved a bar down to meet her big toe, and then from the side, he moved a second bar against her little toe. "Would the lady prefer black or brown?"

Sarah thought of the dress she was wearing. "Black, please sir, if you don't mind."

He nodded as if bowing and went to the back and soon returned with a pink box and from it lifted one of the shoes. It was shiny black and set up high. A double line of white stitching followed the rounded curve on top of the shoe, with a double line running down the wedged heel. He placed it on the ramp. A shoe horn at her heel glided her foot in. Across the top came two thin straps, which he buckled. He did the same with her other foot, and then he held out his hand. Sarah took it and rose to her feet. She felt tall. For the first time in her life, she felt tall.

"Do they fit?" Mildred asked, and Sarah told her, "Like they had my name on them."

"Why, they did," Mildred said, and they began to giggle.

People in the store looked their way. "We've got our giggle boxes turned over," Mildred said.

"Giggle boxes, we sure do!" Sarah wanted to wear her new shoes home and asked the clerk to throw her old ones away. But when he walked away with them, she called him back. She might need them again. But she looked at her feet and her new ones. She motioned him on.

Outside, she saw Mildred's reflection in the window. For a second, Sarah wondered who the woman was beside Mildred. There was a smile on the woman's face that connected to a body that was not fat.

Sarah was looking at herself.

Mildred needed to go inside Woolworth's. Sarah remained outside beside a mechanical horse and sneaked glimpses at herself in the big window and grinned.

"Got another surprise for you," Mildred said when she came from the store, holding a paper sack high. She got inside her automobile, and Sarah followed, the bottoms of her new shoes slapping against the concrete like they were clapping.

From the sack, Mildred pulled two long runs of shiny fabric in swirls of bright red and yellow and white. They were kerchiefs. "We're movie stars," she said and tied one around her head.

Sarah removed her hat, brought the silky cloth down her face and tied it beneath her chin. Two little girls stood near the horse now. They looked to be friends. One of them climbed on, and the horse began moving. The little girl trusted it to take her somewhere good. "Them words you said to me in that store about our giggle boxes being turned over, that other friend I had that one time, Mattie, it's what she used to say to me when we had fun." Sarah pressed the bottoms of her shoes into the floorboard and then lifted up her feet, bringing them together and holding.

"We've got more fun!" Mildred took out matching sunglasses, large with thick white frames. They looked like the outside of eggs prepared sunny side up. Both women put them on.

Their giggles turned into full on laughter, enough to blast through the confines of the automobile to the rest of the world that surely could hear them.

But, then, just as hard as Sarah had been laughing, she began to cry.

"Oh, dear. I didn't mean to upset you," Mildred said and dabbed at Sarah's face with the ends of her kerchief. "We don't have to wear these."

But Sarah shook her head. "No, it ain't that. It's just that all this time I've been thinking it was my husband, Harold, that cheated on me. But it's just come to me that it was Mattie, too. She cheated on me, too. And that was worse. She was supposed to be my friend."

Mildred reached for Sarah's hand. Mildred was not wearing gloves, only bringing forth her skin, her bare skin.

Sarah wanted that. She removed her glove and took away any cloth between them.

. . . . .

Luther Dobbins did not let his boy ride the bus to school that morning. Luther drove him there himself, let him off at the front door and leaned across the truck seat. He wanted to kiss LC good-bye. But his boy was out the door. It slammed so hard, the jowls of Luther's cheeks shook.

He had made a list of what he could do to show he was good. One was taking his boy to school. But kissing him was not on the list. That had come freely.

He lit a cigar and put it in his mouth and wondered what life would have been like if he'd always treated his boys this way. Mildred, too. He had pretended to be someone he wasn't when he first met and married her. He'd quit school when he was fifteen, hitchhiked to the next town over, Greenville, answered an ad for a Fuller brush salesman and in two years became the leading salesperson, and, as such, could treat himself to any restaurant he wanted. The finest in town was at the Poinsett Hotel, where he took himself one day after a sales call he knew had gone too far. He'd talked a woman into buying bubble suds, when she didn't have a tub in her house. He considered resigning and wanted to mull it over at the Poinsett, where he sat at his favorite table along the far wall, positioned so he could best study the way people spoke and dressed and behaved, such as this one young lady who sat at the table next to him. She was cutting her eyes over at him like she wanted him to ask her out, but Luther had lots of girlfriends and thought she wasn't pretty enough to join his herd.

"Yes, good sir," Luther told the waiter, "I'll have the roast beef with new potatoes and steamed green beans with the slightest slivers of almonds and pimentos." Luther didn't know what pimentos were the first time he ordered the beans, but he'd heard others do so.

The girl ordered the exact same. "And put that gentleman's charge on Daddy's bill, too," she said and looked Luther's way.

"I can pay for my own," he told her and pulled out his billfold and showed her a stack of money, a half inch thick.

The girl smiled. "You're rich like my daddy, then."

He broke out in a sweat.

"I'm going to be a movie star one day," she said and held her head at an angle, as if someone was making a photograph of her.

Their food came, and an older man, dressed in the finest of suits, joined the girl at her table. "Daddy," she said and pointed towards Luther, "that gentleman there is rich like you."

The man extended his hand. "George Hampton here, good sir."

Luther rose from his seat. "THE George Hampton who owns this hotel?"

145

The man nodded.

"Luther Charles Dobbins," Luther told him.

"Dobbins. Dobbins. What business are your people in?"

Luther felt moisture bead up around his mouth. "Agriculture, sir. The agriculture business."

"Smart man, your father must be. Nothing more valuable than land, especially pastureland."

Luther asked the girl out. Her name was Mildred. On their first date, she told him her father's hotel had suites, and Luther thought she meant candy and asked, "What kind of candy?" She laughed at him. He thought about not asking her out again, but she was a rich man's daughter.

They married within six months at the Poinsett under a chandelier that cost more than Luther's father had made in a lifetime. He did not invite his family.

Within two years, Luther made enough money to buy his own farm, seventy-one acres of pastureland. When he did, his father and mother surprised him with a late wedding present, the dust bowl cow the Allgoods had given his father, the cow a year and a half old and on the cusp of fertility. "Get you a herd started with her, son," his father had said and laughed. His father had the nerve to laugh. After all those years, laugh. They smelled of smoke that day, the sooty kind, the worst kind, smoke from a tiny house and woodstove and his mother's outside black iron pot she stayed bent over, boiling water to wash their filthy clothes, stirring with a throwaway stick from the mighty Allgood yard. "Get the by God out of my clean yard," he had told them that day. He'd not seen them since.

Luther pulled air through his cigar, lighting its end in fire, then took it from his mouth and flung it out his window onto the dirt of the school yard, where echoes of children's laughter from years past skipped and bounced. But never from Luther when he had gone to school there, because Emmanuel had not been there with him. He was not allowed to go. Luther wondered if LC ever laughed there, with friends, maybe even the Creamer boy. He put his hands on his steering wheel, wrapped them around the large round ring and squeezed. He couldn't add Cletus and Ethel Dobbins to his list. They were both dead. But the dust bowl cow, Old Splotchy, was still alive, as far as he knew. Her calf, the Creamer steer, might be another matter. He thought about driving out to the Creamer place to check on it. That was on his list, the steer's welfare. He was afraid his going, though, would be too obvious and point to him as the likely heavy. That's what villains were called in cowboy movies. But he was the heavy. And a coward. He drove home.

Thrasher was waiting on him by his truck. He was on the list, too. The man had his arms folded across his chest and his head hung low.

"Good morning to you," Thrasher said in a flat voice. "I've come to tell you something."

But Luther cut him off, not for reasons of before, but because all he could see was LC's face if the steer died. "How's that Creamer steer doing?"

"Don't reckon I know."

Luther found that hard to believe. He'd never known this man to lie.

"But, listen," Thrasher said, "I need to speak with you." He talked as if he was trying to gather steam to get up an incline.

"You *need* to come with me." Luther did something he never thought he'd do. He grabbed the man's arm and pulled him towards his truck. "Bloat's serious."

They started to the Creamer place. Luther told himself he would let the man blabber on about what he always blabbered about, the latest cowboy movie he'd seen. But the man said nothing, just sat against the door and stared out the window. And he was not wearing his cowboy hat. It lay in his lap.

"You sick?" Luther asked him.

Thrasher shook his head. Luther had never seen his full head of hair, only the bottom curls that always hung beneath his hat. His hair looked like the waves of an ocean. Luther was glad he had his hat on. He would keep it on.

He turned into the Creamer driveway and drove past the house to the barn, pulled up to the fence, and there was the steer on its feet with its head down. He was eating. *The steer was alive.* Luther had been spared again. His fingers, numb from squeezing the steering wheel, relaxed. "He looks good," Luther said and waited for Thrasher to say the same. Luther needed him to, not because Thrasher knew anything about cattle, but because Luther believed him to be a good man.

But all Thrasher did was look the opposite way towards the house. A Model A sat in the yard. That must be the vehicle Mrs. Creamer was driving Saturday night.

"I'm hanging up my spurs, Mr. Boss Man."

Luther turned his head so fast, his neck popped.

"Yes sir, I'm quitting. That's what I come to tell you. Ain't cut out to be no cattleman. Maybe I'll dust off my Bible and do some preaching again. "

Luther had thought he would want to do cartwheels if he'd ever heard these words. No more pushing people off from visiting his ranch on Mondays for fear they'd see this wannabee cowboy, who would surely announce he was Luther's hired hand. But he couldn't take his eyes off the little man, huddled against the door like a child, scared of his father's hand. And what came out of Luther's mouth both surprised and embarrassed him. "What you believe about salvation?" Luther's voice was quiet, just up from a whisper.

Thrasher put his arms under his knees and brought them up in the air. His boots were no longer shiny. "Once saved, always saved. At least I hope so." He kept his head towards the window. His words left a fog on the glass. Luther watched it disappear the way his own breath had disappeared when he was a boy and would breathe on that one window in their tenant house. After Emmanuel left, Luther was scared the boogey man would come get him in the nighttime, and no one from the outside would be able to see in, only the other family, and they were as helpless as his. The day he learned to spell "help" in school, he'd come home and breathed on the window and written that word. Then he watched it disappear.

"But how do you know if you're been saved *once?*" Luther asked. "What if you get that part wrong?"

"A person knows his heart. If it's clean or filthy."

"Then or now?"

"Both."

"*Then,*" Luther said, "I was a just kid."

"Reckon you're saved."

Reckon you're saved. Reckon you're saved. Reckon you're saved. And this came from a preacher. Luther wanted to make a fist and slap it against the man's upper arm like men do, but he might knock him out of the truck. He was more delicate than Mildred.

But he'd also said "now." *Wasn't his heart getting a little cleaner now?* Having a preacher around would help keep it that way.

"You can't quit," Luther told him.

"Yes sir, I'm quitting." The man's knees shook. His cowboy hat bobbed up and down.

"No, sir. Ain't going to let you. You're really coming along as a cattleman, and we've got big doings today, got a weaning." Luther knew his voice was getting loud but not in that mad way.

Thrasher turned his head Luther's way. "You mean that?"

Luther swallowed. "Yes, I do." He'd told a lie and that was wrong, but he did it to try to make the man feel better. Luther turned his head away. He wanted to wipe his coat sleeve across his eyes, but doing so would signal that he needed to wipe his eyes.

He brought up his arm and wiped.

"You mean doggies," Thrasher said. "You mean we've got to wean them doggies today."

"That's right, doggies," Luther told him and cleared his throat. Calling cows that name wasn't a lie.

He looked back at the man. He had restored his hat to his head. It sunk low over his ears, making the vaulted top seem higher, a kind of dome, but not as round as a ladybug with its protective shell. Or was it a shield that God had given them to protect? After all, they were little.

. . . . .

LC hid in the bushes along the back of the school. It couldn't have worked out better for his father to bring him that day. If he'd ridden the school bus, it would have been harder for him to hide.

When all got quiet inside the building, LC bent low and ran across the yard. He was headed to earn some money to give to Emerson Bridge, and LC needed a family who did not know his father. He'd heard him speak of an elderly couple who lived near Drake's Store, people his father called Catholics, a kind of church his father didn't believe in. Their last name was Spinharney.

LC knocked on their back door. A woman answered. "Hello, ma'am. I'm needing to earn some Christmas money and was wondering if y'all've got anything I can do?"

The woman wiped her hands on her apron. "You're not in school today?"

"Need to earn some money."

A gunshot sounded behind him.

"My husband's killing a hog today. He's got some of the colored helping him, but you might go ask him if there's anything you can do."

LC grabbed on the railing beside him and called up in his mind Emerson Bridge's shoes.

He headed to the barn, where he saw the animal being hoisted by ropes tied to its back legs. Blood ran from an open slit in its throat and puddled onto the dirt below.

LC wretched.

He collected himself and asked for work. His first job was to keep enough wood beneath the big black pot to keep the water boiling. And, after the hog bled out and was placed in a large wooden barrel, his job shifted to delivering buckets of the scalding water for the men to pour over the animal to loosen its hair.

The work took until early afternoon. Mr. Spinharney gave him a silver dollar. LC wondered how much a pair of boy's shoes would cost. He held the coin in the flat of his hand and told the man, "Golly, this is a lot. I sure thank you, sir."

"What you give is what you get. And you gave a lot today, son."

LC's father killed hogs when the weather got cold, too. He'd not done it yet this season. Or rather, Uncle hadn't. Uncle always used his father's pearl-handled .32 pistol. It always looked little in Uncle's hands. LC was surprised that his father had a gun that small. But even little guns can kill.

LC took himself to the man's pond and walked out in the cold waters to its deepest point, almost shoulder high. And then he began to move his hands over his body, full of blood and scalded hairs.

He washed himself clean.

· · · · ·

Mildred pulled into the Durham Shopping Center on North Main and parked in front of Martin's Children's Shop. Straight ahead, in the big glass window, Sarah saw boy's shoes displayed.

She removed her sunglasses.

There were oxfords and work boots and fancy cowboy boots. She curled her toes in her new shoes. She had room to, unlike her boy, who had outgrown his brogans last spring. She'd taken a knife and cut through the leather to allow his toes for more room. He was the one who needed new shoes. She took her feet from her new ones.

"Next stop Richbourg's," Mildred said and opened her automobile door.

Sarah knew she looked a sight with her eyes puffy and red. "What if I just stay here?"

"No, ma'am." Mildred stepped out.

Sarah couldn't disappoint. She put her shoes back on and set her hat on top of her kerchief and stepped out into the air, full of the smell of bread from Merita Bakery across the road. Her stomach made a rumbling sound.

Mildred got a buggy and pushed it to the back of the store, to the meat counter. "Why, they've taken Charles's picture down and replaced it with the new winner." She pointed to a framed photograph hanging on the wall beside a swinging door. It was a boy with a big grin and pale skin.

The door swung open, and a man stepped through, wearing a white full-body apron, covered with splashes of bright red. Some of the red looked to be wet. It was blood. "Mrs. Dobbins," he said and wiped his hands down the front.

"Why, Mr. Bowen, I was just telling Mrs. Creamer here that I see Charles's picture has been replaced."

"The Glenn boy, yes. We're late getting it up. We got used to having Charles back here."

Sarah's eyes moved to the left of the photograph, to some words etched on a shiny brass plaque as large as a mirror a rich woman could hang in her hallway. "Proud to say Home of the Grand Champion." The smell of meat and refrigeration went up her nose. She felt a rush of blood shoot to her head.

"I hope Big LC never comes in here," Mildred said. She was giggling, as was the man.

But Sarah was not. She was reading the individual plates, lined up in vertical rows beneath the words. The first one said Edwin McClain, 1941. The next nine listed L. Charles Dobbins, Jr., with the corresponding years 1942 to 1950. The final name was Neal Glenn, 1951. The space beneath it sat empty and ready for the next boy's name.

Sarah's heart was racing now. Surely they weren't meaning they butchered the grand champion and brought him here for sale? Surely this is not how he was honored for being the top cow.

"Sarah, dear, what kind of meat would you like?" Mildred asked.

Sarah lowered the netting over her eyes.

"We'll get Mr. Bowen to cut it up and wrap it special for you."

Sarah looked through the pattern of tiny squares, outlined in thin black lines. It felt like a screen. She wanted to be behind a screen. "You've done too much already." She took a step back.

"Why, fiddle dee dee. How about a nice rump roast for Sunday dinner and two nice steaks and some hamburger for a good meatloaf? A fryer, too. How does that sound?"

Emerson Bridge hadn't had meat like that since he was five years old. She pictured his ribs. She pictured him with a plate full of meat. His little belly would be full.

Sarah swallowed. She began to nod.

The man went back through the door.

Surely, "home" meant Anderson as in Anderson was the home of the grand champion. Or "home" as in mothers of the grand champion boys do their grocery shopping here. Mildred did.

When the man returned with the meat, Sarah asked him, "Excuse me, sir, but do the mamas of the other boys that won, that McClain boy and the Glenn, do their mamas trade in here, too?"

"From time to time, yes ma'am."

There it was, her answer. She let out a deep breath. It made no sense to kill the grand champion. He was the hero. That would be like killing Scarlett O'Hara, because she was the top actress in that movie. Sarah lifted her netting.

The man placed four packages, all wrapped in white butcher paper, in the buggy. Stamped across each one were words in purple that told the type of meat. The cost was written with a black grease pencil. Sarah added them up. Two dollars and thirty-two cents. That was almost a full dress.

Outside in the automobile, Sarah kicked out her feet in the floorboard and told herself her boy wouldn't have new shoes just yet, but he would have meat. She balled up her fist and put her finger on her first knuckle and called that December, which would be the next month, and then began counting forward, dipping down for January and back up for February and then down again for March. That was four months away. The day he won, she'd bring him here and buy him a pair of every kind of shoes in the window in front of her.

"Shoes tell a person," Mildred told her, her voice flat now.

Sarah realized she'd not smelled peppermints all morning.

"The day I met Big LC, he was wearing a fine suit, but his shoes were covered in so much dust, you could write your name in it. I knew he was trying to be a rich man, and I felt sorry for him. All of my other beaus had been the same, perfect and perfectly boring. Thought I'd take him on as a project, teach him how to be. I started with his shoes, took him to my daddy's shoeshine man at the hotel and got his shoes shined so spiffy, I tried to see myself in them."

Sarah waited for more, but nothing else came. "Well, did you? Did you see yourself?"

"I was blurred."

Sarah couldn't remember Harold's shoes the day she met him. "What about love? Your husband love you?"

Mildred stayed quiet but then said, "Let's put our sunglasses back on. We're movie stars, remember."

They returned them to their faces and headed back down Whitehall. Sarah was hoping that Mildred didn't answer her question because Big LC loved her so much, Mildred didn't want to make Sarah feel bad for having a husband who cheated.

At the grain elevator, Mildred pulled off the road. Sarah was thinking she must be ready to talk, but Mildred pulled a shiny, almost flat, container from her pocketbook and unscrewed the top. She had a drink, a long one. "I feel a sore throat coming on," she said and held it out for Sarah, who shook her head. It smelled like Retonga. "Let's run by the house and get Big LC's Kodak, so we can have this day forever." She popped a peppermint in her mouth.

Mildred put the automobile back in gear, but it did not move. "I told you a story, Sarah. I don't have a sore throat."

Sarah raised the netting all the way. She reached for Mildred's hand.

The women squeezed. Their skin against each other was just skin, equal skin.

Mildred pulled back onto the road.

She drove to her house and ran inside for the camera.

Sarah removed her sunglasses and found herself squinting in the bright sunshine. She heard sounds, loud ones like cries, in the direction of the barn. She loosened her kerchief knot beneath her chin so she could hear. They were from cows, lots of them.

When Mildred returned, Sarah asked her, "Is something wrong with the cows?"

"Oh, that's the mamas and their babies," Mildred said as she backed out the driveway. Today's what they call weaning day when they separate them."

Sarah felt her stomach turn over.

"I've heard it so many times over the years, I don't hear it anymore. I did way back. Odd how you get used to it."

Sarah didn't understand how a person could get used to that.

"Big LC says it's the natural order, because the mamas already are pregnant and need the milk they are making for their new babies."

The sack of meat in Sarah's lap felt heavy and cold. Chills lined her body. In all that sunlight, she was cold.

She put her sunglasses back on.

At home, Mildred had Sarah lean up against the automobile. "Do it like a movie star, like you are without a care in the world." But Sarah didn't know what that position would be like. So she just leaned straight back. Mildred snapped her picture.

Then Sarah took the camera and Mildred leaned. She held her body straight from her waist down but her upper body at a slant.

Mildred left the driveway. She honked her horn most of the way out.

Sarah waved to her in her new shoes, the sack of meat in the crook of her right arm. Dust coated her new shoes. They were already dirty.

She looked for Lucky. He was on the ground.

A note was stuck in the screened door. It was from Duke Power. "Disconnected until payment received" was printed across the top. She still had a nickel's worth of kerosene.

Her boy needed food. Tonight he would have a feast.

Sarah brought the meat inside and fired up the woodstove. She had no ice for the ice box. She would need to cook it all. She would wear her new shoes and cook it all.

· · · · ·

Sarah filled her boy's plate with beef roast and a steak and loose hamburger meat, along with a leg and breast from the fryer.

When he sat down to eat, she told him, "Cooked you a plate of meat. You hungry for meat?"

He shoved the plate aside and returned to the outside.

Her boy wasn't hungry. This is what she told herself.

She was still wearing her new shoes. She wanted to put her old ones back on, but that no longer was an option.

Sarah shoved her plate aside, too.

From the fence, the mother cow watched her young, his body prone to the ground. He had gathered on his feet that day, but had returned to the earth. She listened now as his hooves scraped the dirt, his rhythm familiar, one she had known at his birth, when, in time, she had gained what she needed to set herself high again and return to him.

As darkness fell, he set himself high again and made his way to her, his head tall enough now to rise above the top wire. She licked his face and moved her mouth down his body, while inside the mother cow, her new young lay, now the size of a cat and halfway through its journey towards home.

The gentle wind and her little one were no longer there, but they had been. The mother cow had grown accustomed to them, especially to the gentle wind, who often brought handfuls of grass and slices of pears.

I started to go hide from you, Mama Red. Not come out here no more and talk to you, because my mind was trying to go down some real bad tracks. My boy, too. But he just come running in the house saying Lucky was on his feet, and that's cause for me to come hug your neck and his.

Can I tell you I'm feeling like I might be in over my head a little bit with you and him. I guess you can tell I don't know nothing about your kind. But I want to. I brought you a slice of a pear. I like feeling your lips against the palm of my hand. Kind of tickles.

I appreciate you listening to me talk. Did I tell you I have a new friend, Mildred? She lives at that place where you used to. She made me remember that I wasn't always that bad word I told you my mama called me. Slittail. There was a time when I was the exact opposite. There was a time when I was some kind of woman, I was, Mama Red. It started the day my first friend, Mattie, walked into my cold chicken bone of a life. That was April 9th, 19 and 38. That could have been the eighth day of creation and written up in my mama's Bible. It'd say, "And God created Sarah and Mattie's friendship. And saw that it was good." If ever there was a time when Jesus might have give me the time of day, it was then, because any kind of good I had in me, Sister Mattie brought it out like dried beans soaked good in water and made all plump, so they'd be fit to eat.

After I had that baby girl and that doctor took her away, I took to the bed. But, after about a month of that, Harold brought this woman into our room and said, "Sarah, this here is Mattie. She's our new neighbor from across the yard. She's a woman. Maybe she can help you."

He left the room, and the space opened up between me and her. She was standing at the foot of the bed. She was a scrawny little something. I saw right quick I made two of her. "I'm fat," I told her.

"I'm skinny," she said.

I saw her dimples, how they were sunk deep into her cheeks, and I knew there was something she was happy about. "You got you any children?" I asked.

She shook her head. She had a little nose so delicate you'd think it would break. "Me and Billy Udean ain't been lucky like that yet," she said.

I told her about Little Claudia and that I couldn't never have no more.

She stepped up towards me, and through the air come her hand like it had a purpose to it. "What about if I wash your hair?" she asked me.

"It's filthy," I told her. I was embarrassed of it. It was plumb soaked through in grease.

But her hand was still held out. For me. I took mine from under the covers and grabbed onto it.

I was a little weak, but I got myself to the kitchen, to the sink, and she drew water and washed my hair. When she finished, I made me a bun.

She told me she wished she knew how to do that. She said, "Billy Udean hates that my hair's all stringy."

I told her I'd teach her, and that's what I set about to do. Harold come in, and Mattie froze up like she was scared. But I reckon he saw that we were doing female business and went on back outside. Mattie said to me, "You ain't scared to carry on like this in front of him?"

I told her, "He can't stop me from having a friend." And when I said that word, "friend," I got goosebumps go all over me.

Her dimples sunk in deep.

I didn't want no secrets between us, so I told her, "I ain't saved. Tomorrow's Sunday, and I don't go to church."

I watched her to see if she'd leave me cold, but she didn't do that. She stayed right there and said, "I don't either. Billy Udean likes to fish on Sunday."

We went to laughing. Mama Red, we did. "Our giggle boxes are turned plumb over," she said to me. And they were.

That was the beginning of us, me and Mattie. That right there was.

I think back on our beginning, mine and yours, and I want you to know I wouldn't do nothing on purpose to hurt you. Do you know that? My bones got rattled some today, but I'm thinking now I might have been borrowing trouble. I don't want to borrow no trouble.

NOVEMBER 24–26, 1951

This was a momentous day, Luther was thinking at breakfast that Saturday. "Hammer-mill time. Just me and you, boy. Gave Uncle the day off."

Mildred's hand came his way. "He's got a cold, Big LC. Maybe he needs to stay in and rest."

On the tip of Luther's tongue were words that reflected the old Luther, words like, "Was I talking to you?" but he did not let them unfurl. He took a deep breath and in a voice that he hoped was pleasant said, "Us Dobbins men have Dobbins work to do."

This was day six of living as a good man. He knew he still had some kinks to work out, so he wasn't too alarmed that he'd felt some anger towards Mildred just then. The key was not acting on it. A lot could be accomplished in six days. God had created the world in that length of time.

He felt the morning's sausage high in his chest. All night he'd stayed awake going over in his mind how to operate the hammer mill, something he'd never done before. He wanted to prove to LC that he could do it by himself. Uncle had already connected the belt to the tractor drum, and all Luther had to do that morning was start the tractor and engage the gear that ran the belt that made the knives in the hammer mill begin moving. It would be easy.

He slid his chair back from the table and slapped his boy on his shoulder. "Let's go," he said and headed outside and marveled at the sky of that perfect shade of crystal blue

But his boy did not follow him. That was even better, he was thinking. It would give Luther time to get the tractor started. He'd only done it once before, and that was the day he'd bought it in 1946. It was a hand starter, a John Deere H. He wished now that it had an electric starter like the new tractors of the day. Fleet McClain and Joseph Allgood had electric starters.

He stood between the tractor's left big wheel and the flywheel, a solid circle of metal about the size of the steering wheel. Then he reached over, moved the throttle and pulled out the choke, placing his hands on the flywheel and finding the two grooves that Uncle had said. His hands were sweating, but he tried to get a good grip and give it all the muscle he had.

It moved some but did not crank.

The back screen door slammed. There came his boy.

He gripped the flywheel tighter and hollered, "A grand champion animal requires grand champion actions, boy." He closed his eyes and pictured Uncle's hands. He had turned the wheel the wrong way.

His boy did not come to stand beside him but upfront on the other side of the tractor, near the hammer mill. He was sure his boy was watching. Luther leaned his full body to the right and turned the wheel, the engine making a slight sparking sound. He wiped his hands down his pant legs and grabbed on again, heaving the biggest turn he could muster. This time it cranked, sending forth that blessed sputtering sound.

But then it began to fade.

"Push the choke back in, Dad!" his boy called out.

Luther pushed it in. The sputtering became stronger until it kicked in full and settled into a steady stream, Luther now standing on his tiptoes and looking over the tractor at his boy. He wanted to hear words like, *Good job, Dad,* but his boy said nothing. LC wasn't even looking at him. He was kicking dead corn cobs with his feet.

Maybe he was waiting for Luther to engage the belt. Luther climbed into the tractor seat, placed his foot on the clutch, and slipped the gear to the side. The belt began turning. He could hear the wheel of knives spinning inside the hammer mill, all ready to grind. He would stay in the seat until his boy looked his way. Luther waved his hand to get his attention, but LC had already resumed his place at the end of the feed table, ready to shovel in the ears of corn. Luther had not told LC where to stand, but that's exactly where he wanted him. Luther wondered if the billy shovel would be too heavy for the boy. It was about as tall as LC in length and almost twice as wide at its scooping end.

Luther dismounted and took his position, securing a burlap sack to the downspout of the sacker funnel. It was only a matter of twisting a lever. He hollered, "Shove them in, boy!!"

LC, no more than ten feet away, scooped up some cobs and brought the shovel's wide mouth into the air, his arms wobbling some, but he managed to empty the corn onto the table, a man's arm's length and running on a slope so the corn could easily fall into the opening that fed to the knives.

"There you go," Luther called out as loud as he could, but his boy had his back turned, scooping up another load. LC was a hard worker.

The sound of the machine grinding made Luther clench his fists with joy and ram them into the air, and when the ground corn begin falling into the sack, he shook his head at the magic of it all. Yellow chaff now occupied the space between Luther and LC, their clothes covered, as well as their skin, and Luther felt a communion with his younger blood that bonded them beyond anything Luther had ever known with his first namesake. He took his hands from the bag and wanted to put them on his boy, touch his yellow shoulders and leave his fingerprints on him. But his sack was nearing filling, and Luther held his hand up to signal his boy to stop. He disconnected the sack and set it against the wall of the shed. Uncle would be proud. Luther had left about eight inches, enough room to bunch the burlap and tie it with twine.

A big racket sounded behind him like the machine was tearing up. The scoop end of the shovel was sticking out of the hammer mill, which was jumping, the shovel jerking as if in a fit.

"Turn it off!" Luther yelled. The shovel must have been too much for his boy and gotten away from him.

But his boy did not move. He stood at the end of the table with his arms folded and looking at Luther with eyes unwavering.

His boy had thrown in the shovel on purpose. "I said by God, turn it off!"

Still, his boy did not move.

Luther ran to the tractor and threw the gear in neutral, the machine grinding to a stop, the shovel bouncing, then falling off the side of the table as if it was a tongue, long tired and dry.

"What's the matter with you?" Luther said.

His boy shrugged his shoulders.

Luther grabbed him there and shook him hard. "What'd you do it for? Huh?"

"Felt like it," his boy said. His face showed no expression.

Luther slapped him and then balled up his fist and let it hover just out from his boy's cheek. "I feel like beating you to a bloody piece of nothing." Luther's hand was shaking.

"Do it, then," LC said.

He hit his boy's face. He hit him hard and knocked him into the pile of corn. "Charles never would have pulled such a baby stunt."

His boy got on his feet. "What?" he hollered. "You don't like what you made? Somebody just like *you?*"

"Somebody like *me* wants to win. And how do you expect to do that with the hammer mill tore up?" Luther slid his boot up a couple of cobs and kicked them hard his boy's way.

"I don't want to win!" his boy yelled and came at Luther with his fists clenched.

Luther caught them and held them stiff in the air. "Is that all you got?" He shook his boy's arms. "You want to be a little baby and pitch a fit, is that it? Well, let me treat you like one then." He held his boy's wrists with one hand and spanked him with his other, as LC tried to twist away. "And I want you to know that your do-gooder self didn't get away with what you pulled the other night, either. I might have been born at night, but not last night. If you want to call yourself sneaking out, try to sneak out of a one-room nigger shack, where you and your mama and pop all sleep on the floor on boards that are so rough, they put splinters in your ass. And it gets so hot in the summertime, you keep a coat of sweat on your body the white folks call nigger shine. I kept a coat of nigger shine on me, boy. Did you hear that? I lived like a goddamned nigger. A white boy, living in a goddamned tenant house like I was a goddamned nigger." Luther's hand had become hot. He stopped and squeezed LC's shoulders. "You got it easy, boy."

He released LC and walked away. "No, you ain't me," Luther told him. "You ain't nothing like me."

LC came after him, screaming, "I don't want to be like you!" and shoved Luther towards the tractor, but Luther made himself stiff. He barely budged.

Luther pushed him into the corn cobs. "You go get you an ax," he said, his entire body quivering. "Or for all I care, my by God pearl-handle. And you can either shoot up or chop up what you're laying in, into pieces no bigger than a tip end of a by God bullet." Luther gathered saliva in his mouth, more than was possible, and aimed it at his boy. It hit his forehead.

He turned from his boy, pulled a cigar from his pocket, and lit it. *I'm done, way past done, with trying to be saved. Bring on the damned fires of hell.*

· · · · ·

"How bad is it?" Luther asked Uncle, who was leaned under the hood of the hammer mill, examining the circle of knives.

"Afraid two or three are bent pretty bad, Mr. LC."

Luther kicked his foot in the dirt.

"Ike Thrasher reporting for Monday morning hired hand duty, Mr. Boss Man." He was at Luther's back. Luther made no effort to turn around.

"What seems to be the problem here?" Thrasher asked in that cheery voice of his.

"You're fired," Luther told him and kept his back to him. It wasn't that Luther was afraid to tell him, he just didn't want to have to lay eyes on him ever again. He was of no use to Luther. The man had no respect with the Creamers.

"Pardon me?"

Luther could feel his scalp sweating beneath his hat. "I said you're by God fired. Shoo fly. Don't you ever prance back over here to or at the Dobbins ranch again."

"May I ask why?"

"Because you get on my nerves. You get on my goddamned nerves."

· · · · ·

Ike Thrasher opened the door to his chifforobe. His Rider shirt and jeans outfits, six of them, hung pressed and ready. He was wearing a set, which would make seven and give him one for every day of the week. He removed the first set and folded the two pieces and laid them on his bed. He thought about giving them to Emerson Bridge to keep until he reached Ike's size, but by then the boy would no longer be playing dress up. He was a smart boy. He would have moved on to adult wear.

Ike's hands were shaking. He needed a cigarette. He opened the drawer in his nightstand and removed one from the pack of Lucky Strikes. He put it in his mouth and took the small box of matches, tucked under the cellophane, struck one against the box's rough edge, and brought its fire to the cigarette's end, drawing inside heat, unparalleled heat. Ike had never smoked until he became a preacher. But no one in his congregation ever saw him do it. He only smoked in the confines of his bedroom. It wasn't that he thought smoking was a sin, not smoking by itself. It was the pleasure the Lucky gave him when he took one between his parted lips.

He finished folding the rest of the outfits and saw, at the end of the rod, what he'd always meant to keep in the shadows, his one and only suit. It was dark navy with stripes of gray so slight, they could be missed. This is the suit he wore on the last Sunday he preached. He'd given all of his others away.

He lifted it now and brought it into a ray of sunshine as wide as his old preaching Bible. He laid it on the bed and unbuttoned the coat, folding back both sides. He was heavier then, easily claiming the space high in the pulpit, where he delivered the word. He was good at it, too. At least one person came to salvation or to recommitment every Sunday. Not every preacher could claim that. In fact, he knew some to be jealous.

He mattered to those people.

Ike let himself have that thought. He wanted to matter again.

He put his arm in his right sleeve. The smell of his former cologne, Old Spice, filled his nostrils. He never liked the smell. He only wore it because that was the fragrance that preachers wear. He was a liar back then, and he wore that fragrance and that suit, and he preached the word.

He removed his arm. He would not be a liar again. Like Mr. Dobbins. Mr. Dobbins was a liar, too.

Ike returned to his truck and drove back to see Luther Dobbins, found his former boss and Emmanuel still bent over the hammer mill. He marched up to the machine. "You're a liar, Mr. Dobbins," he said. "And our heavenly Father doesn't like liars."

The big cattleman looked at him this time. "Thought I told you not to never step foot on the Dobbins ranch again."

Ike took a deep breath. "Should have quit last week. Should never have let you talk me into staying. You weren't on the level with me when you said I was a good cattleman. I'm not about to take the Lord's name in vain like you did, but I have strong feelings, too, about you and about what you've done."

Mr. Dobbins drew back a fist, but Ike held up two fingers and kept going. "You've told me wrong twice, sir. The first was about that full feed and the second was to get that steer to lay down. The boy went along on the first one, and that's why our steer got in the fix he did. But, thank the good Lord, the boy had enough sense not to listen to me twice."

Mr. Dobbins shook his fist in Ike's face. "I ought to beat you for saying that goddammed nonsense and on my land, too."

Ike worked to gather spit in his mouth. It wasn't much, but it landed on his former boss man's shadow, tiny at that early hour of the day.

"Your hired man there, Emmanuel, he's the one that runs the show around here. He deserves better than you. But I reckon because of the color of his skin, he's stuck here. With you. Bless him. There'll be jewels in his crown." Ike tipped his hat. "Good day. I'll see you in March. May the best steer win."

He returned to his truck and drove straight to the Creamers. Telling Luther Dobbins the truth made him want to keep going with it.

When he got to their house, he knocked on the door. But Mrs. Creamers did not answer. Her automobile was parked in the yard. She must be sewing. He had barged in her house before, but he would not do it again.

He walked around to her bedroom window and saw her sitting before her machine, her body bent towards it like he used to bend towards his pulpit. He did not want to scare her, so he waited until she stopped pedaling and then gently tapped on the window.

She looked his way and showed him not scared eyes, but tired ones. She rose from her chair and lifted the window. "Mr. Thrasher," she said.

"I'm afraid we're in a heap of trouble, Mrs. Creamer. I don't mean to worry you, but—"

"So, it's true?" She put her hands on the window sill, as if bracing herself. "That I've been fired? How did you know?"

She lifted her hands and crossed them on her heart.

"This is real hard to say, but that two dollars a week Mr. Dobbins gave me is going to be missed in my pocketbook. I'm about to run through all my money, and I know it costs a whole lot to feed that steer. I never meant to let y'all down. I'm sorry."

"That's what you found out?" she said. "That you ain't working there no more?"

He nodded. The scarf around his neck felt tight.

He had expected her to cry, because girls are free to do that, but all she did was look beyond him, off towards the lot where the cows were.

He put his hands up to loosen the scarf, but, once he did, he removed it altogether. "We both know I ain't no cattleman."

She brought her eyes back to him. "You're very much of one."

He felt his face go hot.

He waited for her to laugh, to show him that what she'd said was a joke. But she did not. She kept the same look on her face, her eyes as steady as they come, and from him spilled words only known to himself and God. "I've never told you why I wanted to win with the steer so bad, Mrs. Creamer. It's so I can prove I'm a man, a real one, and be able to step on my daddy's land over there. And so he'll—" He looked across the road. "So he'll love me."

"But you're a man *now*," she said.

"No ma'am, not enough of one." He shook his head.

Under her eyes, he saw bags, deep ones, her skin discolored like a bruise. "When was the last time you had a good night's sleep?"

"Why, Mr. Thrasher, I get a good one every night. I'm alive. My boy's alive." She returned her hands to the window sill. "And so is Mama Red. And Lucky."

For the first time, Ike could see that she had the makings to be pretty. If she had been born into an easy life, into money or privilege, she might even be considered striking with her high cheek bones that could be set off by just the right shade and amount of rouge. "You're a good mama, Mrs. Creamer. All boys should be so lucky."

She took her eyes away and stepped from the window. "Better get back to that dress."

162

"No, come back," he said, the words slipping easily from his mouth. His face flared red. He could feel the heat of it.

She had returned to the window, even leaned in some. "I'll pay you back, Mr. Thrasher, every red cent I owe you."

He wanted to touch her arm, but there was a screen between them. And she was wearing a brown sweater over her dress. He realized he was letting in cold air. Still, he raised his hand and held his fingertips against the screen. He'd never before had feelings for a woman. He'd been on a few dates early on, but none had panned out, so he'd let that part of his life go. But this woman, her gracious self, and her heart, the way she loved her boy, all of this stirred in Ike Thrasher possibility.

She looked behind her. "I believe somebody's knocking on my door. Would you excuse me, please?"

"Let me go around there and see," he said and started for the side porch but then froze in his steps. What if it was a burglar? He tied his scarf back around his neck and began slinking his body outside the shrubbery. A truck was parked behind his, and just out from the porch steps stood a man that looked familiar. Mrs. Creamer had the screened door open. It was the younger Allgood from the FCX. Mrs. Creamer had her head down.

Ike extended his hand towards the man. "What's the reason for this call, Mr. Allgood?"

The man pushed his eyeglasses up his nose. "I was just saying I'm afraid we can't extend credit any longer."

Ike tensed his right butt cheek, where his billfold was.

Mr. Allgood turned his head towards the barn. "I've come to strike a deal with you, Mrs. Creamer. I happen to know that you do have that splotchy-face mama cow."

Mrs. Creamer's body looked like she'd been slapped, but she regained herself and put an expression of such certainty on her face that Ike leaned towards her. "Yes sir, we do," she said. "And I didn't mean to lie to you back then, but that's *my* mama cow." Her voice had muscle.

"Tell you what," the man said. "You give her to me, and I'll forgive your debt, all sixty-eight dollars and thirty-two cents of it. Plus, I'll supply all the mixed grain and anything else your boy's steer can eat until the show. We got a deal?"

Mrs. Creamer stepped towards him. "No sir, we ain't got no deal."

"Thought you wanted to win, ma'am." He pushed his glasses up the bridge of his nose. "Can't do it without feed. And lots of it. It's all free choice at this point, which means you give him all he can eat. With the grain at $2.50 a bag, and he'll probably eat four to five bags a week, and then the molasses to mix in to make it sweet, along with linseed meal for protein and bales of hay, we're talking $80, $90, upwards of $100 a month. And you've got close to four months to go."

"I'll tell you this, Jeremiah Allgood, and I'll tell it to you strong. This woman named Sarah Creamer will scrub every woman's floor out here in the country before I'll let you take my Mama Red."

"And I'll, I'll," Ike began, trying to find equivalent words. "I'll protect the floors of this here woman." Both Mrs. Creamer and Mr. Allgood looked at Ike, who swallowed hard. He didn't know what his words meant, but he did know he wanted to keep going. "And furthermore than that, I'm going to make sure Mrs. Creamer here gets to keep her Mama Red."

"She wouldn't be that far away," the man said, "just down the side road by New Prospect, the first farm on the right after you go around the curve and climb the hill, then start back down towards the creek."

Ike pulled out his billfold. He had only two one-dollar bills, but he handed them both to Mr. Allgood and told him, "I'll go to the bank and come by later today with all I got to my name, $50.02. You can have it all."

"But, Mr. Thrasher," Mrs. Creamer said.

"He can have it all," Ike said in a voice that had grown stronger.

Mr. Allgood cleared his throat. "Keep your two dollars, but y'all know I can't sell you no more feed until you catch your total bill up."

"We'll find us a way," Ike called out as Mr. Allgood made his way to his truck.

"Yes sir, we will," Mrs. Creamer said.

Ike tried not to think about having a zero balance in his account. Maybe he could take out a loan.

Mrs. Creamer turned towards him. "Mr. Thrasher, you said you wasn't no cattleman, but I'm here to tell you that you are. You're every bit of one."

Ike could feel himself blushing. Beneath his shirt, he flexed his muscles.

The temperature that day was fifty-two degrees, a cow's ideal. The mother cow and her young stood together near the fence, their mouths to the earth, the grass soon to go dormant.

You staying here, Mama Red, I'm here to declare that. When you come in my life back in the spring, you gave me reason to keep on going. Like I was with Mattie, when she come in my life. That morning after that Saturday when I met her, I had a reason to get up out of the bed, went to stand at my kitchen sink, and looked over at her house. That one right over there behind you. I didn't see her that morning, but I saw a man I took to be Billy Udean. He was skinny as a stick and had quick moves. He looked to be putting something in the back of a truck that was parked out front.

Harold was sitting at the eating table. I told him, "Mattie says her husband goes fishing on Sundays. Why don't you go with him? Think he's getting ready to go now."

Harold didn't say nothing. I'd never known him to fish.

Me and Harold hadn't had any relations since I'd took to the bed. But I knew that he liked it, so I went over to him and run my hands down his chest and said, "I like men that fish."

I watched him go across. I watched them leave.

As soon as they were out of the driveway good, I went over to Mattie's, but it took me a while to get her to the door. And when I did, she wouldn't let me in, just stayed on the other side of it and told me she looked a sight. But finally she showed herself to me. Her mouth was all swole up. "Billy Udean didn't like my new hair," she said. It wasn't up in a bun no more. "He's jealous of you, Sarah."

When Harold and Billy Udean come home from fishing, Harold had him a string of four pretty good-sized catfish. I asked him how many Billy Udean got. He said six but that he threw all his up on the bank so they could die. Said his wife wasn't no cook, said he was over there starving.

I got me an idea. I told Harold to go over there and ask them to come eat supper and tell Billy Udean how good a cook I was. "Tell him I'm handy."

It worked. Billy Udean went for it. I got busy cleaning fish, fried them up good and crispy with some French fried potatoes. Billy Udean brought several of his Pabst Blue Ribbon beers he liked. Harold drank my sweet tea.

I got another idea when we were sitting there. I said, "Boy, some coleslaw would be good with this fish." Then I reached over and felt Harold's arm and told him, "Maybe a big, strong man could plow up that little spot between our houses out there, and we could have us a nice garden, plant some cabbage and potatoes and green beans and such." Harold had a big grin on his face.

Mattie picked up on it and said, "Billy Udean could plow it up himself with a good shovel or a sharp hoe."

We got us a garden. That next Saturday, Harold and Billy Udean were out there with a mule they'd borrowed from a Mr. Brown down the road. Me and Mattie both watched from our yards. We'd decided not to give Billy Udean anything he could fuss about. But as the morning wore on, we started getting braver and coming on in towards each other. Before you knew it, we were standing together, right there in the dirt, fresh plowed.

The men took that mule back, and me and her took our shoes off and grabbed hands and ran through what our men folks had broken for us. We giggled and ran like schoolgirls, Mama Red, with not a care in the world. We went to skipping, holding hands, and swinging our arms. I could have swore I was a little girl again, but this time I wasn't sitting off by my lonesome at recess, I had me a friend, and we played.

I asked her if she had any sisters. She didn't. I told her, "Wonder if we could be?"

"Sister Sarah," she said and grinned.

"Sister Mattie, Sister Mattie," I said like I was singing.

Sisters for life, we were. I knew it in my bones.

Like me and you, Mama Red. In my bones. For life.

Mr. Merritt wrote the words to the 4-H Pledge in a large hand across the blackboard. He had never done that before. LC felt a rush shoot up his body.

"In case any of you boys don't know it by heart," he said and asked them all to stand.

LC was sitting beside Emerson Bridge. LC whispered to him, "Put your hand over your heart," and then brought his own up, a couple of his fingers his mother had bandaged in white gauze. The continued use of his father's ax to chop the corn to his father's liking kept blisters on him.

"I pledge My Head to clearer thinking, My Heart to greater loyalty," LC read along with the other boys, but mostly kept his eyes on Emerson Bridge. "My Hands to larger service, My Health to better living, for my club, my community, my country and my world."

Neal Glenn hollered, "Hey, Little Dob, trying to be a boxer with your hands all taped up?"

LC balled his fist up as much as he could and shook it at the boy.

"We're not going to have this, boys," Mr. Merritt said. "Especially not today."

There it was. *The paper to sign.* LC's heart began to race.

Emerson Bridge sat down and folded his hands on top of his desk. He had no idea what was coming, but LC had to stop it. He was thinking he should pull him out to the hallway and give him the Christmas present LC carried in his pants pocket.

"I wanted to remind y'all of the importance of 4-H before I pass out what I'm about to," Mr. Merritt said and picked up a stack of papers. "What y'all are doing with your steers is serious business."

LC leaned towards Emerson Bridge and whispered, "I need you to go out in the hall with me right quick."

But Emerson Bridge whispered back, "I hope we don't have to spend more money."

"Because, let's be honest," the county agent said, "what you're doing is raising your steer to be somebody's next meal."

LC saw his friend's eyes open wide, then close down hard. LC tried to think of a way to make something more of the word "meal" like he had done for "deep freeze."

But he came up empty.

LC jumped to his feet. "Mr. Merritt!" All eyes turned towards him, but he didn't know what his next words would be. "I was wondering, since Christmas is coming up, if we can go ahead and get out so we can . . . can . . . go to town to . . . do our trading?"

Laughter filled the room.

"Boys!" Mr. Merritt said and slapped the papers against his hand.

"With your mommy?" the Prater boy yelled.

LC shook his fist again, but Mr. Merritt came to stand beside him. The papers now were within reach. He wished he had his ax. He'd gotten good at chopping things to smithereens.

"Last year, we had a little misunderstanding about what kind of show this is."

LC grabbed the papers, but Mr. Merritt grabbed LC's shoulder. "You can't stop it, son. We'll just type up some more." Mr. Merritt held his hand out, but LC threw them in the floor, some flying off like birds. *Fly off. Fly off.*

But none got away. Mr. Merritt gathered them all and said, "This is a terminal event, boys, which means at the conclusion of the show, an auction will take place where your animal will be sold to enter the food chain. That's where your money comes from." He held up the jumbled papers. "This states that you and your parents acknowledge what I just said. I need both you and them to sign it and bring it back at our January meeting."

LC looked at Emerson Bridge. He'd been afraid he would see tears in the boy's eyes, but he did not. His friend appeared to be looking straight ahead, his eyes, almost blank. He had his feet out of his shoes and crossed and his hands still folded on the desk like a dutiful student.

Mr. Merritt began passing out the papers.

"You ain't going to tell us what we should be doing next with our steers? For the sake of Pear Boy back there." It was the Prater boy, and he was pointing to Emerson Bridge.

LC stood. "You should already have him halter broke and tying him to a post or a tree a few hours a day. It's time now for you to lead him, if you got the knack for it. And you know to 'break him in rope and show him in leather,' right?"

"That's quite enough, LC," Mr. Merritt said.

"Catch this, Mr. Knack!" the Prater boy yelled and slammed a balled up piece of paper that bounced off of LC's forehead.

LC got in the boy's face. It was full of freckles, and LC wanted to spit at them, see if he could hit every one. But Mr. Merritt said, "LC, don't."

LC spit at the boy's face.

The Prater boy wrapped his arm around LC's head, placing it in a hard lock, and then threw LC in the floor, straddled him, and beat him in the face. Boys gathered around, cheering on the Prater boy.

But, in the midst of it all, LC heard Emerson Bridge call out, "Stop! Don't hurt my friend!"

Mr. Merritt managed to break up the fight and dismissed the meeting and told LC and the Prater boy to stay. LC remained on the floor, Emerson Bridge kneeling beside him and using his coat sleeve to wipe blood from LC's face.

When LC sat up, he slipped his hand in his pocket and brought out two silver dollars, one from the hog killing and the other from his mother for his recent birthday. "Merry Christmas," he said. He had wanted to give enough to cover the cost of a new pair of shoes, but his father had stopped his allowance until the new knives were paid for.

"But I ain't got you nothing," Emerson Bridge said.

"LC!" Mr. Merritt called out.

"You're my friend," LC said. "That's a whole lot."

He got up off the floor and joined Mr. Merritt and the Prater boy. "I could disqualify you both right now," the county agent said.

"Do it, then," LC told him but kept his eyes on Emerson Bridge, who was leaving the room, his head hanging low.

. . . . .

Sarah was on her way to pick up her boy from 4-H when she heard a knock on the porch door. She wondered if Jeremiah Allgood had returned, bringing the law with him this time to lock her up for lack of payment. Mr. Thrasher had withdrawn his $50.02 and applied it towards their debt, but he was unable to get a loan, since he had no employment. Sarah felt her insides jump like hot milk gravy popping in a pan. What if he was there to outright take Mama Red? She rushed through the porch to the screened door.

But the man was not Jeremiah. The man was the last person she'd ever expect to see, Billy Udean Parnell, and he was standing on the other side of the screen. She knew she should swing the door open and greet him, but she did nothing and said nothing.

He held his head like he was studying her. His customary cigarette dangled between his lips. He was still bone thin, maybe even more so.

He took his cigarette from his mouth. She knew words were coming, and they would not be pleasant. They might even be mean. But what if he knew about Emerson Bridge and wanted to take him away from her? She widened her stance on the concrete.

But all he said was "I'm sorry, ma'am," and shook his head like he was trying to shake something free. "I was thinking you was somebody else."

Sarah felt a flush over her body.

"There was a family that used to live here, a man and wife, good people, Harold and Sarah Creamer. I thought you was Sarah."

She stayed quiet. He was a better mirror than the one on her chifforobe.

The pock marks on his face had grown deeper. She'd not seen him since a year before Mattie died.

He pointed behind him across the garden. "I used to live over there in that house with my, my . . ." His voice trailed off.

Sarah put her hand on the doorjamb. Here it comes, the part about Emerson Bridge. She was glad he was at school. If Billy Udean ever saw her boy's dimples, he would know.

"Anyway," he said and shoved his foot against the dirt, "I've been gone a long time and her sister was about to sell the place, but thought I might try to see if I could make a go of it here again."

He returned his cigarette to his mouth. Sarah watched as he took another one from his shirt pocket and put it beside the other. She'd never seen him smoke two at a time.

Her hands were perspiring.

His were shaking. "Anyway, don't mean to bother you none, ma'am. Forgive my manners. My name's Billy Udean Parnell." He removed both cigarettes.

Sarah knew she had to say something now. "Clementine" slipped from her mouth.

"Clementine," he repeated.

Sarah swallowed. She wanted to show her manners and say, *Nice to meet you, sir,* but she would say nothing more. Her voice was still fat.

His eyes showed him to be an old man, not just with the wrinkles that fanned out like bird wings outside his eyes, but the shine in them had gone flat. Sarah understood that. He'd lost his Mattie, too. And that made her do something she regretted as soon as she did it. She swung open the door, as if to invite him in.

He took a step back as the door went past him. Sarah wished she could let the door return home, but that would be too much of a show. She caught it and held it open. A couple of feet of wide, open space now between them. She felt naked.

He looked towards her new automobile, parked to his right, and then to his left towards the barn, where a fence and two cows now stood. He was taking in the changes, and she let him.

"Reckon I was fooling myself to come here," Billy Udean said.

Sarah wanted to nod, but she kept her head still.

He turned as if to leave but then stopped and looked at her again. "It's odd. You kind of sound like her. Like Mattie's Sarah."

She held her breath.

He kept his eyes on her for a bit longer, then walked on, stepping into the growth of the old garden, which soon swallowed him. And then she heard a vehicle crank, a truck. She watched it leave. Maybe he would go back to wherever he'd been, now that he'd seen that nothing was the same. Because nothing was the same. Nothing.

· · · · ·

Emerson Bridge did not see his mother out in front of the school. He had wanted to run into her arms, but that was not possible now. She must be sewing and had lost track of time. He folded the piece of paper, put it in his coat pocket and ran towards home, his hand holding the coins.

When he approached Drake's Store, he saw his mother's automobile speeding towards him.

He waved his arms for her. She pulled off the road and threw open his door.

"Sorry to be late, hon," she told him and pulled him to her. How did she know he wanted that? He had been right when he used to wonder what she smelled like. She smelled like biscuits but also sewing machine oil and her cloth, which made his nose tickle. Sometimes she smelled like Mama Red, and that was his favorite, because it was the way Lucky smelled, too.

She reached for his hand. How did she know he'd like that? He took the paper from his pocket, but he could feel her shaking. Her face, its pale color, looked like his papa's before he died. Was she sick?

He'd wait to tell her about the paper. But he could tell her about the silver dollars. "Look what LC gave me for Christmas." He held them out for her.

"That's nice, hon," she said and squeezed his hand.

When they turned in the driveway, she kept her head turned to the left like she was looking for something.

She went inside the house. He wanted to do that, wanted to get up under his bed and hide. But it was time for Lucky's afternoon feeding, time to pour in the remainder of the fifty-pound sack of grain. Time to make him even fatter.

He leaned towards the ground and threw up.

He found Lucky with his head in the bin, eating. He grabbed the sides of the animal's halter and tried to lift his head. But Lucky kept bobbing it away.

The top of the wooden trough came halfway up Emerson Bridge's chest and sat on a platform a couple of feet off the ground. It was about as long as he was tall and shaped like a flat-bottomed boat, its ends and sides sloped to help the steer eat. Emerson Bridge moved to the far end and placed his hands on the boards and pushed upwards with all his might. He managed to tip it up off the ground, but Lucky was still eating. He yelled, "Stop, boy, stop!" as he walked his hands down the boards until it teetered on its other end. He gave it one big shove.

It landed upside down. And closed.

· · · · ·

Sarah looked out her kitchen window that Saturday morning towards Mattie's. The truck Billy Udean had driven away in the day before was not there, nor had it been any time she'd looked out. Mildred was due in eighteen minutes to take Sarah to a Christmas singing and ladies luncheon. Sarah had been thinking she wouldn't go, if Billy Udean's truck had returned. But she was thinking now she could trust that he was gone for good.

She found a dish towel with only one hole in it, draped it across her hands and brought it to a pan, where she laid in the towel like she was laying a baby in a crib. The pan was round, one that she and Mattie had used to gather green beans and such from their garden. In its center, Sarah placed four pears, one for each member of Mildred's family. Her fall harvest had been good, but these four were all she could spare.

Mildred's knock came at the exact time her letter had said, "8:45 in the morning on Saturday." She smoothed down her dress, the same one she'd worn on their last outing with the shoes, and called out towards Emerson Bridge's room that she'd be back in a while. Mr. Merritt was due for his monthly visit that morning.

Sarah told Mildred, "Merry Christmas," and handed her the pan as soon as she got outside. The towel was red and white. She hoped that would make it look Christmas enough.

"Why, aren't you the sweetest?" Mildred ran her gloved fingers along the pears. "Yours is coming a bit later, Sarah."

They got inside the automobile. "You all right, dear?" Mildred asked. "Your skin's a little pasty, and you're weak-eyed."

"Oh, I'm good," Sarah told her. She'd been feeling more tired than usual, but she'd gotten little sleep the night before worrying about Billy Udean trying to take her boy away.

Mildred crossed over Whitehall and proceeded towards New Prospect, passing the cemetery and Harold and Mattie. Sarah looked out towards their graves. *Emerson Bridge is mine. Y'all know that, don't you?*

Mildred turned in towards the small white clapboard building and stopped.

Sarah felt a thousand pin pricks all over her head. "We're not going inside, are we?"

"Why, yes." Mildred opened her door. "I've got a special Christmas present waiting for you in there."

The outside air felt cold enough to snow. "I ain't good enough for God," Sarah whispered.

"Well, if you're not, none of us are." Mildred was not whispering.

"Nobody wants to see nobody fat walk the aisles and take up too much room on the pews."

Mildred closed her door. "You'll take up the room you'll take, and my friends will be proud to see you walk in."

She could feel Mildred's eyes on her. "Why do you do that?"

"Do what?"

"Act like you don't see the bad in me."

"I'm not acting."

Sarah allowed herself to look at the stretch of stained glass windows down the side of the church. There were four of them, stretching as tall as a person. She couldn't make out a distinctive pattern like the flowers in her mother's church windows, but these carried more colors, the colors of the dresses Sarah had made.

"You asked me one time if Luther loved me." Mildred's voice had gone quiet. "The answer is no. He does not love me. He just wanted me for my money, and I knew that, but still went right ahead and married him. I was nineteen years old and afraid I'd wind up an old maid. But turned out that's exactly what I became anyway, old and a maid."

"No, ma'am. Turned out you became my friend."

"Friend, yes," Mildred said.

Sarah did not smell peppermints.

"Let's go get your Christmas present, Sarah."

Sarah opened her door and stepped out. They walked to the front of the church, where she placed her foot on the bottom step. "My mama's church had twenty steps up the front of it. Twenty steps to Jesus, I'd always say."

"A tall one," Mildred said.

"A tall one."

"We've only got two."

"A short one," Sarah said.

"A short one."

They giggled.

Sarah had never thought this day would come, when she could step inside a church. But this day had come, and it was thanks to her new friend, Mildred Dobbins, who might have married a man who did not love her, but Sarah loved her, and she suspected a lot of other people did, too.

They walked the steps. Mildred opened the large door and held it for Sarah, who stepped inside, her eyes taking in the windows, the stained glass, the colors. Her mother's words returning, *"And that pretty colored glass all around out where the crowd sits, they's three windows right beside each other, and right in the middle of all three, they got flower petals. Four of them. Two straight up and one on the right and one on the left. It looks like a cross, the kind Jesus died on for our sins. For our real bad ways. He wiped them all out. All the bad we do. Every bit of it. Every blame bit of it."*

From a door up front walked five ladies, each bearing the colors of red and green. "Merry Christmas, Sarah Creamer," Mildred said and held out a box the size of a five-pound bag of Dixie Home sugar.

But Sarah didn't take it. She didn't want to be selfish and the only one getting a gift.

"Open it!" several of the women called out.

Sarah took the box. It was wrapped in shiny green paper with curly red ribbons. Inside laid a measuring tape, a tablet, a fountain pen, and money stacked as high as rolled dough for biscuits.

"Merry Christmas to all of you," Mildred said. "I've been telling you about my special friend, Sarah, and her masterful sewing ability. Some of you have even bought her dresses. I hope she'll do you the honor of measuring each of you for a new one."

"Oh, yes," the women said, and Sarah wanted to say thank you, say it louder than was possible, but her lips trembled so, she could only open her arms.

As she stood in the midst of all that color, it came to her that what her mother was doing that night when she'd talked of the stained glass was asking for Sarah's forgiveness for not letting Sarah go to church and get saved all those years. Her mother was saying that Jesus forgave her, so maybe Sarah could do the same.

Sarah did the same.

. . . . .

Emerson Bridge was hiding beneath his bed when Mr. Merritt's truck came past his house that morning. The county agent called his name. And then his mother's. But Emerson Bridge stayed quiet.

A knock came on the screened porch door. His heart raced against the wooden planks. Mr. Merritt called their names again. Emerson Bridge wanted to forget names. He put his hands over his ears and pressed, and, in his mind, a new name formed, one he thought he could pass for, too, Roy Rogers, Jr. He had dark hair like the King of the Cowboys, and dimples like him, too. He'd noticed them on that big screen at the State Theatre with Mr. Ike. They flashed as big as slivers of moons.

He listened for Mr. Merritt's truck to leave, and when it did, he ran to his mother's room, to the mirror on her chifforobe, and made himself smile. There they were, his dimples. His mother didn't have them, nor did his papa. But Roy Rogers did. He had been thinking he didn't want to go that morning to the Roy Rogers Riders Club meeting with Mr. Ike and the cowboy picture show afterwards, but now he did. He wanted to see Roy Rogers's dimples.

He returned to his room and put on his Rider shirt and jeans and, in his shirt pocket, slid his Roy Rogers Riders Club rules card. On his collar, he fastened his special clip with a picture of Roy Rogers himself on it and then slipped LC's two silver dollars in his pocket.

Mr. Ike came at the appointed time of 10:30 and stood outside the porch. As soon as Emerson Bridge started down the steps, he asked Mr. Ike, "Guess what my new name is?"

Mr. Ike hunched up his shoulders.

"Roy Rogers, Jr.!"

Mr. Ike giggled, not like he didn't believe Emerson Bridge, but like he did, and it was their secret. They both galloped to the truck like they were on horses.

On the way to town, Mr. Ike asked him what Mr. Merritt had said about Lucky.

"Not much," Emerson Bridge told him and pressed his foot against the floorboard like it was the gasoline pedal. He wanted Mr. Ike to drive faster.

At the State Theatre, Emerson Bridge pulled out one silver dollar and held it for the attendant in the admission booth. "For two real cowboys, ma'am," he said. But Mr. Ike gently moved his hand away and paid with his own dollar bill. Emerson Bridge knew the man was not his papa, but at that moment, he wanted him to be and reached for the man's hand. Mr.

Ike looked surprised but then smiled and settled in by swinging it high, then low.

The stage was full of people and shiny equipment and wires. Always before it was empty, except for the life-sized poster of Roy Rogers and a table with a sign that said "State Theatre Roy Rogers Riders Club." Mr. Sanders directed Emerson Bridge to the right side of the stage, where at least a dozen boys huddled, and then told them of a special Christmas present. "The good people at WAIM Radio are broadcasting our meeting live today." The boys began to clap, and so did Mr. Ike, who was easy to spot. He was the only one wearing a cowboy hat. "As soon as we're on the air," Mr. Sanders said, "I'm going to say a few words about our club, and then I'm going to ask ten of you lucky boys to come to the microphone and give one of the rules."

"Me!" several of the boys said and thrust their hands into the air.

"Me!" Emerson Bridge called out and looked to see if Mr. Ike was watching.

He was.

He wished LC was there that day, but LC wasn't a Riders Club member. His papa wouldn't let him, said it was "too common."

"Do we have a preacher in the audience?" Mr. Sanders asked and held his hand above his eyes to shield the bright light. "I usually read Mr. Rogers's prayer myself, but since today's a special day, I thought we'd see if we have a preacher among us."

No hands were raised. Emerson Bridge knew that Mr. Ike used to be one. "My Mr. Ike!" he called out and pointed the man's way.

Mr. Ike put his hand on the top of his hat and lowered his head. He was shy like that.

"And he knows it by heart, too," Emerson Bridge called out. Every time they'd been to a meeting, Mr. Ike always said the words along with Mr. Sanders.

"I bet Mr. Rogers would really like it if a preacher did it," Mr. Sanders said.

Those words drew Mr. Ike's face forward. Mr. Sanders waved him up on stage and then began tapping boys on their shoulders and calling out a number. He tapped Emerson Bridge and said, "7." "My name's Roy Rogers, Jr.," he told the man and flashed his dimples.

The boys lined up in order behind the microphone. Mr. Sanders told them, "Go ahead and get your cards out and learn your number by heart so when it's your time, you're not reading but saying it like you mean it, the way Mr. Rogers would want you to." Emerson Bridge removed his card and located number seven. "Be kind to animals and take care of them." A flush shot up him.

"Ladies and Gentlemen," Mr. Sanders said, "we are thrilled to be broadcasting live from the State Theatre for the Christmas meeting of the Roy Rogers Riders Club, a club that gives our young boys wholesome rules to live by. We honor Mr. Rogers's wish for us to begin with his prayer."

Mr. Ike bowed his head. "Lord, I reckon I'm not much by myself," and Emerson Bridge knew he should close his eyes, but, instead, he whispered to the boy in front of him, "Want to trade with me?"

The boy made no sound.

"Please," Emerson Bridge said and reached for a silver dollar. "I'll give you this." Mr. Sanders looked his way and shook his head fast.

Emerson Bridge felt like he might cry.

Mr. Ike was saying, "And when in the failing dusk I get that final call, I do not care how many flowers they send. Above all else, the happiest trail would be, for you to say to me, 'Let's ride, My Friend.' Amen."

"Let's ride, My Friend, indeed," Mr. Sanders said into the microphone.

Let's not ride, My Friend, let's not, Emerson Bridge wanted to scream.

The line moved quickly, the boys saying their words and stepping away. Emerson Bridge thought about running off the stage, but the space in front of him opened, and he stepped forward, the shiny microphone aimed at him like a pistol.

He got as far as "Be kind" before his throat closed, and he could say no more.

"That's right, son," Mr. Sanders stepped in and said. He put his hand on Emerson Bridge's shoulder. "But be kind to what?"

Emerson Bridge no longer could see anything. He took a deep breath and said "animals," then grabbed his stomach, bent double, and fell onto the floor.

. . . . .

"Sorry I'm late," Merritt told Luther, who stood near his lot with his boot pressed on the bottom strand of barbed wire. He shoved a small tin box filled with Mildred's fruit cake cookies towards the county agent.

Merritt took the box but did not open it.

"It ain't a bribe or nothing. Just some Christmas cheer," Luther said.

Merritt kept his eyes towards the ground. "Sure hope everything's all right with the Creamer boy. LC probably told you, but I handed out that paper to sign yesterday. Should have told him his steer's fate from the start." He kicked at the dirt.

LC had not told Luther. He'd get right with him after Merritt left. LC was with Uncle at the hammer mill, shoveling in corn cobs the way they should be shoveled. His boy knew better than to try any more monkey business.

Luther took a cigar from his pocket and stuck it in his mouth and lit it. He'd let the man keep going with his words, hoping he'd address how the steer was feeding out.

"The feed trough was turned over, and I couldn't get anybody to the door," Merritt said.

Luther pulled hard on his cigar and tilted his chin up. Buzzards circled above. Maybe the Creamers were dead. Killed themselves at the whole drama of it. Luther blew a smoke ring. It was almost perfect.

"Older boys don't seem to have a problem with it. They get used to it. Every year, they get a little more numb. But young ones like the Creamer boy, and even yours, Luther, they're *little*."

"Hey, is this a Creamer convention or something? You're supposed to be over here telling me that *my* boy's slaughter steer is going to leave the others, including that Creamer one, in the by God dust."

Merritt appeared to look into the lot where the steer was tied to his post.

"LC!" Luther yelled and waved his arms like a wild man until his boy looked his way. "Merritt's about to praise your steer. On the double now!" Luther clapped his hands at the pace he wanted his boy to run. "It's important to put boys through this. Look at that boy coming here. It's making him into a man."

"That year I competed, '41, when that McClain boy won, I was just a boy," Merritt said. "It's a tough row to hoe. Sold out my best friend."

"Must not have been too tough. You advise other boys now how to do it."

Luther brought LC around in front of him. He wished that Charles was there, too, but he wasn't coming home for Christmas. Charles was so smart, Clemson College was sending him out west to tour some big ranches.

"Am I in trouble about yesterday, Mr. Merritt?" LC asked. He sounded like he had a smile on his face. "I think I deserve a punishment."

Luther knew his boy had been in a fight, had come home with a bloody lip, but all Luther had wanted to know is if the other boy looked worse.

Merritt shook his head. "Beats all I've ever seen."

The words Luther had been waiting for. He had picked a good one for his boy.

"Yeah, that Creamer steer has made a full recovery from the bloat, and if they can get enough feed in him between now and the show, that's what—ten, eleven weeks—he'll be the one to beat. He's got the best frame I've ever seen. Just a matter of finishing him out."

Luther clenched his fists. "I asked you how *my* boy's steer looks."

"All right," Merritt said. "He looks all right." He started towards his truck.

"You sure I ain't in trouble?" LC called out.

"Just all right?" Luther hollered and made long steps to get in front of the man. He pointed to his own chest with his hard finger and said, "My boy's the one to beat."

"I've told you before, Luther, the Creamer steer was a real down-the-roader." Merritt stepped around Luther and kept walking.

Luther shouted at his boy, "Hey, get out there with that beast and show off how good he can do. Show him how you've made him follow you around like you're a king."

Merritt's door closed.

"And bring him over here and let Merritt get a look at the meat cuts on him. Show him his rump. Hurry up, boy!"

Merritt cranked his truck.

Luther ran hard towards it, flung open the driver's door, yanked Merritt from the cab and threw him on the ground, where Luther straddled him like a horse, his knees pinning the man's arms to the dirt. "I said by God look at my boy's steer!" Luther jerked the man's head towards the animal, which stood silent with LC twenty feet away. "Tell me *he*'s the one to beat. Tell me!"

"Dad!" LC called out.

Luther grabbed the collar on Merritt's coat.

"I can't do that, Luther!"

Luther shook him. "I said say it!"

"Maybe the second one to beat."

Luther felt sick to his stomach. He took a swing at Merritt's face, while Merritt tried to move his arms from beneath Luther's knees. Luther pressed them stronger. The man's legs began kicking and soon bucked Luther off, the two men now rolling across the dirt. When they stopped, Luther regained his position in the saddle. "So, why do you do it, then?" Luther yelled and tasted blood on his lips. "If it tore you up so bad, why do you put more of them through it?"

Merritt's body became almost limp. "Responsibility," he said. "It teaches them responsibility." The man's eyes looked glassy and full. He turned his head and spit a wad of blood.

Luther gave Merritt's shoulders one big push and then removed himself.

Merritt got on his feet and brushed away the dirt. "At least that's what I tell myself." He returned to his truck.

LC and the steer were no longer in sight. Nor was Uncle. The hammer mill was silent now.

Merritt drove away.

"I got your one-to-beat-down-the-roader!" Luther called out, his bottom lip stinging.

But then a thought came to him. How about *a down-the-road goner?*

He kept those words to himself and returned to the fence. Merritt had left the cookies on the ground. Luther picked up the tin box, full of color. It showed a scene with snow and fancy horses and fancy carriages in front of a fancy house, a king's house.

You put them through it, Luther told himself, *because it'll make you a king. A by God king.*

. . . . .

Ike Thrasher picked the boy up and carried him to his truck. The boy wrapped his arms around Ike's neck.

On the ride home, Emerson Bridge stayed pressed against the door. Occasionally, he whimpered like an animal that had been hurt.

When they arrived at the house, the boy got out of the truck and went inside. Ike wanted to go with him, but he was not invited. He did not know how long the boy's mother would be, but he would wait in the shadows until she returned.

He moved his truck to the road, put his vehicle in reverse and backed up to just beyond his father's house, where he pulled off to the side and parked. "Don't you worry, I'm not about to touch your land." He said those words out loud.

Snow flurries danced through the air. He could see his breath from the cold.

"This probably is a git-up I've got on, too," he said and ran his hands down his denim-covered thighs. "But, Daddy, it's all I've got."

He spotted his mother's trellis, visible from this side of the house. It was covered in vines, gone dormant, but still alive. His teeth began to chatter. "The people across the road, they're good people, Daddy. The boy and his mama. And don't laugh at me, but I'm trying to take care of them."

Where the boy had sat, his Roy Rogers Riders Club card remained. It lay crumpled.

Ike took a deep and abiding breath. "Lord, I reckon I'm not much by myself," he recited. "I fail to do a lot of things I ought to do. But, Lord, when trails are steep and passes high, Help me ride it straight the whole way through."

And then his own words, from his own prayer came forth. "Lord, watch over those people. And help me to do my part good."

. . . . .

Sarah stepped inside her house carrying five sacks of fabric and notions and patterns. The clerk at Gallant-Belks was kind enough to place each woman's

180

materials in separate sacks, along with her name and measurements. Mildred's box sat on top and still carried the stack of money. Sarah had expected to use it to buy what she needed for the dresses, but Mildred paid for everything and said the money in the box was "for you, just for you." Sarah had not counted it yet, thinking it would show her too desperate if she had fingered the bills, lingering with each one, in Mildred's presence.

She laid the sacks on the kitchen table, opened the box, and picked up the money, one hundred dollars in ten-dollar bills. One hundred dollars. Twenty dollars a dress. And there was the promise of more dresses to make, if the ladies were pleased. She thought she would scream and jump into the air, but all she did was pull her chair back from the table and sit in it, her body folding forward. *Why do you love me like you do?* she whispered and could feel her fists so tight, her fingernails cut into herself.

The smell of ambrosia from the luncheon returned to Sarah's nose, the tangy citrus of oranges and the coconut, shaved into tiny, tiny fingers. Emerson Bridge's had been tiny. The first time he wrapped his around her thumb, she felt a spark of heat rise through her that she knew was life itself.

He was going to the show with Mr. Thrasher and should be back by now, but she'd not seen him in the yard. With all this money, she could buy him a Christmas present now, a real one. Perhaps a bicycle. She could pay for it outright and not even think about layaway.

She jumped to her feet. "Emerson Bridge!"

She heard nothing in return. She went to the porch door and called his name.

He did not respond.

She went to the lot and to the barn but did not see him.

Snowflakes were falling all around. Most were as big as nickels, some like quarters. A quiet was setting in like no other. She felt something stir in the pit of her belly, something that made her run and run fast to the house, where she made her way to her boy's room. She stood in the doorway but did not see him.

But she heard him. Sounds, quaking ones, coming from under his bed.

She laid herself flat on the floor and looked through the tassels on the bottom of his bedspread. There he was, his small body heaving. She slid her hand towards him and touched the outside of his arm. "What's got you all torn up, sweet boy?"

From his hand, fisted as hard as a grown man's, he released a piece of paper, twisted like a candy stripe.

Sarah brought it out into the open air and hurried to smooth it against the floor. Some words in bold hovered above blank lines. She read out loud, "We hereby acknowledge that the 1952 Fat Cattle Show & Sale is a terminal event and that the steer we enter will be sold afterwards as a market steer." She didn't know the word "terminal," but she knew "market" as in supermarket.

"I got to kill Lucky, Mama," he said.

Sarah stretched her hand towards him, the tassels off-white and dirty, splayed against her upper arm. "No sir," she told him. "You don't, we don't. We don't have to do this. We don't have to do this at all." Her words came fast.

"But we do, Mama. We need the money."

"We don't need nothing that bad," she said, as her fingers tore the paper into as many pieces as her fingers would allow. And then she slapped the pile, scattering all the tininess across the wide, wide floor.

The world was becoming white and the noise of the day, softening around the mother cow and her calf. Each sought refuge beneath a tree that had long ago grown in the midst of cotton, the farmer allowing it, even praising it for its courage. The mother cow on one side of the fence, her calf on the other, both nestled under the arms of limbs stretching tall and wide.

I need to be put somewhere by my lonesome, left in some pitch-black space that I'd make smell so bad, you'd have to cover up your nose with blankets as thick as you could stand. But even that wouldn't wipe out the wretched smell of me. You'd have to stick your nose in mud, Mama Red, in the hopes that somehow that stench would evaporate on out of here. But it won't, no ma'am. It'll only start sinking down to the lowest room in my mama's Jesus's hell that's already got my name on it. Yeah, right there on that bottom of the bottomest door, my name's already written out. Clementine Florence Augusta Sarah, it says right there on it.

How could I not have known? Mama Red, how?

The heart ache I brought on my boy and almost on you. I was so desperate to feed him and be a good mama, I was about to . . . I ain't going to say. Some words don't need to be spoke. Like fences that don't need to be up. This one right here, between you and your boy, it's coming down.

Mine's coming down between me and my boy, too. That man that came to see me yesterday, that Billy Udean, I'm scared he's going to find out or either already knows about Emerson Bridge and try to take him from me. Ain't seen his truck back over there, though. But now that I say that word "scared," let it be out with us, you wouldn't be, would you, girl? You wouldn't be scared at all. You'd just do whatever you had to when the time come. There you go again, teaching me.

It's good to see our boys playing in the snow. That snowball Emerson Bridge just made—did you see it? I got a rock in my room that I practice with. I'm going to practice some more, and one of these days real soon I'm going toss it to him, and he's going to toss it back. You just wait.

I've missed playing. Me and Mattie liked to play. When we planted potatoes that first time, me and her got on our knees in the dirt, and I started digging a hole with my hand and said, "This is our baby," and I picked up a potato slip and told her, "And, look, we're putting her to bed." I laid her in just as soft and brought up her covers, that was the dirt, to just below her eye. That's how you plant potato slips, eyes up.

Mattie went to digging her own hole. "We got two babies, look, Sister Sarah," she said and put her one in and covered her up good. Harold hollered over that we weren't putting in them slips deep enough, but me and her kept on. We were putting our babies to bed.

That right there, Mama Red, that was the best of us. Like me and you, girl, the best of us, here together under this big tree, that fence coming down and watching our babies play.

DECEMBER 25, 1951

On Christmas day, inside the Creamer house at noon, in a room the woodstove made exceedingly warm, Sarah Creamer and her boy sat at the kitchen table, a feast before them of fried salmon patties, milk gravy she'd made from the grease, boiled white rice and green beans, seasoned with not one, but two pieces of fatback. Sarah had splurged with Mildred's money, this she knew. But it was her boy's first Christmas without his father.

"You want some more, hon? More beans and rice and gravy? And what about another salmon patty or two?"

She watched as her boy's dimples pushed his cheeks closer to God. She didn't always think of Mattie when she saw him, but this day, she did. Harold, too. They would be proud. She was providing nutrition for their son, not just Mattie's and Harold's son, but hers, too, and she was as happy for that as the present she had for him hiding along the side wall of her room. Sarah rose into air, saturated with the smell of good frying grease, and filled every empty space on his plate.

"You eat, Mama," he told her, and she realized she'd barely taken a bite.

She slid her fork under a mound of rice, topped with a good blanket of gravy. But when she brought the food to her mouth, she yawned and shook her head to try to wake herself up. Only a few hours sleep in three days was telling on her, and she only had two of the five dresses to show for it. "Staying up waiting on Santy Claus last night must have made me sleepy, hon."

He looked towards the hallway. A grin came across his face. "I want to give you your present now. Can I?"

She'd planned on giving him his after they'd eaten, but she found herself grinning back and saying, "If I can give you yours, too." She said it as if she was a schoolgirl, and the only problem before her was where to draw the lines in the dirt for hopscotch.

He ran towards his room. She loved getting his pine cones from the yard. Last Christmas he'd filled a paper sack with them and placed red berries from the holly bush on top. Harold had laid off his liquor that day and joined her boy and her at the table for this exact meal.

"Close your eyes, Mama!" he called from down the hall, and she shut them tight the way she did the bins on the woodstove to keep flies off her leftover food.

"Okay, open them!'

She flung them wide and saw in his hands, a present that appeared to be a box the size of a man's cigar. It was wrapped in Christmas paper of blue and white.

"Merry Christmas, Mama!"

The present was as light as a biscuit. She removed the paper, full of horses and sleighs filled with people who looked to be having a good time. The box carried words written in bold along its side. "Miles Nervine," she read out loud.

"To help you get some sleep. You put them in water and let them fizz, Mr. Drake said."

"Mr. Drake?"

He giggled. "I ran there yesterday when you went to town. He wrapped it for me and everything."

"Thank you, hon." She had hoped to keep her tiredness from him. But she had failed.

"Take one now," he whispered in her ear.

She didn't want to disappoint him, but she had to shake her head. "Got to keep on with my sewing, hon. But I appreciate it, and, when I can, I'm sure going to take me one, I am." She slid her chair back from the table. "Now, you close your eyes."

But she saw that he had lost his dimples, and she sat back down and opened the box and took out a tablet, while he poured her a glass of water. He was right. It did fizz, enough to almost overflow the glass. He giggled, and she said to him, "Your giggle box is turned over," as she turned the glass up at her mouth and drank. It fizzed around her teeth.

She went to her bedroom, where, against the wall, leaned a bicycle, a pretty blue one, which she'd bought at B. F. Goodrich for $43.95, paid for it with money she could have spent turning the lights back on, but they had learned to live without them. With the $12.05 she had before Mildred's money and the $51.06 left of the $100, she had $63.11 remaining. She needed to repay Mr. Thrasher and Mr. McDougald and Mr. Scarboro. With the land, the steer, the burial and the automobile, she owed $284.50. But she no longer needed all that money to buy so much feed at the FCX.

She rolled his present across the hallway and into the kitchen, where her boy stood with his hands over his face. The wheels made a wispy sound, and she wondered if he could tell what it was. "All right, open them!" she said and watched as his eyes lit up like they were light bulbs, and good electricity had just hit. "That word says Schwinn there," she told him and pointed to the long part between the seat and the handle bar, "that's the make of it and the very best there is." The sales clerk had told her this. She kicked out her foot towards the back tire. "Them are training wheels. They're to help you get started."

He swung his leg over and straddled the seat.

A knock came at the porch door.

"Reckon Santy's come back?" She scooted that way. It was Mr. Thrasher. She had not yet told him about not doing the steer competition. She had wanted to give her boy a good Christmas first.

"Mr. Ike!" her boy called out and ran to the porch door to let him in.

Sarah took a deep breath.

"Come look what Santy brought me!"

"Then get ready for number two," Mr. Thrasher said and stepped into the kitchen, in his hands a present, a box the size of a bread pan but thick like a sheet cake and wrapped in shiny red paper with a big green bow. He set it on the table. "Tear into it!" he said and nodded towards it.

Her boy caught the end of the wrapping paper and yanked it across the top. He and Mr. Thrasher were laughing. She wished now she'd invited him to eat. They had plenty. She'd added four pieces of loaf bread to the salmon to stretch it. Three nice-sized patties remained on the plate.

But then her boy's laughter stopped, and he pushed the box into the plate of salmons and ran out the door.

"Where's your manners?" she called after him. "You tell Mr. Thrasher 'thank you.'"

But he was outside now.

"Hey, he don't have to like it. I sure didn't like every present I ever got." Mr. Thrasher giggled, but Sarah knew it wasn't a true one.

"I'm sorry, Mr. Thrasher."

He was trying to put the wrapping back on the box. She read "Pistols" across the top of the gift, "Roy Rogers Pistols."

So that was it.

She went outside and found her boy in the lot with Lucky, his arms around the animal's neck. "Mr. Thrasher didn't know, hon," she called from the fence. "None of us did. It was innocent. Like we all are."

The time had come to tell Mr. Thrasher. She motioned for her boy. "Let's don't hurt his feelings. Come on back inside and thank him."

He kissed the side of Lucky's face and then returned with her to the kitchen. Mr. Thrasher had restored the wrapping to the gift. Emerson

Bridge apologized and thanked the man and held out his hands like he wanted the present back.

But Mr. Thrasher did not give it. "Everybody don't want to be a cowboy. I'll go get you something you like, maybe one of them show halters for your Lucky."

"Oh, we don't need that no more, Mr. Ike. Lucky don't have to be in that show now."

"I was going to—" Sarah began.

"The Grand Champeen show?" Mr. Thrasher said.

"Yes, sir."

"I was going to tell you, Mr. Thrasher, I'm sorry. Didn't mean for it to come out like this."

Mr. Thrasher sat down. He made a sound when he hit. His eyes were blinking fast as he kept looking from Sarah to Emerson Bridge and back again.

Sarah heaped food onto a plate. "It's cold, but I'll give you all I have." She set it in front of him.

He made no move towards it. "Why? Can I ask y'all why?"

Sarah thought she saw his bottom lip quiver.

"They wanted to put him in somebody's deep freeze," her boy told him.

"Deep freeze? To eat?"

"Yes, sir. After the show, they sell them, and then they do something awful. They kill them. But Mama said I don't have to do that." Emerson Bridge threw his arms around Sarah's waist.

Mr. Thrasher was shaking his head.

"Hon, how about going to ride your bicycle?" she said and helped her boy take it outside.

Mr. Thrasher was standing when she returned. "It doesn't make any sense. Roy Rogers would never do that."

"I aim to get a few dress orders from some church ladies in the next few weeks. You'll get your money back."

His eyes went wide. "That sign out beside that steer in front of Richbourg's back in the spring, it said to come see him in the meat department. I was so gung ho about it all that I was blind to that part."

"We all were," Sarah said.

He walked to the door and pulled back the curtain.

Sarah knew he was looking at his father's place. "Mr. Thrasher, I know what this means to you. And I sure hate that—"

"Daddy didn't have cows, but he had hogs he sure killed and we ate like they were a crop." His voice was low and little.

187

As glad as Sarah was for her boy, she was that sad for this man. "Mr. Thrasher, I sure hate that—"

"We can't kill Lucky, Mrs. Creamer. Don't mean to cut you off, but sometimes other things come up, bigger things. And that's what's happened here."

"But—" Sarah started.

"But nothing, Mrs. Creamer." He shook his head hard. "We all love Lucky. We don't need to say no more."

Sarah didn't know if she'd live long enough to ever understand what line he had to cross in order to feel like a man. To her, he was more man than any man she'd ever known. She wanted to kiss him. And not like she'd wanted to kiss Harold back when she was a girl. She wanted to kiss Ike Thrasher's heart.

· · · · ·

Ike put the gun and holster set back in his truck. He had used his last dollar to buy it.

Emerson Bridge was not on his bicycle. He was talking to a man just out from the house at the edge of an area that was overgrown. Clouds were beginning to gather, but over his father's house, he thought he saw a touch of blue. He walked that way and went to stand in the middle of the road.

He had dreamed the night before he was holding something made of wire that spanned about a yard in length and a foot wide. But along the two long sides, there were gaping holes every few inches. He tried to fill the empty spaces with little metal cowboy hats he'd cut from a thin sheet of metal. Ike needed to fill them all.

"It's not going to be, Daddy," he said out loud. "But that's going to have to be all right. I'm letting it go now." He thought about removing his hat and moved his hands high to do so, but his head would be naked. And his head could not be naked.

· · · · ·

Emerson Bridge was on his tenth trip down the driveway, the ground slushy from the melted snow, when he heard, "Merry Christmas!" It was a man's voice, but not Mr. Ike's. This one was deep like his papa's had been. Off to his right stood a man he'd never seen before.

"Look what Santy Claus brought me!" Emerson Bridge called out. "Ain't it swell?"

The man started his way. He was about as tall as Emerson Bridge's papa but skinny.

"That is swell," the man said from the garden's edge. He was smoking a cigarette, held at his mouth like he was pinching it. His papa didn't smoke.

"You live over there in that house?" Emerson Bridge asked.

"Used to."

He sounded sad like he didn't have any friends.

"I live in that house right there," Emerson Bridge said and pointed behind him. He did not see his mother at the kitchen sink. Maybe she was asleep by now. "Say Mister, you wouldn't have any work for me, would you? I'm out of school all week and need to make some money for me and my mama."

The man pinched on his cigarette again and then took it from his mouth. "How about everything? I need help with everything."

"Swell!"

The man's eyes looked to be on Emerson Bridge's face hard. "You got dimples," he said.

"Yes sir, I do."

He released smoked from his mouth. "My wife had dimples."

"So does Roy Rogers."

He dropped his cigarette on the ground and put his shoe on top of it. "My name's Billy Udean." The man extended his hand.

"Mine's Emerson Bridge, Mr. Billy Udean."

"Emerson Bridge," the man repeated. "I like that."

"I like yours, too. We both got us two names."

"Guess that means we should be working together, then. Show up at 0800 sharp—that's eight o'clock—tomorrow morning, and we'll get busy clearing out where this old garden used to be." He brought his stiff hand up to his forehead.

Emerson Bridge brought his hand up the same.

The man's hand was shaking.

He turned to leave, and, when he did, Emerson Bridge took off running to tell his mother the good news. Inside the house, he tiptoed towards her room in case she was asleep. But when he got close to her door, he couldn't hold back any longer. He ran in and hollered, "Mama! I'm going to make us some—" but he stopped.

His mother lay crumpled in the floor.

· · · · ·

Ike heard his name being called in a tone that scared him. He was still in the middle of the road. It was Emerson Bridge, and something was wrong, the boy in the yard, waving his hands like he was on fire. "I think Mama's dead!" he called out.

Ike began running.

He found Mrs. Creamer on the floor, got down beside her, and checked for a beat in her neck. "She's going to be all right, son. But we need us an ambulance out here."

"Go see if that new man over there has a telephone. I was just talking to him. I'll stay with Mama."

Ike was at that man's house in a flash. He banged on the front door and hollered through, "We got an emergency and need to make a telephone call."

The man led him to the hall, where a telephone sat on a small table. "Just got it hooked back up."

Ike dialed o for the operator. "We need us an ambulance out here at the Creamer Place on Thrasher Road, second house on the left. Mrs. Creamer's passed out on the floor." Ike felt himself become faint with those last words. He thanked the man and started for the door.

"Excuse me, sir," the man called after him, "but did you say Creamer? The *Creamer* place?"

"Why yes, sir, I did," Ike told him and ran back to the Creamers, their name cycling through his mind like a wheel on the boy's new bicycle, how the name starts out hard but then goes soft by the time it's over.

The mother cow heard loud sounds and lifted her head from the bale of hay she and her young were sharing. They came from the gentle wind's little one and from the man with the high hat.

She lowered her head back to the hay and resumed eating.

Another sound, this one high pitched and from afar, came in, the sound getting louder. She kept her head high. The sound and a light, flashing, approached. She positioned her body in front of her young.

Then all sound was gone.

Someone she was not familiar with, a man, skinny, came to stand near the top fence. Tiny swirls of smoke came with him. The mother cow could feel him watching her. She watched him back for a while, then moved to the side of her young, bringing him forth. She was free to move, now that what had divided them had gone away. Her calf had nursed her twice since then, but, mostly, he ate grass and grain and hay.

This was fortunate for the mother cow. She needed to keep her nutrition for herself and her growing calf inside her, now the size of a small dog and out of reach deep in her womb.

DECEMBER 26–31, 1951

Luther, dressed in his best suit of clothes, walked into the South Carolina National Bank at 8 A.M. sharp on the day after Christmas and asked the lady behind the polished counter to see the president himself, Mr. Donald Brown. "Tell him it's Luther Dobbins." When she told Luther that Mr. Brown wasn't yet back from the holidays, Luther wanted to say, *Fa la la,* but kept his mouth shut and slid two one-dollar bills her towards her. "I need two of the shiniest silver dollars you ever thought about seeing." The four days had given him a lot of time to think his plan through and get every piece of it perfect.

He straightened his tie and looked around the lobby. Two other men stood at the counter, but neither had on a suit.

The teller placed two silver dollars on the counter. They sparkled like his floors after Mildred waxed them.

He left the bank and stood outside on Main Street, lit a cigar, and sent his attention south towards Church Street, two blocks down. That's where a lot of negroes lived and congregated, even Uncle after old man Allgood threw him out. And Luther had seen a Church Street address for a fair number of negroes in the police section of the newspaper.

He began walking that way. That was another part of his plan. Driving his truck could help identify him. He was careful not to walk with purpose, but to stroll as if he was killing time. He passed the women's window at Sullivan Hardware but stopped to look in the men's side. Shovels of all sizes were displayed. He threw his cigar on the sidewalk and used the bottom of his dress shoe to grind it into a splattered piece of nothing.

When he passed Kress's Five and Dime, a bum with a nasty beard was leaning against the glass. In the man's coat pocket, the top of a liquor bottle protruded. *The drunk.* If Luther wasn't on a mission, he'd go to the police chief and tell him to lock the man up.

Luther turned down Church Street, and, as soon as he did, a sweat broke out. This was not part of the plan, his being scared. He had his trusted pearl-handle with him, had it stuck in the waist of his trousers. He knew it could kill a hog. Surely it could kill something on two legs.

He looked down the street, where a preponderance of two-story houses Luther thought of as "negro hotels" lined both sides, along with an occasional shack and a café or two. He saw a couple of older uncles talking near the road. But mostly he saw chickens, red ones, roaming as if they owned the land. Above them, curls of blue rose from chimneys. The place was saturated with smoke, with negroes and smoke. He could smell them. They were everywhere. He just couldn't see them yet.

Merritt's words "The one to beat" floated through his mind. *Ha! How about the one to eat?* He was on a search for a couple of negro boys, and not just any. He needed two that looked comfortable with trouble. It would be easier to find country negroes for what he needed, but they might know him. Over the years, he had transported several to his farm to work in his fields. He moved his wrist against his waist and felt his pistol and then took a few steps down the street. The men seemed to hold their eyes on him. Luther's hands shook so, he brought his arms up and crossed them in front of him. If he squeezed his muscles tight enough, he could stop them from shaking. The beauty was it sent a signal that he was tough, and maybe the uncles would scatter.

But the opposite happened. Negroes came from everywhere, a thousand of them peering from around the side walls and through windows and beside trees and in trees. They huddled, mostly, like packs of dogs. Luther was losing. He had to do something. He took a deep breath and yelled, "Here now!" and braced himself, should he need to take off running.

But he didn't have to, because they shrunk back like he was a mighty wind. He held his shoulders back now, letting his power settle into his bones. For a moment, he forgot what he'd come for, but the sight of two negro boys leaving the front door of a shack reminded him.

"Hey, boys," he said when they passed near him. One looked to be about the age of LC and the other, three or four years older. "What's y'all's names?"

The older one crossed his arms and looked at Luther sideways, but the younger one said, "I'm DeWitt, and this here is my brother Hosea."

"Didn't ask what your mama named you. Asked what your family name was."

"Williams," the older boy said and stepped closer to the younger one.

"Williams, huh?" Luther had seen some negro Williams listed several times in the police section. This was good.

Most of the lurkers had gone back to their business. He could take his time now, make sure he could trust these particular ones. He lit another cigar. The smoke from it snaked up through the air like it was dancing, which negroes were free to do. He wondered if the boys would start a jig. He'd heard they couldn't help it.

"Y'all got a daddy?" Luther asked.

"Yes, sir."

Luther could see that the older boy was going to do all the talking now. "He ever been locked up?"

"Yes sir."

"He locked up now?"

"Yes sir."

Luther couldn't be more pleased. "For what?"

"They say he killed somebody, but he didn't."

"We on our way to see Pop now," the little one said. "He's at the chain gang camp."

Luther figured that had to be close to five miles away. "How y'all going to get there?" He made sure he kept his voice low.

The young one kicked out a foot. "We gone walk."

"That's a far piece," Luther told them, and in his mind knew he'd found his boys. If they could walk to the stockade, they could walk about the same distance in another direction, to the Creamer place.

He stepped in closer. "How would y'all like to make a whole silver dollar a piece?" He held up the two coins, wet from his perspiration.

The boys' eyes grew wide.

Luther felt like he'd put a pole in the water, and two catfish had just bit down on a dangling worm.

"Here's what I need y'all to do. Tonight after dark—and I mean way, way after the pitch black—I need y'all to go out in the country and steal a steer and then get rid of him. Get one of your people to kill him right quick and cut him up and throw a big party and eat him. Use its hooves for balls to throw." He watched their eyes to see if either of them had taken any pleasure at the thought of what he'd described.

He saw it in the older boy's. It was a yearning that Luther recognized as wanting to leave this place and better himself.

The sound of a chicken squawking came from the yard beside them. And then the sound of wings flapping hard. Up through the air came a hawk with a chicken hooked in its talons.

"It got my Sally," the little one said, his hand pointing.

Chickens everywhere came running. They cowered behind a board propped against the trunk of a water oak. None of the birds made any sounds.

The little one's bottom lip trembled.

Luther now was rethinking his choice. Just what he needed, sensitive negroes. But he'd already told them too much to back out. "Which way y'all go to the stockade?"

"To the viaduct," the older one said, "and follow the tracks to the grain elevator and then head off over the hill towards town."

Two uncles appeared from behind the boys' backs. Luther lowered his head. But all he'd done was ask for directions. He raised his head back up when they walked the other way.

"All right," Luther said, his voice almost a whisper now, "when y'all get to the grain elevator, that big concrete building that rises in the sky, instead of going towards town, y'all go the other way, out towards—" He had to stop and think what town negroes would know out in the country, but there was nothing. So he said, "Y'all need to go that way," and pointed with his left hand.

"You there, older boy. Hold out your arm and show me you're getting this."

But the boy did not move. "We're going to need the money first."

Luther wanted to slap him for insubordination, but that would draw a scene. He took a deep breath and tried to calm himself and then said, "Hell no, *boy.* This is *my* show."

"We stepping out for you, Mister." The boy talked in a normal voice. "Money first."

Two women now gathered in a side yard. One had a big stick, stirring a black pot of boiling water that set up over burning firewood. He wondered if she had muscles in her arms like his mother had from lifting and stirring.

"We could buy Pop some smokes with the money, he likes to smoke," the younger one said, his voice dreamy and his eyes open with possibility that told Luther he still believed in Santa Claus. His own boy's eyes on Christmas morning had been flat. LC no longer believed.

Luther clenched his fists, making the coins dig into his skin. "Y'all get the job done, do it tonight, and when I hear of it, y'all will get your smokes money." He opened up his coat and let them see his pearl-handle, then let his coat close, choosing not to address the rope he had wrapped around his waist. "Like I was saying, *boys,* at the grain elevator, turn out towards the country and hustle for a long half hour or so until you come to a church, a white one, sitting atop a hill. It'll also be on y'all's left." He held out his left hand and watched the older boy hold his out the same way. They were back on track.

"Then at that church, turn down that road in front of it and hustle five or so minutes till you come to the second house on that same side we've been talking about, the left. It's just a shack of a place with a barn behind it. The steer's in a lot beside the barn." He opened his coat again and watched the boys put their eyes on the gun like flies on a cow patty, then unwrapped the rope and held it out in front of them.

The older boy reached for it, but before Luther let him have it, he told them, "This is between the three of us. If I ever get pulled into it, I'll come hunt y'all down and kill you dead faster than y'all can strip a chicken leg." He popped the rope.

More negroes were out and about now. "Tell y'all what. When I leave out of here, I'm going to toss this thing by the side of Kress's on the corner. Y'all can pick it up there."

Luther headed towards Main Street. "Hey Mister," he heard called out. It was the young one. "Our Pop's got new legs!"

Luther told himself to keep walking, but he needed to put a stop to this. "So?" he said but kept his back to the boys.

"So, that's why we going to see him." The boy's voice was louder now. "He lost both his legs working on the chain gang, and some nice white man made him new ones for Christmas. They plastic and have shoes on them."

Luther stiffened his legs and turned toward the boys. "What's that got to do with anything?"

The little boy lowered his head. "Nothing." His voice sounded like a mouse.

"Our Pop's gone walk again," the older one said. "That's what it's got to do with."

Luther took a step towards them. "Then y'all get that gall dang job taken care of. And do it tonight."

These boys loved their father. How dare they rub it in his face. Luther resumed walking, his feet flat on the pavement, but in his heart, he was climbing stairs on Christmas morning, LC having already opened his presents, Luther going to his bedroom, where he looked out the window at all that he had amassed, but his eyes fell to the sill, to a ladybug that had come in from the cold, sought refuge inside Luther's house. Luther had put his finger against it, this time gently scooting it, as his mind played out what he wanted to do, call his boy upstairs, his boy running to him, Luther pointing to the bug and saying, "Get that red crawler there, and eat it," but LC putting his hand over his mouth and beginning to laugh, small at first but then taking off like he had wings. Luther knowing he had him then. Luther laughing, too. LC bending low towards the bug and saying, "He's got spots on him, and I can count them, too, Daddy. Watch!" LC counting all the way to ten and LC laughing again, laughing like he was free to laugh and tender enough to laugh, even enough to carry into his whole life. Luther hoping it so.

Then Luther had taken a deep breath and called his boy's name, calling "LC! Got you another present. Think you'll like this one."

Luther had listened for footsteps, eager ones, climbing the stairs.

But he heard none. Absolutely none.

Only the back door slamming. He looked out his window, his boy coming into view and then running across the field with arms wide open towards Uncle's tiny house.

．．．．．

Ike Thrasher looked in on the boy and found him asleep and no longer crying. His mother lay in the Anderson Memorial Hospital, *worn out.* That's how Ike thought of her condition, although the doctors had used big words, called it "exhaustion" and "dehydration." "I'll take care of the boy," Ike had told her before the nurses pushed him from the room. "We ain't got no lights," Sarah was saying as they closed the door.

The light from the moon fell onto the boy's pillow, just above his head. It looked like an angel's halo. Ike knew this was one of those rare moments when God delivered a direct sign. He would provide the light.

The boy feared his tablet had done this to her, but Ike had tried to put him at ease, telling him it did not. They stayed in the front lobby all through Christmas night and much of the next day, but Ike began to worry that the boy would begin to suffer like his mother and insisted they go home. By kerosene light, Ike warmed up a supper of leftover Christmas food and told Emerson Bridge, "As soon as they get her built back up, she'll be good as new." The boy had begun to cry.

Ike now dropped to his knees beside the bed. He started to put his arm around the boy's shoulders, but Emerson Bridge beat him to it and threw himself against Ike. The boy held on with a fierceness that made Ike tremble.

"Them last words in Roy Rogers's prayer, about riding, Mr. Ike, can you say them to me?"

Ike knew the boy was thinking his mother was going to die, but he wanted to do what the boy asked. "And when in the failing dusk," Ike recited, "I get that final call, I do not care how many flowers they send. Above all else, the happiest trail would be, For you to say to me, 'Let's ride, My Friend.' Amen."

"Let's ride, My Friend," the boy repeated.

"But your mama's going to fight her way back to you. She's that kind of mama." Ike felt the boy's body relax. At that moment, he felt more like a preacher than he ever had.

"Back to us, Mr. Ike."

Ike's eyes began to fill like Reedy River, where he'd baptized souls in search. He imagined his own head going under water and coming back high into sunshine and blue. Ike Thrasher had found salvation.

He removed his hat, held it in his hand away from himself. His head now naked.

. . . . .

A sound woke Ike. He had made himself a pallet on the kitchen floor. He wanted to scream. But he stayed still, trying not to breathe. He'd forgotten how dark it got out in the country.

He should go outside and patrol the house, take a quick run around the premises. But he needed a weapon. Mrs. Creamer's frying pan sat on top of the woodstove. It was made of cast iron and could hurt someone. He picked it up, wrapped both hands around its handle and stepped out onto the porch, where he stayed still and listened.

He felt the coldness of the night but heard no sounds, except the rapid beating of his heart.

He stepped out into the yard, starting to his right and passing the boy's room. Shrubbery, tall enough to hide him, gathered in spots. He moved in behind the first bunch, then quickly scooted to the next.

Another sound came. It was Mama Red, her voice deep, and then whispers from humans in the direction of the barn. He wanted to faint.

Lucky snorted. Ike was sure of it, and now dark shapes moved his way. Someone was stealing the boy's steer. "Stop!" he called out and ran towards the sounds, the pan held high. It was two negro boys, and they had Lucky on a rope. "Let him go, or I'll flatten y'all to smithereens." He lifted the frying pan high and charged at them with all his might.

The boys ran. They let go of Lucky and ran.

Ike kept the pan in the air, holding it like he was hanging from a cliff, and this was all that was saving him. But then it came to his mind that he had just saved Lucky. *He* had. Isaiah Ferdinand Thrasher, Jr.

He brought his hands down and stood with the animal, the two of them in the pitch black beneath a sky of sparkling pin lights he could swear were winking at him.

He knew what he had to do. He had to call the law, and he would do so from that neighbor man's house. He saw no lights on there, but Ike would knock and the man would answer.

But, first, he picked up Lucky's rope and led him home. Behind him, off in the distance, sat his father's house. It had no lights on, either, but he would not go knocking there that night. In fact, he would never go knocking there again.

. . . . .

Billy Udean was already in the garden that morning when Emerson Bridge approached him with his hand up, stiff. "0800, sir," Emerson Bridge said.

The man put his cigarette in his mouth and brought his hand up, too.

"Sorry I'm a day late, Mr. Billy Udean. Been at the hospital with my mama."

"How is she?"

"Still in there." He and Mr. Ike had decided not to tell his mother about the boys trying to steal Lucky. She had enough to worry about.

The man took a long pull on his cigarette. The end lit up bright red. "So, when's your birthday?" the man asked. "Got to make sure you're old enough to work."

"June 22nd."

"Yeah?" He blew smoke from his mouth in a circle. "What year?"

"19 and 44."

He pulled even longer now.

"I'm seven and half way to eight." Emerson Bridge tried to make his voice go deep. "Please say I'm old enough."

The man removed his cigarette and used it like a stick to point out towards his front yard. "Got a burn pile going over there. If you'll start gathering up these limbs I'm cutting and then go throw them on it."

He resumed work on a small tree with a large hand saw. This man was strong, moving the saw in a blaze.

"Does smoking warm you up, Mr. Billy Udean?"

"You cold?"

He was, but he didn't want the man to know. He might make him go inside. "No sir," he told him and crossed his arms over his chest. He thought he saw the man looking at his arms. "I'm strong. Watch!" Emerson Bridge gathered an armful and ran with them to the burn pile.

Each time he went for another load, he noticed the man studying him. Emerson Bridge thought he must be doing it wrong. "I'm sorry," he said.

"For what, son?"

"For not doing it right."

"Not doing what right?"

"What you asked," Emerson Bridge told him. "Taking these limbs and burning them."

The man took off his cap and brushed back what little hair he had and then put his cap back on. "Son, you're doing it right."

Emerson Bridge smiled. He liked being called "son." His papa had called him that.

When he returned for the next load, the man asked him, "What's your mama's name?"

"Sarah."

The man made a sound with his nose like he was breathing in something hard. "Creamer?"

"Creamer. Yes sir."

The man had a knot in his neck like his papa had. Emerson Bridge saw it move up and down. "My papa's name was Harold. But he's dead now."

It moved again. "Sorry to hear that, son. He been sick?"

"He coughed a lot, but Mama said he died of hard times." Emerson Bridge thought his eyes might fill up, but he took a deep breath and made himself stop. "I'm the man of the house now."

The man's eyes looked kind. Emerson Bridge bet his papa would have liked him.

"We've got Mr. Ike helping out some, and he tries real good. He wants to be a real cowboy like Roy Rogers, but me and Mama know he's really not. But don't say nothing to him about it." Emerson Bridge brought his finger up to his mouth and said, "Shhhh."

The man dropped his cigarette, ground it into the dirt and pulled out another. "Roy Rogers, huh? He's the one that's got dimples like you."

Emerson Bridge could feel his own sinking in all the way to his teeth. "Yes sir."

The man put the cigarette in his mouth and struck a match and then cupped his hand around the fire and brought it to the end. It was like he was whispering a secret.

Emerson Bridge gathered another load and started for the burn pile.

"So, your dimples," he heard at his back, "where'd you get them from? Your mama or your papa?"

He turned and looked the man's way. He had his cigarette pinched at his mouth, and his voice wasn't so strong anymore.

"Neither one." He ran on and soon returned for another armful.

But the man had not cut anymore. He faced Emerson Bridge and dropped his saw to the ground. His hands were shaking. He brought one up to Emerson Bridge's left cheek, to his dimple, and brushed it soft like it might break.

· · · · ·

From near his side shrubbery, Luther heard the automobile slow, then pick up speed. The afternoon paper had arrived. He had been keeping his ear out for such. Nothing about a steer theft had been reported in the morning paper.

Luther retrieved the paper and then went inside the house, as he did every afternoon to read it. Mildred was in the living room, taking down the Christmas tree. He started to shoo her away, but having her in there might be an advantage. It showed that he had nothing to worry about.

He sat in his easy chair, lit one of his Tampa Nuggets she'd given him for Christmas, and propped his feet on the ottoman. She had a nice fire going. He set his cigar in his ashtray stand and opened the paper, making sure he kept it high enough for Mildred not to see his face, in case there was bad news. But he needed to stop his hands from shaking.

He scanned the front page. Fighting continued in Korea, snow in Chicago, navy fighter planes lost in the Santee swamp. Nothing. His eyes moved to the "Today in Anderson" column. The big news was the annual rabbit hunt without guns, only dogs and sticks, where "a number of kills were made." A new Anderson hospital admission record, hip surgery for an old lady who tripped on her grandchild's Christmas toy and teenagers practicing basketball at the Recreation Center. Nothing.

Luther wiped his brow.

When he'd spent enough time on the front page for Mildred to believe he was reading it, he turned to the inside to more local news on page three, and there his eyes saw the headline "Negroes Steal Turkeys." He sucked in his breath. What if the paper had gotten the animal wrong? But then he read it was old man H. S. Hanks, who was known for raising turkeys, hundreds of them. The law had enough on their hands with this turkey theft. Luther was home free.

But, there, down lower, appeared the headline, "Negro Boys on the Loose after Attempted Steer Rustling." Luther's hands dropped, crunching the paper so loud, Mildred looked his way. He jerked his hands up high again.

He read to himself. "An attempted theft of a 4-H steer belonging to seven-year-old Emerson Bridge Creamer, son of Mrs. Sarah Creamer, of Route 2 in west Anderson, occurred late Wednesday night. The sheriff credits Mr. Isaiah Ferdinand Thrasher, Jr., of McDuffie Street, with stopping two negro boys from stealing the steer. "I was under a commitment to protect the Creamer place," Mr. Thrasher said. *Ike Thrasher was the reason they were caught?*

He wanted to ball up the paper and throw it in the fire and let Mildred's flames consume it the way the lure of her money had consumed him. But he knew he needed to finish reading in his usual fashion. Of all days, this had to be a Thursday when the paper was as thick as a Dobbins slice of bacon with all the grocery advertisements.

But what if the negro boys knew who he was? Why did he have to wear a suit that day to try to impress Donald Lee at the bank? He should have worn clothes that were common. If they could walk to the Creamer place, they could walk to his. His wasn't as far. They had nothing to lose. They could kill him. But maybe they'd just come for the money he'd promised. What if he left the coins on the front porch? But how would they know where he lived?

He balled up the paper and threw it into the fire. "Ain't nothing ever in here worth reading."

He walked the stairs to his bedroom and took his gun, his pearl-handle, from beneath the mattress and then went outside to his truck and placed the gun under his seat.

"What'd you put in there, Dad?" It was LC out in the yard and not in the lot where he was supposed to be, working with his steer.

Luther wanted to backhand him, but he liked that his boy was man enough to question him. He pulled the gun back out and held it between them. "Can't trust niggers. They'll steal you blind."

The fading sun caught the silver barrel and made it appear to shine. Luther, though, preferred that his boy see the handle, see that he could afford a pearl-handle. He slid his fingers forward and let the sun cast the pearl as white as teeth. Luther looked at his boy, in his eyes, to see if they glistened, too.

But they did not.

LC turned and went to the lot, to his steer, which he touched, running his hands, flat and full, along the side of the animal's neck. As if he loved him, Luther thought, as if he loved him.

Luther put the gun back under the seat.

It was a tad early for him to go to his garage, but to his garage he went and touched his drinking glass and bottle of almighty whiskey, running his hand flat over them.

And then he poured himself full.

. . . . .

Merritt pulled into Luther's driveway before Luther had finished his breakfast. "LC, get your lessons and get out to the road. The bus'll be early today, being the first day back at school."

He took a deep breath. He knew why Merritt was there.

He went outside to Merritt's truck parked near the barn. Merritt rolled down his window. "And what do I owe this momentous gigantic enormous pleasure?"

"On my way to the Creamers to check on that steer, Luther. Was out of town last week when it happened. You know any more?"

Luther felt his body jerk. "All I know is I got to kill a hog today as soon as Uncle gets here." The hard part was over now. Merritt wasn't on to him. There'd been nothing more in the newspaper about the negro boys.

"So you don't know anything else?" Merritt said.

Luther wanted to spit in the man's face but chose to cast it on the ground. "Got my own boy's steer to worry about. Don't make it my business to follow the Creamers like you do. Run after every time they twitch their little pinkie." Luther motioned with his last finger in front of Merritt's baby face.

"Attempted rustling is hardly twitching their little pinkie, Luther."

"Well, *Paul*," Luther told him and made sure he said the man's name with the same heaviness the man had tried to use on him. "Who says that jelly didn't make it all up? Bet he did it to get attention. Everybody wants to be in the paper. Surprised he didn't insist on them taking his picture with his little cowboy git-up on."

Merritt took a deep breath and let it out real slow.

"Why you asking me for, anyway? I ain't got nothing to do with your prized 'down the roader.' You think I'm that Houdini or something and can pull that stuff out of the air? Or that man with them memory powers the paper says is coming to the Recreation Center that can name the exact population of every town in the whole state? No, sir. I'm just a poor country boy trying to run a farm out here, if you'll excuse me." Luther took a couple of steps away.

"I'll tell you who's poor," Merritt called out. "That little Creamer boy. Dog, if he don't have the hardest time."

Luther shot his eyes towards the lot, where his boy's steer was tied. He hoped Merritt would follow his lead.

But all Merritt said was, "Should have paid him more attention. Gone around there more."

Luther could feel his body tensing up.

"Don't go getting your dander up, Luther. Not showing favoritism, if that's what you're thinking." Merritt was backing up and chuckling. He'd never heard Merritt chuckle. "Everybody knows you've got a dynasty out here."

Luther made a show of drawing up air in his nose. "What's that smell?"

"Manure?" Merritt said and stopped.

Luther drew up more air. "Why, the smell of money."

Merritt was moving again. "By the way," he called out, "they approved moving the Fat Cattle Show & Sale from the fairgrounds out here to your farm. You got what you wanted. Nobody can challenge you."

Merritt left. Luther had thought he would revel at the county agent using the word "dynasty" to describe what he had built, but Luther wondered if the man had said it in jest. Like he didn't believe it for half a second. And that they were moving the show to his place, so that when LC's steer that Luther had selected didn't win again, everyone could laugh and do so on his Dobbins property, where the laughter would seep into soil, staining it and causing nothing to ever grow there again.

The mother cow had not seen or heard the gentle wind. The mother cow kept watch.

"Morning, Mr. LC." It was Uncle. He watched the man go towards the barn, where the hog was penned up with a big slop trough, getting fat. It was certainly cold enough for hog killing, highs in the forties that day, and he could trust Uncle to do it right.

Luther felt a rush travel to his head like a bullet. He needed a better plan, one he could trust.

He went to his truck and retrieved his gun. He would give it to Uncle to put a bullet in the hog's head, but Uncle would also be using a second bullet.

Luther found him in the barn. "I need you to go do something for me tonight. Need you to go out to the Creamer place and get that blame steer and get rid of it." He shook the gun in front of Uncle's face when he said the last part.

Uncle dropped his eyes towards the ground. "Mr. LC, I—"

"*I* is right. *I is going to do that for you, Mr. LC.* That's all you need to say."

"You know I can't do that. That's not—"

"That's none of your business. You work for me. You'll do what I tell you."

The Adam's apple in Uncle's neck bobbed from a big swallow. Luther pointed the gun there. "Maybe the business end of a gun is a superior talker than I am." Beads of perspiration peppered the man's brow, sprinkled about like the little pin holes in the tin roof of the tenant house he grew up in.

"It's wrong, Luther."

At the sound of his outright name, Luther felt his body tense. He pulled the hammer back. "I'll tell you what's wrong. Wrong is you getting above your colored raising. I'm *Mr. LC* to you. And you ain't nothing but a nigger."

"You don't mean that."

"I do," Luther told him. "I mean it as strong as, as—"

"As strong as what?" Uncle said and moved closer to the gun. "As strong as you were that night to tell on my mama? Make Mr. Allgood throw us off his place just for taking care of one of your kind?"

Luther's hand was shaking. "What was she doing with a white baby anyway?"

"A white lady she did laundry for died giving birth, and her husband didn't know what to do with it and asked my mama to take care of it until he could get him another woman to marry."

"Don't look right for negroes to have white babies."

"Like it didn't look right for whites to live as negroes?"

Luther moved the gun until it touched Uncle's skin. "I said go get that by God Creamer steer and get rid of it."

"No, sir." Uncle pressed his neck against the barrel. "Go on and shoot me, because I ain't going to go do it. It's wrong."

Luther could feel beads of perspiration on his brow now.

"You can't pull that trigger. You make everybody do your dirty work for you, *Luther*." Uncle backed away from the gun and put his hand on the barrel and pushed it aside.

He walked away.

"Don't you walk away from me," Luther called out. "You do that, and you'll never be hired on with me again."

The man kept walking.

"You hear me?" He aimed the gun at Uncle's back. "Should have known you never were my friend. That I couldn't count on you when I need you. When I need you the most."

Uncle now was halfway across the field. He was heading to his house.

Luther ran after him and got in front and put his hands on Uncle's shoulder to make him stop. But Uncle stepped around him and resumed walking.

The gun in Luther's hand shook.

He watched Uncle become smaller and smaller.

He watched Uncle go inside his house.

Luther stood still and waited for him to come back to him. Life could resume then. Luther's life.

But Uncle stayed inside.

Luther lowered his gun.

He walked back to his truck and returned the gun beneath his seat. Then he went to his garage and found his whiskey bottle, turned it up at his mouth and did not stop until all of the liquid was gone.

. . . . .

Sarah's boy sat between her and Mr. Thrasher on the ride home from the hospital. It was late morning and a school day, the first after the Christmas holidays, but her boy had stayed out in the hopes that this would be the day she'd get to come home.

They held hands.

Mr. Thrasher was not wearing his cowboy hat. She wondered if he'd lost it and couldn't afford to buy another, with all of the money he'd spent on them.

Six days was a long time to be away and an expensive time, too. Her hospital bill totaled almost two hundred dollars. Sarah had worried they'd not let her out until she paid it, but the man there told her as long as she could make a monthly payment, he wouldn't turn her over to Collections. "And you don't want to be turned over to Collections," he'd said. "They'll try and take whatever you have." She needed to get back to sewing those dresses as soon as she stepped in the door, but her doctor told her she needed bed rest for at least another week. She did not tell him, but that would not be possible.

As they approached her house, she saw Billy Udean's truck in his driveway. She squeezed Emerson Bridge's hand. *My boy,* she thought and rested her head against the window.

Mr. Thrasher stopped in front of his old home place and turned her head and body towards it. A "For Sale" sign was out front. She didn't know how much a cowboy hat would cost, but this seemed extreme. But then she remembered on one of his visits, he had asked about her bill, and she had not wanted to talk about it in front of her boy. It called for talking about it here. "I want you to know I'll get my hospital bill covered," she said and made sure she had a lift in her voice.

"Mr. Ike said he don't need it no more, Mama."

"But, don't you—" Sarah said.

"That's right. Don't need it no more." He let off on his brake and turned into their driveway, pulled up to the house, and came around and opened her door. The sun fell just right on his face, and she saw in it a peace that she'd never seen in him. It was as if an iron had removed all of the wrinkles, smoothed down his skin and made him young again.

She waited until he brought his eyes full on her, and then she told him, "I can't let you do it. But thank you."

"It's already done." He bowed towards her like the gentleman he was and extended his hand. She felt like Scarlett. She'd always wondered if Rhett Butler was wearing cologne in that movie. She thought she smelled it now and drew it up her body, took his hand and stepped from his truck, which could have been the finest carriage.

"I think it's time we started calling each other by our given names," he said. "What do you say, *Sarah?*"

Hearing her name sent a ripple through her, not the kind she got when she first met Harold. That one had ridden the surface of her skin like a child's foot running through a fresh-plowed field, its slight weight barely moving the warm dirt. But this one, this one ran deep, churning soil that lay hidden and bringing it high to see the light. "I say that'll take some getting used to. But, yes sir." She paused before she said his name. "Yes sir, *Ike.*"

"Mama! Come on," Emerson Bridge yelled from the steps. He had the screened door open.

Ike Thrasher bowed towards her and stepped out of the way as if clearing a path for her. She took a few steps, but then her heart began to race, and she thought she might faint. She bent over, putting her hands on her knees. Her boy rushed to her side, and, in no time, he and Ike had their hands holding around her waist. With their help, she resumed walking, making their way to the house and up the steps and to the kitchen, where a cake sat on the table. It looked to have chocolate frosting.

"Look what me and Mr. Ike made for you, Mama!"

Sarah brought her hands to her mouth.

Her boy threw his arms around her. "I'm glad you're home, Mama!"

"Me, too, hon."

"Make that three of us," Ike said and reached for her hand and her boy's.

They all held like that, giving those words their own space, which made the words grow even bigger, while light from the outside world shined through the curtains over the sink, shooting through in long rays that seemed to want to reach as far as they could.

. . . . .

Luther returned to the spot where he and Uncle had last stood together. He sat in the pasture grass and weeds, long dead, and watched Uncle's house. He had a hard time sitting up. The whiskey made his body feel like jelly.

In time, Uncle and his common-law emerged, both loaded down like mules. They looked to be dragging bed sheets, filled as fat as ticks. Uncle was pulling a wagon, the one he used to collect drink bottles along the roadside for extra money. "Hey!" Luther tried to call out and get on his feet but fell. "Hey!" he tried again from the ground, his head bobbing like a baby just learning to lift. "Why didn't you never come back to see me when you left way back then? Just to say hey. Why didn't you? We were just boys then."

Luther watched them until he could see them no more.

And then he kept working until he got back on his feet and could go to the barn, where he fetched his can of kerosene and set back off across the field.

When he got to his tenant house, he poured kerosene all around the outside. Then, he took his matches from his overalls pocket and struck one hard against the rough tarpaper, a light tan. He'd selected that color over the dark gray, tan being closer to white. He wondered if Uncle ever noticed that Luther had done that for him.

He threw the burning match to the ground.

And then he stepped back and watched it all die.

I laid up there in that hospital bed and thought about all you've taught me, Mama Red, and about something I still ain't done with my boy. I ain't played with him. Asked my nurse for the biggest piece of paper they had, so I could wad it up and throw it in the air and practice catching it. But she made me stop.

I see Billy Udean has come back. His truck is still over there. Has he been over here? You seen him talking to my boy? I see part of the garden's been cleaned up. He must be coming back for good. But he will not take my boy away.

Wonder if he still likes his beer? The last catfish supper we all had together was the night before he packed his suitcase and took off walking to town to join the Army and go across the big waters to kill what he called "slant eyes." He'd been making fun of Harold for not going, calling him "four eyes." All around his plate, Billy Udean had lined the bottles of beer he'd finished off while he was eating, lined up like he was making a wall out of them. There was 10 of them. Mattie tried to get him to back off a little bit, and he slapped her mouth so hard, he knocked her in the floor. Harold picked up Billy Udean and threw him out the door into the yard like he was a sack of potatoes.

Funny I say potatoes because that was the first sign, after Billy Udean left out of here, that we were all starting on sewing a new kind of dress. That very next Sunday night, we picked right up with our fish supper. Mattie come over, and it didn't take Harold long to make that first stitch. He said, "I don't like the way you make Mattie cut our French fried potatoes."

"Like what?" I said.

"Like fingers," he went and held up one of his in the air.

"That's how they supposed to be, Harold. Longways," I told him.

"Only thing that's supposed to be longways is a woman's hair," he said. "I like a woman's hair hanging long." He used his hands to touch his shoulders.

He'd never known me to wear hair that way. Mine was always in a bun. Mattie's too. I'd done it up for her in a bun that day.

"I like my potatoes cut round, sliced thin and cut round," Harold kept going.

"Sister, I don't mind cutting them round next time," Mattie said. She always cut them while I fried the fish.

"Longways is how they're supposed to be," I said. "That's proper."

Mattie kept cutting them longways for a Sunday or two. But then she started cutting a few of them round. She'd mix them in with what was cut proper, and, once she'd fried them all, she'd set a couple of the rounds off the side of the plate and aim them straight at Harold. He'd see them and grin.

Then Billy Udean stopped sending his army paychecks home. "You know how much he likes his beer," is all Mattie said about it, but I could see worry lines streaking her face. I'd seen my mama sew enough to know how to run a stitch or two, so I asked Harold to get me a sewing machine, and I set about sewing dresses and selling them and giving Mattie the money. Harold took them to work and sold them to some men for their wives. Two dollars apiece.

But then they did a leap frog one Sunday night while we was eating our catfish. Harold up and said he'd found Mattie a job, said the telephone company needed operators to connect calls, called them Hello Girls.

"Sister don't need no job," I told him. "She's got my dress money."

Mattie didn't say a word.

"Billy Udean never would stand for her getting no job," I told him.

"Billy Udean ain't here." Harold was talking in a voice more stern than I'd ever heard.

"Then I want one, too," I said.

Harold slammed his fist on the table. Made his beer bottle bounce up in the air. He'd taken to drinking him one or two. "You're stout," he said. "And handy around the house."

"Y'all," Mattie said in the slightest little voice. "I do think I would like to try to work." She had her eyes on Harold.

Harold picked up his beer and took a big swallow.

In two days' time, they started riding to work together every morning and coming home together every afternoon. And in a week's time, Mattie had her hair down, hanging longways.

Harold went to catching less and less fish. It seemed like every Sunday he'd come home with one more short of the Sunday before, until this one Sunday in September, the one before his birthday, he came home with just one. Mattie was standing out in the yard with me when he pulled up. I said to him, "What you trying to do? Starve us?"

Harold didn't say nothing.

"One fish ain't going to feed three people," I said, but he stood there like a bump on a log.

That's when Mattie popped up and said, "He don't like to fish."

"What you mean he don't like to fish?" I said.

She looked at Harold. "Tell her, Harold."

"You tell her," he said.

Mattie twirled a piece of her long hair with her finger. "Harold don't like to kill nothing," she said.

"He don't like to kill a fish?" I said.

Harold had his head hung down.

"Harry just went along, just because," Mattie said.

"Harry?" I called out.

"I meant Harold," she said and started for the house. "I'll start cutting up the potatoes."

But I'd seen her eyes, and they told me everything.

JANUARY 2–3, 1952

Sarah rested her body against the kitchen table as she bent over it, pinning the thin paper pattern to the fabric beneath. This would be her second dress since she had come home from the hospital two days before. She had finished the first one by alternating between staying in bed and sewing, at first resting for two hours and then working for 15 minutes, but over the two days, she had built up to almost equal time.

A knock came on her screened door. She wasn't expecting Ike, and her boy was at school, but he wouldn't knock anyway. Maybe it was Mr. Allgood, again, wanting his money or worse, Mama Red.

She heard a name being called. She heard Clementine. It was Billy Udean. She drew in her breath. He couldn't see inside, but what if he decided to come through the porch like he used to and knock on the big door? He'd be able to see her, the shape of her anyway, through those bare curtains.

She tiptoed backwards to the hall and hid against the inside wall, pulling the darkness around her like a blanket. But what if he was in trouble like she had been in trouble on Christmas day, and he needed her?

She smoothed down her housedress, tucked in her stray hairs, and went to the porch. But he was no longer there. He was approaching the garden. "Excuse me," she called out.

He turned towards her and removed his dark hat, holding it in front of his chest like a gentleman. Sarah had never seen this in him. Maybe he wanted to scratch his head. That would be more like him. But he didn't.

"Left something for your boy there on the steps," he called out, "if you'll kindly see that he gets it."

Sarah grabbed onto the doorjamb. He'd said "your boy." Had they been talking?

"And I stacked some firewood against the house there for y'all to burn. Your boy can bring it in for you. He's that kind of boy."

They had been talking. Billy Udean knew him. Had he seen his dimples? Surely, he'd seen his dimples.

She should tell him thank you, but she'd have to use her Sarah voice.

He resumed walking towards the garden. Sarah eased open the door and saw the sack. It was rather large and had Sears & Roebuck on the outside of it. The gift was for Emerson Bridge, she knew, but still she picked it up and peeked inside and saw a garment of some sort. She removed it. It was a coat, a nice one, brown, and made of some kind of leather. Even the lining was nice, a lighter shade of brown, and made of rayon that in itself cost good money. Fifty-eight cents a yard was the last she had paid for it.

She would risk it. She called out, "Thank you. That's real nice of you."

He was in the garden now. He threw up his hand to acknowledge her words. A big section of it had been cleared. He started back towards her, and Sarah wanted to run inside the house, yet also go forward into the yard to greet him. But she stayed where she was and settled her feet over the stains from the blood that Mattie had left the night she crawled out that door.

He came to stand just out from the bottom step. A wave of tingles climbed Sarah's body.

He took his cigarette from his mouth and held it down by his side. "Didn't know what size to get him but thought that looked about right."

Sarah nodded. "It's very right."

He took a step towards her. She squeezed the door jamb. "He's a hard worker. In one of the side pockets, he'll find the money I owe him for helping me try to clean up some of that old garden over there."

They *had* spent time together. But her boy had not said. "A hard worker, yes. Thank you very much." She was speaking full in her Sarah voice. He did not want to take Emerson Bridge from her.

Billy Udean pulled long on his cigarette. Sarah felt like he was pulling her.

He returned his hat to his head and tipped it towards her and turned to leave.

She didn't want him to. She swung open the door and went down the steps after him.

He stopped but kept his back to her. His shoulders were quivering.

They were no more than two feet apart. Sarah felt a circle around the two of them, the two of them alone, sectioned off from all doings and sounds of the rest of the world.

"I became a better man while I was over there," he said, his voice carrying waves. "People that knew me before I went across the big waters would see that I'm a different man now."

Sarah wanted him to turn around, but that would put it all on him. She needed to do something now. She moved around in front.

He had his head bowed, and she didn't know if he was a praying man now or just afraid to look at her. But what she did know was this was a different man. And this different man *knew*.

"We was in gunfire in France, and there, out in the middle of a field, was this milk cow that was bawling." Sarah kept her ear out for him to call her name. She told herself that when he did, she would say it was so. "The cow needed to be milked. Her sack was so full, it looked like it might bust wide open. The way she was hollering, it got down inside of me and made me start to shake. I ran to her, put my gun down and took her teats in my hands and went to milking her."

Sarah felt a tug at her nipples.

He removed his hat and held it upside down. "Used my helmet as a pail like this and let that good milk run into it and keep it there, all safe. Bullets were flying all around me like a flock of birds, and not one of them hit me. Or her." He brought his eyes up to Sarah's now and locked in. "I felt like she was my Mattie."

Sarah felt a jolt start at her feet and shoot skyward. She widened her stance to steady herself, but not because, as times before, when she feared what was coming, but because she welcomed it, welcomed it full.

"God protected me, and I told him, 'If you keep me alive and let me go back home to my Mattie, I'll do her right, I promise.' But I didn't get that chance. Sometimes you don't get another chance." His entire face was wet. "I just wish Mattie could have seen me now."

"I do, too," Sarah told him fast, and when she did, she knew she had crossed the line. She wanted to scream *My name's not Clementine.* But he knew that already.

They held their eyes on each other, both staring truth head on.

"Mattie would have loved him, your boy," Billy Udean said. "His dimples, especially."

Sarah felt every nerve in her body become like a soldier and salute. This is what it felt like to serve, she thought, serve something bigger than herself. She would risk it now, the whole truth. "Yes, she would have. And his dimples, yes. They can hold a whole lot of happiness. She would see it."

She wanted to put her arms around him. She wanted the two of them to stay up for the rest of the day and night and talk and then go clear the rest of the garden, and come spring plow it and run through it barefoot, and when they'd felt all the fresh dirt they could stand, plant it in potatoes and corn and green beans. And her boy could join them.

She held up the sack. "He'll be getting off the school bus this afternoon right at four o'clock, if you want to give it to him yourself."

"Appreciate that, but I'll be gone by then. There ain't nothing for me here. Time to let her sister finally sell this place and me to move on. Been down on the coast with a buddy from the war ever since I come off my war bond tour, which the army put me on right quick as soon as they whisked me away that day." He put his hat back on and tipped it towards her, stepped around her and started for the garden.

She wanted to scream, *She didn't kill herself because of you. She did it because she was stained. And she couldn't live with that.* But who was Sarah to say? She realized she did not really know Mattie. Still, she wanted to take the burden from this man before her.

But all she called out was, "I lost Harold last March."

He stopped and turned back towards her. "Your boy told me. Sorry to hear that."

"And Mattie." The words slipped from her lips, and she did not wish to call them back.

"Mattie," he said, his voice not going high with a question, but staying down low, accepting.

But his eyes said the most. They said, *This is what we have now. This.*

He turned and continued on across and got in his truck and drove away. She imagined he had killed some people, maybe even some slant eyes, but none could have the bite of the deaths that had taken place here at home.

She began to shake all over. It was like all that she had hidden was fighting to be freed. She opened her arms, stretched them wide, and her feet, she set them apart. Sarah opened her mouth and flung back her head. The skies above were blue and full of puffs of clouds like the smoke from the cigarettes of the men she had loved—her papa, Harold, and now Billy Udean Parnell.

. . . . .

"Hey!" Emerson Bridge called out to LC, who was up ahead in the hallway at school. This was Emerson Bridge's first day back, and he hustled towards his friend and told him in a rush, "I don't have to sign that paper. Mama ain't going to make me."

"You're lucky," LC said, his voice flat.

Emerson Bridge thought his friend would be happy for him, but LC had his head lowered and was gritting his teeth. *Big mouth,* Emerson Bridge was thinking. LC didn't have a mother who would do this for him.

"My dad would kill me before he'd not sign that paper." LC's eyes looked bloodshot.

Emerson Bridge felt a sweat move through him.

"He keeps a pistol under the seat in his truck. He'd kill me dead with it."

"You don't mean that."

He saw LC swallow.

"Do you mean that?"

"He hates me," LC said.

"You know he don't hate you."

"He hates me. My dad, my daddy hates me."

Several girls walked past them. Emerson Bridge thought how lucky girls were to only have to make curtains for their 4-H project.

LC moved from being out in the open to the wall, which he hugged up against. "If I don't win this year . . ." His voice trailed off.

"Then what? If you don't win, what?"

LC moved his forehead against the wooden boards. He looked to be grinding it in.

"He'll holler at you?"

LC made no response.

"Give you a whipping?"

LC turned to look at Emerson Bridge straight on, his forehead dark red. "Kill me."

"Boys," their teacher called out from the door just beyond them. "Almost time for class."

LC slapped his hands over his ears and stomped his feet. He had become moody, but never like this. He balled up his fists.

Emerson Bridge thought LC might hit him, but his friend put his hands flat over his face and pressed and said, "I hate him. I hate him. And I will not win for him."

"Well, then don't," Emerson Bridge told him.

"I won't. You're right, I won't." LC wrapped his arms around himself like he was cold and scared and every bad thing there could be. "I've thought about taking my steer and running away." LC was whispering now.

"Where would you go?" Emerson Bridge whispered back.

"Nowhere to go. He'd come find me and kill me with his pearl-handle."

"What you talking so much about killing for? It scares me."

"Just a fact. What's wrong with a fact?"

Big mouth, Emerson Bridge told himself again.

"Starting tonight, I'm going to sneak out to the barn and take away the afternoon feed. Put it back in Luther Charles Dobbins's feed sack that I'd like to cram down his throat, make him choke on all that roughness, scratch his insides out." LC began to cry.

Emerson Bridge put his hand on his friend's shoulder.

"Boys," the teacher said again. "It's time."

"I don't mean that," LC said. "Forget I ever said it. I love my daddy." He took off out the front door.

· · · · ·

The material was an emerald green gabardine and thicker than most fabrics Sarah worked with. Pinning patterns to this material required something more. She was grateful. She needed something more. Billy Udean had been gone less than an hour. Sarah was standing at the end of the kitchen table where he'd always sat for their Sunday night fish suppers, her body now leaning where he had kept his empty beer bottles lined up around him. Mattie always sat to his left. Sarah looked there now and pushed a pin through, the two pieces now together. Even if a wind blew, the two would stay.

Like mothers do. Mothers stay. Mama Red had taught her this when she had to separate her from Lucky back in the fall. Sarah would see her eating alongside her calf, four lines of barbed wire keeping them apart, yet not at all. Mattie was a mother. But she had not stayed. *How could you, Mattie? How could you leave your little boy? You took the easy way out. Mamas don't leave.* Sarah pushed another pin through and thought of her own child, the little girl she let the doctor take away.

She raised up from the table. She didn't even know where her baby was buried. And there she was, finding fault with Mattie.

Sarah had to find her baby. She had to find her that day. She got her pocketbook and was out the door to her automobile. Where she was going, she did not know. But, when she approached Dixon Road, she found herself turning left and making her way to Mildred Dobbins. Sarah pulled beside the house and stepped into air that was not fresh and fragrant but smelled of something burning. She glanced around for anything on fire, but saw nothing out of the ordinary, only a man who looked like Mr. Dobbins leaving the garage. He appeared to stumble but then righted himself.

"Why, Sarah!" she heard as she stepped up onto the Dobbins front porch. It was Mildred with a broom in her hand. She was sweeping.

Sarah rushed out the words, "Would you happen to know where a doctor back in 19 and 37 might have buried little babies whose parents didn't go to no church? Some place south of town?"

Mildred propped the broom by the front door, reached back and untied her apron, and ran into the house. Sarah's fast words had scared her friend off. "I'm so sorry. Where's my manners?" she called into the house. "I meant to say hello first." Why hadn't she just driven on to town? Then she wouldn't have lost her new friend.

She turned to leave and heard Mildred's shoes tapping across the hardwoods behind her. "So sorry, dear," Mildred was saying, "had to get my pocketbook and put on some lipstick. I want to take you somewhere."

There were no words between them as Mildred drove.

It began to rain.

They drove through town and just south of it to White Street to a cemetery where they went under a curved archway that carried the words "Silverbrook Cemetery." "There's a baby section here," Mildred told her. "Some ladies at the church keep it clean."

Sarah pictured an area with a fence, a pretty white one and so low to the ground, a person could step over it. But there was no fence, only tiny markers lined up in crooked rows like children's teeth and all following the downward slope of the earth. The tips of her fingers and toes tingled.

The rain was not a hard rain. Sarah could see through the glass on her window with ease. "There looks to be a hundred of them," she said.

Mildred parked along the road under a large oak tree that grew at the top of the hill, its bare limbs like bones piled up in the sky. Sarah stepped out and extended her hand as if she was reaching for someone's hand. She was reaching for Harold's. She did this without thinking.

The markers were a dark gray metal and no more than two inches high. They set in the ground on spikes and carried the name of the funeral home, McDougald's, along with a date, most carrying only one. "There ain't no names," Sarah said. "Nobody's got them a name."

She started down the hill. "January 19th, 19 and 37," she called out. "That's the one I'm looking for. It was a Tuesday."

The graves seemed to be organized by date. Mildred began on the far side. Sarah moved through the early '50s and then the '40s and began the '30s. Her pace picked up.

About halfway down the slope and three graves over from the road, she spotted a marker with January 19, 1937. Beyond it, she saw dates in 1936. This was the only marker for her date. "Here she is!" Sarah called out.

Mildred came running. Sarah dropped to her knees. "Here's my . . . here's my daughter." She had never said that word. "My *daughter*, Claudia. Little Claudia. Claudia Creamer."

Mildred joined her on the ground.

"Everybody hear me?" Sarah called out. "Her name is Claudia!" She put her hands on the sides of the marker and squeezed. "Everybody deserves them a name."

It was raining harder now.

"The doctor didn't let me hold her. 'Attached,' he said. Said I'd get attached. What's wrong with getting attached? Tell me!" She was screaming now. She imagined the little girl in her arms now, awake in her arms, her naked bloody skin no longer blue but a deep red, her body no longer limp but squirming and her mouth hungry for her mother's milk."I'm holding you now, little Claudia. Mama's holding you now." Her sounds were guttural.

But then Sarah took her hands from the marker. "You ain't got you one good mama bone in you, girl." Sarah mimicked her mother's clipped tone, even moving her hand like she was holding a fly swatter.

"Why, you're a very good mother, Sarah," Mildred told her.

"No, I ain't. I let a man, a complete stranger, take my little girl off. Told me to forget her, said he'd 'handle this.' *This? This* was my baby girl, and I let a stranger take her away. Didn't give her a name. Didn't give her a burial. Didn't give her nothing. Mamas don't do that."

She got up on her feet and ran for the automobile.

"My Little LC talks about you all the time," Mildred called out. "About how kind you are."

Sarah got in the automobile, water dripping from her hair and face and hands.

Mildred joined her but didn't crank the engine. "Sometimes I think my Little LC wishes you were his mama. I've even been a tad jealous of you, Sarah. You don't realize how strong you are. I'm not as strong as you."

"Strong wouldn't have let him take her away."

"You were doing what the doctor said. Any mother would have."

"But I ain't any mother. I was Little Claudia's."

She thought of Billy Udean's coming and going and now Little Claudia. "It seems like my days past are reaching back to me and saying 'Hey there.' It's like they're trying to get me on the telephone line so we can talk." The rain beat down hard on the automobile's roof like the fingernails of a thousand babies.

"You a good friend, Mildred. You are. And a good mama, too."

"Good mamas protect. And I don't do a good job of that. Big LC's hard on him. Little LC's a bag of nerves, especially lately."

Sarah thought of her papa and the way they managed through Sarah's mother. "Laughing. Laughing helps out a lot."

"And peppermints," Mildred said. "I know you've smelled my peppermints."

Sarah did not smell them now.

"That Retonga is 36 percent of what my husband would call the devil's drink."

Sarah heard Mildred take a deep breath and then another.

"Can I tell you what I'm afraid of?" Mildred whispered. "I'm afraid that my Little LC might crack up. One minute he's laughing. The next he's crying. It's like he's living in two different worlds."

Sarah thought of Mama Red, what she would do. "Stay close to him. Even if there's hard wires between you." She looked back towards her baby's grave. Rain drops streaked down her window. "So the rain can run off."

"Off what, dear?" Mildred asked.

"The hill that they put these babies on. They're on the side of it. So the rain can run off, forget that it was ever there. But that ain't right. They deserve to be on level ground so water can sit on them. And stay."

The mother cow took into her mouth some of her calf's mixed grain. She ate it most days, now that they could share the feed trough, but she could only eat a little, given her two remaining teeth on the bottom and gum pad up top. This day, her chewing loosened further one of her last two. It fell from her, while in her offspring's mouth, his last baby tooth had just come in.

Sarah was waiting in the yard for Emerson Bridge when the school bus let him out that afternoon. By then, the rain had packed its suitcase and left, leaving behind a patient sky of blue that showed itself full and strong. In her hand, she held a rock, the one from the blue blanket. She had squeezed it so, its jagged edges brought blood. She wanted it to bring blood. She thought of the cuts on Mama Red when Sarah met her.

He ran up the driveway towards her, and when he got to within good sight, she tossed the rock into the air a whole foot high. She cupped her hands together and caught it.

"Want to play rock?" she called his way and held it out for his view. She didn't know what he and his papa had called the game.

Emerson Bridge ran faster. "Swell!"

Before she tossed it, she studied his dimples, sinking deep, and told him, "Your dimples there, Emerson Bridge Creamer, they could hold a whole lot of happiness."

"Throw it, Mama," he yelled, his hands, ready.

She swung her arm back.

It was because of you, Mama Red. You. You and your boy taught me to play. There I was thinking I'd go into the night with a heart so heavy for my Little Claudia that I wouldn't be of no use to my boy. But look at how it turned out. It started down low and went up high.

Me and Mattie, I believe we went the other way.

218

Six weeks after Harold's birthday, she was too sick to go to work. Said for Harold to go on. I found her hanging off the side of her bed, throwing up in her slop jar. I got a wet rag and held it to her forehead. When she was feeling better, I went home and put a chicken on to boil to make her some good soup. She went back to work the next day.

But the next Sunday night, when she come over for our fish fry, as soon as she stepped into the kitchen, she went to gagging. Threw up all over the floor. I wanted to get her to a doctor, but she wouldn't have it.

"The smells," she said, "the smells."

I walked her back home, and, when I come back, Harold had him four beers lined up around his plate.

After another month or so, Mattie started being too sick to go to work again. Then, on up in the morning, she'd get all right and we'd sit at her eating table and talk about things she'd overheard people say on the telephone. But one morning I went over there, and she had her hair up in a bun again like mine. She'd been wearing it long. She saw me looking at it as soon as she raised up from her slop jar and brought her hand up back there and pressed on it like she wanted it to stay forever.

That's when the light come on for me, Mama Red. Right then. Right then I let myself know what I'd been trying not to know. None of us did. None of us wanted to hit it straight on like that. Billy Udean had been gone for a good year by then. Mattie was carrying my husband's baby. It didn't take too much figuring.

She eased herself back down on the bed and pulled the covers up high.

I had all kinds of jumbled up feelings. I was hurt, because my husband had stepped out on me. And I was scared because what were we going do with that baby? And jealous. I was jealous of what the two of them had shared and would keep on sharing. Where was I going to fit in? But all I can tell you is that I loved her, and I couldn't never have me another baby. I was thinking she could do it for both of us. We was close like sisters. Wouldn't sisters do that?

Her hair had a hard shine to it from grease. I said to her, "I want to wash your hair, Sister. Can I wash your hair?"

She went to shaking her head and slapped her hands up top like she was blocking me. But I just put mine right on top of hers.

"I don't want to take my hair down, Sarah. I want to keep it like this. Always keep it like this." She had her eyes squeezed shut.

"Call me Sister, Sister Sarah. Always call me that." My voice was speeded way up.

But she stayed quiet.

"Please," I said. "Please call me that."

I told myself I would sit there for the rest of time, if that's what it took. But, soon, there she went opening her eyes. She whispered to me, "One time. It wasn't but one time."

"Call me Sister, Sister Sarah. Say it."

"Sister Sarah," she said, and I let them words coat me like plentiful flour on my hands. "One time, Sister Sarah. One." She held up her finger. It was shaking.

"Harold's birthday," I told her.

The sun was coming through her window, fell in like a knife cutting its way in.

"Let me wash your hair, Sister," I said.

"He was sweet to me. That was the reason, a pitiful reason, but that was the reason." She took her hands off her head, slid them down under mine, and I was left holding on.

I washed her hair and put it back in a bun.

When Harold come home from work that day, I said to him, "Teach me how to drive." I smelled whiskey on his breath.

"A woman don't need to know that," he told me.

"This woman does. This woman needs to take Mattie, our Mattie, to the doctor."

He hadn't been looking at me, but he turned my way when I said that. I started for the door.

He give me a lesson. He give them to me all afternoon, and then I called myself knowing how to drive.

I come in the house and got Mattie on the telephone and told her to be ready that next morning, that we was going to the doctor.

She sat between me and Harold. I drove. Not a word was said. We dropped Harold off at work. Before he got out, I asked him how to get to Greenville. That was the next big town over. I figured we needed us a stranger for a doctor. He pulled out his billfold and handed me two one-dollar bills.

We found us a doctor. He said it was so, said Mattie would have the baby in June of the next year. My nerves started at the top of my head and came on down my face and my arms and my legs to my toes.

When we got back in the automobile, tears, big ones, filled up Mattie's eyes. "I'm sorry about them potatoes, Sister," she said, "cutting them round like I did sometimes. And right in your face."

I pictured them round like little tires that could roll. And what I told her back was the only words I could say. "I can carry it, Sister. I can." And I took me a deep breath and held on until I got her back home and me across the yard where not a soul could see me or hear me.

JANUARY 7–13, 1952

The letter came in Monday's mail. Sarah was at her sewing machine running a long stitch when Emerson Bridge came in from school and handed it to her. She was thinking it was the hospital, wanting its money.

He was wearing his new coat. She especially liked the way its ribbing hugged his wrists. She reached over and circled his right one with her fingers.

"Look, Mama! You can fit all around me." He giggled.

She saw his breath. Her room was cold. She'd meant to put another stick of firewood in the woodstove before he got home. She told him, "I'm glad that coat's keeping you warm, hon."

This was her fifth and last dress. She would go with Mildred soon and deliver them. She had $38.22 left of Mildred's money. She'd use $10 of it to pay on her hospital bill. The handwriting on the envelope looked personal and not business, and it carried no return address. This was her mother's handwriting. She dropped the envelope in her lap.

"Who's it from, Mama?" Her boy's eyes were wide. He'd asked about her mother before. She'd told him she lived "far, far away."

"Somebody you don't know, hon." She wished he would leave."You seen Lucky yet?"

She resumed pedaling. She tried to put her mind on running a straight seam, but how did her mother know where she lived? Sarah had told her the day she left she was moving to South Carolina, but she'd never said where. And her married name, how did she know that? Harold told his name that first night, but that was fifteen years ago.

Then it came to her. That letter she'd sent her mother, *You finally got you a boy. You got a grandboy.* Her mother had received it and kept it. Sarah picked up her hook for removing stitches and caught just under the envelope's back flap, moving the hook across the top like she was pumping water from a well. The paper inside was thin. She read to herself, "That first name you got, that Clementine name. That come from a song your papa used to sing to me back when he loved me. Mama."

Sarah felt a tightness around her eyes.

"What's the matter, Mama?"

"Nothing, hon. Just got a letter from my mama." She whispered those last words.

"Your mama from far, far away?"

Sarah nodded and squeezed the material she was sewing, a pretty orchid color in rayon taffeta.

"What'd she say?" he asked.

She felt like she was that fabric, and her mother was trying to put a stitch in her, trying to make some kind of connection. The two of them. Because her mother had saved her letter. And her mother knew where she lived and knew her name. "She said she loves me," Sarah told him.

Her mother was coming for her. After all this time, coming for her.

. . . . .

Sarah set her black hat upon her head and on her hands slid her black gloves. It was six o'clock in the morning on Saturday, and she stood before her chifforobe mirror. Darkness hugged all around her, but in front, where she held the kerosene lamp, a bright light lit her like a baby sun. She wondered if her mother would recognize them, the hat and gloves. They certainly were not plain but carried a distinguishing mark, a ridge that ran along the top of each finger like the railroad tracks that would soon take her home.

She'd made herself a new dress, a chestnut brown organdy with wide lapels at the V-neck and turned-back cuffs at the sleeves. Buttons in a gold offset ran up the front. She had thought it all too fancy at the store, but her mother had saved the letter and remembered her name and where she lived.

Her boy was still asleep. She went to the woodstove and put on a pot of water to boil. She would make him grits, and she would heap helping after helping onto his plate.

When daylight began to show itself, she went to her boy's room, held the lamp over him, and saw the shape of his body beneath the four blankets she had placed on him the night before. She put her hand on his shoulders and nudged him. "Me and you's going on a trip today," she told him and watched his eyes let in the light.

"Where we going, Mama?"

She wanted to tell him, was about to bust wide open to do so, but she made herself just say, "It's a surprise. A big one, too."

She had new clothes for him laid over the back of his chair at the kitchen table. She felt like Santa Claus had come all over again. J. C. Penney's had a cash-and-carry sale that week, and she'd spent all of a ten dollar bill on a pair of dark blue thickset corduroy slacks and a long-sleeved plaid sports shirt of blue and green. The clerk told her both were "sanforized-shrunk and vat-dyed for safe tubbing." Sarah liked that. It sounded like the clothes would stay around a long time. But what she was most proud of were his shoes, oxfords with extra thick rubber soles.

She led him to the kitchen. "Them pants has got double pleats, look," she said and held the lamp out in front, where the pleats extended down three inches from the waist band. He wouldn't know their purpose, but she did. They made the garment more sturdy.

They left the house at eight o'clock. Sarah had a small suitcase packed for them. If she was lucky, tomorrow morning she would hear the church bells across the road from her upstairs window, where she was sure her mother would want Sarah and her boy to sleep that night. She'd give him her old bed, and she would sleep beside him on the floor. It would be their first vacation.

"We going far, far away, Mama?" Emerson Bridge asked as she drove.

"We are."

The train station was located on Main Street in the back of Lawrence-Brownlee Insurance, just up from the courthouse. She'd been there to buy their tickets the day before, had spent $8 for the round trip. Subtract out the price of her boy's clothes and shoes and Sarah had $7.09 to her name. Mildred came down with a cold after the visit to the cemetery and had not yet arranged the delivery of Sarah's dresses. The ticket man told her to arrive by ten o'clock for their 10:30 departure, but Sarah couldn't wait that long. The big clock on the courthouse said it was almost 8:30.

When ten o'clock came, they went inside. The train arrived shortly, and they were led down a flight of stairs, along with four other people. A man in a dark suit stood by the second car down from the engine. He extended his hand to take the tickets.

"Can we sit in that first one there, Mama?" her boy asked.

"I don't see why not." She handed the man their tickets and started for the first car.

The man stopped them. "It would be the second car for you two, ma'am."

"But my boy here wants to ride in the first one."

"It's closer to the engine!" Emerson Bridge said.

The man stepped in closer. "That one's for the colored and baggage." He took her suitcase and nudged her towards the second car and told her, "You wouldn't want it anyway. There's no coal heat, and it's noisy and more dangerous."

Before she stepped into where she was supposed to go, Sarah removed her coat of dark brown, the same one she had worn to Anderson when she married Harold, and handed it to the ticket man, asking him to make a present of it to a woman of his choosing in that first car. Sarah's mother would make her a new one, a black one, to match her hat and gloves.

The train soon left the station, its wheels churning the way Sarah's belly felt, flipping over on itself and then returning. In a little more than four hours, she would be in Gainesville.

Her boy kept his face pressed against the window. She liked that he was taking in the sights, the rows of white houses that lined the track and then the tall pines near the grain elevator, followed by wide-open fields and pastures. They were headed to Seneca, only twenty-five miles away, where they would pick up a second train that would take her home.

She saw his shoulders bobbing and was thinking the train was jostling him, as it did her. But then she saw the wetness on his face. "What's the matter, hon? You don't want to go to Grannie Teenie's?" She'd never said that name before.

He covered his face with his hands.

"You hungry? Or cold, is that it?"

"Lucky, Mama," he said through his fingers, and she leaned in close to hear his words. "What about Lucky and Mama Red? Who's going to take care of them?"

"Why, hon, Mr. Ike. And he's even going to stay the night, to look after things."

He slid his hands down.

Her mother didn't know they were coming. It would be a surprise, and her mother would meet her grandboy, and she would be happy. Maybe even for the first time in her life, be happy.

She thought of this and allowed the noise of the train to fill her ears.

. . . . .

The smell of smoke from Uncle's burned house no longer filled Luther's world. This is what he was thinking as he emerged from his garage that Saturday morning, his flask and body full of whiskey. It had been two weeks and a day since it had finished burning and its bones collapsed to the ground and Luther had telephoned Walter Moorehead and told him to bring his bulldozer over. "I need a big hole dug and for you to push a big mess into it."

Luther that morning breathed in air, clean now, and then exhaled and stumbled to the ground.

"Breakfast is getting cold, Big LC!" It was Mildred. She'd already called him three times. LC was running the hammer mill, and its sound helped drown her out. Luther wished it would drown her out forever. No, he didn't. He didn't wish that. He didn't want everyone to leave him.

He picked himself up and waved his boy over, but LC ignored him and threw in another shovel full of corn.

He went inside the house and began his breakfast of sausage and eggs and grits. Mildred sat with him and had a cup of coffee. "I'm going to have to start buying our sausage and fatback at Richbourg's, Big LC, if you don't get my freezer restocked by the middle of next week."

Luther stopped chewing.

"And I know you don't want anybody wondering why we're not eating the almighty Dobbins hog."

Luther slammed his fist on the table, making her delicate china jump like it was spooked.

But Mildred didn't even blink. She dabbed her mouth with her napkin, got up from the table, and began clearing it.

Luther intended to kill the hog that very day. It would be easy. The animal was still in the fattening pen where Uncle had put him before Christmas. But what Luther needed first was another drink. That way he could hold his hand steady when he fired the pearl-handle. He slid his chair back and started for the door. Mildred shot her eyes at him like she was trying to show him how to shoot his own gun. Luther hollered, "How dare you think I can't do my own dirty work," and raised his hand to her.

He thought she'd slink away, but she stayed where she was and pulled a bottle from her apron. It looked like one of his, except it wasn't as fat. He thought he was seeing things. "That cough syrup?"

She took the bottle from her mouth. "You could say that." She raised it towards him. "You want some? It'd save you a step or two from going to that garage."

Luther slapped the bottle out of her hand and sent it across the room to the wall, where it broke wide open. Then he grabbed her arm and threw her on the floor.

At the back door, he put on his coat and stepped out into the symphony his hammer mill created, his arms opened wide, the music surrounding him.

LC was really coming along. When he finished the grinding, his boy would move on to his next task, teaching his steer to follow him. Luther had given him an apple early that morning and told him to put it in his back pocket.

Luther went to his garage and turned his whiskey bottle up at his mouth. It was empty. He threw it on the dirt. He had one more hidden behind some old tires.

But no bottle was there. He knocked the tires over.

He went to his truck, took his pearl-handle from under the seat, and made his way to the pen. The hog was eating from the mash trough. "Raise up that fat head of yours and look at me," Luther told him, but the hog continued to eat. He fired a shot into the air. The hog jumped back.

"See, I can do my own dirty work." He aimed the gun at the hog's head, but the animal snorted and charged at Luther, who fell into the mash. But not the gun. He had kept his hand high.

Luther wondered what Uncle was doing. He bet he went back to Church Street and pictured Uncle in one of those negro hotels with rooms so little, it would be like living in a box of matches. Luther bet he was sad and missed his farm life. And missed Luther, too.

He managed to free himself from the trough, and he and his pearl-handle went back to his truck and headed to town, where he parked a block away from Uncle on Benson, outside Dickson Ice Cream. He would hate for his former hired hand to see Luther's truck and embarrass himself by running to it and jumping in.

Luther walked up to South Main and took a right and headed towards Church. He struck a match to light a cigarette, but it couldn't hold its fire against the stiff wind. He tucked in face first in the alcove by the front door of Kress's Five and Dime. Something heavy tugged in his coat's bottom right side. It was his flask. He pulled it out in celebration and sucked it dry. The flask was real silver and decorated in a pattern of loops that dazzled.

He wiped his mouth with the sleeve of his coat and tasted mash. He spit it out and remembered he'd forgotten to light the cigarette. People milled around inside the store. He could see them through the glass. He could see himself, too. He'd forgotten to shave again. And where was his hat?

He moved from the alcove to the corner and looked down Church Street, where he saw two little girls playing hopscotch in the middle of the road. Beyond them, ragged-looking boys bounced a ball off an old rusted Model T. What if the two negro boys he'd engaged saw him? He turned up the collar on his coat and slouched his shoulders from their usual high stance. Surely, Uncle could still pick him out. They'd known each other almost four decades.

Past the girls, Luther saw a gathering of uncles. In the center stood his. Luther wanted Uncle to see him. He would risk it. He turned down his collar and held his head up high. Uncle had his head thrown back, laughing. Luther felt himself unsteady. The wind was stronger in the cross current. His wet back made a chill move through him.

He waited for Uncle to look his way, but Uncle did not. Maybe he didn't recognize him. Luther stepped further up the street and lifted up on his tiptoes. But all Uncle did was continue to hold court with his new friends. Luther kicked his foot towards the gathering. He didn't need Uncle anyway and held out his hand like he was holding his pistol. "And don't think I can't, either."

Luther needed a drink. He knew where the liquor store was, even though he'd never been inside. It was only one more block south and fronted West Market. He could see it in his head. It was a small place like they tried to hide it.

He took himself there and told the man behind the counter, "I want your very best, top-drawer, top-shelf, fit-for-a-king whiskey."

The man looked at Luther like he was inspecting him.

Luther held onto the counter.

"That would be either Carstairs or Calvert." The man talked with an accent like he was from up North.

Luther didn't like doing business with Yankees, but he would make this exception. "Which one do more real businessmen buy?"

The man set two stand-up placards just out from Luther. "You can read about them in these advertisements and let me know."

Luther picked up the one showing a man in a nice suit. The words were a tad blurry, but he could make out the beginning, "The man who cares says Carstairs." But what sold him were the words buried deep into the writing. "This is the one I want," he told the man. "Says it's tailored by Society Brand."

"They're talking about the man's suit."

Luther cleared his throat. "All the better. Give me two of the biggest bottles you've got."

But the man made no move. He wasn't a midget like Luther had seen at the county fair one time, but the man was short and acted like he was tall. Luther slapped his hand against the counter.

"Two would cost quite a bit, sir," the man said.

Luther pulled out his billfold and held up the twenty that topped a stack of one's. "Would this cover it?"

The man sat two bottles on the counter. "The largest we sell is the 4/5ths. That'll be $4.50 two times and nine cents tax for a total of $9.09. Are you sure you want to purchase them?"

Luther slapped his hand against the counter again.

"Very well, then." The man gave Luther his change and put the bottles in separate sacks.

"I want you to know I can do my own dirty work," Luther told him.

"Oh yeah?" the man said but did not look at him.

Luther gathered the bottles in his arms, cradled them like he did his boys when they were little and a father could still do that. They would wrap their legs around his waist and lay their heads on his shoulders. They did it like they loved him.

Luther returned to his truck. A family stood outside Dickson's Ice Cream, a man, a woman, and a young boy. The woman looked like Mildred, small and fragile and with feet that shuffle when she walked. At times like now, Luther wished he loved her. The man and boy were holding hands. Because they could. There was no blood on them.

He took out his flask. No longer did the pattern dazzle. Luther now saw antlers, a whole network of them, of deer running and leaping, their white tails stiff and high in danger.

He knew what he had to do. He would not be killing the hog when he returned home. He would be taking LC hunting. But this time Luther would kill. He would show his boy that he could. And then they would be on level ground like this father and son before him. They could hold hands again. Couldn't they hold hands? And maybe return home and look for ladybugs.

· · · · ·

LC slammed off the tractor throttle and killed the belt that ran the hammer mill. Then he spanked his hands against each other, intending to send the yellow dust that clung to him far away.

But it stayed.

His steer remained tied to the post that had become his home. The air around the animal was clean.

LC ran to him and found the steer eating, his head in the grain bin. LC kicked it, hoping to make the animal stop, but he continued to eat. He was gaining more than two pounds a day now and well on his way to three. His father had a man haul in some scales and weighed the animal in at 802 pounds. Charles's steers were always way over a thousand by show time. The bin contained corn and molasses and would fatten, unlike the apple LC carried in his back pocket. His father had forgotten that he'd already given him the apple lesson. He'd been repeating himself a lot lately. LC had planned to eat the apple himself, but it occurred to him that maybe the steer would stop eating the grain if he ate the apple. LC held it in front of the animal's face.

The steer paid it no attention.

LC bit into it, hoping to release its smell, the animal now lifting his nose and sniffing, his breath hot against the cold and creating a cloud that LC imagined carrying them both far away. But then the steer shifted his gaze to LC, who saw in the animal's eyes a sadness like he was scared.

LC reached for the animal's face. It was solid white, unlike the rest of his body, which sported the Hereford red brown. LC began tracing the outline of the white, running his finger up the animal's jaw, cupping around his eye and then making a sharp turn towards the back of his head. He looked like an old man balding, like his father, the way his father's hair covered the sides of his head but left the top exposed and naked.

LC smelled something strong and sour behind him. It was his father, standing no more than six feet away. LC jumped. "Thought I'd reward him for doing so good following me," LC said and held the apple at his steer's mouth and waited for his father to hit him.

But his father stayed quiet, and LC was so struck by what he saw, he thought he was seeing things. His father was not wearing a hat. He said, "Look, Dad," and pointed at the animal. "Without your hat, y'all look alike."

"I can do my own dirty work." His father was swaying. "I want you to know that, boy."

His father headed out of the lot and waved for LC to follow. LC was thinking he must be talking about the hammer mill, but his father did not lead him there but to his truck.

The smell inside was so strong, LC thought he might gag. He rolled down his window. Two paper sacks with the tops of bottles sticking from them set between them. His father had been spending a lot of time in the garage since Uncle left. His father now seemed lost.

They drove through town, the truck jigging and jagging, and headed south on the same road that took them to that bad place, and LC felt his insides tense up as tight as his father's knuckles wrapped around the steering wheel. He pulled up on the door handle and tried to push the door open.

"What you doing?" his father hollered, grabbed LC's arm, yanked him from the rushing wind, and swerved to the right shoulder and stopped.

"I know where you're going, and I don't want to go." LC tried to wrestle his arm away.

"You don't know nothing."

"I do, Dad. I know a lot. You've made me know a lot." LC jerked his arm free.

His father gunned the engine, got back on the road, and soon delivered them to that same field. He reached for the pistol beneath the seat. It was the pearl-handle.

"Can that do the job, Dad? That little jelly thing?"

"Don't you call it that, boy." His father got out of the truck and slammed the door.

"What? Jelly?" LC yelled through.

His father was walking towards the woods. LC got out of the truck, ran after him, and jumped on his father's back. "I learned a lot from you. I *am* you."

His father knocked him backwards. LC hit the ground but got up and came at him with clenched fists.

"You ain't me, you're your mammie." Luther spit on the ground. "And I'm going to show you who I am, too."

"What? A Dobbins man?" LC screamed. "So you can feel what it's like to kill and be marked?" He moved his two fingers in the air like he was moving down his father's face, but his father did not see. He was headed for the woods. He was running.

LC was breathing hard.

The bones of the deer lay on the other side of those trees. He imagined buzzards had feasted on the animal, taken what they wanted and left the rest to rot. He imagined his father had reached the opening now and had seen the bones. He hoped they lay before him. LC stomped his foot and felt tears well up. He didn't want his father to kill another one. *Don't let one come across,* he prayed.

He ran as hard as he could and found his father standing at the wood's edge. He had the pearl-handle drawn, both hands holding it, and pointed towards the field that lay open, the grass no longer green but brown.

"I'm going to count them for you, how many I've seen," his father said. "One, maybe three. I got to decide which one I want. There goes another one, four. Come on and count with me, boy."

LC, for the first time, saw his father as a little boy. He was as scared as his steer.

"You can count to ten, can't you?" his father asked. "Come on and count for me. You do it."

LC got in behind him and stretched his arms around to his father's. They were shaking "Come on, Dad. Let's go home."

He had thought his father would resist, but he lowered his arms and let go of the gun. It fell to the ground. Then his father turned towards him and wrapped around him the way a child might. "No, you ain't me, LC. You're better than me."

. . . . .

Sarah and Emerson Bridge arrived at the Gainesville station at 2:50 in the afternoon and stepped out into the cold. The skies were thick with gray. Sarah set their suitcase down and pulled the zipper on her boy's coat as high at it would go. Her dress was hardly enough to keep her warm, but she was on her way to see her mother. The walk there was almost three miles, straight up Mountain Highway. It would warm her up.

She'd last seen this town in November of 1936. No longer could she smell the smoke from the fires the April tornado set off. Nor was there rubble piled here and there and buildings reduced to splintered planks. Her old place of employment, Cooper Pants, in the next block up, looked to be thriving. Her town had rebuilt itself.

And so had she. She took her boy's hand, and they set off north.

But she soon became winded and stopped to rest. Her boy offered to take the suitcase, but he was just a boy.

It took them close to two hours to arrive at Sarah's street, "C" Street. "Number 8, up the hill, fourth one on the left." She could smell already the air full of frying grease in her mother's house. Sarah wondered if it would be chicken or cubed steak or even salmons. She bet her boy was hungry. They'd not had anything to eat since the grits at breakfast.

When they reached the fourth house on the left, Sarah pointed across the street to the green-and-white church. "Twenty steps to Jesus, boy," she said.

Her boy's eyes grew large.

"Tomorrow morning, maybe you can run up and down them. It'll be church Sunday."

She looked for any signs that her mother was home. The curtains on the front window were closed. They never had an automobile, and none was parked out front now. The house was a duplex and not as large as she remembered it. Her family had lived on the right side.

She rested her hands on his shoulders. Her hands shook but not from the cold.

A cat ran from under the house.

Sarah took hold of his hand, and together they climbed the concrete steps, three of them, and all with moss growing and cracks where grass and weeds lived.

At the door, she set her suitcase down and, with her freed hand, smoothed down Emerson Bridge's hair. She'd cut it that morning and combed through Harold's tonic, giving her boy a nice part on his left side. "You're handsome," she told him and wondered if her mother heard her and was standing already at the door.

She placed her boy in front of her. Her mother would see him first.

Sarah ran her hands down her dress and wondered if her mother would recognize her. The skirt had quite a flair. She brought her gloved hand up to knock. "Mama? It's your girl." Her voice sounded like a schoolgirl, high and silly.

Her boy stood on his tiptoes and bounced.

But Sarah heard nothing from behind the door.

She knocked again. "Mama? It's your girl. It's Sarah." She tried to talk louder.

Still, nothing came back.

It couldn't be more than five or so in the afternoon, the sun having begun to set, but it was too early for bed. Maybe her mother had moved. Maybe that's why she'd written but had forgotten to say.

Sarah swallowed. "How about Clementine, Mama," she called through. "Clementine."

"*Sarah*, Mama," her boy whispered. "Your name's Sarah."

She patted his shoulders. She loved his innocence.

A twinge in her belly told her maybe she shouldn't have brought him here. She moved him behind her.

"Somebody out there?" she heard. It was her mother.

"Yes ma'am, Mama. It's your girl."

"Ain't got no girl."

"You do, Mama. You got me." Sarah could feel her heart racing. "You sent me that letter the first of the week, told me where my Clementine name come from." Her words were coming fast. "And I brought you a surprise." She moved her boy back in front of her.

"Had a girl one time, but she up and left me."

Sarah swallowed. "I've come to see you, Mama. Come a long way. Let me in." She didn't mean to, she wanted to be strong for her boy, but her voice had cracked some.

"It ain't locked."

Sarah opened the door and saw a room of darkness, except for the light the door brought in. Her mother sat in a wheelchair in that light and held her hand up over her eyes.

Sarah stepped inside. The smell of urine and rotten food covered her like a coat. She brought Emerson Bridge up alongside her. "This is my boy, Mama." She tried to talk without breathing. "My boy, Emerson Bridge. That's his name, Emerson Bridge." Their shadows ran through her mother and cast large against the back wall.

"Y'all see my kitty out there?" her mother said. "Here, kitty kitty!"

Sarah nudged her boy forward. His hand was pressed to his nose. "You got you a grandboy now, Mama. You always wanted a boy. Look here, here's you a boy."

"Kitty kitty! Kitty kitty!" It was as though her mother was singing.

"Yeah, Mama, my boy here's got him on some brand new shoes. Show them to her, hon." He picked up his left foot. "They're sturdy, Mama, look. The clerk said so they could handle plenty of scuffing. Scuffing, that's the very word he used."

But her mother wasn't looking at the boy's foot. She had her eyes closed now and was making a sound like a baby, running a finger over her lips and humming.

Maybe her mother hadn't heard her. Older people's hearing can fade. Sarah would soon turn thirty-four. Her mother was seventeen years older, putting her at fifty-one. Sarah cleared her throat. "Mama, I said my boy here's got on some new shoes." She reached down and pulled up his pants leg for better viewing.

But her mother did not open her eyes.

Sarah let his pants fall back in place.

Heaps of empty tin cans and empty loaf bread bags surrounded her mother. Labels showed pork n' beans and tuna fish. On a table beside her, Sarah saw stacks of unopened cans of the same. She wondered if her boy was hungry. And her mother, too. "Anybody hungry?" she asked.

"Y'all didn't see my kitty out there? It's about time for her supper." Her mother was craning her neck left and right, trying to see around Sarah and her boy.

It was a mistake to come. Sarah let herself have that thought. She tapped her boy and motioned with her head towards the door.

"Say them are new shoes?" her mother said.

So her mother had seen, and her mother could hear. Her mother wanted her there.

"Yes ma'am, Mama." She pulled up his pants legs again."They're brand new, look. Came from J. C. Penney's. That's a big store. Cash and carry, Mama. I paid cash and carry."

Her mother was running her finger and humming again.

Sarah was holding the suitcase. She thought about asking Emerson Bridge to take it up the stairs to her room, and she could holler up, "That was my room, my room when I was a girl."

"Your old man have dimples like he's got?" her mother asked.

Sarah felt a jab in her belly.

"Must have. Because even if you had them, nobody could see them in them fat cheeks of yours."

Sarah touched her cheeks. She felt her bones.

The fat from her mother's waist draped over the arms of her chair. She looked to have more than doubled in size. She was wearing a nightgown and house coat, both a shade of pink and both threadbare.

"Yeah, believe my kitty's found her some babies up under the house."

"You letting her do that, Mama?" Sarah's words coming fast like a fly swatter coming down. "Letting her have babies?"

"She's company. It's lonesome around here. Your papa got blowed off by that bad twister, and you up and left me for a sweet-smelling, sweet-talking man."

She could feel saliva starting to collect in her mouth. She wanted to gag. She looked back at the door.

"That's right," her mother said. "Go on and leave me. You didn't want to come no way."

Sarah felt a hardness rise up in her that made her clench her fists. "I'd smush them, Mama? Them babies. Is that what you mean? This slittail would smush them?"

Her mother lurched towards her. "You watch your mouth around that boy."

"That's what you used to say, Mama. Girls were slittails. That's what you called me, a slittail."

"I said watch your mouth."

"What'd you send me that letter if all you was going to do was beat me up some more? Why, Mama? Why?"

Her mother began moving her finger again.

Sarah put her hand at the top of her boy's back and felt his little bones like wings. She wanted him to fly. She hoped the whole rest of his life, he would fly.

"I was foolish enough to think that you wanted me to come see you. Must have been out of my mind." She tried to calm herself, but that got her more riled. "We got hard times back where we live. Don't know how I'm going to keep food on the table and clothes on my boy's back. My husband's dead now, and I got a boy to raise, a precious one, too." She was screaming now. "Don't know how, Mama, but I'll die trying to give him what he needs." She pulled her boy closer.

Her mother took a can of tuna fish from her pile and stabbed it with the sharp end of a can opener and started working it around. "Here," she said and held out the can. "Y'all hungry?"

Sarah said nothing.

Her mother rolled towards her. "I'll give y'all the whole can."

Sarah shook her head. "It was never food that I needed, Mama."

A cat ran past Sarah's legs and jumped in her mother's lap and began eating from the can. She was skinny and mostly gray in color. She ate like she was starving. Sarah remembered eating like that when she was a girl. "But I reckon that's all you could give me, wasn't it? It made me fat." Sarah took a step towards her. "But I ain't fat no more."

Her mother ran her hand down the cat's back as if she loved her. The animal arched to meet her mother's touch.

"Why didn't you never answer my letter back? Huh, Mama? You know, when it rains in the dead of summer, even an asphalt road gives something, gives that steam that rises up. *Something,* Mama. It would have been like tipping your hat to me that said *I* was something."

The room was losing light.

"That letter come eight long years after you left me, girl. Why didn't you send me one after that first baby of yours come, the one you didn't think I knew about inside of you when you left out of here? And where's that one anyway, huh?"

Sarah swallowed. She knew her boy would hear her, but that was going to have to be all right. "Because that first one, Mama, didn't make it to this world. She died inside of me." She reached for her boy's hand and pulled him towards the door.

She motioned for him to go stand on the porch. Sarah stood in the doorway and faced her mother. "That wasn't right what you did with that mama dog way back. Or with me. Wasn't right at all."

The cat jumped on the floor and scurried to the outside past Sarah.

"Bye, Mama," she said and closed the door and turned towards the road.

"I was wanting you to know I got me a kitty," her mother called through.

Sarah quivered. The kitty was not in sight. Sarah wanted to lay eyes on her, see what might have drawn her mother to the animal. Maybe it was the kitty's good mothering. Maybe her mother was trying to learn, too.

Sarah thought about what she wanted her mother to know. The answer came easily. She turned her body sideways to the door. "I've missed you, Mama," she said.

When the response came, it came loud and echoing. "Here, kitty kitty," her mother called out.

Sarah swallowed and straightened her body, turned it full towards the road and her boy. "Every day of my life, I have."

The setting sun threw its remaining light on the stained glass at the church. The reds, yellows, greens, and blues appeared more rich, now that the sun was casting its crumbs. The colors themselves had to do the work, had to bring forth. She took her boy's hand. Together, they walked down the steps.

The sound that steer had made that night came to Sarah. She knew now why his cries had found their way to her bones. Like him, she had been calling for her mother. Been calling her whole life.

But hers wasn't coming. Ever.

$$. . . . .$$

They arrived back at their house as the sun was waking the next day. They'd returned to the station and caught the next train that would take them home. It left at 2:20 that morning. Emerson Bridge's mother stayed quiet the whole time, except for her coughing and the only words she said, "I told you she lived far, far away."

He had wanted to ask her about the other baby, but it was not the time. She had called her "she." He could have had a sister. He would like to have a sister one day.

His mother pulled in beside Mr. Ike's truck and got out and started for the house but then dropped to the ground. Emerson Bridge ran to her. She was on her knees, her body moving up and down like she was opening and closing. She called out a word that she held onto like she didn't want to let it go. She called out "Maaaaamaaaaa!"

She did this over and over.

Emerson Bridge knew what he had to do.

Lucky was in the lot. He was eating from a bale of hay. Emerson Bridge went there and waited for the steer to lift his head, and then he placed his hands on the sides of the steer's face. He could feel the animal's muscles as he chewed. Lucky was strong.

Emerson Bridge told him, "Me and you's lucky, boy. We got us mamas that love us. But my mama don't. Hers is mean."

He could see her though the fence. She was still on the ground.

"I give you that name, Lucky, on purpose. Because I was lucky to have you and hope to be lucky enough for you to win and get that money for me and Mama. But then I found out what that would mean, and Mama said you didn't have to do it no more."

Emerson Bridge swallowed. He knew that what he was about to say would change the course for them all. "But you do have to do it, boy. You got to save her."

He could see himself in the steer's eyes, the morning sun catching them just right and showing him how small he was in the animal's round largeness. The steer lowered his head and went back to eating. Emerson

Bridge buried his face in the thick hair of Lucky's neck and told him, "Thank you."

He returned to his mother, who lay curled up on the ground now, her knees tight to her chest. He laid behind her and cradled her.

"It's all going to be all right, Mama," he told her. "Lucky's going to do this for us."

She shook her head hard and said, "No, no, no."

"Yes, yes, yes."

"No, hon, no."

"Yes, Mama, yes."

"We can't."

"We have to."

She stayed quiet but then rolled up on her knees, folding her upper body down on top. "Oh, God! Oh, God!" she called out and beat her fists against the dirt.

Emerson Bridge stood and looked back towards the lot. He was glad God gave Lucky a good coat for the cold weather. He was counting on God to give him everything else he needed, too.

The mother cow saw the gentle wind and the little one return and saw the gentle wind drop to the earth and heard the gentle wind's voice, calling.

How am I going tell you what I got to tell you, girl. How? How am I going to get words out of me to come across this cold-as-ice air to you? And you standing there all still and me down on my knees with my hands wrapped around a wire and squeezing. I feel like my head's between two big rocks with no place to go. Like Mattie must have felt that night. No place to go. Either pick she made, I reckon wasn't no good in her mind. I'm trying to stay all one piece so that part of me don't fly off somewhere and go to bed and pull the covers up.

Maybe if I tell you the rest of mine and Mattie's story, I'll be able to tell you the rest of ours, mine and yours. Yeah, if I could just tell you about that night.

The telephone call came way in the night. "It's time, Sister," Mattie said. And all through my head came a thousand bumble bees swarming. We had us a plan. We wasn't going to have no doctor. I was going to do it, me.

I put on some water to boil and drove the truck over to get her, brought her back here and told her to lay up on our eating table, where I'd already set every towel I had in the house. I went out to the barn to get Harold. He was drunk and in no good shape to come, but I told him to get on his feet and be a man, be a papa. He tried, but I had to prop him like I had to prop him by the door when we got inside. The whole time I was telling myself, "I can carry it, I can."

There was a light bulb hanging on a cord from the ceiling over Mattie. It looked like a bald head to me that night, a baby's, naked and upside down.

When the baby come out, it was all red in color and not that bad blue, and that meant alive, and I hollered, "Your baby's alive," and then I seen he was a little boy and I said, "A little boy, Mattie, and he's alive." She busted wide open into tears and held out her arms for him. He was slick with blood and connected to her by her life cord. It didn't have much play in it, but I was able to stretch him up to her, and there came her dimples, which I'd not seen in a long time. They went in deep like he'd poked his two little fingers in her cheeks. She had the top of her nightgown undone, and she put his little mouth on her nipple. "You a mama now, Mattie," I said. "You happy?"

Harold went to sliding down the door. He'd stayed propped that whole time. Then Mattie went to hollering, "Cut him loose of me!" And I was thinking she meant Harold, but that baby wasn't at her nipple no more. She was holding him straight out with her stiff arms like she wanted me to take him. "Get you a knife and cut him loose of me now." She was meaning the baby. "What was in my head?" she said. "I can't keep him. Billy Udean will kill me and this baby, too."

I didn't have a knife. Hadn't thought to have me one out. Harold grunted. He was laying full on the floor now, and it come to me that I wanted Harold's. His pocketknife. His. "Give me your knife, Harold," I hollered. "I mean it. You hear me and give me your knife." I went to kicking him, but he wasn't offering up nothing, so I fished it out myself and brought it to that life cord and cut it and took that baby. Mattie was trying to get herself off the table, and that baby was in my arms, and what was I going to do?

There Mattie was on the floor now and crawling over Harold. When she got clear of him, she said to me and it would be her last words, too, she said, "It ain't the child's fault he was born." And that's right, isn't it, Mama Red. It wasn't. He didn't ask to be brought into . . . into all this. He was crying, he was hungry, and you know what? I wanted to feed him. I did. I'm going to tell you that right now, Mama Red. I started unbuttoning my dress, there at the top like Mattie'd done, and there was that baby alive and awake in my arms and with his eyes all fighting to get open to look at me, I thought, and I said to him, "Hey there, little boy. You hungry? You want to eat?" and I got my brassiere away from me, and I put his little mouth at my nipple that was getting all ready for him, like a funnel so he could wrap his mouth around it like yours does you, but he wasn't wrapping around, so I took my finger and put it right up to his lips. "Come on, sweet baby," I said and had my finger moving around. "Come on, I'm going to teach you." And there his lips went to working. I could feel him sucking. I would have give him my whole hand, if he'd have wanted it. He could have pulled every

238

inch of Clementine Florence Augusta Sarah right inside of him. I brought him back to my nipple, and there he went, his little lips working, working, working. But then he went to crying.

I didn't have nothing for him. I didn't have no milk. I ain't no mama, I was thinking. I ain't. And what's the matter with me for thinking I could be? But here comes the part I've lived with all these years and what I'm so ashamed for you and him to know. I told that little boy, whose belly was as empty my cupboards have been, "I don't want you, I don't. You ain't my baby. I ain't your mama."

I didn't want him, Mama Red. I thought it. And I said it. And I took him back. And I know he hadn't been in this world but a few short minutes, but they were long minutes, because he had to hear me, he had to take them words into his clean heart. And what gets me is he came into this world thinking he was not wanted. His mama give him back, and I give him back. We both give him back. He did not think he was loved. And don't a baby deserve to know that? Don't we all?

I got to take me some deep breaths now and get up off my knees and look at you in them soft eyes of yours and tell you the rest of what I come out here for.

Remember them tracks I told you I was on? Them bad ones I thought couldn't be but turned out they was, so we all got away from them. I come out here to tell you we can't get away from them. No ma'am, we can't. I can't. I can't carry it all no more. By myself, I can't.

I know I've done y'all like a yoyo. Y'all together, then apart, then back together. What I'm saying is I'm going to have to pull y'all apart again. Except this time it won't be no fence separating you. It's going to be more than that. A whole lot more. My boy's ribs, they stick out like somebody had their hard fingers curved around him. Always before I thought they were Harold's. But them are my fingers, Mama Red, mine, my fingers curved and ready to pick him up, lift him high. I'm his mama. And I want to take him high.

But that means you losing yours. I'm going to have to put him in that show we talked about, and I'm going need you to go live with somebody else, a man you know. It's where you started out. His name is Allgood, Jeremiah, like in the Bible. He's been wanting you back, been begging me, but I've put him off. But I can't put him off no more. No more.

I'm going to have to live with what I'm doing. For the rest of my born days live with it. I am. With what I'm doing to you and to your boy. And to mine. To my boy.

And I won't never, Mama Red, I won't never get it out of my head. Or heart. Ever.

JANUARY 14, 1952

The mother cow, alone now.

She was carried away in a sound, unfamiliar, and delivered to land she had once known, having accepted her first steps following her transport from the west, where continual winds sent her, then a four-day-old calf, and her mother east to green pastures.

These were the green pastures.

The train that brought them there let in long slats of light running the way the cows' bodies ran, head to tail, the light becoming long slivers each night. She was her mother's last, the cows having been packed in so tightly on transport, her mother was squeezed to her death, while she managed to tuck in beneath her mother's belly. With no room to fold down, only stand, the cows around her mother helped hold her high, until the train stopped and the cows were offloaded and her mother fell to the floor.

This night, the mother cow folded down onto the land of her infancy, the light above her appearing as dots, an expanse of dots, glistening, like grass in the setting sun after a rain.

Under those same dots, her calf folded down, too. Alone now, too.

MARCH 10, 1952

On the night before the show and sale, LC went to the barn. It was just after supper and already dark. "LC, dear, you sure you want to go out there?" It was his mother, calling at his back. "And don't you want a flash light?"

He did not turn around, but the answer was yes, he wanted to go. He had something special he wanted to say to his steer, something he should have said long before now. And, no, he needed no extra light, not with the moon and stars accompanying him in the yard. But when he entered the barn, he entered the way he wanted, alone and in darkness. His father had placed fresh straw on the ground that afternoon for the show the next day. It crackled beneath LC's feet.

His steer lay bedded down in the back stall. The animal made a sound, which LC took as a greeting. "Hey there yourself, boy." He sat near the animal's head and touched the steer's face. The whiteness of it helped him place his hand there. The thickness of it made him wish his hand could stay and hide. "In church," LC told him, "I learned about a man who died for all the bad stuff us people do. He had a name. It was Jesus. And I've been thinking if you're going to give your life for my daddy and me, then you at least ought to have a name. I was wrong not to give you one. I want to call you my favorite name. I want to call you Shortcake. Can I do that? Can you be my Shortcake?"

The animal's breath warmed LC's arm. The smell of sweetness floated up to his nose. Shortcake liked his name.

LC knew his own had come from his father, who put Jr. at the end of Charles's name and III at the end of his. He had been jealous when he was little, thinking Jr. placed Charles closer to his father. But he was not jealous any longer. There was a lot he wasn't any longer.

He leaned in close. "Can I tell you something, Shortcake?" He wished his voice could be strong. "The little boy I used to be and the man I've been trying to be for my daddy, I'm neither one of them. I feel like I'm nobody no more. *Nobody.*" LC kissed his face, letting his lips linger in the thickness. "But I don't feel that way with you."

He made his way back to the house. He smelled pines. His father had hired someone to cut them down that day.

He readied himself for bed. When his mother kissed him goodnight and was about to turn off his light, he whispered, "What if I don't win, Mama?"

She gathered him up in her arms. "All a little boy can do is give it his best, dear."

She'd called him a little boy. He missed being little.

"Would you do something for me?" he asked. "Could you call me Little LC one more time?"

. . . . .

On the night before the show and sale, Emerson Bridge took the kerosene lamp, lit with the last drops of kerosene, to the barn. Lucky was inside for the night, lying down. He was tired. Emerson Bridge had stayed out of school and worked him hard that day and the many days prior, teaching the steer to follow him and stand four-square and be quiet about it all. They'd both done what they'd been asked. Emerson Bridge had broken him, and Lucky had let him.

Emerson Bridge sat in front of the animal on straw taken from one of the bales that his papa used to sleep on. Mr. Ike had wanted to get some fresh straw from the FCX, since they supplied the Creamers with whatever they needed at no cost, now that Mr. Allgood had Mama Red. But Emerson Bridge had wanted to use what his papa had supplied.

The light from the kerosene threw the animal's head against the back wall, made it appear large and dark, but robbed it of anything that distinguished it, like that one spot of red brown that sat alone in all that white at the top of his head. Emerson Bridge put his finger there. "You look like your mama, boy. You sure couldn't miss that." He brought his hand to his own face, to his dimples, pushing in the one in his right cheek. "Maybe my mama had dimples when she was little, too, and they went away when she got old. Wonder if mine will?" He pictured her face. She had a big forehead. He slid his hand up to his own and laid it flat. His whole hand fit. "Here's where I look like my mama, Lucky."

The steer was licking Emerson Bridge's wrist. "I'm glad I never took your name back. And I'm glad I called you Lucky, because that's what I was, lucky to know you."

He knew he'd just crossed a line. He was talking of a time when Lucky would be no more. He nestled his face in the animal's deep fur. "Now, listen. You're going to be hearing God say something to you. He's going to say, 'Let's ride, My Friend.' And when you hear that, you go on with him. All right? He'll take good care of you."

Strings of saliva dripped from his steer's lips. Flecks of corn peppered his skin. Lucky thrust his chin into the air and released a low, short sound, one that Emerson Bridge had come to know was meant for him. He saw that Lucky was missing a tooth, the one in the middle on the bottom, and a new tooth was growing in at an angle. Mr. Merritt had talked of baby teeth before, said that cows have them like humans do. Emerson Bridge wondered if the tooth fairy visited cows. He hoped so.

There was one more thing he needed to say, words that had caused Emerson Bridge the most struggle, his papa's urging Emerson Bridge to be kind. *The Bible says to be kind. 'Be ye kind, one to another,' it says. I wasn't always, but I hope you will be, son.* What he was asking of Lucky was not kind to Lucky or to Mama Red. He wished his papa was there to help him with it. But then his papa's words, telling Emerson Bridge he was the man of the house came to him. He felt like that's what he'd been when he'd made the decision to go forward with the show. Because don't men take care of who they love like his papa had done with him and taught him to shave. "For when the time comes," his papa had said.

The time had come.

Emerson Bridge rose to his feet and took the lamp to the back of the barn, where his papa's John Deere tractor mirror still hung on a nail. Below it, on the one remaining bale of straw, sat his papa's shaving kit and beside it, his papa's mug, filled earlier that day with water from Lucky's pail. Inside the mug, propped against the side, was his papa's brush, getting softened, too.

First, he needed lather. He stirred the brush fast and made a white cream appear and then stepped up onto the bale and looked straight ahead into the mirror. He could not see the top of his head. He had grown. He lifted the mirror from the nail and held it high, then closed his eyes and remembered his papa's moves, the way he had brushed on the lather, covering up his bones.

He brushed on the lather, stopping just beneath his eyes. All that white made his eyes of green more green. That's what he got from his papa.

He picked up the razor and began covering territory.

MARCH 11, 1952

L uther that early morning, standing on his back porch, shoved his hands into the pockets of his suit pants, hoping no one would notice them shaking. But then he wondered if the suit would draw attention to him, to his hands, since judges wore suits, dark ones, as if they were going to a funeral. Mr. C. V. Richbourg, too, the man who always bought Charles's grand champion, would wear a suit. Always before, Luther had worn all-over khaki that Modern Cleaners had prepared just right with medium starch, but the show was at his place today, and he wanted to look the part, so he remained in his suit and claimed that exclusive territory.

He stepped out from his house, the sun having cleared the horizon but God seeming a tad stingy with his daylight. Where was the promised blue? In two hours, the 1952 Fat Cattle Show & Sale would begin, and in less than an hour after that, the grand champion would be named. He had sent Charles a letter the month before, asking him to come home to help put the final touches on LC's steer, making sure it stood four-square and giving any tips for calming the animal in the ring. Luther did not mention the straightness of the steer's back, but if Charles had any assessment of its structure, he would welcome it. Charles had not responded.

Luther headed for the lot to see LC and look over his steer one last time, when two trucks, transporting contenders and boys sporting big smiles like they could break into laughter, drove past him. Luther pushed his hands further into his pockets and retreated to his hammer-mill shed, where he stood beside his machine, now silent, its pitiful work done. He kicked it. LC's steer had weighed in at 987 pounds the day before and should be at 990 today, but that was at least twenty pounds lighter than Charles's winners.

The smell of manure drifted towards him, as more trucks were coming in now. But it was the smell of something else, its tanginess, that not only found Luther's nostrils but burrowed inside. The smell of pine. Luther had hired a man to cut down the row of pines that grew alongside Luther's house and grind them into sawdust to coat the lot, enough to outdo the fairground people, who were stingy with their scattering of the lumber cast-off. He stepped a few feet to where the first pine beyond the shed used to loom tall. It was now a stump, flat on top, and on it grooves from the man's chainsaw. Luther put his foot there, his dress shoe, new wingtips, and thought he saw a ladybug. He bent towards it, only to see another one climbing up the three inches of bark. He looked towards the lot, thinking he could spot LC, thinking the two of them could look at the bugs and share a laugh before things got so serious. Couldn't they share a laugh? And this time, he wouldn't hurt the bug, he'd be tender the way LC would be.

He would practice before he called his boy. And this would steady his fingers, his hand. The one cresting the stump now and on the flat surface, that one Luther chose, the bug having done the hard work of climbing and now could relax for the level, straight surface. His finger against its red shell, the dots of black arranged in rows. Luther would count them as his boy would, one, two, three and then one, two, three all the way up, Luther hearing his boy's counting ring out. Luther's finger now pushing, but the bug having no place to go with the high wall of the groove to its right and left, but Luther wanting to play, so he moved his finger behind the bug and pushed it forward. The animal survived. Luther laughing.

He ran towards the lot now. An automobile drove past him carrying three men in suits. These were the judges. Luther thrust his hand into the air. "Welcome, gentlemen," he said and noticed the other men, the farmers, in common overalls or khakis like Paul Merritt, who had just pulled up.

He waited until the judges stood on his land and then scanned the lot for LC and saw him with his steer near the post where the animal had lived most of his days in the last few months. "Hey, boy!" he said and looked to see if any of the judges were listening. One looked his way, Luther now calling to LC, "Run that hand of yours over its back and tell me if it's not straight as a gun barrel." His eyes juggled between the man and his boy. "Wouldn't hold a drop of water, would it, son?" He listened not only for his boy's words to confirm but the conviction in his voice to carry his words.

"No, sir," LC yelled.

There it was. Both.

But the judge's back was turned.

His boy was running now towards the gate, and Luther thought running to him, but it was to the Creamer boy and his steer. The boys stood so close, Luther thought they were going to hug, but then they extended their hands and shook them like men, like gentlemen. Luther's eyes, though, concentrated on the Creamer steer, larger than LC's and its back as level as level could be, *the one to beat* cycling through Luther's head. He moved to the front of the lot, just out from his barn, where he'd paid a man to build a platform, part of the $200 he'd sunk to get his place ready. He climbed the steps, taking two at a time, and soon stood perched high above. "A palace," he told himself, "a by God palace," and watched the contenders below him scurry like ants on the thick coat of his sawdust.

Merritt stood in the back left corner, where the boys, including LC, and their steers were gathering, some of the animals head butting. The judges would mark them down for that behavior, this Luther knew. LC's steer looked to be well-behaved. A short woman carrying a notepad and a big camera approached the boys. This was Martha Sheely from the newspaper. Sneezy, she went by. She had covered all of Charles's wins.

Luther made his way there and picked up Merritt saying, "I told y'all at our first meeting that your only job was to finish your steer. Animals have a purpose, and part of growing up is understanding the greater purpose of livestock. You've all done your part and done it well. You should be proud."

Luther wasn't sure he'd told his boy how proud he was of him, but he would do that.

"Some quick reminders," Merritt said. "Keep your steer's head up with your rope pulled tight." He demonstrated with his arm up in the air. "Your arm might get a little tired, but the judges look for head up, even when you're walking with him. And he needs to walk like he's free and not on a rope and certainly not being pulled."

"Round, roly-poly, and short legs, like my boy's steer here," Luther called out. "That's what judges like." He waited for everyone to look at him, and then he put his eyes level with his boy's steer's back. "They'll be looking down its top ridge here and feeling of it." Luther put his hand there. "Three to four inches of fat, pure fat, people. That's what they want." He slapped where he'd been touching. "Like my boy's here." He looked to see if Sneezy wrote that down.

Her pencil didn't move.

"Soft like jelly and with muscle hard like a spreading knife." It was Thrasher. He wasn't wearing his hat. "That's quoted verbatim, ma'am, from a judge's mouth in your own newspaper last year."

She moved her pencil.

"And when you stop with your beef," Luther called out, "make sure its feet are four square, especially its back feet. That'll make their haunches look bigger, so the judges can see the kind of meat cuts they carry. And I'll go on record now and say that it's going to take a whole lot of onions to smother the T-bones the butcher's going to get from my boy's good deep freeze steer."

"Excuse me," the newspaper woman said and held her notepad in the air. "Do we have any first-timers here?"

The Creamer boy raised his hand. The woman stepped his way. Luther did, too.

"So, what have you been doing to get him ready?" she asked the boy.

"Petting him," he said, his fingers fumbling with the rope.

Luther rolled his eyes. All his worry for nothing. The steer might have the right frame to hold the product, but he wouldn't know how to behave during the show. He would drag that boy from one end to the next.

"Then after the show," the woman said, "what are you going to do?"

The boy's lips began to quiver, and then he took his eyes off the woman and put them on his steer beside him. The boy could have been Luther's the year before, LC's lips right before the show, but Luther had clenched his hand and hit LC's arm and yelled for him to stop. Luther took his hand from his pocket now, opened it, and moved it the Creamer boy's way, while the Creamer boy placed his hand on the animal's neck and brought his eyes back to the woman. "I'm going kill him."

Sneezy lifted her pencil.

Luther's hand froze. He shifted his feet.

"You love me, Daddy?" It was LC.

Luther turned towards him and took in his boy's face, his eyes held open. "Come with me," Luther said and started through the crowd, LC following.

"Boys, if I could have your attention, please," came from the megaphone. It was Merritt on the platform, where the men in suits now stood. Luther continued on through the crowd, his eyes fixed beyond the hammermill shed.

"If y'all would go ahead and bring your steers to the front here," Merritt was saying, "we're going to have our official weigh in, and then the show and sale will commence in a few short minutes after that."

Luther was thinking they'd have time to see the ladybugs and share a laugh and then his boy's steer could be weighed. Luther running now. But his boy was not following. Luther stopped and stretched up on his tiptoes to see. No LC. Luther started back through.

"Hey, think you'll get your dynasty going again this time, Luther?" some man said.

"Have you seen LC?" Luther asked him.

The man shook his head.

"Have you seen LC?" Luther began asking as he passed through, his voice getting louder.

"Where's Charles?" someone else said.

247

"Folks," Merritt was saying, "while the steers are being weighed, we're honored to have Miss Anderson, Miss Virginia Marie Lollis, perform her winning talent number, "Jesus Paid It All.""

The crowd became quiet.

"Anybody seen LC?" Luther yelled.

"He's getting his steer weighed, Luther," Merritt said from up top.

Luther heard snickers. He stayed still.

The woman began singing. She wore a crown on her head, her hair blonde and plentiful and arranged like a note of music above the words in the Baptist hymnal. On her feet, high heels sparkled in the same color as her dress, a turquoise blue with a shine to it. She sang without music with a voice that Luther had heard better, but she sang as if she was free. He was standing near his water trough. He had made sure LC filled it to the brim. The water glistened.

CV Richbourg himself and the Dixie Store man and two buyers for big meat companies in the Midwest, Steve Prater and Bob Cathey, along with Jeremiah Allgood, all stood around Luther. He could see LC now near the scale. They had run out of time for the ladybugs. They would do it after the show.

The woman finished singing, and Merritt took the megaphone. "Ladies and Gentlemen, welcome to the 1952 Anderson County Fat Cattle Show & Sale. We begin with the show and then will move into the sale, followed by the removal." He called the boys and their steers to line up in the large open space in front of the platform. Luther moved to the front and off to the side near the fence, where he could set himself apart.

His boy stood on the opposite end from Luther and in the number one position, exactly where the judges always placed Charles. The Creamer boy stood on the end closest to Luther and afforded Luther a sustained look at the steer. He could feel himself relaxing. The steer had a definite dip in its back. It would hold tons of water.

The boys moved with their steers in what Luther thought of as the beef parade, one at a time parading their finished beef in front of the judges, who stood with their clipboards at the edge of the platform. Nineteen steers, a record number, had entered this year. Luther needed a better view. He took the steps up high. Merritt shot him a look, but this was Luther's place. He saw Thrasher and his sidekick woman standing way in the back where they belonged. Her automobile out behind his barn had weeds growing up through it. The afternoon before, he had positioned his truck longways in front of the eyesore to hide it. Beside them stood another woman, Mildred.

One of the judges moved to the far end to Luther's boy, another somewhere in the middle and the third to the opposite end with the Creamer boy, whose steer was standing in a perfect four square with his head up. The animal stood so still that, if his eyes weren't open, Luther would think he was dead. The Creamer boy, though, had his eyes closed.

Luther felt sick to his stomach. He looked down at his own boy, whose eyes were on his judge, his steer moving like it was dancing. The judge's hands were on the animal, checking for fat under its ridge, then moving to the shoulders and feeling for pot roast and short ribs, then down its front legs for brisket and then rising to feel along its ribs for rib eyes and T-bones and sirloin. The final check came for rump roasts on the animal's rear. Luther had schooled himself well in the meats. Charles would be proud of him. Luther tried to read the judge's expression and thought he saw a smile. Luther imagined he was checking the boxes for outstanding. In all areas, outstanding.

When the judges finished examining the steers, they walked outside the lot to a large dogwood tree that was just budding in white. The men huddled like football players. Luther watched them to see if any looked back towards his boy, which they had done with Charles.

None did.

But, when they climbed back onto the platform, one of them, Luther was sure, looked at LC. His boy had it.

That same judge took the megaphone. "First of all, we want to say that all of the steers have a bright future in somebody's deep freeze. We judge on a level back, hind quarters that run deep on the leg, a full chest that drops between its two front legs, short-legged, and a raw-boned frame."

Luther nodded his head. That summed it up. These men knew what they were doing.

"The Grand Champion we've named has the body I've just described and, besides that, his coat has a nice sheen. The kicker, though, is we find him very quiet and broken to be led."

Luther felt like he'd taken a knife to his stomach.

"The 1952 twelfth annual Fat Cattle Grand Champion belongs to young Emerson Bridge Creamer of the Centerville 4-H for his Hereford steer, weighing in at 1,032 pounds. All three of us find this animal perfectly finished."

The flash of the newspaper woman's camera went off as applause broke out everywhere.

Luther shot a look at his boy, who already had his eyes on Luther and who held on him, as if he was looking for an answer. Luther raised his fist. There was his answer.

The Creamer boy stepped out of line, rubbing his winning in everyone's face and saying, *Look at me, I won the big blue ribbon.* Then he and his steer turned back into the crowd, which parted for him like Moses did the Red Sea. They went to Luther's water trough where the animal began splashing its head.

Luther looked down at his boy, but he was no longer there.

"What do you know!" Merritt said, his voice booming. "Looks like our Grand Champion likes to play in the water."

Laughter filled the place, moving in waves and growing larger as more people joined in and gathered around the winning steer. Luther snatched the megaphone from Merritt and yelled into it, "Y'all shut up!"

The laughter stopped. And so did people's movements. Everything went still.

Luther looked out over the crowd. He still did not see his boy. *Just like him to tuck tail and run.*

A gunshot rang out.

Luther jumped.

The sound came from behind the barn in the direction of his truck, the crowd no longer quiet but deafening loud with its screams.

He saw Mildred running. He dropped the megaphone, saying, "Oh, God, oh, God," and hurried down the steps towards his truck, where people were running like cattle being herded, mothers and fathers screaming their children's names, even the Creamer woman, with arms outstretched and calling out, "Emerson Bridge! Emerson Bridge!" A man with wild eyes running up to Luther and saying, "He had his knees bent like he was riding a horse or something. And then he said something about some kind of shortcake and I saw the pistol. I'm sorry, Luther!"

Luther threw the man to the ground.

Up ahead, a crowd gathered in tight, layers stacked on layers. Several people looked Luther's way, their hands pressed to their mouths. They began stepping back, pulling others with them, and then others more, until there was a parting, giving Luther a clear shot of what lay twenty yards in front of him, just outside the open door of his truck, Mildred, clutching LC, who lay in her arms as limp as a coat.

Luther charged towards them but stopped. He felt all eyes on him. Mildred's, too.

"You did this!" she shouted. "*You* did!"

His pearl-handle lay just out from them in a puddle of blood.

She rose to her feet. She did so in one fluid motion, their boy still in her arms.

She came to stand a foot away. Blood covered her face and neck and hair. A drop fell from her nose. "You killed *my* boy," she said.

Sounds of shrieks peppered the air.

"I should have stopped you," she said. "God forgive me for not." Her hand shot into the air and found Luther' face, the hard tips of her wet fingers wiping down his left cheek, then his right.

Luther smelled blood.

"You are marked now," she said. "You. *You* are."

. . . . .

Sarah and Mildred sat just out from the open door of Luther's truck, both women rocking their boys against their bosoms, both releasing steady streams of cries. They sat in dirt, full of dark red with swirls of yellow. It was springtime.

Others stood around them in a circle. From them came only whispers.

The only other sounds were the approaching sirens, growing louder, before falling silent.

. . . . .

There was no auction held. The men who intended to bid got together and bought the whole lot, paying 55 cents a pound for the Reserve Champion and 42 cents a pound for the steers that did not place. That was a nickel more than the 1951 prices. Emerson Bridge's Grand Champion brought a dime more, brought 73 cents per pound. C. V. Richbourg wrote him a check for $763.36.

The removal took place as planned. Trucks pulling trailers arrived to transport the steers to slaughter at Walker's Abattoir off the Liberty Highway, all except Emerson Bridge's. C. V. Richbourg sent his own personal truck to carry the grand champion to his farm to stay the night, before being taken the next day to Richbourg's Supermarket and put on display out in front of the store.

When the Richbourg truck pulled in, Emerson Bridge broke away from his mother's arms and watched Lucky being loaded. He told the newspaper woman, "There goes a whole lot of love, ma'am."

. . . . .

Ike Thrasher brought Sarah and her boy home in an empty bed truck. No one spoke a word.

When they reached the house, Ike told them he couldn't stay. He needed to go change out of his clothes. Sarah and Emerson Bridge needed to change out of their bloody ones, but all they could do was stand in the yard and hold hands.

"I can't even begin to know how hard this day was for you, hon," she told him. "It was a day too big for a little boy."

"Papa said I'm the man of the house now, Mama."

"You are. But it was a day too big for the man of the house, too."

Sarah knew he had shaved again. There were cuts on his face. They weren't as deep or as long or as numerous as the time he had shaved a year ago. Almost to the day, a year ago.

She felt him shaking, the whole space of him shaking.

"We're rich now, Mama," he said and lifted the folded check from his shirt pocket, his eyes of butterbeans no longer clean and shiny.

"That's an awfully steep price to pay. I broke your heart. I did, I broke your heart, just to be able to put more than a pitiful pear on your plate."

"Lucky said he would do this for us, Mama."

She ran her fingers through his hair. She had not cut it since their visit to Gainesville. She could see more of the red in it now. "You're the kindest soul God ever made, Emerson Bridge Creamer." She dropped to her knees and leaned her head back to look up at him. "It's not just food you need, hon. I know you need more than that. Do I give you more than that?" She swallowed and waited for the answer, whatever it was.

"Yes, ma'am."

"Because I want to. More than anything, I do."

"You do, Mama, yes ma'am."

She pulled him to her, wrapped her arms around his back. Before Mildred had folded herself into that long, black automobile, her son's body lying covered with a sheet that was too starched and too white, Mildred had told her, "You've got a mother's heart." Sarah thought about that now. The night she laid Mattie's and Harold's baby outside Mattie's front door, the baby had cried, calling out for someone to come take care of him, to please come take care, because he couldn't do that himself. The words *I came for him* whispered from her bones. She told him, "I want you. Do you know that I want you and that I'll always come for you, hon. I always will."

"I know that, Mama."

Mama she heard and repeated that word down inside of her, where it had lived since it was born that late afternoon with that mama dog. For the first time, Sarah wanted to move that word to the outside. "Mama," she said out loud and noticed how the word carried.

She thought of Mama Red and looked towards the lot, empty.

Her plan, if they won, was for her and her boy to get in the automobile and go to the bank and cash the check and then go pay everyone she was beholden to and then stop by Drake's and buy her boy anything he wanted.

But that didn't seem so important now.

"Need to ask you something, hon. What do you think about us using some of that money to go get Mama Red and bring her home?"

She could feel his head nodding, the sound of his hair rustling against her. "Lucky would like that."

She had seen Mr. Allgood that morning. She called up in her mind where he'd said he lived, down the road by the church. She would find it. She and her boy started for her automobile.

A truck came up the driveway. She was thinking Ike had returned, but it was Mr. Allgood, Jeremiah Allgood himself, and in the back of his truck, Mama Red.

Sarah went running, met the truck before it made it halfway up the driveway. She wanted to tell him she was on her way to him to fetch the mother cow home and pay him whatever he wanted, but she could not talk, only run along beside the truck to the barn, where it stopped, and she could lay eyes again on that glorious face of red brown and white.

"She belongs with you," Mr. Allgood told her.

· · · · ·

Luther did not see the undertaker slide his boy into the ambulance. Nor did he watch the removal trucks come and go. Luther Dobbins sat in pine needles that blanketed the ground around the first tree stump, the marks on his face drying, his skin tight and shrinking.

Luther watched the ladybugs.

The man who had cut the pines advised against it, saying they were too young and innocent for lumber, but Luther told him they weren't for lumber, they were for dust.

They were for nothing, he was thinking now. *Nothing. Like me.*

His boy's eyes had held on Luther after the announcement, eyes so dark, they could be black. Like the spots on ladybugs. Luther knew what his boy was asking, asking if Luther loved him, *"Do you love me, Daddy?"* as he had asked outright before the show.

"Here's Daddy's answer," he called out, "here," and raised his hands, his open, unclenched hands into the darkening air, stretching them towards the lot, where his boy had been, his boy who was tender, too tender for what Luther had asked him to do. *Too tender to have a daddy like me.*

The mother cow looked for her young but did not see him.

She called but heard no answer.

As darkness fell, she bent to the earth, laying her body down on it, while dots of white, even twinkling white, sprinkled above her and around her in patterns of order and beauty. The top of her tail now having risen, her lower back softened, her ligaments and tissues made supple. Her baby no longer lay on its back but had followed the natural course and moved from its high place near the mother cow's tail, past her pin bones to her womb, deep inside her womb, where her baby now, just now, under dots of twinkling white, is rotating to its belly for the rest of its journey.

part 4

LEARN

MARCH 12, 1952

My boy's ribs, they filling out some now.

I know that might be hard for you to hear, Mama Red. Because your own boy, I know you miss him. Here you are laying down out here in the grass by your lonesome. And you keep lifting your head and moaning and you got your hooves cutting up the ground.

You've been back a day, and I was thinking I'd just let you be with your sadness, but me and you's got some unfinished business, and I want us to have a clear line between us. You mind if I have a seat? Rub your face. I see God's already getting you ready for hot weather. Your hair's thinning, getting that slickness to it. But it's a little chilly out here now.

What I come out here this morning for is to ask you to forgive me for what I had to do with your boy. Can you do that, Mama Red, can you forgive me? I'm sorrier about that than I can ever say.

You looking down towards your tail. And your moans are getting louder. You breathing heavy. I see your tail's getting all hiked up, and you holding your legs straight out and stiff. Wait a minute. Are you . . . Mama Red, you having a baby?

You are. You having a baby. There's its hooves hanging out of you, two little black ones, like rocks. You about to be a mama again.

But you feel all cold back here, girl. Your legs, they're cold and not sticking out like your front ones. That mama dog, all her legs were sticking out. And where's your baby's head? Don't the heads come out first? Them puppies did. Head first on their two front legs like they were diving in a pond.

You in trouble, girl, ain't you? And hurting, you hurting. I got to get your baby's head out. Oh, mercy.

It's too tight for me to get my hand in there over them hooves. I'm going to have to push them back in. It's all warm up in there. And your mama squeezes, I feel them. There's its legs. I'm just going to follow on up. Got my whole arm in now. There goes another squeeze.

I feel its head, I do. It's turned backwards like it's trying to look at you. That's why it couldn't come out.

Got both my hands in now. I hope I'm not hurting you, got one holding onto to its legs and the other one straightening out its head. I'm trying to hurry, girl. You're doing good.

Got it all lined up now, so on that next squeeze you give, I'm going to pull. That's what I had to do with Little Claudia for that doctor. You squeeze, and I pull.

We're doing it, girl, we are. The tip end of its hooves are back out. But your squeezes are getting a little softer. I need you to keep them going hard. I know you getting tired.

That's right. Squeeze for me.

Them hooves are out now, and I see the tip end of its nose.

My hands keep slipping. I need some help pulling. Like maybe a rope. That Mr. Allgood hung one on the fence over there. Let me get it. Hold on, Mama Red.

All right, here we go. I'm tying one end to one leg, tying a sewing knot, and the other end to the other leg and now slipping the rope behind my back and having me a seat on the ground and making it real tight around me. Going to work one leg at a time. Like walking. Come on, little baby, that's right, come on, let's walk, let's walk on out.

Got my heels dug in good, cutting in the earth like you, girl. Come on, little baby, that's right. Let's walk on out. We doing it.

There's its nose and part of its head now, Mama Red, you looking? Come on, little baby. Mama's got you, hon. Mama does. Oh, mercy, I said 'mama.' Not papa, but mama. That's right, come on, let's walk. Mama ain't going to let you fall. I got you, hon. Come on.

Its whole head, Mama Red, oh, its sweet whole head and its shoulders. Come on, baby. Almost. Mama'a got you. You almost there.

There it is. Mama Red, your baby. Full out. You want to see? You lifting your head.

She's got all kinds of wrapping on her, some clear, some white, but she looks kind of blue. I believe she might be blue. And I don't believe she's breathing. I don't see no rise and fall. That mama dog licked that sack off of hers. Mama Red, you going to get up and do that? No? Then let me clear her nose and her mouth out with my fingers.

I still don't see no rise and fall. Oh, mercy. I'm going to breathe in her mouth, I am, and run my hand down her body, trying to get her going. Come on, little baby. Wake up, little baby. Let's take you a breath.

She just coughed. Mama Red, your baby just coughed. She's alive, your baby's alive. Raise up and look at her. She wants to see her mama. You too tired to lift up now, is that it? I'll bring her to you, then.

She's heavy. I'm going to have to slide her a little bit on this new grass.

There's your mama, little baby, there she is. I'm going to hold her up to your mouth, Mama Red. That's right, lick that baby girl clean.

That good mist is coming from your mouth, girl.

Look at her, trying to get her eyes open. She wants to see you. And look, she's trying to work her legs, wanting to stand already and just a few minutes old. Listen to me, calling her a little girl.

I bet she's hungry and wants to nurse. You going to stand up for her, Mama Red? Or you too tired? That's all right, I can help you. I see your milk sack's all full for her. Let me get some in my hand, but let me wipe them down my dress first. Got some cuts from that rope.

I'm picturing how your little boy pulled on you. He wrapped his mouth around you and yanked. That's what I'm doing. Oh, your milk is so warm. Am getting me a handful. And now bringing it to your baby. Here you go, hon. I'm going to have to help you learn to suck. My boy, I had to help him, too. Going to dip my finger in some milk and hold it up to your lips and run my finger around.

There you go. You doing it, you sucking. Now let me get some more of your mama's good milk.

Oh, she's lapping it up. You watching your baby drink, Mama Red?

The markings on her face. Another little pattern of you. Different from your boy's. His gathered up more in the bottom on the left, but hers is gathered more on the right. Looks like somebody's made a fist and then stuck her thumb up to show that everything was good. Do you see that?

Mama Red, you're scaring me. Open your eyes. Can you? I know you're tired. You're just tired. Ain't that right?

She's working her legs, trying to stand again. There she goes, getting on her feet, all wobbly. Oops. She fell down. But there she goes again. She's a fighter. Back on her feet now and coming up to see you. Smelling your face.

Believe I'll have a seat up there with y'all. Oh, you want to prop your mouth up on me, girl. That help you see your baby?

You breathing on me, Mama Red. That mist. Your mist. That morning after you come them four miles through the pitch black for your boy, I watched you put it on him, and I was wanting it on me, too. You just put it on me, too. I don't mean to be whispering, but I feel like God himself is right here with us. Right here.

No preacher's ever dunked me in what my mama called holy waters, but I feel like what you just did, just saved me. Coated me in your holy waters and saved me.

You breathing's slowing down, girl. And your eyes keep opening and then closing.

You leaving, ain't you, girl? That mama bone of yours, the best there ever was, you done used it plumb up, ain't you?

That question I asked you when I first come out here about you forgiving me. You do, don't you? You forgive me enough to leave your little girl with me, even after what I done to your boy, you trust me that much with your girl. Me. Clementine Florence Augusta Sarah Creamer. I'm going take that down inside of me. For the rest of time, I am. That right there, girl, that right there is going to see me through, and I promise you, my teacher, that I'll take care of her with all I got. With my mama bone. My mama bone. Mine.

Mama got it wrong. I do have a mama bone in me.

And I believe, Mama Red, I believe it might even be a good one.

By the time the mother cow no longer could open her eyes, the long shadows of the day had begun to show themselves.

She released sounds, low ones. They rose skyward, towards the gentle wind's face.

Around them, in grass, newly green after its long and cold sleep, her newborn calf kicked up her back legs and ran. She was a girl. She was becoming strong. The gentle wind's little one ran with her and filled the air with shrills.

By the time the mother cow's sounds faded into silence, the night air approached, and the wind began to call.

A sound emerged from the gentle wind. She wept.

It carried.

Because, when the nighttime air and the winds get just right, a sound can do that, carry. It can carry across land that is foreign. And across barbed-wire fences made to hold. It can even carry across a lifetime, sounds sent in infancy and in youth and a body grown.

And across lands that are foreign. And barbed-wire fences made to hold.

ACKNOWLEDGMENTS

One morning, in light so early it still could be considered dark, I caught a glimpse of the divine. I caught it in a gathering of mama cows, a dozen of them, all huddled and straining against the corner of an old barbed-wire fence on my daddy's farm, each cow with her chin shoved high into the air, sending forth sounds. They were guttural.

I was standing some ten feet away in my pajamas and boots. Their sounds had drawn me from my bed. Mostly, I could see their eyes, their lids pulled back and showing a vast sea of white that surrounded circles of deep brown. One cow stood nestled in the corner. She cut her eyes my way and bellowed. Above her mouth, a mist hovered.

I would not see it yet, but she and the others had pushed the end post forward with such force that it angled out like an arm waving at something familiar.

And it was. Their babies. They were some thirty yards away, at the other end of a grassy lane. They, too, stood huddled, and they, too, sent forth sounds. Deep ones. Long ones. They were steers, neutered males, aged six to eight months. My daddy the afternoon before had separated them from their mamas. It's called weaning.

This is what farmers do. Just like later that morning, a trailer hitched to a truck would pull around to where the steers stood, and a man would herd them and load them and take them to the other side of town to the cattle barn to be sold. For slaughter.

One of the mothers, the one nestled in the corner, cut her eyes my way again. I knew what she wanted. In my bones, I knew. She wanted me to get her baby back. She wanted me to knock down fences, hers and his.

But I couldn't.

But, then, something came to me—I could tell their story. I could tell about the way they love their babies, about their bond, this maternal one. This piece of the divine.

I made a promise to her, and *One Good Mama Bone* was born. She became my Mama Red, and we've been looking for champions, and they have come, acres and acres of them.

We send thank-you's, deep, guttural ones.

Beckey Badgett, who will never know how much her daily question—"How's the gang?"—fed my soul and kept me going.

My siblings. Brother Jamie McClain, who takes care of Mama Red for me and helped me get the details right. Twin Linda McClain McCall, who stops whatever she is doing to listen to me read sections to her and always says, "Oh, Bren." Sister Renee McClain Morris, who has been patiently waiting to read this story.

Jana Sasser, the blessed daughter I never had, who invested as much in this novel as she does her own, which makes me one awfully blessed writer.

Others who offered glorious feedback. Butt Glue Charleston members Shari Stauch, Jacquie Gum, Frances Pearce, Allison Gregory, and Lee Cox. Nashville writers Lily Wilson, Bob Mangeot, Jonathan Price, Pam Jones, and Terry Price. Sandra Johnson with monthly check-ins. Lorin Oberweger, my freelance editor, who set me on a new course when she told me, "We need to see Sarah's magnificence."

Writers. Dorothy Allison, who told me I needed "prodding." Robert Olen Butler, who noticed me shaken in 1988 at the first writers conference I ever attended and took the time to gently point me forward. Ben Fountain, who encouraged me and believed in me, a complete stranger. Lee Martin, who reached across the table in Vermont, held my hands, and said, "It will happen, Bren." River Jordan, who threw her strong arms open and welcomed me into her Nashville tribe, including the fabulous writers in our Dutch Lunch club.

Folks who do the work of God, farm sanctuaries around the world. Specifically, Farm Sanctuary, the Gentle Barn, Indraloka Animal Sanctuary, Catskill Animal Sanctuary, and Woodstock Farm Sanctuary. Bless you all!

Folks with helpful cow and 4-H information. Mell Gerrard and Janis Gerrard Hunter, who let me ask tons of questions, as did Fleet McClain, Jr., and Laura McClain Lipe. Dee and Jessica Davis, who walked me through how to straighten a calf's head for birth. John McGlone with the Boyd County Kentucky Fair.

Folks who gave me work and provided a financial foundation on which I could give myself time to write. My buddies, too numerous to mention by name, but you know who you are. The businesses you represent: BellSouth, Cingular Wireless, Kentucky Association of School Administrators, Equifax, Cox Communications, CableLabs, Clearwire, the American Society of

Mechanical Engineers, Outdoor Advertising Association of America, Ciba Vision, UCB Pharmaceuticals.

Gwen and Frank Hughes and family, who always believed. Gwen, get your dress ready!

Pattie Welek Hall, whose joy lifts me higher and whom I told the day after I sent Story River Books my manuscript, "I feel like I'm stepping in to what has been set up for me."

My Story River Books family. Jonathan Haupt, my editor and the pivotal champion delivered to me so I could make good on my promise to Mama Red. Linda Fogle and Suzanne Axland, who make the business side of publishing a teetotal pleasure. The late Pat Conroy, who birthed Story River Books with a heart as enormous as his talent and who yelled, "The cow!" when I thanked him for publishing this book. Mary Alice Monroe, who provides the door into this novel, and what a most glorious, generous door it is.

Ron, a former neighbor in Atlanta, who gave me the seed of this story in 1992, when he called me to his porch and told me a secret he'd been carrying for fifty-four years about a baby who was born one night in 1944, the mother's husband off at war.

And, finally, to Mama Red, who is still alive at this writing, all twenty-five years of her, I want to say, "With the help of all of these champions, I made good on my promise to you, girl. I delivered. We delivered your piece of the divine."